THE RAVEN'S CRUX

JULIE BOGLISCH

Black Rose Writing | Texas

©2024 by Julie Boglisch
All rights reserved. No part of this book may be reproduced, stored in a retrieval system or transmitted in any form or by any means without the prior written permission of the publishers, except by a reviewer who may quote brief passages in a review to be printed in a newspaper, magazine or journal.

The author grants the final approval for this literary material.

First printing

This is a work of fiction. Names, characters, businesses, places, events, and incidents are either the products of the author's imagination or used in a fictitious manner. Any resemblance to actual persons, living or dead, or actual events is purely coincidental.

ISBN: 978-1-68513-367-2
Library of Congress Control Number: 2023943966
PUBLISHED BY BLACK ROSE WRITING
www.blackrosewriting.com

Printed in the United States of America
Suggested Retail Price (SRP) $24.95

The Raven's Crux is printed in Minion Pro

*As a planet-friendly publisher, Black Rose Writing does its best to eliminate unnecessary waste to reduce paper usage and energy costs, while never compromising the reading experience. As a result, the final word count vs. page count may not meet common expectations.

To all those who have supported me for so long during all my ups and downs, you all have a special place in my heart. Particularly my ever present, ever encouraging and ever loving parents. Patti and Glenn, Mom and Dad, you two mean the world to me.

To my publishers and editors and readers: you all are amazing people. Find the answer to the mysteries in your life and keep moving forward. You'll find what you seek in the end!

And of course, to my adorable pets, Jasmine, Paisley and Nelson. Keep being your chipper and friendly little selves.

THE RAVEN'S CRUX

CHAPTER 1

Aiden leaned against the window, peering out at the dreary landscape. Rain pounded against the glass, as wind rattled the aged wood. The surrounding trees resembled reaching fingers, leaves holding on through sheer force of will alone.

It seemed nothing in this town was actually surviving.

"Spot something?" Noah popped up next to him, amusement shining on his face.

Aiden jerked, startled. "Of course not," he grumbled, peering back out.

"I was wondering, considering you've been staring out the window the whole time since we got here. You haven't even unpacked. I mean, Dad's almost done."

"How have you already done that?" He turned to Noah, taking note of their little room.

They went from having separate rooms to once more being forced to share a room. The wood paneling of the walls saw better days, but, Aiden had to admit, the rug was soft. The beds were placed on either side, giving them space in the middle to walk. His stuff was still thrown all over the place, some landing on the bed. Unlike Noah's side, his walls were still bare of anything. He could hear movement and rummaging from across the house, the door open enough to reveal a hallway barely lit by an exposed bulb. Guess Dad was still busy.

Noah, on the other hand, was finishing putting his own things out. A few band posters of some music Aiden wasn't fond of and one or two Anime posters that added a splash of color to the dismal room. A blue patterned quilt lay over the bed and the desk already had a lava lamp set to one side.

"What do you take me for?" Noah peered over toward Aiden. "You?"

"Oh, funny." Aiden shook his head, peering back outside. "Ugh, I don't know how you can stand this place."

"I can't, I'm making do."

At those words, Aiden turned back just as Noah took a seat on the bed. His cropped reddish-brown hair hung around his ears, as amber eyes stared back at Aiden.

Aiden sighed at that, taking a seat on his unmade mattress. He knew his brother was right. All they could do was make do. Didn't mean he still couldn't grumble about it.

To be honest, he should be used to constantly shifting locations. His dad was always moving around from place to place. You would think he worked in the army or something, but, no. He was a detective, an investigator, or so Aiden was told.

This was just their newest relocation. A dreary town out in the boonies. Driving through, it felt like he was in a ghost town. People barely traversed the streets and the rain seemed to fall endlessly from the sky.

The little house they ended up in was near the edge of town. An old rickety place that was at least big enough to house the three of them.

It had a kitchen with an old stove and a microwave that appeared to be from the 80's and was probably broken. The TV might as well have been busted, with how old it was… it still had an antenna. The house was a one-story, with a single front entrance which was a ridiculous fire hazard. A single long hallway broke off from the main kitchen and dining room. Their room was closest to the kitchen, their father's being at the end of the hall. The only other rooms were a living room, which had more dust then anything, and one shared bathroom that had a clawfoot bathtub.

There was a surprising lack of spiders.

It wasn't the worst place they had been in, but it was certainly close.

"Aiden, how long do you think we'll be here?"

Aiden glanced up and shrugged. "Hopefully not long, maybe a few months, maybe only a week or two." He paused at that and slumped. "I wonder if there is even a decent school here."

"If only Dad had time to homeschool us." Noah chuckled. Aiden rolled his eyes, but didn't argue.

"Boys, are you done?" Dad's voice echoed into the room as he knocked on the doorframe, glancing in with a wide grin. His face was grizzled, his posture tall and proud.

"I am." Noah waved. "Aiden's just been staring out the window the whole time."

Dad turned to Aiden with a raised eyebrow. "I know you like to procrastinate, but that's a bit much."

"And you, Dad?" Aiden crossed his arms over his chest, a little annoyed. "What brings you here?"

"I was checking on my boys, what else?" He stepped in, glancing around. "A bit smaller than I would have liked, but we'll deal with it like normal."

"Why are we even here?" Aiden brought up, catching his full attention. "There's nothing out here."

Dad just quirked a brow at that and gestured. "There are a lot of things out here. A whole plethora of opportunities."

Dad always said that. Noah believed him, but Aiden certainly did not.

"Really?" Noah sat up, staring outside.

Dad nodded, grinning as he adjusted his cloak, fingers tugging at the nicely trimmed beard. "Contrary to your brother's belief, there are all sorts of things here. It's a whole town and forest to explore with mysteries galore." His expression softened. "Just, you know the rules;

no going out at night, no going out by yourselves and stay close to a home, any home."

"We know, Dad." Noah smiled. "Hey, maybe we can find a clue on Mother. Wouldn't that be awesome, Aiden?" Noah turned to Aiden, who quickly looked away.

Aiden didn't miss how Dad's smile became strained as he leaned against the doorway. "Maybe… Still, in this case, be aware of yourselves if you go into the town. Part of my job here could get dangerous, so I want you two to be careful, understood?"

Aiden nodded. "One of those cases?"

Dad hesitated. "I don't know the specifics, but what I've gathered makes it something to watch out for." His gaze flicked to the window before he turned back to Aiden and Noah. "But that's not for you two to worry about. You know how to take care of yourselves, just remember what I've—"

"Dad, you literally just repeated it," Aiden pointed out. "We'll be careful."

"I'll remember the salt." Noah chuckled as Dad blinked before letting out a laugh.

"You're learning." Dad stepped in, ruffling Noah's hair. "Now, let's get going. We'll grab dinner and pick up some groceries tomorrow. Sound good?"

"As long as it's not overly greasy," Aiden muttered.

"I can't promise that, but it'll at least be homey," Dad piped up.

Aiden groaned, face in his hands as Dad waved before stepping away again, footsteps echoing over the creaking wooden floor.

Aiden was already hating this place.

•　　•　　•　　•　　•

Noah peered over to his brother's slumped form, noting he was silent again. It wasn't unusual, Aiden was the more quiet of the two of them. It was something Noah had gotten used to over the years.

That's what having a twin was. Even though they looked alike, their personalities couldn't be more different. He glanced out the window, mentally humming at the thought of what could be out there.

He wondered if it was haunted and almost chuckled out loud at the thought. It was always fun, exploring new places and seeing the sights. He knew he should be bored of it by now, Aiden certainly was, but he couldn't help but be excited for each new leg of the journey. Though he did hope to settle down at some point. Especially since, even though Dad always said there was so much to learn and explore, they rarely got to go very far.

His expression faltered. Sure, he always told himself that all he needed was his father and brother, but he couldn't help but think of Mom. He missed her. Mother had been gone for a few years now, disappeared as if she never existed. Noah didn't doubt she was still out there, but he knew Aiden did.

If anything, Noah had a feeling Aiden wouldn't forgive Mom, even if she did come back. Noah wasn't sure how he would feel if he saw Mom again. He supposed it would just be nice to know the truth.

He probably took that from his dad.

"So, what investigation do you think he's doing here?"

"Who knows, probably just following reports of cheating again." Aiden glanced over, reddish brown hair falling around his face, slightly longer than Noah's own and a bit messier as well. "Though he did mention it might be dangerous, so it could be a missing person situation. I wonder if he wanted to pick up harder or more dangerous missions again. They do usually pay better." He paused, glancing toward Noah with pursed lips. "What, are you going to try to find out?"

"Well, of course." Noah smirked, getting an annoyed huff from Aiden.

"Aren't you curious?"

"You know the answer to this, it's the same every time." Aiden shook his head. "And that's a big fat no."

"If you say so." Noah stood. "You should probably get your bedding set up. I'm taking a peek outside."

"In this rain? Are you… Yeah, no. You're crazy." Aiden waved. "I should have known. At least bring an umbrella this time."

"That was ONCE." Noah glared, getting a faint smirk from Aiden. Noah huffed, stuck out his tongue and left the room. The air was somewhat stagnant, the house probably having not been used in a long time. Dust still clung to a lot of the furniture, something he would have to worry about later, once they had cleaning supplies. Dad was throwing on his work boots, heavy raincoat in hand.

He glanced up. "Hey, Noah. What brings you out here?"

"I wanted to take a look around."

Father hesitated at that before nodding. "Here." He passed a raincoat over to Noah. "Just stay close to the house for today. I still haven't put up the barriers, though don't tell your brother." He winked and Noah smiled.

It was their own little joke. Dad always said that to make Noah feel better about a new location. Dad would go around the house, making random sigils and throwing salt every which way. It was ludicrous and silly. Aiden always scoffed at it, but Noah appreciated the little gesture.

It was calming, knowing that even when Dad was away for long nights and weekends, there was something still 'protecting 'them. It was the thought that counted.

Maybe it would stop anyone else from being whisked away like Mom.

Still, he wasn't dumb, he knew it didn't actually do anything. He was thirteen. It was childish. He was finally a teen after all.

That didn't stop Noah from holding onto it though, unlike Aiden.

"I'll stay close."

"Good. I shouldn't be gone too long." Father stood, patting Noah's head. "I'll put it up when I get back from talking with the mayor. Along with your mother's cross." He paused. "After the rain dies down a bit."

Noah chuckled at that. Yeah, doing it in the rain did not work, or so Dad told him before. "Alright, see you later."

Dad waved and left, pulling his hood up. The door creaked as he opened it and stepped outside. He hurried over to the car, starting it before heading into town. Noah pulled his raincoat on as the door closed with a click. Shoving his feet into a pair of boots, Noah grabbed an umbrella and slipped outside. The porch groaned slightly under his weight as he took a step out, hopping down the stairs and almost splashing into the mud. Unlike the house, the air outside was fresh and filled with the pleasant smell of autumn rain. It was open, so much less gloomy than peering through a rain-coated window. The clouds above moved quickly, as if racing each other. Noah started to walk around, taking in the place. There was a garage to one side where the car had been parked earlier. The garage itself was small, more of a shed than anything. Noah meandered over, peeking inside. There was room for a car, once all of the junk was moved.

There were barrels and old tools scattered about on tables both metal and wooden. The door, like everything else, creaked upon opening. The handles and hinges squealed from a need to be de-rusted.

Noah supposed he wasn't surprised, this place was old.

A faint chill filled the air and he frowned. Was the air conditioner on? Wait, was there an air-conditioner? He glanced around before stepping back out, closing the door behind him. The rain that slipped past his umbrella felt warm. He shrugged it off. It was probably just his imagination. Plus, it seemed like the garage wasn't open much, it's possible it retained a cooler temperature because of that.

It wasn't like it was freezing.

He continued around the house, gazing into the surrounding forest. A fence lined the way on three sides, just barely blocking the trees and clearly broken in some areas. Vines curled over the aged wood, bits of white paint showing what it used to be like. Noah walked to the far side and, spotting a familiar window, grinned.

He crouched slightly, staying close to the side, noticing as light spilled out and faint music echoed from within. A rhythmic thrumming, followed by a blazing guitar solo rang out. Noah quietly chuckled and, keeping low, peeked into the window.

Aiden was cleaning, humming quietly to himself. Boxes littered the floor where he left them, clothes piled around as if he was debating where to put them and just threw them to the side. Noah began to hum, a tune he remembered from an old horror anime he watched recently. Aiden stilled, furrowing his brow before peering outside.

Now, his brother didn't believe in horror or paranormal. Noah thought it was interesting and could understand how it would be difficult to believe, but he couldn't deny that it was a thing. Or, at least, part of him kind of hoped it was, it would be cool.

He let his humming get louder and lightly thrummed against the wall near the window.

"Noah, if that is you…" Aiden's voice echoed with annoyance, footsteps moving closer.

Noah waited, the rain soaking past his hood since the umbrella was closed. He ducked below the window and, moving to the other side, rapped against it.

Noah heard his brother yelp and poked his head up, seeing Aiden stumble back. The shock turned into a heavy glare. Noah chuckled as Aiden stomped forward and, unlatching the lock, lifted it up.

What Noah hadn't noticed was the book he was holding. Noah yelped as Aiden swatted down, smacking him in the head. "That was for scaring me." He pulled back, revealing the book he was holding, one of Noah's manga.

"You didn't have to hit me," Noah groused, flipping his umbrella open. The spray of water spattered Aiden, who twitched, a glare flashing over his face before disappearing. "Plus, you almost ruined my manga! Do you know how expensive those are?"

"It's fine." Aiden put the manga back down. "What do you expect me to think? This place is brand new and you know our luck. Remember that burglar from two years ago?"

Noah winced and shrugged. "Yeah, and Dad came home at the same time and had him dragged to the police station."

"Or the time a drunkard tried to come in through the window?"

"Okay, that one was weird." Noah grimaced. "But, seriously, we're in the middle of nowhere, like you said. There is, literally, no one around. Believe me, I checked."

Aiden pursed his lips, an odd expression on his face. "Just get inside. Even with the raincoat, you are going to get soaked."

"Fine." Noah huffed as he stepped away. Aiden reached up, closing the window. Or, at least trying to. He frowned, tugging at it as Noah watched, confused. A moment later, it slammed down, rattling the glass, startling both of them. Aiden blinked as Noah tilted his head, glancing up at where it had been.

There was a click as Aiden shrugged and flipped the lock before stepping away, closing the curtains as he went.

Noah hurried around the corner, racing back into the house.

He finished his exploration anyway and was feeling a little unsettled, being outside by himself, especially since Dad JUST reminded them to make sure they were together. He glanced toward the forest before snapping the door shut, locking it as he went.

CHAPTER 2

Aiden paced over to the bed, shivering slightly. A cold wind blew through when he tried to close the window, some of the rain splashing in, hitting against his sweatshirt.

The window itself stuck, pretty hard. So it was surprising when it suddenly crashed down, almost shattering the glass. Everything in this house was old and decrepit. It made Aiden curious why his father picked it, but then, he wondered that for every place they stayed in.

He swore, every house they ended up in had some old aspect to it, whether it was a never-used attic which his dad would blockade or something like this, where it hadn't seen public or private use since over a decade ago.

He took a seat on the bed, finally made with the proper bedding, and stared at his pile of clothes that he knew he needed to put away, but couldn't convince himself too.

The sharp knock on the window caught his attention. Rolling his eyes, he stood with a hint of annoyance.

Really, Noah? He told his brother to come insi—

The front door closed as wet footsteps echoed from the hallway. Aiden stiffened, not sure where to go. He darted toward the door and held it as the handle turned, his attention split between the door and the window.

The handle rattled before something slammed into the door near where he pressed his ear. "Aiden! Let me in already."

At that, he swung the door open and pulled back, gaze flitting to the window, the curtains still closed. He would have blamed the knock on a nearby tree branch, but he knew the forest was a good ways away.

"You didn't see anyone outside, right?"

"Ugh, I already told you, there wasn't anyone." Noah groaned. "Relax, would you?"

Aiden hesitated, a strange chill running down his spine. He KNEW he heard knocking. He glanced toward the window, noticing Noah's raised eyebrow of amusement.

"You know, Aiden, you can't pull that on me."

"I'm not trying to." He walked over, convincing himself it was just his imagination as he opened the curtain.

A girl, drenched to the bone, stood outside, face pressed against the glass, gold meeting his gaze.

Aiden snapped the curtain closed as Noah let out a startled scream. A second later, there was that tapping again and Aiden turned, glaring. "No one?" he hissed, voice going up a notch.

Noah just stared, shocked. "Where the heck did—I didn't see her." He shook his head, joining Aiden. "She's soaked, we should probably let her—"

"Are you insane?" Aiden snapped, pulling away from the window, that chill not leaving his bones. "Do you remember what happened last time you thought it would be a good idea to let someone in?"

"That was once! Dad was there that time anyway, so—"

Tap, tap… Crash!

Both boys whipped around, backpedaling to avoid the shattered glass as it scattered over the wooden floor, the curtain blowing as wind howled through.

A hand reached through, feeling for the lock, dark as night skin seen in flickers past the billowing curtain.

Aiden moved, dancing over the glass, wincing slightly as it cracked under his boots, now grateful he hadn't taken them off. He grabbed the nearest thing to him before slamming it down, a strange terror running under his skin. The girl retracted her hand as another book, this time a textbook, crashed down where her fingers were. "Who the hell are you?"

Silence met his demand, the curtains fluttering back into place.

Noah grabbed a nearby broom he had been using to get the dust off the floor and, extending one end and staying well away from the glass in his socked feet, pushed the curtain out of the way.

The girl was gone.

Aiden observed the shattered window as Noah shrunk back slightly.

"I'll… uh… call Dad," Noah stammered, pulling out a phone.

Aiden nodded, guard up. They didn't have a means to barricade it and the wind was strong. "Noah, get your shoes on and help me pull this over. It'll block most of the water and her trying to get in again." Aiden hurried over to one side where a bookshelf stood. "We'll clean up the glass after."

Noah nodded, placing the phone against his shoulder as he quickly threw on some shoes before joining Aiden, helping him pull the worn bookshelf over. Aiden was grateful, shoving it forward wasn't the easiest thing, but it would do in a pinch.

In the meanwhile, the phone clicked in. "Noah? Everything okay?"

"Oh, uh, Dad, there was this strange girl outside. She shattered our window. Aiden and I have blocked it with a bookshelf, but—"

"Shit." Dad's swear startled Noah. "I'll be back soon. Don't go outside and don't open the door to anyone, you hear? Stay away from the windows and go to my room. I left your mother's cross there." There was a pause before Dad let out a sigh. "How do you two have such strange luck?"

"Don't know." Noah shifted from foot to foot. "Do you know why I didn't see her outside? Or leave?"

"You most likely just missed her. It's pretty dark outside, you probably hadn't noticed." Dad paused. "I'll be back in a bit. Stay inside for now, alright?"

"Alright, fine." Noah clicked off, turning to Aiden. "You probably heard that, right?"

Aiden nodded, glancing toward the window with a furrowed brow. It really was their luck. Every time, it seemed. He sighed and, after quickly sweeping up the glass, hurried to Dad's room. Some lights that resembled candles were placed around the room and near the window was the cross. There wasn't any salt or anything, meaning that Dad hadn't gotten around to doing that weird occult stuff that Noah and Dad were so fond of.

Noah hopped onto the bed as Aiden closed and locked the door. He was used to going to Dad's room. More often than not, they ended up finding themselves staying in there as Dad looked for whoever came into the house. Though Aiden always heard him muttering in frustration about having protected their room and failing. It made no sense to him, so he often ignored the strange mutterings.

It was ridiculous and he knew it didn't happen to other people his age… probably… admittedly, he never asked. Movies and TV said that it was not normal to hide away in your parents room at their age, but that didn't always mean much.

He meandered over to the window, lightly fingering over the cross. It was weird to think this was all that was left of Mom.

He heard faint footsteps along with the splashing of mud. His body froze as something reflected off the glass. The girl stood outside, watching quietly. Shit, Dad said to stay away from the windows. Idiot. He pulled back, but noticed that she didn't come closer. She didn't move away either. Her black tangled hair was matted down and only one eye shone, a shimmering gold iris that gleamed in the rainy night. Aiden tugged at the ratty curtains, closing the window, just barely managing not to knock the cross off.

"Aiden?"

"She's still out there." Aiden let out a breath, stepping back. It didn't seem like she was close, like with the last window, but it was still unsettling.

Who even knew they were there? He supposed it was a small town, so it wouldn't be surprising if news traveled fast. He heard pounding footsteps from outside and the door unlock and slam open. "Noah! Aiden! You okay?"

"We're fine," Noah called from where he was fiddling with some of the strings of the threaded quilt draped over Dad's bed.

More footsteps and then a faint tap on the door, followed by another. Aiden unlocked the door, recognizing the sequence. Dad stepped inside, water still dripping from his raincoat, the hood down as he glanced between them. "Sorry about that, boys. I didn't expect people to already know we were here."

"It is a small town," Aiden pointed out, getting a hum from Dad. He ruffled Aiden's hair, causing Aiden to pull away, annoyed.

"True. Now, why don't I take a look around. Where did you last spot her?"

Aiden just pointed out the window, causing Dad to frown. "So close?" he muttered before glancing toward the boys. "I'll be right back. Oh, and here." He tossed a bag which Noah caught. "I got some donuts to munch on before you called." At that, he stepped back out, closing the door firmly. A click sounded from the other side, indicating he locked it.

"Oh! Hey, our favorites." Noah pulled out a chocolate frosted with sprinkles and a blueberry glazed. "Here." He handed the blueberry over before snacking down on the chocolate.

Aiden took his, noting it was a homemade-like glaze. The donut wasn't bad, actually. He took another bite and peeked through the window. Father stood outside, staring out into the forest, the raincoat back on properly. He turned and spotted Aiden, giving a thumbs up before moving on.

Aiden snorted, but felt a smile twitch over his lips. His dad was so corny.

Soon enough, Dad came back in. They returned to the twins 'room with a piece of plywood and some nails from the shed. Dad chuckled at the sight of the bookcase. "Good thinking, Aiden."

"How did you know it was Aiden?" Noah huffed.

"I know my boys." He helped push the bookcase aside, peering over the broken glass with a strange expression, muttering something softly under his breath. He shook his head, grabbed the plywood and quickly nailed it into the sill, wincing as one rusted nail broke under the hammer. Once done, they pulled the bookcase back over before heading carefully to the car to grab some dinner in town.

"I think she's gone, for now. I'll have someone over to fix your window when I can," Dad said as he pulled the seatbelt on. Noah took the passenger seat, leaving Aiden to sit in the back.

At least it was more comfortable than on the way here, with all their supplies around Aiden. One of these days, he'd get in before Noah.

The town was quiet, the rain finally dying down and turning to a faint misty drizzle. Lights glowed inside houses as they passed. It was getting late and the air was starting to grow a little colder. A gentle breeze passed through as they stopped at a small, warmly lit diner. Noah hurried inside, using his hand as a shield as Aiden, grabbing an umbrella, stepped out and walked calmly after him. Dad stayed even, humming a jaunty little tune as he locked the car doors.

The inside of the diner was like any other diner Aiden ever saw. Plastic seats decorated the windows and aisles and a counter with stools took up one side. The tiled floor was slightly wet. A waitress was talking with a customer in the back corner of the room. She glanced up and smiled. "Why, welcome," she called. "You can sit wherever ya would like."

"Thank you, ma'am." Dad nodded in her direction, causing the woman to blush and turn back toward the customer.

Dad was always a charmer. Aiden followed his brother, taking a seat beside him as Dad joined them and let out a tired breath, taking his own seat.

Aiden could only hope to get some of his father's charm. According to Dad, however, they resembled their mother more than their father.

Aiden reached toward his chin, feeling sad when he noticed there still wasn't stubble. Hopefully, it would grow in soon. He wanted a beard like his father's, trimmed, but still full.

Noah didn't seem to care too much about that, thrumming his fingers on the plastic table as he hummed.

How were they so different from each other? Aiden couldn't help but wonder. They were identical twins, right?

Noah glanced toward him, curious. Aiden just shook his head.

Footsteps clacked over the linoleum flooring, catching his attention. He turned as the waitress stepped up. She was blonde with long curls, tanned skin and a nice figure, probably in her mid-twenties, early thirties. Though, Aiden wasn't certain. Dad appeared to be in his mid-thirties and was almost fifty, so he never really could guess.

"Hi, how can I help ya?" She spoke up, a slight lilt in her tone. "Haven't seen ya strangers around. New here?"

"We were just passing through and happened to stop in," Dad said, lie falling easily from his lips. "My name is Roger, Roger Marcus Raven."

"What a unique name." The woman chuckled. "It's a pleasure, Mr. Raven."

"Please, call me Roger." Dad nodded, getting another giggle from the woman before she quickly composed herself.

"Yes, well, sorry about that. Welcome to Herisdell. Not much here, unfortunately, but we're glad to have ya, even if ya are just stopping by." Her gaze flitted toward Noah and Aiden. She smiled. "Here is our menu. Let me know if anything catches your eye." She placed three menus down. "Any drinks?"

"Water's fine." Dad spoke up.

"Same." Aiden nodded.

"I'll take a diet coke," Noah said. Aiden stared with a bemused expression crossing his face. Of course his brother would get a soda this late at night. Noah clearly noticed. "What? I haven't had one in a while."

The woman nodded and hurried off.

Other than the other customer, a guy off to one side minding his own business, the place was quiet. Aiden wasn't surprised. His gaze flitted to the clock, ticking nearby. It was almost nine o'clock. No wonder he was so hungry, even after having that donut. He pulled up the menu, flipping through it. It was typical diner fare, stuff he'd had at least a hundred times by now.

They ordered as the rain finally ended, the storm clouds breaking apart above, showcasing the slivers of a moon, poking through.

The other customer stood and, barely giving them a glance, left, hurrying away.

The waitress came over, dropping off their drinks before confirming what they were getting for dinner. When she returned with the food, Dad raised his hand.

"I'm sorry, ma'am, but I have to ask. Why is it so quiet at this time? I know it's late, but usually a place like this would be busier."

The woman sighed, a strained expression on her face. "Ya'll don't know? Oh, well, I suppose you wouldn't." She shifted, hands pushed into her apron as the three of them listened, Noah occasionally snapping up a fry. "Ah, well, a few weeks ago, there be some strange happenin's around town. People disappearing in the middle of the night. Chill winds blowing through in the middle of the day, all that creepy shenanigans." She shifted once more. "Supposedly, the mayor called in a private investigator to figure out what's been going on after something about a failed previous investigation. I don't know the details. It would be nice to go about town again without fear of them strange happenin's."

"Thank you." Dad smiled. "I suppose that would be worrying. I bet that investigator will figure things out."

"I sure hope so, the last one disappeared." At that, she tilted her head and scurried off.

"Disappeared?" Aiden snapped, turning to his dad, voice pitching up slightly. "You hadn't mentioned that."

Dad gave a smile that seemed a little off. "I only recently learned of that little bit myself. The message hadn't spoken of it. It was only when

I met the mayor briefly earlier that he told me." He sighed. "It just means I, and you two, will need to be more careful." His gaze flitted to Noah. "No exploring until we have more information, got it?"

Noah slumped at that, nodding. "I know how this works…" he grumbled as Aiden sent him a worried look. That was going to be rough on Noah, but they would make do.

He turned back to Dad. "The last few were cheating cases, this is very different from that. Why did you choose it?"

"Aiden, we are in need of money and cheating cases, while decent, weren't paying what I needed. I had to get back into the bigger and more dangerous cases like before…" He paused, as if he was about to say something else before letting out a breath.

"You are at least getting paid accordingly, right?" Aiden sighed, munching on his tuna melt. "Some before, some after?"

"The pay honestly should have alerted me." Dad grimaced and Aiden let his head hit the table. Noah patted his back. "Don't worry, kids, everything should be fine." He reached forward, ruffling their hair again. Aiden pulled away as Noah lightly slapped Dad's hand, a hint amused.

"So… how much?"

"Ten grand for coming, One hundred and fifty dollars a day and then another twenty grand on successful completion." Dad gave a faint smile as both Noah and Aiden stared at him before glancing toward each other.

"That didn't clue you in that there was more than a little problem?" Aiden frowned.

Dad placed his food down with a strange tiredness that seemed to press down on his shoulders. "I was well aware." His expression softened. "I figured going out to a more rural town after the city would be a nice change of pace. We would figure out what's going on and rest for a bit before moving to our next location. The amount of disappearances, however, is making that option much less, well, optional." Dad glanced toward the window, staring outside for a bit. "I guess I also have to remember how much you two have grown up and, while I would love to have you stay with someone, your mother and I were only children. There really isn't any place I feel comfortable sending you."

Aiden paused at that, but mentally agreed. All his grandparents were dead or... well, let's just say he was glad Dad was no longer with them. They didn't have any aunts or uncles to stay with.

It was just the three of them.

The food didn't taste as good now, almost like burnt ash in his mouth. He knew his father tried, but it wasn't quite the same. Why had Mother disappeared? Did she just leave them? Was she dead?

Aiden didn't know and the thought soured his mood. Either way, she wasn't coming back. He knew that.

"Kiddo? Everything alright?" Dad's voice pulled Aiden from his thoughts and he just nodded, getting back to his melt. He needed to stop thinking about this.

Dad watched quietly before speaking up once more. "So, I was able to talk to the mayor and he agreed to set you two up in the nearby school. It's not far, so you should be able to walk there no problem and when I was driving around, I checked out the route, it seems safe enough." He dug into his bag and handed two necklaces to them. "I have a gift for you. I know you broke your last ones in the previous city, so I made you some new ones."

Aiden twitched, staring at the little wooden cross. It was set on a threaded piece that he knew would make his skin itch.

"Thanks, Dad." Noah pulled his over, flipping it on. It settled over his shirt and against his chest as if he always wore it. Noah fiddled with it, a faint smile on his lips, as Aiden grudgingly took his own. Aiden hated wearing them. It was stupid and made no sense, but his father had a knack for knowing when he wasn't wearing it. He would always have this strange worried and disappointed expression.

"Thanks, Dad," Aiden muttered, getting a soft smile from their father. Aiden slipped it on, stuffing it under his shirt. Maybe that way, when he put it in his pocket, he might have an excuse for why Dad didn't spot it.

His dad was so weird. He believed in these random supernatural or paranormal, he supposed, gimmicks. Noah was enraptured by it. Aiden? Not so much. His dad was an investigator; he found missing people and dealt with cheating cases, occasionally diving into more dangerous cases like murderers or rapists, but that was less common. His job was to prove the impossible was possible. That, no matter how supernatural it might seem, there was always a reason, a cause.

So it made no sense to Aiden why his father, who was quite good at his job, believed in the supernatural. An inherently impossible thing, even more so since crosses were religious, not supernatural, yet he combined them as if they were. It was nonsense.

He shook it off as Dad paid the bill, leaving a tip for the lady before they made their way back outside. The air was crisp and cold, the moon now clearly out, the clouds passed. The drive back to their current home was quiet. They did briefly stop at a little shop that seemed to be open 24/7. Though the shopkeep was a nervous fellow that Aiden thought was a little strange.

He'd met strange people, that wasn't unusual. He knew people from almost all walks of life at this point, or so it felt like.

They bought some quick breakfast supplies, Dad promising he would buy some proper groceries tomorrow.

After saying good-bye, they headed home. Aiden surveyed the area as they arrived, wondering if that girl was here again.

"Hey, Dad, why don't you park in the garage? It's open enough." Noah spoke up.

Dad waved it off. "I'm too used to not having a garage. Maybe once I clean it out, I might start using it, but, for tonight, I think I'm good." He slipped out and went inside. Noah and Aiden exchanged glances, shrugged and followed. It was their first night in a new location. Aiden thought he would be used to it by now.

He never was.

CHAPTER 3

The bookshelf was still in place when they got into their shared space. Dad observed the bedroom with a strange attentiveness before he nodded. "I'll make sure the front door and windows are locked, as usual before I head to bed, I have an early morning tomorrow so I may be gone before you two are up. Is that okay, boys?"

"How is that different from usual, Dad?" Aiden huffed as Dad just smiled, ruffling their hair. Aiden quickly moved away with annoyance as Noah chuckled, lightly slapping at the hand.

"Like Aiden said, we'll be fine."

"I know, I'm just a paranoid old man, what can I say? Now, get some rest. If I'm not here in the morning, I'll leave you a note in my room, as usual, okay?"

"Alright," Noah piped up, smiling.

"And school?" Aiden asked. "Didn't you say we were starting tomorrow?"

Dad paused at that and nodded. "Right, almost forgot." He shook his head. "School doesn't start till nine. Hopefully I'll be back in time to pick you boys up and bring you over so you can find your way a bit easier next time. You two are usually up early anyway."

"You mean, how I have to drag Noah out of bed." Aiden's eye twitched as Noah smiled sheepishly.

"Not always. Quite often, it's you that sleeps in, actually," Noah pointed out, a faint smirk on his lips as Aiden glared.

"I sleep in, sure, but I don't have to be literally dragged out when I do." Aiden gestured, letting the annoyance slip into his voice. Noah was something sometimes.

Dad gave a faint laugh and nodded. "I trust you boys, just make sure to remember what I've told you."

"We can defend ourselves, Dad." Noah spoke up, one hand on his hip as he gestured with the other. "We're not children."

Dad seemed to hesitate at that before stepping forward and ruffling Noah's hair again, causing him to yelp. "I know you aren't, but you are still my boys. Isn't it a father's job to watch out for his sons?"

Noah pouted, but didn't argue. Aiden let out an amused snort, arms crossed over his chest. His father was so weird sometimes. "Fine. I'll keep an eye on Noah."

"I know you will."

"Hey! I can keep an eye on myself, you know." Noah's pout became more exaggerated as Dad chuckled.

"Well, either way, good night." With that, he waved and slipped out of the room. Footsteps echoed through the house followed by a series of faint clicks and thumps before the creak of Dad's door closing met their ears. Aiden checked the door before taking a seat on the bed. Noah plopped onto his back.

"Thanks for that, Aiden." He huffed as Aiden shrugged. A moment of silence developed between them before he continued, voice softer. "So, a new town. A new place." He turned toward Aiden. "Do you think this time, things might be different?"

"Why would you want that?" Aiden pulled off his shoes, not looking at Noah. "Different doesn't mean good."

"I know." Noah sat up, expression evening out. "I know it doesn't, but I can hope for that for both of us, right? A new school, a new environment… we might be able to…" He trailed off as Aiden paused, fingers freezing on the laces before he finished, tugging them off.

"I guess," he finally admitted. "But I don't expect much." After all, he wasn't sure what different would entail and he was almost afraid to know.

·   ·   ·   ·   ·

The fresh air perked Noah up as their father gathered them outside, checking his watch with a slight frown before pulling them into the car. Unlike the day before, the sky was clear. The air was dappled with the early morning sun's rays. The ground was still slick with the previous rainfall and their boots slid in the mud as they hurried over. People were already starting to move about in a languid silence.

It was strange, Noah noted, for such a beautiful day, the area still had that dreary quality to it. He supposed it made sense with the fact that there were a bunch of disappearances.

That would dampen anyone's mood, especially in a small town like this.

"Just make sure to take a right here and then a left at the next fork." Father gestured as he drove slowly through town, giving them a chance to take in the route. Noah wasn't even bothering, Aiden would be able to keep track anyways. Noah hummed, both to wake himself up and to lighten the mood a bit.

Aiden's gaze flicked to him, amused, before returning his focus to the streets.

"So, what do you think of this place?"

"Same as usual. We haven't been here long enough to know." Aiden flicked Noah in the side, causing him to huff. "Though at least the last place had a bit more sound. Notice how there aren't any birds?"

Dad's gaze flickered to them briefly at the words before he focused ahead once more.

Noah paused both at Dad's reaction and his own realization. He noticed it was silent, but now that Aiden pointed it out, the lack of birds made the place almost eerie. He reached up, fiddling with his cross at the thought. He wasn't a fan of the silence like this. "Yeah, okay…"

Noah frowned. This did happen occasionally when they went through a town. Dad mentioned it was because animals can sense when something is wrong. "How much farther?"

"Almost there." Dad spoke up, voice a little tense as they rounded another corner, moving past a two-story home that could almost fit in a suburban neighborhood if it got a new paint-job.

Honestly? That was most of the residential homes around here. Everything felt like it needed a fresh coat of paint.

Noah glanced up to see a school ahead, farther down the road. It was a two-story building with multiple wings. It probably, at one point, held kids from most of the neighboring towns. Now, only a small trickle of students stepped into the double-wide doorways. With how big it was, it made sense they just made it into a joint middle and highschool. Didn't mean he had to like it though.

Dad pulled up to one side in front of a set of gates that some of the students were running through and turned to them, one hand draped over the back of the seat. "It's pretty straightforward, do you think you'll be alright getting home?"

"We'll be fine, Dad." Noah shrugged, grinning. "Aiden has the directions anyways."

Aiden rolled his eyes, but didn't argue.

Dad chuckled as Noah opened the door, stepping out. "Have a good day at school, alright? Keep your heads down until we have more information, but still, enjoy yourselves, okay?"

"That's easier said than done." Aiden spoke up as he slipped out of the other side, joining Noah.

"I know, Aiden, but I'm going to worry anyway. Still, call me if you need anything, alright? I have to go." He glanced at his watch again, frowning slightly.

"Sure, Dad, get going, we'll see you later." Noah waved as Aiden nodded. Dad smiled before turning and heading down the street toward the inner part of town.

"Guess we're here." Noah spoke up when Aiden didn't say anything. "I'm not excited about this, but…"

Aiden examined the school quietly. "I am," he finally admitted. "I just hope they are ahead for once. I don't want to retake the same class again."

Noah winced, thoughts flicking to the last few schools. "Oh, right. That sucked." He placed his hands in his pockets, peering up. "Well, hopefully, I can meet someone to talk to, a cute girl or maybe a handsome boy would do."

Aiden clearly caught his grin, returning the expression with his own deadpan, if soft, one. "Of course you would say that." Aiden shook his head as Noah waved, chuckling. "Just… well, you know."

Noah's expression softened. "You know I will be careful, I am aware of what to watch out for now." He winced, mind flashing to the previous school, the incessant questions and… He turned toward the new school. "Anyway, it's one of the few things that keeps school interesting, meeting new people. I know you're not fond of it, but, seriously, it can be helpful."

"If you say so," Aiden's voice said it all in regards to his feelings on the matter. Noah huffed, but didn't push as they stepped inside. He didn't miss the attention directed toward them, which Aiden was clearly ignoring as usual. Still, it would be so nice to be able to keep in contact with someone more than a few months at a time.

Noah pulled out his phone, flipping through it. He gave his number to a few people in the last town, but no one had yet to check on him even when he contacted them. It made his heart clench and fall.

He supposed he was going to have to delete those names off his phone just like all the others.

A finger lightly tapped his hand and he glanced over toward Aiden. "I wouldn't worry. One day, we'll be able to find a place where we can settle and then we can find people to talk with."

"I want that one day to be soon," Noah muttered, but pocketed his phone anyway. Aiden said nothing to that and Noah knew he couldn't. Both of them felt the same way to an extent, though Noah had no doubt the thought was much stronger for him. A home to call his… it would be nice.

They wound their way through the school, eventually finding the principal's office as bells chimed above, a dainty little tune. A secretary sat out front, busily flipping through some papers as he knocked on the door to the principal's office.

The principal, a heavier set man with balding hair and a thick beard stepped out. "Ah, you two must be the Raven twins. Your father spoke to me over the phone." He walked forward, extending a hand. "I see you made it here. Welcome."

Noah took the principal's hand, noting a faint smell of orange and cinnamon as a slight shiver ran down his spine from the chill in the air. It would certainly explain why the secretary was in a thicker sweater, even though it was fairly warm out. Aiden bowed his head. "It's a pleasure, Mr. …" He furrowed his brow and the principal chuckled, releasing Noah's hand.

"You may call me Mr. Henderson, I am the principal of this school." Mr. Henderson took a step back, nodding to the secretary. He stayed glued to his paperwork, barely acknowledging as he handed over some folders. "Thank you, Mr. Clark." Mr. Henderson glanced over the pages, curious, before nodding. "Ah, I see, even with all of the traveling, you two manage to maintain steady averages, almost top of the class." Mr. Henderson hummed. "Unfortunately, it seems like you're slightly ahead of most of our younger students, I hope you don't mind." At that, he walked over, handing them both a schedule. "Well, I hope you enjoy your stay at our school. I must be going." He waved and headed back inside his office.

The secretary never changed his position, just continued to flip through his papers.

Noah glanced toward Aiden who was scrutinizing the schedule. "Of course," he muttered, folding it up before turning to him. "How is yours?"

Noah shrugged, standing up and heading out. Their footsteps echoed and cracked over the linoleum flooring as they started down the hallway. Fluorescent lights hummed above and lockers lined the side. A few stickers were placed here and there and there were some posters on the wall, but, like the rest of the town, it was dreary. Aiden continued to inspect the schedule as Noah stayed at his side, peeking over his shoulder every so often.

Aiden stopped in his tracks before groaning. "Ugh, not again."

Noah blinked, catching Aiden's schedule and promptly wanting to follow his brother's cue.

None of their classes were together.

"This always happens," Aiden muttered. "You would think they would want to try to keep us together, but NO."

Feeling sheepish, Noah gently nudged into Aiden's side. "Hey, it shouldn't be too bad. We'll try for today and talk to Dad tonight, if it's too much of an issue."

Aiden hesitated at that before sighing. "Easy for you to say." He paused. "Sometimes I wish I could have a little of that enthusiasm you always seem to hold, then I remember how annoying it is."

Noah stuck out his tongue, but was relieved to see a smile flit over Aiden's lips. "Mean, but true."

"I know." Aiden stopped. "I think this is your room."

Noah peered over, noting that he could hear quiet chatter from inside. He turned to Aiden, nodding.

Aiden waved and continued on, disappearing down the hall.

Noah took a deep breath and knocked on the door.

A hush settled over the room as the teacher walked over and opened the door. It was a young woman, remarkably similar to the one who worked in the diner. She blinked. "Ah, you must be Noah." Same lilting tone, they must have been sisters, probably, or maybe just a lot of people in town had that accent. It was hard to tell sometimes. "You'll have to sit in the back, alright?"

Noah nodded and stepped in, noting an empty seat on the right hand side of the room. The class was small, only about fifteen kids around his age. They all stared at him in a way that was way too familiar to him. He just smiled and walked to the back, taking a seat. He pulled his stuff out, settling it on the desk.

"Well, class, as I said, we have a new transfer student who will be staying with us going forward. Please be nice and help him if he asks any questions." The woman nodded and then turned to the blackboard, beginning the class.

The students around him kept glancing his way and he heard a few girls chattering quietly.

This was going to be a long day… and he could only imagine how his brother was feeling.

CHAPTER 4

Aiden withheld a glare as he walked to the last class of the morning. He usually liked school. There was a certain atmosphere that made it interesting and he didn't mind learning new things; but when the principal said the other students were behind, he didn't think they would be that far behind. He already learned non-linear functions and equations last year and they were just starting on that topic. It was going to be a uselessly long stretch of time.

Guess he was going to have to borrow a computer or something again, some online learning would probably work.

Thankfully, while the school was large, most classes were held in the same wing, so it was easy to find Noah again. To none of Aiden's surprise, he was already chatting with some of the other boys from class and a few girls. Aiden shook his head as he followed behind on the way to lunch. Noah glanced over his shoulder and blinked, grinning, before quickly saying something to the others. They waved before heading off and Noah came to a halt, waiting.

Geez… he didn't have to do that. Aiden joined Noah, giving him an unamused expression. "Already?"

"I've gotten a lot of questions, as usual, between classes. You should hear some of the stuff that goes around here." Noah shook his head, both amused and annoyed. "It's super weird."

"I don't want to know."

"Of course you don't," Noah said as they headed into the lunch line to grab some food, staple meals like chicken tenders and fries. They found a seat on one of the long tables, getting a few looks their way.

Ugh, just because they were twins didn't mean everyone had to watch them. It was annoying. Aiden's frown deepened as Noah plopped down, already munching on a fry. "Come on, relax."

Aiden slumped as Noah's expression shifted to a nervous one, belied by the faint upturn of his lips. Aiden at least managed the facsimile of a smile. "Nice mustache."

Noah blinked before quickly wiping at his upper lip, smearing the ketchup over it even more. "Aiden!" he huffed, grabbing a napkin as Aiden just grinned, munching on his own food.

Thankfully, no one came over, though he did briefly spot someone peering into the room before walking away.

It was strange, because he didn't remember hearing the door open, but suddenly there was this blonde-haired girl that seemed to be from the high-school wing peering in. Their eyes met and she quickly pulled back, disappearing. Aiden groaned.

The people here were really weird.

Soon enough, lunch ended and Noah waved before they split. The rest of the day passed fairly quietly until right before the last class.

He had gotten lost, which was odd, that was normally something Noah would struggle with, not him. He glanced toward the west wing, which he hadn't been to before, shaking his head and turning away.

"You are the new kid." A voice caught his ear and he jerked, turning. It was the same girl from lunch. She had long messy blonde hair that trailed over her shoulders and was a little older, probably around fifteen. She walked toward him, a slight limp to her step as a few students rushed past, as if ignoring her or not seeing her. She had a faint, yet odd smile on her lips. "Why is someone new here?" Her expression slipped. "Don't you know it's dangerous?"

Dangerous? What does… the disappearances? I guess others probably were aware of it too. Still, why was this random girl talking to him?

"Considering you said it as a statement, not a question, you already know." Aiden huffed, walking toward her since that was where he needed to go for his next class. Instead of letting him pass, she turned, staying in step with him.

"What's your name?"

"Why are you asking?" Aiden sighed and glanced sidelong. The girl's attention was straight ahead.

She paused for a moment before turning to him, shoulders tense with worry. "How about this? My name is Lynn. Is that better?"

After a moment of silence, Aiden spoke. "It's Aiden. To be honest, you should talk with my brother, Noah. He would be more willing to speak with you." Once more, Aiden increased his pace, spotting his classroom up ahead.

"Wait, brother?" Lynn blinked as she caught up, surprisingly agile with her limp. That worried expression increased. "Do you look alike? I think I saw him as well."

Aiden finally came to a stop, realizing this girl wasn't going to leave him alone. "Yes." He turned, annoyed. "It's clear I don't want to talk to you, why do you keep bothering me?" She stared at him quietly, long enough to make him feel uncomfortable. "Look, sorry, I'm not a fan of new places or people. Endless questions like this is—"

"It's fine." She softened, extending a hand toward him. "It's good to be wary, it might save your life." She appeared almost sad. "I wonder… if she really was right."

She?

Lynn must have noticed Aiden's confused expression because she shook her head and waved before quickly rushing away. Aiden found himself staring before annoyance flared through him. Why did he always get the strange ones? He turned toward the door, glancing up as the bell rang. He groaned, stepping inside. A hush fell over the room as all attention darted to him. He ignored it, finding one of the few empty seats. Thankfully, the teacher hadn't arrived yet. He settled in, peering toward the window which let in clouded sunlight. He could hear quiet whispering and felt steady gazes on him.

"Isn't that the new boy?"

"Yeah, did you see him earlier?"

"He was talking to himself, it was weird."

Aiden stiffened, glancing toward the girl who spoke, noticing her quickly turn away, words becoming more hushed. Wait, talking to himself? What were they talking about? That girl was a little older than Aiden, sure, but she was clearly a student and the school wasn't so big for an underclassman not to know an upperclassman or was it they didn't notice her since it was right before class? Aiden felt unsettled at the thought, it wasn't the first time he's talked with someone people didn't recognize, though he usually never saw them again. Maybe that would happen this time too.

He really did get all the weirdos.

There was a tap on his desk which startled him out of his reverie. A boy, sitting in front of him, leaned back, one finger lightly tapping at his desk. He had shorter blonde hair that seemed to resist combs with how messy it was, lightly freckled pale skin and a curious expression on his face. In some ways, the boy almost reminded Aiden of Lynn. "Oh, hey, we're in a couple classes together. You're that Aiden kid, right?"

Aiden nodded, already tired of introducing himself.

"The name's Phen. Full name, Stephen but… I don't much like it. I prefer Phen." He grinned, green eyes filled with a strange mischievousness. "Anyway, not much exciting happens around here, so it's nice to see new faces."

Aiden stared at him, not sure how to respond and Phen hummed, gaze flitting to the desk before turning back to him. "I heard you had a twin? Don't see many of those around here." He made it sound like they were an exotic animal or something. "I live pretty close to the school, where do you live?"

"Nearby." Aiden spoke up, already wanting to be out of this conversation, unfortunately, his mind wandered and a few questions arose. They said he was talking to himself, but he was clearly talking to that girl, though it was right before class started. Now he was curious. "By the way, how well do you know the students here?"

Phen raised an eyebrow, smirk on his face. "What, someone already catch your attention? You're a quick one."

Aiden barely resisted slapping a hand to his face. He kept his voice quiet, not wanting to stand out any more than he had to. "Not in that way. No, there was this girl who wouldn't stop talking to me. She said her name was Lynn."

The boy's expression froze at those words, stuck in a smile. "That's impossible. How do you even know that name?"

Aiden furrowed his brow. "Because she told me?"

Phen stared at him, impassiveness in place of the earlier chipper mood. "Liar."

Aiden sighed and shook his head. "Whatever."

He was used to this. People calling him a liar for knowing things he clearly was not supposed to know. That's why he didn't like talking to people. It wasn't his fault that people liked to talk to him for some reason. He knew he wasn't personable, so it made no sense to him.

To Aiden's surprise, instead of turning away, Phen continued to scrutinize him, a strange curiosity flitting on his face, along with a slowly growing hope and fear. "Wh… What did she look like?" Aiden found himself unable to respond, startled. Phen seemed to notice his expression and continued, "A lot of weird stuff has been happening recently. Our town is kind of known for oddities, but lately, things have escalated. You are a stranger, but… look, I know I called you a liar just a moment ago, but this is the first time I've heard that name in a while." His voice dipped to a whisper. "I was startled, but it's clear you weren't faking. You shouldn't know that name anyway, being so new, so…"

Aiden felt himself relax at that. "I appreciate it." He analyzed Phen quietly, debating on whether to speak or not. "She was probably about my height, long blonde hair and clearly from the high-school wing. She had a sort of limp to her step as she walked." Aiden watched as the boy nodded along before freezing at the last words.

His gaze snapped to Aiden, shock and horror in his expression. His fingers curled into the desk and he took a sharp breath, a hissing whisper, different from before. "Wait, you saw her? You talked to her? She was just outside?"

"Yes?" Aiden felt himself back up slightly at the sudden outburst. Phen was trembling, staring out the door. A few students turned to them before going back to whatever they were doing.

Where the heck was the teacher?

"Impossible. That's impossible…" He kept muttering, his gaze distant. Aiden groaned. Well, guess he wasn't getting any information now.

That proved to be the case as, a few minutes later, the teacher walked in, appearing more than a little disheveled. She quickly adjusted her jacket and walked to the front of the class to begin the lecture.

Aiden didn't miss the faint redness to her cheeks. He did not want to know.

Thankfully, class passed quickly after that. He stood, prepared to meet Noah, when a hand grasped his arm tightly. He winced, immediately pulling away, only to still when he realized it was the boy from earlier, Phen. He seemed to have calmed down, but had a strange expression on his face.

"I'm sorry." He pulled away. "That girl you spoke with, Lynn. Can you tell me where you last saw her go?"

Aiden hesitated. He wasn't necessarily doing anything else today, and it was clear the boy was going to keep insisting. That persistence strangely reminded Aiden of Lynn again and he slumped, nodding. Plus, it would be funny to tell Noah he already 'made a friend'. "I didn't see much, but—"

"Anything, anything you can tell me." Phen spoke up.

Aiden let out a breath, heading for the door. Getting out of the musty smell of the room to slightly more fresh, if still metallic air was a godsend. Most of the class already left. The teacher was busy filling out papers, letting out a huge yawn.

Aiden didn't miss Noah's surprise when he walked out with Phen at his side. Nor did he miss Phen's shock as his attention snapped between the two of them. "Oh… you really are twins." Phen's gaze settled on Noah, who chuckled, before turning back to Aiden. "So?"

Aiden blinked, confused as Noah snorted. "Sorry for my brother, my name's Noah, yours?"

"Phen." Phen turned back to him. "Your brother said he would help me find someone."

Noah's eyebrows rose sharply, clearly shocked by the words. Aiden crossed his arms over his chest, glaring. Noah quickly waved his hands, defensive as a sheepish smile crossed his face. "Sorry, that's… anyway, who was it?"

"Someone I've been searching for. She's been missing for a few days now."

Noah's expression froze, gaze meeting Aiden's in a 'seriously, again?' expression. It wasn't Aiden's fault this happened. Though it was rare for someone to join them. "Really… Anyways." Noah turned back to Phen as Aiden shifted on his heels, heading toward the west wing where he first met her. He heard scrambling and a sigh from Noah. "Aiden, wait!"

"I'm showing where I last talked with her." Aiden spoke, voice even. "Let's just get this over with."

"You are way too blunt sometimes." Noah's jesting tone only slightly overshadowed the worry in his voice. "Anyway, so your name is Phen, what got you to talk to my brother in the first place?"

"Oh, uh… that's…"

"Noah, leave him alone." Aiden peered over his shoulder, noticing the way Phen was staring past him, clearly distracted. Noah backed off as Phen glanced toward Aiden with a grateful look before his attention shifted forward once more, observing everything with a strange degree of wariness.

"The west wing?" Phen spoke up, hesitant. "I've never been this way myself and there are almost no classes this way even with the joint school…" Aiden observed the area quietly. The hallways changed slightly. The lockers were a bit more rusted and the walls slightly more dilapidated. "I mean, the occult club will sometimes meet here, but most people avoid it."

"You have an occult club?" Noah perked up as Aiden loudly groaned.

"Yeah, my sister was part of it," Phen replied, staring down the corridor. "I found this place creepy, so I would always wait by the school entrance instead…" he trailed off.

Aiden couldn't help but get a bad feeling, his stomach twisting slightly. Noah's expression dropped, becoming serious. His attention returned to the hallway, now quiet with the students having left the school. A faint creaking groan echoed through the hall.

"You said she was this way, right?" Phen asked. When Aiden nodded, he took a deep breath and started walking forward. Noah and Aiden, startled, stayed a few paces behind.

CHAPTER 5

Aiden shivered, noticing as Noah did the same. The hallway was slightly colder than the rest of the school and the sound of their footsteps echoed oddly off of the walls.

"Lynn! Lynn, are you there!" Phen started shouting, startling both of them.

That twisted feeling grew.

"Phen?" A voice echoed back, causing all three of them to jump and turn. Standing in one of the doorways, a dark room beyond with the vaguest impressions of black curtains caught Aiden's attention. That is, before a girl stepped out. It was the same one as before, a slight limp to her step and hair a light blonde trailing passed. Noah shifted back, clearly recognizing her. He must have seen her at lunch as well. Lynn ignored them entirely, gaze focused on Phen, who stood frozen. "You can see me, right?"

"Lynn?" Phen took a step forward, and then another. "Is that really you?" His voice was shaken, giving Aiden no time to think of what the girl just asked.

"Of course it's me." She smiled, expression watery as she extended a hand toward him, just like she did before for Aiden. "I'm sorry, Phen. I never meant for this to happen."

"What? Why are you apologizing? What do you mean?" Phen hurried forward, reaching for Lynn who pulled away. "Just come home. I've been looking for days! Why… why didn't you say something if you were still in the school?"

Lynn's expression shifted, pained as she turned to Aiden. "I didn't believe it when she said it. She felt it, felt you. You really are able to save us." She spoke softly, tears trailing down her cheeks. "Please, help my brother find me."

"What? But you're ri—"

Lynn smiled and took another step back, disappearing into the darkness. Faint words hummed in the air, a mere whisper. "Buried within…"

Phen darted forward as the words faded. "Lynn! Sister!"

"What?" Noah spoke quietly, confusion clear in his voice. Aiden wasn't much better, thoughts churning. He cautiously meandered forward, glancing inside the room, only to still.

The only one there, breathing heavily, was Phen.

Lynn was nowhere in sight.

"Where is she?" Phen's voice was broken. "She was right here." He whipped around and darted forward, startling Aiden. He grasped Aiden's shirt, tugging him almost off his feet. "Where is she? I wasn't imagining it, right? She was here, right?"

"Hey, panicking isn't going to help." Noah stepped in, as Aiden glared.

Phen loosened his grip, letting Aiden go. Aiden adjusted his shirt and crossed his arms over his chest. "We should talk to Dad. He would probably be able to help."

"Your father?" Phen asked, shaken. "Could he really help?" He stared down at his hands, pale. "My sister. She looked exactly the same as she did when she disappeared."

"How long ago did she disappear again?" Noah asked as Aiden stepped back. The chill faded slightly, but the unease still held tightly to his stomach.

"About five days ago."

That feeling plummeted. Yeah… he was going to have to ask Dad.

"She said you could save her. That you could help me find her. I know you don't know me, and I don't know you, but this is the closest I've gotten to knowing what happened to her."

Noah and Aiden exchanged looks before Noah shrugged. "Why not? Dad's busy anyway."

Aiden groaned, face in his hands. Of course Noah would accept. "And where do we even start? She's clearly not here."

Noah went to argue, only to pause. "There might be a clue here, right?"

Phen's expression lit up and he started to scramble around the room. Noah soon joined. Aiden stayed outside, deep in thought.

The words, buried within, echoed in his mind. Buried within? What was buried within? The clue? Something else?

For a morbid moment, he shivered as he wondered if it was maybe her.

He promptly pushed the idea off because it was utterly stupid, inconceivable, really.

Aiden paused as a cold breeze blew past. He frowned.

Tap, tap.

He stiffened and jerked, turning toward the sound. Across the hall was a wall of windows facing a small courtyard where meager light drifted through.

Pressed up against the window, one eye obscured by still wet jet black hair, was the girl who broke their window last night, her piercing golden gaze locked on his.

Aiden did everything in his power not to scream as she tapped again and then pointed.

"Aiden? Did you see something?"

Aiden jerked, noticing as Noah poked his head out the door before following his original line of sight. "You look like you saw a ghost."

"Ludicrous." Aiden spoke before turning back toward the window, only to do a double-take. Once again, the girl was gone.

Where had she been pointing? Why did she leave so quickly? He hesitated before noticing a door that led to the courtyard, half-hidden by lockers.

This was so stupid.

"Huh, I didn't know there was a door there. Phen, where does that door lead?" Noah pulled back into the room.

Phen, who seemed to be scrabbling at the floor, glanced up with a furrowed brow. "What door?"

"That one." Noah gestured toward the end of the hall. Aiden continued to stare at it, not sure what to do.

Follow the creepy girl? Or stay put? The obvious choice was to stay put, but, like Noah, he was curious.

"That leads to the courtyard. No one goes there, it's said to be haunted." Phen hesitated before furrowing his brow. "It's also close to the occult room. Maybe Lynn took it as a cut-through."

He bolted toward the door, Noah calling out in surprise. Aiden hesitated before letting out a sigh and following after, Noah scurrying past.

It seemed the door was stuck slightly, but soon, Phen managed to get it open. Clouds once again covered the sky, but it didn't seem like it was going to rain, it just cast a dim light over everything.

Noah perked up, glancing to one side before heading over. Aiden followed Noah's gaze. The ground dried considerably since the early morning rain, but there were still tracks of mud here and there. However, where Noah squatted, the mud seemed to have been dug up by an animal. Aiden wondered how Noah even noticed before he mentally slapped himself.

Noah was in investigation mode, of course he would notice something strange.

"What are you looking at? It's just earth." Phen glanced over, clearly annoyed.

Aiden paused, gaze snapping back toward the window where he saw the girl from their new 'home', the one with black hair and who always seemed soaked to the bone. She had been pointing this way.

He walked over toward where she stood, as Noah began brushing away the dirt and mud, revealing more of what he must have noticed.

Phen watched, clearly both confused and frustrated. Not that Aiden could blame him. This was his sister, of course he would be worried. Aiden shuddered, he couldn't imagine what would happen if he lost Noah or Dad. He positioned himself where the strange black-haired girl was and followed her line of sight.

The door wasn't visible from this angle, but Noah was.

Noah stilled, paling slightly. "Uh… uh…" Aiden darted over, noticing as Noah suddenly jerked back, turning and throwing up into a nearby set of flowers.

"What are you doing?" Phen, at this point, just seemed angry. "We're searching for my sister!"

Aiden slid to a stop, squatting where his brother had been, as, with the other hand, he patted Noah's back. Something pale shone in the faint light, cloth clinging to it, just visible through the dirt. Aiden carefully brushed some dirt away with his sleeve, hearing Noah gagging behind him.

Aiden didn't say anything, he couldn't as he continued brushing using the sleeve of his jacket. "Noah, call Dad, and the police."

"Al—already on it," Noah coughed out, fingers clicking loudly over a phone.

"Wha—why?" Phen stepped over and Aiden stood, turning toward Phen and shaking his head. Trying hard to not panic at what Noah found was a monumental feat in that moment. Sure, he saw and heard some of Dad's cases, but this was… Phen glared. "Will you stop this? We're searching for Lynn, she was right there. I told you she would be through this door, so why—"

"Lynn isn't that way." Aiden spoke up, gaze locked with Phen. Aiden let out a breath. "Just…"

"How would you know that?" Phen growled.

Aiden clicked his tongue. He wasn't sure how to deal with this. He didn't know Phen, why was he—Aiden pulled away, once more squatting down. He was trying to keep his mind steady, but it was doing a fantastic job of screaming bloody murder. He could hear Noah speaking into the phone, being concise like Dad taught them. Aiden couldn't pay too much attention to the conversation.

After all, they just saw Lynn. Aiden and Phen talked to her, so…

Phen walked over, glancing between Noah and Aiden, only to freeze as Aiden brushed a little more of the dirt away, Aiden's sleeve now covered in mud. Phen collapsed to the ground, staring down at the pale and slightly bloated form of a young woman, only partially visible eye wide in fear.

Aiden wanted to join his brother in throwing up, but held off. After all, his mind was shutting down at the fact that he just talked to Lynn… and yet was staring at the corpse just two feet away.

"Lynn?" Phen spoke hesitantly, shock on his face as he tentatively reached forward. "But… I was just…"

"I know."

Everyone's attention snapped up as Lynn sat down, staring down at her own dead body.

"Lynn? You're alive?" Phen spoke, the beginning of tears threatening to fall.

Lynn's smile was all Aiden needed to know. Or well, all he could know. His mind ground to a halt at the inconsistency before him. How was this possible? Lynn was dead, and yet she wasn't?

"You're a ghost." Noah spoke up, catching their attention as he wiped at his mouth, hand trembling.

Lynn nodded, expression soft and yet so painfully sad.

"Ghost?" Phen parroted.

Yep, Aiden was done, this was too much. "There's no way." Aiden shot to his feet. "Ghosts don't exist."

"Aiden—"

"No." Aiden slashed an arm out. "I'm out of here, you can talk to Dad and the police." At that, he turned to race away.

"Wait." Lynn's voice met his ears and he stilled. If he didn't turn around, he could imagine he was talking to someone normal. "I know it wasn't much, but I've been trying to get back to my brother for a while now. You and your brother gave me the strength to do that, to ask for help. Thank you."

"I don't know what you're talking about." With that, Aiden darted away. If he didn't leave now, he was going to faint.

•   •   •   •   •

Noah watched Aiden bolt off, pained. He couldn't even imagine what Aiden was feeling right now. Sure, ghosts seemed surreal to Noah, but he at least had a slight belief in them, but Aiden… Noah let out a breath, knowing Aiden would be alright before turning back toward the young woman and Phen. Phen was staring at Lynn, tears streaking down his cheeks. "What? Helped? You had been trying to contact me?"

Lynn stood and walked over, squatting in front of Phen. "I'm your older sister, I only meant to make it quick and be back."

"What happened?"

Lynn shook her head. "I don't remember."

Phen curled his hands into fists, digging into the ground. Lynn reached forward, hands gently catching his cheek. Whether it was touching or not, Noah couldn't tell. "I'm glad you found me." Her gaze shifted to Noah. "All of you."

"How?" Noah managed to get out, shocked. He would have found this fascinating, if it wasn't for the implications.

Lynn pulled away, almost floating over the earth, if it wasn't for the faint sound of footsteps. "Your brother and you made me strong enough to manifest."

"Huh?"

Lynn smiled. "You will realize, one day, just know you helped my brother and me today, and that is enough."

"No." Phen stood sharply, taking a step forward. "It's not. I knew when the police gave up almost right away that it was probably pointless, but I couldn't just stop. How am I supposed to believe you're—" he cut himself off.

Lynn turned, body flickering as if she was barely holding on. She was so solid only moments before, but now, as Noah observed her, it was as if she was becoming opaque, almost wispy. "My sweet little brother." Lynn spoke gently. "My dear Phen… don't let him catch you, okay? I researched too deep, knew too much."

Phen stilled and Noah narrowed his eyes, curious on what she meant.

The moment was interrupted as the sound of sirens met their ears. Both of them turned toward the front of the school.

"Good-bye, Phen."

Noah turned just as Phen stilled, only to jerk back toward Lynn. However, Lynn was gone. The only one that remained was the slightly bloated corpse buried in the ground.

Noah was on the verge of feeling sick again, even though he knew there was nothing left in his stomach.

Phen, on the other hand, just collapsed, staring down.

CHAPTER 6

That was how Dad and the police found them.

"Noah!" Dad called, pulling him up into a tight hug, worry clear in his voice. "When you called, I came running as fast as I could." His gaze slid to the police who were already taking pictures of the scene. One was talking to Phen, who seemed to be in shock. "I already told the police I needed to make sure you two were okay before I helped them. Where's your brother?"

Aiden, right. Noah tried to center himself, gaze averted as the police worked. "He's fine. He just needed to get away."

Dad let out a relieved breath as one of the police officers walked over, nodding to Dad before turning to Noah. "You were the one who called, correct?"

"Yes." Noah straightened as Dad put a hand on his shoulder, more as a comfort. He was clearly staying out of it, though. Noah wasn't surprised.

"I'm sorry to bother you, but I do have a few questions." The officer, a taller man in uniform, watched the scene before returning his attention back toward Noah. "Was it just you and the boy, Phen, who discovered the corpse?"

"No, my brother was here too," Noah admitted. He had a feeling Phen would probably say something, so lying was not the best option. "He couldn't stand seeing it and ran."

The officer peered down his nose, suspicious. "Speaking of, how was it you managed to find the deceased victim?"

Noah stilled. How could he explain it was because they had been following what could only be a ghost? "We're new here and Phen agreed to lead us around. He mentioned how this area was haunted, so we decided to take a look. Some animal started digging there and revealed part of her clothing." Noah tried to keep his voice even. He wasn't necessarily lying, technically, it was Phen showing them around… kind of. At least, after Aiden showed which way Lynn went.

"This girl has been missing for a while and you suddenly just come across her—"

"Officer, I will cut you off there." Father spoke up. "As you might recall from the reports I gave you and your team. My boys and I just arrived in town two days ago and I AM working to find out what happened here in the first place. From what I am hearing both now and on the way here, this girl disappeared almost a week ago."

"Right, my apologies." The man actually appeared sheepish. "It's been a long few weeks and suspicions are high, you must understand." He let out a breath, turning back to Noah. "I would like to ask your brother some questions as well. Do you happen to know where he ran off to?"

"No." Noah shook his head.

The officer pursed his lips before turning back to Dad. "Considering the situation, it might be best if your children stay together. If you need to find your son, go ahead and do it now."

"I agree." Dad nodded. "If you need anything else from my sons or me, don't hesitate to ask. Once I am sure they are alright, I will be back to join the investigation on this matter. For now, though, I would like to check on my son. This is a lot for a child."

The officer nodded and turned away. Dad gently pushed at Noah's back, leading them out the door, away from the scene.

"Noah, I want you to stay here." Dad turned once they were away from the officers and toward the front of the school. "I'll look for Aiden, but I know you're still coping with what happened. I'll be right back. If you need anything, there are officers right outside and my cellphone is on."

Noah nodded, unable to do much else as Dad hurried off. He felt terrible. Their first day here and already all of this happened? Part of him was worried for Aiden. After all, if Noah was struggling to come to terms with the situation, how did his much more analytical and skeptical brother feel?

•   •   •   •   •

Aiden stared out over the meadow just beyond the school. The surrounding wall was about waist high, but that didn't matter. He perched himself on top of it, trying to get his thoughts in order. He calmed down, staring out over the green grass littered with flowers and, farther off, trees. Still, his thoughts kept flickering back, back to the visage of the bloated body, back to the marks around her neck… back to her talking to them so casually.

What was she? She couldn't have been a ghost, that was impossible. But, it wasn't a hallucination because all three of them were talking to her. He didn't recall seeing any machine that could have created a hologram and, to be honest, he doubted any hologram would be that high-tech in this day and age anyway.

Yet, he couldn't accept the idea that he had been talking to the dead. That was impossible. There was no such thing, no matter what his brother said, he must be going insane.

He peered up, noting the clouds whipping through the sky. It was either the rainy season, or they just had really bad luck with the weather lately.

To be honest, he wasn't sure how long he sat out there, trying and failing to calm his racing thoughts. There had to be an answer to all of this. He knew he should go back. He technically left his brother with a stranger and a dead body.

He gagged at that and curled up as everything finally caught up with him.

She was only a little older than them. For no one to know she died, that she was buried in the freaking school courtyard? Discounting the whole talking to her part, it was terrifying to think about.

He just wanted to be out of this place.

He heard faint footsteps and paused, glancing over his shoulder.

He expected Noah or Dad. What he hadn't expected, and sent him tumbling off the wall in terror, was the girl from their new home. Water slowly dripped from her frame as that single golden eye pierced through him, as if examining his very soul and he HATED it.

"You found her." The words whispered over the wind. "I thought so."

"Who are you?" Aiden kept the wall between them, whipping the backpack off his back and holding it, ready to swing if necessary. His whole body was tense and he felt a trill of panic run through him. What or who was this girl?

The girl just tilted her head. For a… whoever she was, her skin was incredibly dark and warm. It almost seemed to shine in the dreary light. "Hm, it's been a long time since I've shared my name to the point that I no longer remember it." A faint twitch of a smile curled onto her lips. "But, it's also been a long time since anyone saw me. Nonetheless, you gave me the strength to shatter a window."

"You're making no sense." Aiden spoke, trying to keep his voice level as he glared at her. "There was NO reason to shatter our window."

The girl hummed. "I was just trying to get inside from the rain."

Aiden didn't believe her, knuckles white. "If that was the case, you could have simply knocked on the door. There was no reason to attempt to crawl through our window. That is beyond creepy."

The girl's head cocked the other way, almost like a bobble head and it unnerved Aiden greatly. "You simply don't understand, do you?"

Aiden shifted a foot backward, ready to run. He froze as she suddenly surged over the wall, dress fluttering in the wind as she leapt over. In an instant she pushed into his face, a way too wide grin curled over bloodless lips. "But you are exactly what I need to get home. How else will I accomplish my goal if I don't stick right beside you?"

Aiden, instinct screaming, swung his bag, spinning in the same movement. The girl stumbled back, clearly startled. He finished his spin and booked it, almost slipping over what little mud was left.

A hand grasped his wrist and he was tugged back. The girl leaned forward, chin inches from his shoulder, the black hair almost tangling with his own reddish-brown with how close she got. "Stop running." Her smile was gone. Her form flickered, the wetness slowly drying. A heavy chill ran up and down Aiden's spine as he stood, frozen. "For someone with such strength, you seriously have no idea of your situation. I am barely restraining myself."

"Aiden!" Dad's voice snapped him out of his thoughts and he swung his bag once more, causing her to step back, letting him go. He dashed away, heading toward his father's voice. He spun around the corner, almost slamming into his father. Dad caught him as he stumbled. "Whoa, son, what's wrong?"

Aiden took deep breaths, realizing he was shaking slightly. "It's that girl from yesterday," he managed to force out, peering over his shoulder.

Dad's eyes narrowed. He peeked around the corner, watching for a moment before slowly pulling back, a gentle smile on his face. "She's gone." He placed a hand to Aiden's neck, startling him. "And you're not wearing the necklace…" His expression was sad, almost pained. "Why?"

Aiden shifted. "It's…" He tilted his head. Of course Dad noticed. "I didn't want to. Still, Dad, why are you asking? Aren't there more important things to worry about?"

"No," Dad cut in, startling Aiden. "I don't know what I have to do to convince you, but I want you to wear your necklace. It's for your own—" Dad stopped suddenly before sighing. "I know you don't like it, I get that. Just promise you will wear it from now on? At least while we're here?"

Aiden pursed his lips before sighing and nodding. He dug into his pocket and draped it around his neck, tucking it under his shirt. Dad seemed to relax at that, a gentle smile on his face that promptly disappeared into a more serious one. "What happened?"

Aiden hesitated. He wasn't sure he could explain, or wanted to, but he knew Noah would, so he let out a long breath and began speaking. He doubted his father would believe him, but then he had to remind himself that his dad had a strong belief in the supernatural, which Aiden still thought was ludicrous. His sibling and father were insane, but he had no other way to tell the story. Did he believe it? No, there was no way he could, but he was logical enough to at least give the facts of what he had seen himself.

Dad's expression shifted from concern to worry to a thoughtful silence as they walked, Dad gently pressing against his back. "Was this girl who pointed out the grave the same as the one who spoke with you just a few moments ago?"

Aiden hesitated before nodding. Dad tilted his head down, deep in thought before letting out a long breath that seemed to carry a lot in it. "I hoped this wouldn't happen."

Huh?

"Come, let's get your brother. I will talk with the police later."

Aiden wasn't sure what he thought of that, but let his dad lead him away. He turned, just catching the girl's long tangled hair and piercing gaze before she pulled back. He shivered.

Who was she?

CHAPTER 7

They soon caught up with Noah. Phen had been led away, according to Noah, by a police officer.

They walked outside to find a small crowd watching, curious. Dad led them to one side toward their car and hopped in. Aiden found himself in the back seat, but didn't mind this time, thoughts flaring and roaming. The chill in the air was gone, Aiden noted, and the uneasy feeling that had been tugging at him had passed.

The ride to their new home was strangely quiet, none of them wanted to talk, trying to process what just happened.

"So, the Raven luck strikes again." Dad finally spoke up as they were pulling out of town. "First day of school too, who knew I would be driving you both to and from school."

"It just happened," Noah said. "Aiden actually started talking to a student, his name is Phen, by the way, and it turned out Phen's sister Lynn talked to Aiden, which is weird because—" he cut himself off as silence filled the car once more.

Dad let out a heavy sigh as he pulled up to the garage, turning the car off before getting out. "Come, I believe the living room is cleaned up, at least somewhat. I'll get back to work after this." Aiden exchanged glances with Noah, brow furrowed. Guess whatever it was they needed to talk about was serious.

They headed inside, locking the doors as they went before stopping in the living room. It was small with only a single couch and two chairs on either side of a small wooden table. Noah and Aiden ended up on the couch as Dad practically slumped into one of the chairs. His smile was sad and pained.

"Dad, what happened back there?" Noah asked, voice hesitant.

Dad withdrew into himself slightly, taking deep breaths before he spoke. "That was a spirit, a ghost."

"No way," Aiden cut in, finding himself panicking at the thought. "I know you believe in the supernatural, but—"

"Aiden." Dad's voice was strict, causing Aiden to clam up. "For now, just listen."

Aiden wanted to argue, but one look from Noah, who pleaded with him to stay quiet, caused him to slump.

Dad seemed to take that as agreement because he continued. "To be honest, many of the people you have encountered over the years have been ghosts, humans long departed from this realm that cling to the essence of life."

Aiden stilled at that, thoughts flicking to the multiple visages he recalled seeing.

"Even the drunkard?" Noah blinked curiously.

"No, that was a legit drunkard who needed a good slap in the face." Dad chuckled.

Aiden found himself snorting at that, relieved. At least only most of his life was a lie so far, no biggie.

"So then, who were they? The ghosts I mean?" Noah leaned forward, hands between his legs as he gripped the couch. "I mean, I don't remember seeing any traditional ghosts like those see through or opaque ones on tv or the messed up ones in video games."

"That is—I'm not sure on the specifics of why you couldn't differentiate them." Dad peered toward the window, thoughts churning. "I'm just going to ask, who do you think they might have been?"

Noah clearly seemed to be thinking hard, debating. Aiden shivered. "What about that woman who wouldn't leave me alone?" He asked softly. "She kept trying to touch my arm and hug me."

Dad winced and sighed. "Yes, that was one."

Noah jerked, eyes wide. "So, wait, what about the guy who kept following us at school a few years ago? Or that boy who was flirting with everyone but they all just ignored him? Or that—" He shuddered. "Or those girls who kept staring at Aiden?"

At each one that Noah listed off, their father gave another tired nod. "In order, the woman had lost her child and, when her house caught on fire in her sleep, she continued looking. The man was killed for… reasons I shall not name. He was banished. The young man you spoke of died of an actual broken heart, there was no saving him. As for the girls, I'm not entirely sure on that one. Someone else took care of them." He shook his head as Aiden found himself curling into the couch as each memory flared through his mind… along with so many more.

"That man who crawled through the window after Noah let him in?" He asked softly.

Dad just nodded, absolute fury on his face. "I made sure that one was taken care of, thoroughly. It was a very satisfying case to complete." He let out a tired sigh. "However, I realized early on that they all appeared human to you so, wanting to give you the most normal life I could, I just passed them off as, I guess you can say, creeps. There are a lot of people in the world like that even though they are still living." His gaze flicked to Noah. "And that is why I told you never to let some stranger into the house. I thought you would know better."

Noah actually winced at that, fingers curling inward as he slumped, attention on the floor.

"So, why can we see these things?" Aiden asked hesitantly. He wasn't sure if he could or wanted to believe it, but he needed to know. Especially after learning how much of his life was a lie. Noah nodded along, probably a mix between curious and worried like himself.

Dad hesitated before tapping the floor, the rug muffling some of the sound. "I don't know if you remember, but your mother was a powerful woman. Fierce, kind and gentle." Dad's expression grew distant as he continued, "I loved her, as much as I love you two. That's part of why I became an investigator, for her, to help her. When we had you two, I couldn't help but to find myself with a new purpose." He watched them, expression soft. "I wanted to do whatever I could to keep you two safe, just like your mother would."

Aiden and Noah exchanged glances as Dad continued, "You see, your mother was a powerful psychic, a ghost-whisperer, some would say. I am able to interact with them as well, though not to the same extent as she could." He weakly chuckled at that for some reason. "To be honest, I only have some of the basics in that regard. I have knowledge on them and can somewhat see them, but that's with some concentration. Unlike you two and your mother. Of course, I only realized after she disappeared that you two held her abilities."

"So, we can talk to and see ghosts." Noah's face shifted into a wide grin. "Cool! I thought you were just saying it to make us feel better."

Aiden didn't agree, panic and horror flaring through him. His grip tightened on his jeans as the words finally connected in his thoughts, solidifying into a horrifying realization. Nope, NOPE! He was not listening to this. Ghosts DON'T exist. He tried to focus once more on Dad, knowing he couldn't completely ignore the situation, no matter how much he wanted to. Sure, he just listed off all the types of ghosts they met but… that was a past thing, something he could readily ignore. They were talking present tense, as in, something they could do NOW.

Dad watched Aiden quietly before nodding toward Noah, amused. "I suppose it could be." He paused. "It was only natural that you would be able to interact with them but I always wanted you to be able to live a life that didn't revolve around them. A more normal life where the supernatural and paranormal weren't the most prominent features."

Aiden paused at that, shoulders slumping as a faint realization dawned on him. However, it was Noah who spoke, stunned. "That's why you would 'put up those barriers 'and had us wear these." He showed his necklace, getting a nod from Dad.

"I'm not as strong as your mother with the paranormal, but I know the basics of protection, as I said earlier." His gaze slipped to Aiden. "And I figured a gift would make more sense than demanding you to wear something. Though it seems demanding is sometimes the better option if it means keeping you two safe."

Aiden glanced askance, fingers flitting to his neck. No wonder Dad said that earlier.

"Wait, so these actually do something?" Noah pulled up the necklace, fiddling with it. Dad nodded. "Neat! See, I told you." Noah turned to Aiden before he paused. "Aiden?"

"Why?" Aiden tilted his head up, fidgeting in his seat, not looking at either of them. "I know you wanted us to have a normal life, but did you honestly think we would? What with constantly moving and having random people show up all the time doing weird shit? With people wondering who we were talking to when it turned out we were probably talking to a—" Aiden cut himself off.

Thankfully, it seemed Dad understood. He let out a tired breath. "I was doing what I thought was right." He pushed himself to his feet and walked over. He reached over. Aiden slapped his hand away. Dad paused.

Aiden turned his head down. "It makes no god damn sense. You've lied to us, but how was that protecting us? We could still see them, they could still get to us. I hate the idea, but if we had at least known, we could have protected ourselves better, could have known what to look out for." He curled inward. "Could have known when we were talking to someone that others probably couldn't see. Ghosts, spirits, whatever the hell they are shouldn't exist and now I'm forced to believe that? To believe everything I've seen and heard is a lie?"

It would certainly explain all the strange looks he always got in every school.

"Aiden…"

"No wonder no one believed us." He snapped, staring up at his father with anger. "We're all insane, this situation is insane!"

A hand lightly landed on his head and he went to shove it off before he found another hand wrapping behind his back. "I'm sorry." Aiden paused at his dad's pained words, noticing his dad was shaking slightly, holding Aiden to his chest. "I wasn't sure what else to do after your mother disappeared."

Aiden wanted to be angry and frustrated, he did, but it was rare to see his dad being so vulnerable. He felt stiff, unsure what to do, how to react. That anger and frustration and confusion still lingered, but this was his dad. He sighed and relaxed at least a little bit. "For now... Alright."

Dad held him in a tight hug for a moment longer before slowly pulling away, ruffling his hair. Noah leaned over, almost pushing Aiden off the couch. He shifted, glaring toward Noah who just gave him a weak smile before turning to Dad. "What did Lynn mean when she said we gave her the ability to save her?"

Dad paused at that, brow furrowed. "I'm not quite certain. That's beyond my expertise."

Noah furrowed his brow, but grinned. "By the way, is that why you are so good at investigations? Because you can talk to ghosts?"

"That's a newer thing." Dad chuckled, pulling back, clearly trying to lighten the mood a little. "I always wanted to be an investigator, the ghost thing was an added benefit and curse." He winced. "Just, now that you know, be careful with them. True, they were once human, but they are not anymore. Becoming a ghost twists the spirit and soul, even the gentlest human can become a dangerous ghost if given the right prompting. They can help you and some will." At that, he turned to Aiden before turning back to Noah. "But some are so obsessed with what kept them to this realm, what bound their spirits here, that they won't rest until they get what they want."

"Oh." Noah blinked as Aiden sighed.

"So, what do we do in those cases?" Aiden asked, arms wrapped around himself. He hadn't accepted it, but he couldn't ignore it either. So having knowledge on the subject could be beneficial.

Dad shrugged. "You're smart boys, sometimes you can talk, sometimes you run and sometimes…" He reached into his pocket, pulling out some salt. "You throw salt in their face and laugh, or you try to banish them."

Noah blinked as Aiden felt a deadpan expression cross his face.

Dad chuckled and put the salt back into his pocket, small granules slipping through his fingers. "Well, the salt thing works to a small extent. It sometimes just annoys them though." His expression shifted, almost stern. "However, I wouldn't try to attempt to banish any, which is a completely different process and a complicated one."

"I'm curious on it." Noah spoke up, getting a wince from Dad. "You mentioned one of the ghosts we met got banished, right? Can you show me?"

Dad shook his head. "No, it's dangerous. One wrong move and, instead of banishing, you bind the ghost to you and, believe me, you do not want that."

"That's a thing?" Aiden wasn't sure he really wanted to know what was going on anymore.

Dad nodded. "Let's just say, some possessions are the results of bonds made when a priest attempts to banish and fails. There isn't much that can be done for the victim."

"Oh…" Noah glanced down. "So, what's going to happen now?"

Dad hummed, deep in thought. "Most likely the police will ask for specifics on how you found her." His expression shifted. "I'll cover for you when I get back. What I'm more worried about is what did that to her… or who."

"It should be who," Aiden said quietly. "What shouldn't matter."

Dad's expression was even as he responded, "That's the thing, we don't know. It is possible it could be a ghost or a human. A killing like that, in broad daylight, even in an area less utilized is not something easily accomplished by a normal small town killer. Either we are dealing with a professional or…" He let out a sigh. "Either way, it's not something for you two to think about. Wear your necklaces and you should be protected from them. Once I figure out what's going on, we will leave this town. Believe me, in the two days I've been here, there isn't much reason for me to want to stay." He chuckled. "For one, the weather is atrocious, and for two, this town has more ghosts in it than humans, it feels like."

"Is that a thing?" Noah blinked.

Dad paused at that. "Not that I know of, but it certainly feels like it." He pushed himself to his feet. "Then again, we haven't been anywhere with a storied history, so I can't say. Anyway, I'll make dinner tonight. For now, get some rest. Once I get back from talking with the police we'll get dinner started. Sound good?" He glanced between them, receiving nods from both, though Aiden's was more reluctant. Dad pushed himself to his feet and, with a heavy sigh and wave, he slipped out.

Aiden pulled inward, arms wrapping tightly around himself as he pushed into the couch. He let out a startled yelp as Noah practically fell onto his lap, peering up with an amused, if hesitant, smirk. "Well, I got your attention."

"Seriously?"

"Come on, Aiden, I know that was a lot, but at least we got some information and Dad will be back soon. He only went to collect what information he could and make sure the police were on the way to the next objective or whatever."

Aiden knew that but, he couldn't help but feel off. "Will you get off?"

"Eh… nah, I'm having fun annoying you." Noah grinned, putting his hands over his head and stretching almost like a cat.

Aiden used the movement to kick a leg upward, causing Noah to yelp and quickly catch himself. "Jerk…"

Aiden pushed himself to his feet, unable to hide the hint of amusement as Noah rubbed the back of his head, pouting. "Well, I did tell you."

"Yeah, yeah." He stood, hesitating. "So, I wonder why all those creeps always seemed to focus on you?"

Aiden froze at that. He was trying to ignore that detail. He let out a sigh. "Probably because, if that cross actually did something…"

"You never wore it." Noah let out a huff. "No wonder Dad was always frantic and pissed when he found out."

"And how he seemed to have a sixth sense when it came to knowing if I was wearing it." Aiden grumbled, getting a chuckle from Noah. "Most likely it was because of that."

Noah's expression softened, pained. "Yeah… Um, Aiden?" Aiden's gaze flicked to him as Noah stepped toward the door. "Do you think if Mom was here she would have told us earlier?"

Aiden stilled, mind flashing through way too many thoughts before he turned away and shrugged. "She's not, so we'll never know."

"That's—"

"Just, stop asking. I'm not in the mood to talk right now." Aiden pushed through the doorway, heading to his room. He was just going to work on homework and call it. This was too much for him.

CHAPTER 8

A few hours later, Dad returned looking haggard but relieved, carrying bags of groceries. Noah, silent after their odd conversation, helped him unpack.

Aiden slipped into the room, noting Noah's hesitant expression before he peered over to Dad. "Dad, do you mind if I join you? I can't think straight."

"Of course." Dad actually seemed to light up slightly. "It has been a while since we've cooked together and I brought ingredients for pasta."

"Really?" Aiden perked up as Noah shook his head, amused.

Dad actually chuckled at that. "Come on, I bet you two are probably starved. You are still growing boys, after all."

"Dad!" Noah called, almost embarrassed, but at least no longer oddly silent.

"Considering how much you eat, he isn't wrong." Aiden spoke up, letting a faint teasing tone slip in. It wasn't often that he actually got to tease Noah and it felt like it fit.

Noah huffed. "Fine, I get it. I'll be working on homework." Aiden waved as Noah hurried away.

"It's good to see you teasing, but do keep in mind not to do it too often." Dad reached forward, ruffling Aiden's hair. Aiden reached up to swat him away before letting out a sigh. "Still, the fact that you are relaxed enough to do that makes me feel better."

Aiden turned away, unsure how to respond to that. "So, food?"

"Right, let's get cooking." Dad started rolling up his sleeves as Aiden just shook his head, amused. As much as he found himself aggravated with Dad, he also found himself relieved, a faint smile crossing his face as they worked. Dad managed to get splattered with a little sauce when he accidentally whisked to hard. This was comforting after a day of mayhem and, when they sat down to eat, the three of them around the table as usual, it was almost nostalgic. He knew Noah was probably thinking of Mom but he was just glad to have the family he did.

•   •   •   •   •

The next day, Dad brought them to school, but it was closed due to the investigation. Dad, after making sure they were settled in at home and doors locked, headed off to get back to work. Noah was at least grateful dad stayed home last night, even if both Noah and Aiden had trouble sleeping. It was made a little easier knowing Dad wasn't that far away.

It was also clear that Dad was reluctant to leave, just like the day before, but this time Aiden reminded him that the sooner he found out what was going on, the sooner they could leave.

Dad chuckled at that, agreed and, making sure their crosses were secure and promising a repairman would come soon to fix the window, he left, peering back a few times before hopping in the car and taking off.

Eventually, they settled down, Aiden in the kitchen and Noah in the bedroom, a light on near his bed.

Noah flipped through his homework, smile fading as he worked. A faint clattering sound echoed from the kitchen, telling him exactly where Aiden was. As exciting as all of this was, the fear and shock was catching up to him. Sure, it was a day later, but it was almost as if he was trying to push it to the side and now no longer could. He almost wished he was Aiden, able to shrug it off, but the image stayed in his head. Her glazed eyes, the scratch marks showing she fought, the fear twisting over her gasping bloated face.

He wondered what all the other ghosts they met actually looked like. Dad mentioned how they died but…

What if that happened to one of them? What if he saw Dad or Aiden like that? He wasn't sure if he could handle it. He pushed against the headboard, curling into it. Ghost stories were always somewhat interesting and he did enjoy a good horror story or manga, but this?

This wasn't what he had in mind.

How was it he never realized? He just turned thirteen, for pete's sake. He was fascinated by his dad's work for a while and the supernatural was something he was always interested in.

There was a faint tapping sound from the still broken window, thumping against the plywood. Noah paused, fingers curling around his cross before standing up and walking over, cautiously calling out, "Hello?"

"Hello." A girl spoke from the other side. "I saw you at the school and wanted to talk, especially since classes were cancelled today. Can you let me in?"

Noah furrowed his brow. "I mean, if you come to the front door, I probably could." There was a pause from the other side, a tap, and then faint footsteps heading away.

Noah paused. What was he doing? He just said he would maybe let in some random girl he didn't know. He sighed. He really was going crazy in this new place, especially since Dad just reminded him not to let in strangers. He pushed himself to his feet, heading toward the front door.

Bang. Bang. Bang! Noah jumped, hearing a startled yelp from Aiden. Dang, that girl was fast. He darted past his brother who was standing in front of the stove, staring in confusion and surprise. Noah stepped up to the door, curious. Why did that girl knock on the window first anyways?

Weird…

CHAPTER 9

Noah unlocked the door before peeking out. He froze as a face met his, noses almost touching as the girl from two nights ago leaned close to the door, head cocked to the side, eye locked with his. She smiled, and it was surprisingly pretty, her skin almost glowing in the for once decent light.

"Noah, what are you—" Aiden's voice suddenly cut off as Noah finally snapped out of it, jerking backward. Aiden stood frozen beside him, staring through the doorway, a mixer with what seemed to be cream dripping onto the floor.

The girl tilted her head more. "Have you figured it out yet?"

"Gho—" Aiden took a step back, fear flashing over his face.

Noah blinked and turned to her before his eyes widened. "Wait, seriously? You're a ghost?" The girl seemed to blink at his tone, gaze snapping to him. "You were the girl from the other day, the one who—hey! You broke our window!"

He heard what sounded like Aiden slapping himself as the girl pulled back slightly, confused. "Yes." Her voice came out as more like a hiss.

"Okay, so, why? I mean, okay, I have a lot of questions, but… wait, you were able to pound on the door, right? Can't you just, like, phase through it?"

At that, her visible eye flashed and Noah almost let out a scream as gold met his gaze, frigid cold bit at his skin. It was as if she was pressing herself against glass. Her expression twisted as she hissed. "You think I haven't tried? You and your brother are the same."

"We are twins…" Noah managed to squeak out, though that seemed like such a stupid thing to say. The girl paused at that and slowly pulled back.

"Why are you here? Why do you keep bothering us?" Aiden pointed with the spatula, guard up, beyond tense.

"As I said earlier, I want to go home." She spoke, staring past Noah toward Aiden. "You two have the strength to help me do that."

"What?" Noah asked, feeling a little nervous. If she was a ghost, this was kind of cool, but he was also more than a little unnerved. He noticed, as she stood there, her damp hair was slowly frizzing, as if drying. It was disconcerting to watch. "Also, what do you mean we have the strength to help you? Lynn said something like that too…" he trailed off as her attention snapped to him.

"Noah, close the door." Aiden's voice pitched upward, clearly distressed.

"She's not doing anything and she's soaked." Noah noticed Aiden's tense posture and gestured. "She helped us find Lynn and, sure, she broke the window, but she left us alone after that. Maybe she wants to talk? Plus, I did ask her a question and I REALLY want to know. This is the first ghost we know is a ghost that we can talk too. Aren't you curious as well?"

"It doesn't matter." Aiden glared, spatula pointed forward. "If she is a spirit or whatever, she doesn't belong."

"Oh, come on, like letting her come in is going to be an issue." Noah rolled his eyes. "I mean, seriously, you can come in if you want."

"NOAH!"

Noah waved it off, his brother was too paranoid. Yes, he understood what Dad said, but she was just a girl their age, maybe a little older. The only ghosts they met so far recently were Lynn and this girl. Sure, they had problems in the past with supposed ghosts, but usually they were weirdos and creeps. He didn't see the prob—

He turned as a wide, crooked grin crossed the girl's face. A faint shattering sound reached his ears. It was as if something she was pressing against vanished and she took a stomping step past the threshold.

Ice speared down his spine.

"Whoops?" Noah very quickly backpedaled, fear suddenly twisting his chest into knots as his brain screamed that this was a terrible idea. The temperature dropped as water slowly coated the floor, staining it a dull brown. The air quivered as a giggle sounded from the girl. Aiden grabbed Noah's hand and pulled, causing him to stumble. They bolted.

Laughter met their ears as footsteps echoed after them, faster… faster…

"Where are you going?" The voice spoke up right next to Noah's ear. "You can't hide anymore. You can't run anymore. I'm here now."

Aiden, passing the kitchen, grabbed the salt shaker and wrenched it open, throwing it behind him.

The screech pierced Noah's ears as they stumbled down the hallway. "Where are we going?" Noah found his voice pitching up in terror.

"Dad's room," Aiden hissed, bolting into the room and slamming the door.

Noah briefly wondered what he was doing. Aiden didn't believe in this stuff, but then, Noah couldn't argue. Dad's was always the safest room.

They quickly locked it and scurried back as something slammed against the door. Noah's gaze flicked to the now empty salt shaker as quiet cackling traced from the other side. The faint dripping of water hit the floor like a distant rain. "It has been so long." The girl spoke, voice echoing past the wood. "It's been so long since I've been indoors, so long since I've been able to be in a home, in shelter. The fact that you two know so little and yet give off such warming rays of LIFE. It's irresistible."

"What do you want with us?" Noah shouted as Aiden stepped in front of him. He didn't realize how bad he was shaking until he gripped Aiden's shirt, fingers pale. "What the hell are you talking about?"

The giggling stopped and a humming echoed from the other side. "You are so… so naive." The voice echoed and reverberated through the door as a cold feeling drifted through the walls. "Naive, and so lucky."

At that, Noah felt like he was going to faint as something breathed in his ear. He screamed, slamming into Aiden, causing both of them to fall, tangled limbs flailing as another giggle echoed behind.

Noah whipped around, barely noting he was on top of Aiden. Sitting on the bed, hair and clothes drying as she sat there, was the girl. Noah briefly noted a splash of water against the wall and shuddered. The room was now silent and while the chill was there, it wasn't as sharp.

"Oh man, I've been wanting to scare the living daylights out of someone for so long." At noticing his expression, the girl rolled her visible eye. "Seriously though, you have no idea how lucky you are that it was me you let in and not someone else. Especially since I've been working hard to resist that ability of yours you give off and, before you ask? Don't. I have no way to describe it. It's just something ghosts feel. The closest equivalent would be a feeling of life." She shrugged.

"Noah, would you get off? Your elbow is digging into my back so I'm unable to scream at you in frustration." Aiden growled, coughing slightly. Noah hesitated before scrambling off. Brushing his shirt down to calm his racing heart, he surveyed the ghost. She was observing them and the room around them passively. He felt Aiden shift behind him, one hand gripping his shoulder while the other held the spatula wavering past him.

"And, to be honest, while you two are dumb, your father certainly isn't. I couldn't touch you even if I wanted to." She gestured to their chests where Noah grabbed onto Dad's gift. "Your crosses at least are stable."

"How?" Aiden spoke up, and Noah only noticed the tremor in his voice due to how close he was, the knuckles white. "The door was locked and we heard your voice from the door and then behind us."

"You really don't know much about ghosts, do you?" The girl hummed, gliding to her feet, literally. Footsteps echoed, but she never touched the floor as she moved toward them. "So, to explain in order, now that I've had my fun and am able to soak up your energy, thanks for that, by the way." She gestured, clothes finally drying and hair frizzed as a result—wait, that happened because of energy? Not because she was inside? Did it have to do with the strength or life or whatever they supposedly gave off? Talk about weird. "You let a ghost in, dumb move." She brought a hand up, finger twitching from side to side. "Anyone with abilities like yours should never allow a ghost entry. If one is powerful enough, it can come in, but it'll be severely weakened if it does not have permission. Contrary to that, if it already lives there, it weakens upon leaving the location, or attempting to leave."

She placed her hands back down, patting the bedding as she sat once more, legs kicking back and forth. Now that Noah could get a better look at her, he noticed she was wearing a simple white gown that trailed to just below her knees, long socks covering her feet, but no shoes. The dress flowed around her figure, loose on her shoulders. "Believe me, I learned that from experience. As for the second part, about my little trick? It wasn't teleportation or anything. Ghosts can leave, I guess you can say, markings or residual effects. You—" and she pointed at Noah. "Clearly noticed the water on the wall. That is how I actually came in. You were, at least, smart enough to lock the door which barred that entry, but this entire house was pretty much mine once you let me in."

"So, why are we lucky then?" Noah asked hesitantly. Aiden sent him a glare which screamed shut up.

The girl shrugged at that. "Because you got me?" She twirled a finger. "I have no intention of hurting you or making you mine or some bullshit like that." She tilted her head back, expression distant. "I just want to go home and you are the first ones who have given me even a glimmer of a possibility of doing that. Sure, at first, I thought of the idea of forcing it from you." Her gaze met Aiden's as Aiden's grip tightened, causing Noah to wince. "However, I changed my mind when this one here let me in, even though he clearly knew what I was." Her attention shifted to Noah. "Such kindness and naivety was strange and refreshing. Especially from the living who hold such strength. With that, I'm giving you a chance, a chance to help me."

"Help you?" Noah hesitantly asked, relaxing slightly even though he could feel Aiden's nervousness. "You said you were searching for your home?" She was clearly not trying to scare them anymore and she did mention she changed her mind. He would have to ask Aiden later what she meant by forcing it, but shoved it off.

"Away from here…" She turned to them. "I was brought here, not of my own free will, and killed when I tried to escape. Being bound to the outside world made it difficult to interact with others."

"Oh." Noah paused. "Well, what's your name?" At that, the Ghost stilled, startled. Noah pressed on, hand to his chest. Aiden seemed like he wanted to scream at Noah, but was holding his tongue. "My name is Noah."

CHAPTER 10

The Ghost stared at him before letting out a laugh, this time, one of actual mirth, not so much evil intent. "Oh, man, I would be lucky to get someone like you two." Her laughter died. "Asking a ghost's name, you are a strange one. Though, since both of you did it, I guess it's not surprising." She paused and her expression fell. "I wish I could remember…"

Noah didn't miss the way Aiden pursed his lips, as Noah himself relaxed fully. "You don't remember? But Lynn did."

"Lynn was a newer ghost." The girl tilted her head up, curious. "I'm surprised you figured out my clue, by the way, you didn't watch for long." Her attention swiveled to Aiden. "It was difficult to step into the courtyard, but I wasn't going to leave such a new ghost to her fate. I was a bit surprised you realized it so quickly."

Noah blinked, confused, as Aiden narrowed his eyes. "Why did you help us?" The words came out sharp, almost clipped. "Considering her phrasing, I'm guessing you were the one who helped and spoke with Lynn?"

"Nailed it in one." She nodded, expression pained for only a brief moment before returning to amused. "And, also, because I wanted you to know I wasn't trying to hurt you. Plus, well, I have my own reasons. I wanted to help so I could get help in return. I'm not evil." She paused at that. "Okay, not completely. I rather enjoy terrifying people, but that's beside the point."

Realization dawned on Noah and he chuckled. "Oh, so that's why you tapped on the window the other day, you saw me do it."

The girl nodded, grin spreading over her lips.

"So…" Noah gestured, very carefully trying to pull away from Aiden, only to stop when Noah noticed the tension still in his brother. He didn't understand, but it was Aiden. Aiden was usually slow to trust, so should he really be surprised? Noah shook it off and turned back to the girl. "I have to ask, Lynn said it was difficult to speak to us, but you don't seem to be having trouble, why?"

The girl stared, head tilting to one side, causing her hair to hide most of her face. "The power you give, so willingly, feeds spirits and ghosts like myself which was why I called it 'life 'earlier. Such boundless energy makes it much easier to manifest, even to the untrained eye." She gestured to herself. "You can almost say you 'cleansed 'my form back to its normal state with your powers alone, which is something I must thank you for even if I don't fully understand how you can do it."

Okay? Weird, but whatever. Clearly, she didn't know, so no point in asking. "So, what now?"

The girl surveyed them quietly, appraising Aiden and Noah. "That is up to you two. I cannot touch you while you wear those crosses and while I am able to now traverse in your home, my movement is still limited."

"Well, if you are staying, we can't call you ghost." Noah shifted to lean more heavily on one foot as he pondered for a moment before feeling a smile cross his lips. "How about we call you Mia?"

She snapped her head around, almost literally. Aiden cringed while the girl slowly sat up. "Mia?"

"I think it's a nice name and, well, we need to call you something, like I said."

"Are you insane?" Aiden hissed into Noah's ear. "That thing is a ghost, spirit, whatever. It's not going to stay here."

"SHE doesn't exactly have anywhere, and we can't exactly throw her back outside. For one, we don't know how and for two, that's just not right." Noah shook his head. "I mean, looking at her now, she's just like a normal girl."

Aiden stared past him, right toward Mia. "I dearly hope you don't regret that idea." He kept his voice low. "I don't like it, but it's clear I can't convince you otherwise."

"Nope." Noah shook his head. "And, anyway, it's not like she killed anyone, right?" Noah turned to Mia, only to freeze.

The girl was inches from his face, hissing. "How DARE you accuse me of such a thing! I am not a psychopath, or some freak with a god-complex. I simply want to go home."

"Back off," Aiden snapped as the spatula slammed onto her head, some of the remaining whipping cream getting into her hair as she let out a startled yelp.

"Ow! That hurt!" she whined as she cradled her head, pulling back. She sent a glare toward Aiden whose guard was up once more. "Geez, that wasn't necessary. I wasn't going to hurt him."

"Why do you think I would actually trust that?" Aiden just continued his staring contest. "Considering how our first 'meeting ' went."

Mia pulled back, staring silently before letting out a long breath. "Of course." She shook her head. "I'll just say, while it is no excuse, emotions and obsessions can be powerful things." Her black hair began flicking with agitation. "Your abilities are addicting, like bees to honey. Let's just say, I highly doubt my reaction is going to be the last time you encounter something like that, especially since you were NOT wearing your cross at the time." Her expression was strange. "Though, I am now aware that it is a double-edged sword. Noah, here, would have been the easier target if that was actually my intention."

Aiden gritted his teeth as Noah blinked, glancing toward her warily. "What do you mean by that?"

"Simply? Your brother's abilities are slightly stronger than your own and so, while more enticing, it's more dangerous to interact with since he's able to fight back more than you might." Mia shrugged. "That's simply what I meant. However, like I said, I have no intention of doing anything, not after…" She put a hand to her chest, a flicker of a smile on her face. "Well, I don't think we'll worry about that right now."

"Okay, this is getting to be a bit confusing." Noah huffed. "We just learned, maybe two days ago, that ghosts are a thing and now we're talking to one. While it's cool, I have to say, Mia, it is a bit weird."

"You just learned about us?" Mia blinked, turning to him in surprise. "Really?" Noah nodded as Aiden slowly moved behind Noah. She glanced between them and hummed, shifting away from them. "That would explain a lot. Your father certainly has some abilities, but not quite to the extent of yourself." She shivered. "Powerful though, and well-versed in protection. It was lucky I could even get close to you." Noah suddenly felt relieved; so that's why he always felt safer after Dad put the barrier down. No wonder. "It is odd how he didn't tell you." She paused. "It's understandable, though, especially if he was unaware of how much energy you actually give off, which is possible."

"Okay." Aiden stepped back, eyes narrowed. "This is… a lot at once."

Mia hummed and nodded. "Yes, it is." Aiden glared as she smiled. "However, if I want to reach my goal, I have to keep you two alive, for now." She took a seat once more. "So, might as well explain what I can." Her gaze drifted to Noah once more. "I promise, Noah, that I will keep you two safe as long as you help me try to get home."

Noah blinked and shrugged. "Sure."

Aiden didn't argue this time, though it was clear he wanted to. Mia seemed to relax at Noah's words, an almost gentle expression falling over her face. "Then, thank you for the new name. It means more than you think to me."

"I mean, like I said, we can't call you ghost, or at least, I can't." Noah shrugged, grinning. "Plus, other than trying to scare me, you've mostly just been answering our questions, so I don't see a problem with you staying here." He paused at that, barely managing to keep his expression up. It was his fault she was here anyway, it was his responsibility to deal with her. Dad was already dealing with enough, and so was Aiden. "Just don't hurt Dad if you see him?"

"I can abide by that." She nodded. "Though, I have my own means for him not to notice me, especially if I stay near you two." Her grin widened slightly as her attention flitted to Aiden, who shuddered.

"Stay away from me." He spoke evenly, knuckles white.

Mia's expression was odd, unsettling for the longest time before she nodded. "I will do what I can." The words seemed strange from her lips. "I promise, I will not hurt you, Aiden." Aiden stiffened at that. "I cannot, unfortunately, promise I will be able to stay away from either one of you."

"O…kay?" Noah stared at her quietly. "So, what? You are going to stay in our room?"

"I will not be far." She nodded. "If you are worried, I have no interest in either of you in that way. I simply need to stay near you to maintain form properly." She peered out, eyes narrowed. "And to keep HIM away from you."

"Him?"

"A dangerous thing." She turned back to Noah and Aiden. "A being that exists in this town that has recently gotten stronger. He is the reason behind the disappearances, but that is all I know." She shrugged. "Just keep your eyes open, especially you." She pointed toward Aiden. "He WILL come after you two, especially if what I sense is actually the case."

"What you sense?" Noah put a hand to his head and groaned. "Right, the whole 'life 'thing or whatever. This is getting a bit much. Still, it sounds like you know who this person is." Noah leaned forward. "If you know, tell us."

Mia's expression turned apologetic. "I don't have anything more to tell you. I can sense his presence just like I can sense your strength, however, I don't know who they are or anything. The person could even be a she, I just used him to make it easier." She shook her head. "Ghosts are complicated." Mia actually smiled, though it was strained, before the expression faded. "Though this situation is a bit more so. I'll say, simply, that there is more than one soul there, that's why I can't even tell what gender they are."

Noah gritted his teeth, frustration searing through him. It took a moment before he let out a tired sigh. Aiden still seemed skeptical and clearly didn't think she was revealing everything, but Noah couldn't help but feel she was telling the truth, the words were genuine. He wasn't sure why he was so certain on that, but he was.

She stood and stepped forward, half floating off the ground. "I would advise not telling your father that I am here. Many like him jump to conclusions, which I cannot blame, but it is still quite frustrating." She paused before extending her hand. "In exchange for keeping you all safe, will you help me return home?"

Noah glanced toward her hand, thinking through her words. He was already hesitant to tell Dad that he screwed up by letting her in, especially since they just talked about that very same thing earlier. He didn't want his dad to worry about them more than he had to if there really was such a dangerous person in town. A person that they only knew existed, but that was about it.

"Noah…" Aiden's warning tone made Noah sigh.

He shook his head, but reached forward, taking her hand. It felt surprisingly warm, though not to the same extent as a normal human, but not frigid like he expected. Her grip wasn't tight, if anything, it was rather gentle. "Sure." He stared at her, noting she was staring at his grip with an odd expression, one he couldn't quite name. "Just give us time. We can't do anything right away, obviously, but considering how often we travel, I bet we could bring you with us. It would involve telling Father eventually, but…" Noah shook his head, noting the way Aiden was watching with disapproval and almost a hint of betrayal. "Don't mess with us again." Noah's gaze snapped to her and she stiffened, startled. "You said you wouldn't hurt us, and, it sounds like, you hope to keep us safe. You better keep to that promise." He leaned forward, almost tugging her to him, cheeks almost brushing as he whispered,

"And don't you DARE hurt my brother. He means the world to me and I want him to stay safe, understood?"

She blinked before relaxing, pulling away. "I promise." Something about those words seemed strangely final, but Noah shoved the thought off. "Who knew such a naive one can hold such…" She trailed off before shaking her head. "Still, I will take what I can get. So, for now—" She grinned before a cold wind brushed through. Noah took a startled step back and noticed as she disappeared, as if never there. There was a moment of silence before he turned toward Aiden, who was watching Noah with a strange expression.

"What the hell?" Aiden's voice cracked as he gestured, shuddering. "Are you insane? We don't KNOW anything about these things. Whatever they are. Why are you making promises you can't keep? Especially to someone like that who isn't going to TELL us anything?"

"Aiden, relax." Noah felt his expression soften. "I get it, I do. It's just I messed up when I let her in, so I was going to be the one to make amends. Plus, I truly think she honestly doesn't know anymore than she said."

Aiden stared at him quietly, hands at his side. "I hope you know what you are doing." He turned and, unlocking the door, walked away. "I'm going to finish dinner." The hesitancy in his voice spoke volumes.

Noah pursed his lips, wincing. Great, he put Aiden into a difficult situation, again. He understood, to an extent, his brother's concern. This was foreign territory. Still, Noah felt he was right in what he decided to do. He believed Mia when she said she couldn't touch them, because he trusted his father. He felt bad for Aiden, who was never one to like or understand the supernatural. To him, this probably felt like a nightmare. Noah wished he could do something to help Aiden understand, but what could Noah do when even he was struggling to come to terms with the situation?

Noah shook his head, took a deep breath, and headed for their shared room. So, he was only somewhat startled when he spotted Mia standing in the middle of the room, chest rising and falling as if in breath, one strap slipping down her shoulder slightly. She seemed almost contemplative. He walked over, taking a seat on his own bed as she glanced sidelong toward him, almost twisting her head since one eye was still obscured. She watched him, curious before floating over to the bookcase, tapping it. "I will admit, it was pretty smart of your brother to cover the window like this." She turned. "You two seem very different from each other." She just continued to watch Noah quietly.

Noah let out a breath. "I know that, but he's still my brother."

"I can tell and you, also, kind of told me." Mia's expression softened. "It was clear as day just moments ago how important he was to you. I thought you naive, but I might have been mistaken. Still… I…" She seemed to hesitate in her words, almost stumbling, which was strange to Noah. "Thank you for the name. It's a nice name."

Noah relaxed, smiling faintly. "You're welcome." He reached to his side, grabbing up some homework he hadn't finished. "Still, it's been a long few days. First, we find out we can talk to ghosts and now we're living with one, fascinating how things happen."

"It really is." The words were wistful. Noah glanced up as Mia took a seat on the rug, staring up at the bookcase. "I can't believe I can talk to people. Sure, it's two boys I've never met, but I'll take what I can get."

"Should I be offended?" Noah joked. Mia chuckled.

"Nope. I would say that either way." She paused. "I was well aware that, even if I sought your help, it was possible you wouldn't be able to help me. No one has been, they've only tried to banish me." Her expression grew crooked, the air dropping fast. "They realized fast not to bother me." She shook her head, the temperature returning to normal. "I reacted badly to your brother's presence, so I understand his hesitancy on the situation. Believe me, though, knowing the situation as it is, I mean neither of you any harm. And, so you are aware, most ghosts just want to be left in peace. You don't mess with them, they won't mess with you. Some, like me, might need help. Others…" she shook her head again. "I don't know much about, but I know enough to avoid them. Nothing good comes of meeting them or interacting with them."

Noah thought about that. How many of the ghosts they met in the past were like that? How many were ghosts? "How can we tell if we are talking to a ghost?"

Mia paused. "How do I appear to you now?"

"Uh… normal? If anything, you look like you could be our next door neighbor, especially now that you are 'cleansed 'or whatever."

Mia stared, shock flitting on her face before she tilted her head, and kept tilting. "Really?" She spoke, and Noah was certain if she was normal, her neck would have been snapped. "Fascinating."

"Can you PLEASE not do that?" Noah quickly turned away, feeling the need to throw up. He heard a faint giggle followed by a loud snap. Noah did not turn back toward her. "Okay, duly noted. I will say, though, a lot of ghosts don't do that, from what I've gathered… I think."

"True." Mia moved into Noah's line of sight with a grin, head back in place. "To most people, we appear translucent at best, some more solid then others, but with an opaqueness that makes it difficult to recognize us. A family member could be standing in the room with their dead relative and not even realize." The smile faded. "That's why no one recognized Lynn, not at first, and part of the reason that boy, Phen, could never find her. It was only due to circumstance that Phen recognized her. After all, most would think it was either a trick of the light or someone they should know, but don't. The fact you can see us as clear as a living being is… let's just say, it's unique."

Noah furrowed his brow and sighed. So, that didn't help distinguish ghosts, but at least he now felt better about not being able to tell when he was interacting with one. Actually…

"When Aiden threw salt at you, does that really work?"

Mia twitched, a deep frown cutting over her lips. "Oh, it does. For some spirits, it sends them back to where their souls were bound. For others, it makes them mad, and for others… it burns like a mother effing son of a—." She promptly cut off her curse, muttering more swears under her breath that Noah couldn't hear.

"I'm guessing the third is from experience?" Noah winced as gold snapped up to his face.

"Oh, very much, and that brother of yours got it right in my face. Sure, it did weaken me, making it less likely for me to actually DO anything, but oh boy, did it hurt."

"Noted." Noah blinked, putting the idea away for later. It was good to know such things.

Mia sighed, swirling around for a moment to take in the room. "I think I'm going to get some rest. I can only siphon so much energy like this and, while it feels great, I don't want to use it all at once." She hummed and took a step back. "I'll still be here, but not in this form." At that, she faded away into nothing as Noah stared.

"Cool! And creepy… very creepy."

"Isn't it?" a voice whispered beside him and he yelped, turning to see nothing there.

"Oh, Aiden is going to flip," Noah muttered, falling onto the bed. He knew he should be worried about Mia, especially considering Aiden's concern, but for some reason, now that he spoke with her, he didn't feel he needed to keep his guard up. He felt strangely safe. It was weird.

And, well, Noah did feel bad. To die so far away from loved ones and family? From what someone saw as home? He couldn't help but wonder… did that happen to Mom?

He hoped not, but the feeling, the thought, was starting to grow.

He was out of his depth with all of this.

CHAPTER 11

Dinner that night was good, but quiet. Neither of them wanted to talk and, admittedly, Aiden was still unnerved with his brother's decision to allow a dangerous... Thing into their house. He was too pissed at Dad to mention anything, considering he hadn't said anything about ghosts or whatever in the first place.

He didn't want any part of this, to be honest.

Oh man, his life was ridiculous. Ghosts? Really? It couldn't have been aliens or werewolves or something? At least those made some sort of sense. Okay, not the werewolves, Aiden admitted to himself, but aliens, certainly. It took much coaxing from Noah and his own exhaustion to finally drag him to bed, though he could still feel the eerie chill in the air.

Sleep came to him in waves, the unsettling feeling of being watched ever present and, what made it worse, was he KNEW what was watching. He wanted to snap at the Thing, but also didn't want to anger her.

He just wanted her to stay away from him. Aiden already saw what she could do and he felt sick to his stomach at the thought. It was clear Noah felt fine, even safe, if his snores were any indication. Aiden did not.

He deeply regretted agreeing with Noah about convincing Dad to leave that morning, because Dad didn't come home that night and, when the alarm went off for the next morning, Aiden was exhausted. Physically and mentally.

He glared at the clock which glowed faintly, a tune echoing from the speakers he wasn't even really listening to.

"Huh, not a bad song," a voice echoed near his ear. "Who knew you had good taste in music?"

Aiden tried desperately not to freak, but he did grab whatever was on his desk and swung. This time, he met nothing but air, though the chilled feeling did retreat.

"Geez, I was just saying you had good taste. I wasn't actually trying to do anything." The voice spoke, causing Aiden to twitch. He shifted, legs tangled in the sheets as he sat up, glaring at the Thing. She put both hands up, wincing as Noah groaned, rubbing his eyes tiredly.

"Ugh, it's too early for this." Noah yawned. "Morning, Aiden, Mia."

"Morning, Noah." The Thing flitted over to Noah, allowing Aiden to relax slightly. Aiden pulled himself out of bed, watching them warily as he checked that the cross still sat around his neck. After his father's words, along with that Thing's, he felt strangely comfortable with having it on, unlike before.

"You okay?"

Aiden peered over to Noah, who was watching him quietly. "Fine." His word came out more clipped then he intended as he grabbed his clothes and stepped out of the room. "I'm getting ready for school." At that, he hurried away, noting with relief as the Thing didn't follow him. Noah could deal with her.

He winced, feeling a little bad, remembering Noah's pained expression yesterday when he mentioned how he screwed up. His brother was usually more happy-go-lucky, it was rare to see the serious side come into play, but it happened. Aiden let out a breath, sent a quick text to Dad to check on him before quickly getting changed and starting on breakfast, noting as Noah and the Thing joined soon after.

The process of cooking calmed him slightly, so he was only slightly unnerved at her presence, though Noah's chipper attitude was certainly helping. He felt a faint smile cross his lips as Noah gestured, talking about the latest manga he read with a familiar enthusiasm.

Soon enough, they were on their way to school and the Thing was still following them. Aiden twitched, finding himself shifting closer to Noah almost instinctively. To his surprise, Noah didn't try to push him away, or give him an odd look for his strange reaction.

"So, you are going to be following us from now on?" Noah asked curiously as he glanced toward her. The Thing curled around them, not even attempting to appear human. Aiden shivered, her form appeared serpentine, twisting in ways that bones shouldn't, giving her a wispy and just downright wrong appearance.

"Pretty much. I can't protect you if I don't stay near you, and this way, I know you won't leave me behind. I still want to go home, after all." She paused, curling around them once more with a pleased sigh. "And, well, it is nice to actually get energy for once, not just expend it."

"Do you know how wrong that sounds?" Noah snorted.

The Thing stopped at that, letting out a huff. "I have no other way to describe it, smart-ass."

Aiden shook his head, focusing on getting to school. The town, already dreary before, now seemed worse. Whispers echoed in the streets as people rushed to get inside houses and to locations. The school was no different, if anything, it better reflected the tension. At some point, to his relief, the Thing disappeared, saying something about incorporeal form.

Aiden didn't ask, he didn't want to know.

The students all seemed jumpy and it was obvious why. Quite a few glanced their way, even more so than two days ago.

"Well, we are the ones who helped find Lynn." Noah spoke up after a while, voice quieter and posture somewhat tense. "On our first day too."

"I was worried that was going to happen," Aiden admitted, gaze flicking from side to side. "Be careful, okay?"

Noah paused, startled. He turned to Aiden, a mix of emotions shooting across his face followed by a smile. "Yeah, I'll be fine. You take care as well. I'll see you for lunch."

Aiden nodded and the two split. Classes were… how could he phrase it properly? The closest was that they did not help his already growing stress. It also didn't help that the Thing thought following him was a good idea, even though Noah asked her to leave him alone. Though, he did notice the way she kept flitting around, surprise and hints of joy on her face.

At one point, between classes, when she peered through a doorway with an almost awed expression, he couldn't help but ask, in a low voice, "What has you so excited?"

"I've never been in here before." She grinned, the visible eye sparkling. "Usually I can only get into the surrounding grounds or the courtyard. This is the first time I've actually been inside the school. It's all thanks to you two, really."

"If that's the case, why are you bothering me? Why don't you go with Noah?"

The Thing paused, staring at him before shrugging. "You're more fun to mess with, plus…" Her mood automatically shifted, expression neutral. "You're the one in more danger. Sure, you might be stronger and able to protect yourself compared to Noah, but you are also a magnet for spirits who are drawn and strengthened by that life of yours." She paused at that, her words ringing in his head as he shuddered at the implication. Her expression softened slightly as she continued, "I promised I would keep you safe. That nothing would harm you. I'm going to keep to that promise."

Aiden wasn't sure what to say to that. The Thing mentioned that yesterday. He was in more danger because of what, his power or whatever it was? He felt uncomfortable about asking and the Thing didn't seem inclined to say more as she once more flitted out of the visible spectrum.

Lunch was a quiet affair, at least for Aiden. Noah sat beside him, talking with someone that decided to sit next to him, curious on what happened. Thankfully, the Thing decided to stay away, near the doors of the room to keep watch.

It was when they were getting to the end of the day when Aiden noticed he hadn't seen Phen around. He wasn't too surprised, the boy did find out his sister was murdered.

Aiden shivered at that. He could only imagine what that was like, hoping to find someone, only to learn that they died horribly.

Well, he supposed he could imagine. If they ever found Mom, that was. The thought was a morbid one, but in some ways, he almost preferred that idea to the other one where she just left and never came back; that she abandoned them. He wasn't sure if he could take it and he knew Noah wouldn't be able to.

•   •   •   •   •

That night, Dad still hadn't come home, which wasn't unusual. Both of them were used to their father doing long stretches of investigating at a time and appreciated when he could be there. They tried to call, but it went straight to voicemail, so they left a quick text. The Thing mostly remained silent, often lost in thought.

So, when the next day dawned with a light drizzle, Aiden wasn't surprised to see the Thing hovering over his bed, eye closed and just humming a tune. Thankfully, she was staying a good distance from him, but even then, it was still uncomfortable, unsettling and it deeply startled him.

Barely keeping a neutral face, he got ready and, grabbing an umbrella and handing one to Noah, they left.

The Thing, who dried considerably upon returning to the house, quickly became drenched once more, hair and clothes plastered to her skin. She just glared up at the sky and kept moving, mood downcast.

"Aiden?" On the way to school, the voice caught him by surprise. He turned as Phen stepped out of one of the houses. It was a nice two story home that was actually one of the cleaner places in the town. The little garden out front was nicely trimmed.

Phen himself, however, seemed haggard.

"Phen?" Noah glanced over, surprised. "Are you…" Noah paused, seeming unsure how to continue.

"Are you okay?" Aiden asked. "You look terrible."

The boy blinked. "You really are blunt." He paused and then walked down the steps. "I'm sorry."

"Why are you apologizing?" Noah stared, confused. "Your sister—"

Phen looked away and sighed. "I don't know, I just felt like I needed to." He stopped in front of them, the rain falling over him, soaking through his clothes. Aiden hesitated before extending the umbrella a little to help. Phen seemed startled, but appreciative. "You… thank you." His voice came out a little hoarse. "I wish it didn't end up the way it did, but I'm at least glad to know what happened to her. I think I would always be wondering." He shifted from foot to foot. "I told the officers I was showing you around. Even with everything happening, I doubt they would believe that I spoke with my… my sister." He turned his head up, as if staring past the umbrella canopy.

"I would think you would want nothing to do with us after that," Aiden admitted, not sure what to think of the thanks.

"Same." Noah nodded, shifting closer to Aiden so as to cover him with his own umbrella, which Aiden appreciated. "Thanks, but it is a bit surprising."

"I can see that." Phen glanced toward Noah before turning back to Aiden. "Sure. I was confused and angry at first, but I also know it's not your fault." He slumped. "I know my sister, she truly did believe you helped her and, I suppose, you helped me as well. My family and me." He shifted as a weak smile fell on his lips. "Of course I'm going to thank you." He extended a hand. "To new chances, it's nice to meet you, Noah and Aiden. Hopefully, we can be friends."

Noah's eyes lit up and he took his hand. Aiden just stared. Friends, huh?

He felt a breeze and shivered as a bit of rain fell past. He glared over his shoulder, though he couldn't see the Thing anywhere, before hesitantly reaching forward.

Phen's expression shifted to one of relief as he took Aiden's hand and shook.

"Friends." Noah chuckled. "I didn't think we would make one so quickly." His smile fell. "Sorry it happened under such circumstances."

Phen shook his head, pulling back. "It's just good to know the truth." He hesitated before a faint smile that appeared a bit… off settled over his tired features. "I've had some time to grieve so…" He let out a breath. "We should probably get moving."

Aiden blinked, wondering if that was actually the case. He knew, from experience, that it took time to grieve and it had only been a few days. Could Phen truly be recovered already?

"Are you sure?" Noah asked quietly.

Phen nodded, gaze turned toward the school, though they couldn't see it from where they stood. "I can't just sit around the house. I'm too anxious and it feels wrong."

Aiden shook his head as a faint chime in the distance caught his attention. Great, now he was going to be late for school. He turned, pulling his umbrella back as he quickly walked away. He heard a yelp and a chuckle as Phen and Noah followed behind. He wasn't going to argue if that was the case. He could understand the need to get away.

A moment later, as he took a turn he knew led to school, a faint giggle in his ear made him start. He almost stumbled over the slick ground.

"Will you leave me alone?" Aiden hissed, feeling the tension in his shoulders. Why the heck was this Thing bound and determined to stay near him?

"Nope." The Thing's voice reached his ears, almost chipper. She was using that strange invisibility or whatever. The thought made him want to puke. "Plus, I prefer staying near you." Her voice went softer. "To make amends, and to make sure HE doesn't sense you."

"Because of this stupid ability you talked about?" Aiden forced out.

She simply hummed, but didn't respond.

In some ways, he was aggravated she didn't continue; in others, he was grateful she stopped talking to him. He felt like he was going insane, talking to the air like he was.

Soon enough, they made it to school, Phen and Noah only a few paces behind, trying to catch their breaths. They were clearly talking about… whatever it was they were talking about. Phen followed Aiden as Noah waved good-bye, heading to class. "I didn't realize we had the same first class as well. English, right?"

Aiden nodded, shifting his grip on his umbrella as he shook the water off.

Phen hummed at that, deep in thought.

"Are you okay to be at school?" Aiden asked, trying to follow some of his brother's ability to converse. He was, admittedly, also curious. Sure, he answered earlier, but…

Phen's hesitation spoke volumes. "I will be. I have so many questions that I need to figure out, so much I need to know." His lips pursed as anger flashed over his face. "I need to figure out who killed my sister."

Aiden paused at that. It made sense. He let out a sigh and nodded, getting a flash of a smile from the boy.

They took a seat, settling into class as a quiet chatter filled the room. Aiden hadn't noticed last time, but Phen's desk was actually pretty close to his own. The whispers from the past few days escalated. Aiden found himself sinking into his seat as the second bell rang, beginning class.

The teacher glanced up and stood. "Good morning, class. As you all know, there was an incident on Monday that might have unsettled many of you." Her gaze flipped to Phen briefly before she continued, "First off, no one is allowed to enter the west wing of the school at this time unless with a chaperone or guardian. This includes any clubs that might be stationed in that wing. Second, all students must either go to clubs or return home as soon as classes are over, no loitering in the halls. Understood?"

There was mumbled agreement from most of the class, though they were mostly talking amongst themselves, rumors spreading about exactly what happened. It seemed no one except Noah, Aiden and Phen knew the full truth of the situation. It was unsettling to think about. The teacher tried to get the class 'attention before sighing and starting the lesson anyway.

Aiden listened, only half paying attention to the course, just in case he was called. Curiosity got the better of him and he listened in on some of the quiet conversation happening nearby.

He only really caught bits and pieces. Most of them were talking about Phen and how he must be feeling, but quite a few conversations were about Aiden and Noah. Detective twins or something ridiculous, though a few thought they were the ones behind the incident, asking weird questions like were they murderers? Was it a cult?

Rumors were always annoyingly fascinating.

CHAPTER 12

The day passed into lunch where some of the differences were quickly obvious. No one was allowed outside and the seats were more regimented. Aiden was just grateful he was able to sit near Noah, who was already talking to some girls. Aiden didn't care to ask or know why or how he was able to do that. Knowing Noah, the conversation was probably distraction from what was going on now.

"Phew, it's so noisy sometimes." The Thing took a seat next to him, half in and out of another boy sitting beside him. The boy flinched and shifted over, mentioning something about air-conditioning. The Thing giggled before flitting to invisibility once more.

God damn. Aiden tried to steady his breathing as he took another bite of pizza. "There's a lot of students here. Of course it's loud." He kept his words clipped and short, said softly under his breath so hopefully, others wouldn't hear. "Can you leave me alone?"

"I'm not hurting you or anything," the Thing responded as a chill settled between Aiden and Noah. Even Noah shifted, glancing over nervously before putting a smile back on his face as he returned back to his conversation. The Thing gestured, flickering briefly to visibility before disappearing again. "I made a deal with Noah, after all. Plus the other reason I'm here is to keep an eye on the boy you were with."

Phen? Aiden's attention flicked to where the boy was sitting with some friends.

"With seeing his sister due to your abilities and learning of her death, well, it is easier for him to detect ghosts."

"Is that why you're invisible?" Noah's words caught Aiden's attention, noting that the girls were talking amongst themselves. He briefly heard them mentioning that some of the boys were terrible, pranking others in such a situation. He ignored them, noticing that Noah's attention stayed on Aiden, causing Aiden to let out a breath. He mentally thanked his brother for being willing to talk with him so it didn't look as strange.

"Yes," the Thing responded as a breeze brushed past. "I don't want him to see me, yet. Plus, I don't know who to trust in this school, so it is safer for all of our sakes."

Aiden and Noah exchanged looks before Noah sighed, biting into his chicken. "Trust, huh?" Noah muttered quietly before swallowing. "Well, either way, I would rather have a friend in all of this, even if it is a bit strange."

Aiden couldn't argue. Why was Phen so determined to be their friend when they barely knew the boy? Aiden sighed. People were weird and he was done with all of this. After all, if anything, Phen was probably using them. No one knew much of anything until Noah and Aiden arrived and then suddenly, they found one of the missing people? No doubt Phen thought he could use that to his advantage to learn more about the killer.

The idea sent a painful feeling through Aiden's chest. It would be nice if he could actually get a friend that didn't have any of those types of intentions, but he doubted that would ever come to pass. Noah's attention diverted back to the others when one of the girls tapped him on the shoulder. That smile was back and he was, once again, socializing as if nothing happened.

Sometimes, Aiden envied his brother. Aiden knew he was unapproachable, so seeing Noah so easily able to create relationships was… he wished he could have a portion of that ability. An ability like that was far more useful than this sick joke regarding the supernatural.

The pizza, once tasting good, now was almost sour on his lips as his thoughts devolved into loathing. He shouldn't be envious, he should be happy for his brother, but he also wasn't oblivious. He noticed how those Noah talked to never seemed to contact him back to the point where, eventually, Noah was found scrolling through his phone, deleting numbers in this quiet, pained silence. He supposed that was one thing he didn't have to deal with. If you don't make friends, you don't have to deal with the idea of them leaving you behind.

Still, Phen was the only one he knew here, if Phen was using them, he would just have to watch out for Phen in return.

Decision made, he glanced up toward Phen. So, friends, huh? He knew nothing of what it was like to be friends, but he didn't think he would need to. Noah would take care of that, he would watch without saying anything to Noah. He didn't need to know.

Phen's attention shifted to Aiden and he waved. Aiden turned back to what was left of his pizza.

He wished he could ignore Phen, but that was easier said than done. He let out a tired breath as the lunch ended and they went their separate ways. He was lost in thought, so when he felt a surge of cold, it was his only warning. He jerked, glancing up just as two boys jumped from the nearby doorway, twisted clown masks on their faces as they put their hands up in a 'boo 'format.

He stumbled back, whipping his backpack over his shoulder, barely stopping himself from screaming as they laughed before running down the hallway.

He heard a faint hissing sound by his ear before the cold faded. He stared, shocked, as the boys suddenly let out a shout as if they tripped on something, falling flat on their faces, skidding over the linoleum. Aiden shook where he stood, heart still hammering in his chest. He heard movement as a teacher burst out of a nearby door, spotting the two. Other students stared in shock, some racing away. A few laughed, but quickly stopped as they were nudged by other students or just realized the situation. Aiden looked around wildly. He felt heat on his face and hurried away, not wanting anything to do with it.

His luck was horrendous as usual.

•   •   •   •   •

Noah didn't miss the way his brother was more subdued today as they left school. He heard about the pranks, so when he found out Aiden had been caught in one, he almost turned right back on his heels and attempted to head back inside. Mia, however, quickly told him he didn't need to bother. She was near Aiden when it happened and the boys didn't leave completely unscathed. A teacher spotted them on the ground when they took a tumble with their masks on and, supposedly, both were promptly sent home for it. Noah didn't know how to feel about that, but found himself less tense.

Phen joined them, humming quietly, though he did ask Aiden if he was alright, clearly having heard of it as well. When Aiden nodded, his expression softened. Soon enough, he stepped forward, joining Noah. Aiden, however, stayed back a bit, watching warily. Noah supposed it made sense; usually, it took a little extra effort to get someone to talk to you, but Noah wasn't going to look a gift horse in the mouth.

"So, what is there to actually do around here?" Noah asked, catching Phen's attention.

"To be honest, not much." Phen stared ahead. "We used to have an arcade down the street, but that closed a couple weeks ago. The owner tends to not like kids sneaking in, especially lately, so most avoid it. Then again, most people avoid everything in town." Phen paused at that. "Not surprising, really."

"That would certainly explain why this town is so dreary," Aiden muttered, glancing at his phone briefly. Noah pulled out his, noticing a simple text of, 'Can't talk 'splayed over the screen. It was from Dad. He pursed his lips before he pocketed it. Well, at least Dad responded, somewhat. Did Aiden try to contact Dad as well? If so, did he get a similar message? Noah noticed Aiden watching him. Aiden just nodded, tapping his pocket. *So, I guess he did get something similar as well.* Noah debated for a moment before letting out a breath. It was probably one of those cases again. Hopefully, Dad would contact them properly soon.

"I mean, the diner is pretty good, but that's about it." Phen shrugged, turning to them as he walked backwards, catching Noah's attention. "But, yeah…" his expression shifted. "My sister isn't the only one that's disappeared, you know."

"We know."

"Ah right, because of your father?" Phen spoke softly. "He was that detective from the other day, right? I haven't seen him much lately, though I did spot him walking through town yesterday."

Noah let out a breath. That was good to know. "Pretty much. We tend to stay with Dad when he goes to a new place, though it's sometimes hard to keep track of him." Noah shrugged. "Unfortunately, he didn't realize how bad the situation was this time. Yet, it's Dad. I have no doubt he'll figure it out before anything else bad happens."

A moment of relief flashed on Phen's face before he nodded. "That's good to know." He paused, attention drifting to the hard pavement. "As long as he can take care of whoever is causing this."

"He will." Aiden waved, catching Noah's gaze. "Speaking of, we should head home."

Noah nodded, turning back to Phen. "We'll drop you off at your place."

Phen seemed startled at that. "No, no, it's fine."

"It's, literally on the way home," Aiden deadpanned.

Phen hesitated, thinking it over and then chuckled. "Okay, you got me there. Fine."

With that, they headed back home. Noah found himself chatting with Phen. Most of it was just on some of the basics of the town, favorite tv shows and movies. It was a simple conversation, but one Noah appreciated. It was a nice change of pace.

"This is my stop." Phen paused before turning to them. "Thanks." His smile was hesitant, not fully there, but visible. "I'll have to come over and see your place sometime."

"It's nothing fancy," Aiden pointed out. "Plus, we're really only staying until Dad figures out what's going on here."

"Oh." Phen turned to Aiden, observing him for a while, longer then Noah expected, before he shifted back, lightly tapping his foot. "That's fair." He turned, heading toward the door before peering over his shoulder. "After tomorrow is the weekend. It's not much, but do you want me to show you around town? I need something to do."

"Sure." Noah smiled, getting one in return. "We would like that, right?" Noah nudged Aiden who sighed and nodded.

"Alright, I'll meet you at your place. You'll have to show it to me tomorrow."

Noah didn't miss the way Aiden twitched at that and chuckled. "Works for me." It wasn't like they were inviting a ghost in, they already kind of did that. Waving good-bye, they headed home. For once, the sky was actually clear instead of the punishing rain. It almost made Noah want to go for a walk, but then he acknowledged it would be stupid, especially since Aiden probably wouldn't have wanted to go with him.

If Noah could get through tomorrow, it would be the weekend. He could do with a bit of a break from school, to be honest, though they did already get a day off.

The next day passed quietly and, once more, they found themselves walking home from school with Phen joining them.

CHAPTER 13

Noah chuckled as Phen tried to ask Aiden questions. He felt a little bad, noticing how uncomfortable his twin felt, but at the same time, it was good to witness Aiden actually talking with someone. Mia didn't count since she was staying surprisingly quiet when they were at school or around Phen. They moved past Phen's home and down the street, Phen's voice quieting as they walked. Noah didn't miss the uncertainty as they moved out of town or the way he hesitated.

Aiden sighed and stepped ahead, leading the way as Noah joined Phen, who appeared somewhat nervous.

"You live out here?" Phen asked, peering around.

"It's not that bad." Noah shrugged as they took a bend, their little house coming into view. Phen was more than a little unsettled, almost stiff upon noticing the house.

"Seriously? Here, of all places?"

"You know something about this house?" Aiden asked, glancing over his shoulder.

"Everyone in town knows it, it's one of the more avoided locations for a reason." He peered around hesitantly. "Supposedly, this used to be a cartel base many years ago, like, decades, almost a century or two. No one really knows the exact time frame. It is said that the victims still roam to this day." He shivered and Noah didn't miss how the temperature dropped. Mia must be around. "People speak of a ghost that stands outside, peering in the windows, dark-skinned, dark-haired… pure golden eye."

Yeah, that was Mia to a tee, Noah acknowledged as Aiden shivered, rubbing both arms. Right, his brother was still nervous around her. "That sounds terrifying." He turned to Phen who nodded.

"I wouldn't be surprised if she did exist, especially after seeing Lynn like that." Phen spoke quietly.

Noah's attention drifted to where he could have sworn he spotted Mia. For a brief second, she flickered into existence, almost freezing mid-step. Her piercing golden gaze stayed firmly on an oblivious Phen as she mouthed something. She slammed a hand to her forehead, frustrated. She shook for a moment before vanishing.

He felt a little bad, but he wasn't sure what he could do, or if there was even anything he could do.

"Noah?"

Phen's voice pulled him out of his thoughts and he turned. Aiden and Phen stood to one side, observing him. Noah didn't miss the worried expression on Aiden as he peered around.

"It's nothing." Noah smiled. "I was just wondering what it would be like for the person Phen was talking about if they really were still here. That's all."

Aiden shuddered and shook his head before, clearly wanting a slight change in topic, he turned to Phen. "What was it like?" Aiden asked, and Noah glared back at his brother. He's so insensitive sometimes.

"What?"

Aiden paused, seeming to think through his words before asking, "What was it like to be able to talk to a loved one, even if it was just briefly?"

Noah felt his heart clench in realization. Aiden was thinking of Mom again. He wasn't sure why his brother was saying it like that, but he hoped one day they would see Mom again. Aiden, clearly, thought that wasn't possible.

There was a long pause of silence followed by a weary sigh. "It hurt," Phen admitted, voice much softer, almost quivery. "But I'm glad I was able to see her again, to sort of say good-bye. To think she was trapped as a ghost and I didn't know. At least now I think she's resting at peace, but…"

"You can't help but feel the need to find the one who killed her," Aiden said. "I guess anyone would feel that way."

Noah wondered about that. If he was ever in a situation like Phen's, would he do like Phen was doing and keep going, or would he break?

"Come on, let's go inside." Noah gestured, getting another glare from Aiden. Phen seemed surprised, but nodded. "You should try my brother's food, he's an amazing cook."

"Really? You didn't strike me as much of a cook." Phen turned to Aiden, who just walked ahead, opening the door.

"Appearance is deceiving and all that," Aiden muttered. Noah winced at that, entering inside. Dad still wasn't home and, admittedly, Noah was starting to get worried.

"Huh, I thought this place would look a lot more abandoned." Phen glanced around, surprised. He stepped up to the windows as a chill filled the air.

Oh no, Noah thought as Aiden stiffened, head almost snapping as his attention shifted toward Phen. Phen noticed their change, confused before shivering and glancing back outside.

"Hi there," Mia said as she pressed herself to the glass, crooked smile on her face. It wasn't quite the same terror as before, but it still did the trick of causing Phen to scream bloody murder.

Mia giggled and moved away from the window before stepping through the front door. "I believe you've heard of me?"

Phen collapsed onto his butt, terror flashing across his features. Mia stalked up to him as Noah shook his head.

He was not surprised when something sailed through the air, smacking Mia in the face. Aiden was in a throwing stance, shifting backward slightly, prepared to run.

"Ow!" Mia rubbed her nose as the shaker clattered to the ground next to Phen's foot. "Why do you always do that! You shouldn't even be able to hit me with a projectile!" She pointed toward Aiden, who just sent her a look.

"How the heck should I know?" Aiden hissed, defensive. "This supernatural shit makes no sense, but you WERE being rude and doing this is not helping the situation."

Mia whined as Aiden turned, stomping away. He paused and glanced back toward Phen, specifically ignoring Mia. "Oh, Phen. Do you have any food allergies?"

Phen blinked and shook his head, still staring at Mia in shock. Aiden nodded, turned and scurried away.

"You kind of deserved it," Noah admitted after a moment as Mia huffed, arms crossed. "You know how Aiden feels."

Hesitation crossed her face and she winced. "Right." She turned back to Phen, who was staring up in terror and very heavy confusion.

"Sorry about that." Noah sighed. "She's new and we really don't know much about her. Phen, this is Mia, Mia, Phen." He gestured between them.

Phen still hadn't moved besides nodding, very jerkily.

"If you want to run, screaming, be our guest," Aiden called from the other room. "It's not the first time."

That seemed to snap Phen from his thoughts. "Why—who—how?" He paused. "I didn't know Aiden had such a strong throw."

"Long story." Noah winced, smiling sheepishly. "I kind of accidentally let her into the house and decided to let her stay. As for Aiden? Let's just say he has good aim when he needs it."

"Not wrong." Mia twitched her nose, rubbing her lip now. "Usually, I have fun scaring people, but I need to remember not to do it when that one is around."

Noah shook his head, not sure how to respond to that statement.

"So, you are a ghost." Phen hesitantly got to his feet, clearly not sure what to do with himself. "I mean, I should have expected as much with how they reacted, but…"

"If you are wondering, you are correct, your sister has moved on. She simply wished to say good-bye." Noah never witnessed such a soft expression on Mia's face before. "You had a kind sister."

Phen glanced down, clearly trying not to cry. Expression watery, he smiled. "Yeah."

"Come on, let's take a seat. I know you said you would show us around tomorrow, so it's up to you."

"No. I want to be out of the house for a bit, away from Mom and Dad. Let me call my mom." He dug into his pocket, pulling out his phone before dialing. Noah listened quietly as he explained the situation and that he was staying for dinner. "Yes, I'll be home before it gets dark." He paused and grimaced. "Yes, I'll ask them. I know you're still busy with Dad and the car's actin—yes. Yes. I'll talk to you later, Mom." After another moment, he hung up and turned back to Noah with a tired groan. "So, since I'm staying a little later, do you mind if you bring me home? One, my mom wants to meet you and two, she doesn't want me going out alone and the car's been acting up for the past week. She can't leave until it gets fixed and she's busy with…" He trailed off before shaking his head.

"I don't mind," Noah said.

"Smart woman." Mia spoke up, curling between the both of them. Phen let out a little shriek and Noah chuckled. "I will admit, I'm surprised she let you stay with them though."

"I told her you two helped us find Lynn, though she also heard it from the police, and that you arrived a day or two before that. Plus I might have insinuated your father was here too." He peered around, frowning. "Is he?"

Noah winced at that. "He will be soon. He's still working."

Phen frowned at his words, clearly spotting his reaction but was distracted by Mia who shifted slightly, catching his attention. "Hm, I suppose that would work." Mia pulled back. "Let's hope we don't have to go at night."

"We?" Phen choked, startled. Mia smiled.

"Why? Did you really think I wouldn't come with? I need to watch out for these two."

Phen glanced toward Noah, seeming confused. Noah shrugged. "She has a goal she wants to achieve and I guess we can help her. I don't really know the details, to be honest." He paused, thoughts flitting to the agreement. "Let's just say, I agreed to help if she helped us, quid pro quo and all that."

Phen nodded, clearly a bit overwhelmed. They sat there in silence, the sound of pots and pans rattling from the other room, followed by a beautiful smell caught their attention.

Aiden poked back into the room. "Food's ready."

Noah nodded, hurrying over with Phen a few steps behind, confused.

On the table was a small pile of hamburgers and homemade fries. "I wasn't sure how hungry everyone was." Aiden shrugged, taking a seat. Noah chuckled, following Aiden's example as Phen cautiously took his own. Mia floated above, glancing down in curiosity.

They dug into the food, eating quickly.

"Oh! This is really good." Phen took another bite. "My mom's always come out a little dry." He glanced up. "You are my age, right?"

Aiden rolled his eyes as Noah laughed. "Yeah, it's just that Dad is out a lot, so Aiden learned how to cook. Don't ask me, though, I tried to help once and, well…"

"The kitchen was a mess after. It took an hour for Noah to help me clean it up."

Phen glanced between them and shook his head. "Geez, you guys really have had a rough time, haven't you?"

Noah shrugged, noticing as Aiden bent his head down, munching on his food. "So, where are we going tomorrow?"

"Around town. I noticed you don't have a bike, so we'll have to walk." He paused. "Though, uh, maybe I'll have you pick me up instead of coming here." At that, he glanced up toward Mia, who waved. "I don't think walking here alone is a great idea."

"Nope," Mia chirped before spinning and replicating she was taking a seat next to Aiden. "It would be a very bad idea." Her expression grew serious. "Very bad."

Aiden watched quietly, gaze flicking between Mia and Phen. Noah blinked, feeling more than a little confused. Did Aiden know something Noah didn't? He wouldn't be surprised, it wasn't the first time.

Noah turned to Phen, curious, "So, Phen, this place, it sounds like it's been haunted for a while. Are there other rumors of the surrounding area?"

Phen paused, fry in his mouth as he debated. He quickly chowed down on it before saying, "Sort of? This town in general is well known for being haunted, but people usually pass it off, especially since it's never really been evil." He paused at that. "Usually, a lot of rumors are about hauntings that are more pranks than anything."

"I can confirm that." Mia raised a hand.

Phen jumped at that, staring at her before nodding. "It's only recently that things have changed."

"The disappearances." Aiden tilted his head up.

Phen winced and slumped.

Noah reached over, lightly patting Phen on the shoulder, noting how it startled him. "Hey, we'll figure out what's going on." Noah turned to Aiden, who was suddenly wary. "I mean, Dad's working on it and clearly this guy is dangerous, so why don't we help?"

"No," Aiden argued, anger flashing over his face. "What if something happens that—"

"We haven't heard from Dad in a day or two and, while I know he can usually be gone for long stretches, by this point, he would have at least contacted us more than just once," Noah cut in, finally letting some of his worry seep out. Phen gave Noah a harsh look, which Noah promptly ignored. Yes, he had pseudo lied, but so did Phen so it was only fair. "If the person that killed Phen's sister is the one Dad is searching for and the one Mia warned us about, then shouldn't we try to find him? Find out a way to stop him?"

"How do you propose we do that?" Aiden's voice hissed in a quiet whisper. "We're not Dad. No one's going to believe us—"

"Maybe they will." Phen spoke up, a wide grin on his face, causing both of them to still. "All we have to do is capture whoever is doing this. You said your father was researching him, right? If we capture the guy, then it should give him a chance to put him down."

Aiden pursed his lips, displeasure clear in his tense posture. "Yeah, sure, that's ALL we have to do." Strangely, his words echoed Mia's as she said the same thing in tandem. He froze, staring at her in surprise as she blinked, stilling in the air. Noah found himself stunned by the in unison words.

"Well, that's a first." Mia grinned. "Didn't expect to agree on something already."

Aiden shivered, shaking his head as Noah recollected himself and turned to him. "Come on, Aiden," Noah quietly pleaded.

Aiden seemed to debate before slumping back into his chair with a tired sigh. "Fine. Fine, we'll see if we can find out what's going on. I just think it's stupid, reckless—"

"And can definitely get you killed as both Aiden and I agreed upon," Mia said, voice almost monotone. Her features were creased into an expression Noah couldn't quite identify. "Don't take this lightly. I'm not about to let my one chance at freedom die because of stupidity."

Noah pursed his lips at that, but sighed. "Ultimately, I'm worried about Dad and…" he turned to Phen. "You want to avenge your sister, so we have reason enough to try, at least."

Phen's expression twisted before he let out a long breath, a weak smile crossing his face. "Thanks." He paused. "I should get going."

"I'll go with you." Noah stood. "Your mom did ask us to, after all."

The hesitation was clear, but eventually, Phen agreed. Aiden, groaning, followed, locking the door. The sky was beginning to get dark and the air was much colder than before. It was hard to tell if it was because of Mia or normal weather changes.

The walk was quiet, but surprisingly serene. "I'll have to show you guys the ice cream parlor, they have some amazing mint chocolate chip." Phen glanced over, grinning before the smile faded. "Lynn used to love it." He quickly turned away.

Aiden frowned at that as Noah felt a surge of sadness. It wasn't their fault, but he couldn't help but feel bad. Hopefully, finding a way to deal with the man who did it would help. He could only hope.

When they arrived, the lights were glowing faintly, the front porch alit with a warm yellow glow. The door clicked open and a woman who looked remarkably like Lynn stepped out, relief on her face. "Phen, it's good to see you home. I thought you said you would be home before dark." She bustled forward, pulling the boy into a hug.

"Mom!" Phen tugged, half-heartedly pulling away. "This is embarrassing, but thanks."

The woman pulled away and turned to them. The redness of her cheeks and the faint tear streaks showed the woman was still grieving. Even her smile was barely there, given more out of courtesy, but Noah understood. "Ah, you two must be Noah and Aiden. Phen told me about you two." Her gaze shifted between them. "Thank you for helping us know what happened to Lynn." Her voice hitched as Phen lightly patted her back, watching her worriedly. "I heard you've only arrived recently. Thank you for keeping an eye on my boy."

"Mom." Phen's voice broke slightly and he cleared his throat.

"Of course." Noah smiled, hoping to relieve her a little, even as his thoughts drifted to his own mother.

"Will you be able to get home safely?" she asked, concern taking the place of gratitude. "It's late and it's just the two of you." She peered around. "Why don't you stay here tonight and leave in the morning?"

"We'll be fine." Aiden spoke up. "We don't live far from here—" At that, Phen furrowed his brow, but didn't say anything. "We'll be coming by tomorrow."

"I know you might think it's not that far, but you're still kids. Where are your parents? They should have been the ones to bring Phen home."

"Father's busy." Noah piped up, forcing a bright smile on his face and hands behind his back to portray innocence. Just in case Father came back, he wanted to be home waiting for him instead of at someone else's house. "He's expecting us to be back soon."

The woman's frown deepened, brow creasing with a mix of worry and annoyance, clearly about to argue.

"We'll be fine." Aiden spoke up. "Like Noah said, we don't live that far, right down the street and there is plenty of light on the way."

"Fine, I'll make something for lunch then." She shook her head, clearly not pleased, but finally accepting their insistance. "Now, come on, Phen, you've got homework to do."

"But it's a Friday!"

"Homework first or else you won't finish it." At that, she pulled him inside, nodding good-bye to them. Noah's smile became strained as they left, the air feeling cold now that it was just them.

"She's nice if a bit…." Aiden's voice trailed off, sounding a little odd. "Come on, let's go." Noah glanced over as Aiden headed back down the road. "It's late."

Noah found his attention pulled back to the warmth of the home before he followed. His throat clenched as the cold wind picked up, brushing past both of them.

They were alone like usual. Painful feelings pulled at his chest. What was it like to have that warmth? All they had to look forward to was a cold empty place they couldn't even really call home, but it was the only place they really knew and where their father would be expecting them.

CHAPTER 14

Noah felt a light touch on his shoulder and turned. Aiden watched him, concern flitting over his expression, followed by a faint, if tired smile. It was such a rare sight from his brother that Noah couldn't help but smile back. "Hey, we'll be okay," Aiden whispered. "Someday, for now, let's just get home just in case Dad's looking for us."

Noah chuckled at that. "Maybe we could drag Dad with us, have him retire."

Aiden snorted, reaching up to ruffle Noah's hair, causing him to squawk in protest. "Yeah, I don't think we'll be able to convince him of that even when he's old and using a cane."

"True, he would probably just follow your example and hit people with the cane."

Aiden actually chuckled at that. "I CAN'T imagine."

Noah relaxed slightly. The thought still hurt, aching, but he was able to push it back into place, where it always lingered. He wasn't sure if he could ever fully get rid of it, but he could handle it. "Thanks, Aiden."

Aiden, who turned his attention back to the road, nodded. He tilted his head just slightly to face him. "I figured, if I was having those thoughts, you were too. I wasn't going to let you start spinning into that mess."

Noah blinked at that and shook his head. "You…"

"Should pay attention." Mia's voice crept up on both of them, a hint of concern in her tone. "With it being this late, let's just say, we need to get you two back and quickly."

Noah barely withheld the jump. Aiden shifted, muscles tense once more. "Right." He spoke evenly, gaze flicking to where Mia materialized beside them. "I hate to say this, but for once, I agree with the Thing."

"It's Mia." Mia spoke up, annoyed.

"Thing will be fine for now." Aiden picked up the pace, causing Noah to stumble after him. Noah heard faint grumbling from behind, but figured it was just Mia. Geez, his brother didn't even call Mia a ghost. Though, he supposed it made sense. The supernatural in regards to Aiden was pretty much a conundrum in and of itself. Plus, with Aiden's hesitation around Mia, it wasn't surprising.

He found himself quietly observing the surroundings as they trekked back down the road, the occasional lamp light from above flickering dully in the growing darkness. The beginning slivers of pale moonlight caught on the surrounding houses and forest. The sound of their footsteps over the pavement echoed loudly in his ears. The silence was what got him. It unnerved him when they first arrived, now it just made the night so much worse. A breeze picked up, tugging at hair and clothes as they kept to a fast walk. Neither said a word as Mia floated beside them, a strange wariness causing her to shift between them. "I do wonder why you two were so insistant to leave. You would have been safe in her home for the night."

"I want to get back to the house, just in case Dad comes home." Noah glanced toward her, shrugging. "Plus... I felt uncomfortable just going into a random strangers house. I mean, we know Phen, but only kind of. I don't know, it's just..." Noah wasn't sure how to continue. He could feel Aiden's gaze on him. His brother's expression was somewhat agreeing, if a little pained.

Aiden turned ahead and Noah didn't blame him. He probably agreed immensely with Noah's words. Mia didn't ask again, simply stayed quiet. Aiden continued to lead them through the streets and back to the dirt path toward home. Noah surveyed the surroundings, that unease making his stomach clench and twist; a nauseous feeling overtaking him.

The feeling of being watched crept up on him and he found himself peering over his shoulder. Mia flit urgently, unsettled.

Soon enough, they took the final bend, their new place in sight. That feeling of being watched grew and Noah noticed the way Aiden whipped around, staring into the trees. The barest hint of fear flitted across his face before he turned and, grabbing Noah's hand, bolted. They raced toward the house, their footsteps sounding loud in Noah's ears, competing with the thrumming pounding in his chest at the suddenness.

"Inside, now," Mia hissed, keeping pace as Aiden pulled out the keys, quickly unlocking the door. He dragged Noah in before slamming it shut, locking it.

They stood in silence, breath catching in their throats.

Mia hovered in front of them, and, for a brief moment, Noah saw hesitation.

Then he heard the sound, a faint echoing hum from outside.

"Come on," Aiden whispered, lightly tugging Noah back. They carefully moved through the house to Dad's room. Aiden snapped closed the curtains and locked the door.

Noah's gaze flitted to Mom's cross and he grabbed it as they scurried into the closet, closing the door and burrowing low in the messy pile of clothing Dad never hung up.

They held their breaths, Mia hovering above them, a spectrum of emotions on her face seen even in the darkness.

That humming sounded again, nearby, just outside the window. A slow scratching filled the air, like nails on wood, as Noah gripped the cross tighter. Dad mentioned this before and he was hoping, desperately, that it would help right now. He felt terror thrum through his veins as he pushed into Aiden's side, Aiden holding him tightly, breaths slow and measured in case they had to run.

For a moment, Noah could have sworn he felt a chill run down his spine and heard the faint sound of scraping and clawing, but soon, it was followed by an eerie silence.

After some time of held breath and pounding hearts, Mia put up a finger and drifted out.

He wasn't sure how long they waited, how long adrenaline sang through his veins, screaming at him to run, to get away.

Finally a familiar tapping reached their ears. "It's safe, he's… that thing is gone."

Noah carefully pulled away, pushing open the door. Aiden followed after a moment, pale and shaken.

"Did you see him?" Noah finally voiced out, words hoarse. Thing? Why would… why would Mia call him a thing? Especially when she hated Aiden calling her that?

Aiden hesitated and shuddered, something Noah was noticing a lot lately. It was unnerving, to say the least. "I just saw a shadow through the trees." Aiden placed a hand to his chest, fingers curling around where the cross must be. "I just needed to run."

"That was a good call." Mia spoke softly as she stared out the window. "That thing has gotten stronger. It feels like the human soul is being devoured."

Noah shivered, even though the words didn't make sense to him. "How is that possible? How can a soul be devoured?"

Mia shook her head, staring out the window once more.

Aiden took a deep breath and headed toward the door.

"I would stay in here for tonight. Don't leave this room." Her words stilled him, causing both of them to turn to her. She pulled away. "That cross has been in here for a few days." Her gaze flitted to Noah's tightened grip around Mom's cross. "It's given this room some protection. You'll see what I mean in the morning." At that, she left.

Aiden continued to watch where Mia disappeared to, a deep frown on his face as his fingers twitched near the door handle.

"Aiden? Just for tonight. I know you don't like her, but I feel we should trust her on this." Noah walked forward, putting a hand on Aiden's shoulder, noting how tense his brother was.

"This supernatural stuff…" Aiden brushed Noah's hand off as he turned. "Fine. I'll take the floor." Aiden walked away from the door, grabbing up one of the pillows and blankets scattered over the bed and plopped onto the thin-rugged floor, curling inward.

Noah hesitated, worry settling over him in a wave before he let out a breath. He plopped onto the bed, fingers curling into the sheets. "Come on, Aiden, we can share for tonight."

Noah watched his brother before lightly reaching forward with his socked foot, pushing lightly on Aiden's back. "I will keep bugging you. You need sleep too, especially with how little you've slept with Mia around. It's not the first time we've had to share a bed, I doubt it'll be the last."

"Will you stop poking me?" Aiden grumbled. "I get it."

"Then why aren't you moving?" Noah poked again, almost kicking him at this point. "Look, I know you don't like everything that's happening." Noah felt his words stutter a little and pushed through. "I mean, the supernatural has always fascinated me, but I know you've never believed in it. I can only imagine how…" He trailed off, unsure what to even say. He couldn't imagine how his brother was feeling with all of this. It was stressful already just being in a new place. To add weird things like ghosts and whatever the heck that was outside? That was another thing entirely.

He heard a heavy sigh and glanced over as Aiden slowly pushed himself up. "Fine. You're not going to stop bothering me otherwise."

Noah smiled, both genuine and a little sheepish as Aiden scooped up the bedding and pillow and turned to him. The smile faded as he noted the exhaustion in his brother's features. It made him feel even worse. Part of that exhaustion was because of him.

They set up the bed, placing whatever they could between them and settled down. Noah curled inward, grateful to eventually hear his brother's soft breathing as he fell asleep. Noah relaxed, turning toward the window. He pulled out his phone, staring at it quietly, the bright glow almost hurting his eyes before he lowered it.

Dad still hadn't called or texted and it was worrying him deeply. He wanted to call, but it was late so, instead, he sent a brief text. 'Where are you? There was a creepy thing here. Aiden and I are safe, but I'm scared.'

As soon as those words were typed in, he froze. He hadn't wanted to admit it. After all, he was the one helping Aiden. However, the fear of the unknown, at those sounds he heard outside? It DID scare him. He shuddered as he heard a faint whisper that he wasn't sure whether was wind or breath. There was tapping and a long scratching sound outside… or was it inside?

He sent the text, pulling the phone close to his chest as he let out a breath. Calm down, Noah. This is your thing, if you let it get to you, how can you help Aiden? He shook his head, trying to center himself. It took time before he felt his shoulders relax.

Maybe Dad would text in the morning. He placed the phone on the side dresser and rolled over once more. His pounding heart settled as he let the relief pass through him. After all, Aiden was right there and fine. Strangely, he didn't mind sharing a bed today, especially after the last few days.

CHAPTER 15

As much as Aiden wished he slept well the rest of the night, he knew after the first bit, it was fitful. He could hear his brother shuffling beside him, rolling back and forth in a failed attempt at sleep. There were moments that Aiden could have sworn he heard faint scratching, followed by hissing. A footstep here, a creak there. Wind rustled against the windows outside, pushing against the glass.

With the curtains closed, it took a while before he finally gave up on sleeping, unable to fully tell the time except a faint glow from behind the thick fabric. He briefly noticed that Noah put Mother's cross on the side dresser and shook his head. He wasn't sure what good that did, but according to the Thing, it did something. Anger seared through him at the thought. Pushing himself up, feeling his back crack slightly in the process, he let out a groan that merged into a yawn. A faint whine from Noah caught his attention as he swung his legs over the side of the bed. To be honest, he was grateful to have gotten to sleep in the bed, even if they had to share. Floors weren't the most comfortable locations.

"Aiden, it's early," Noah grumbled, curling in tighter. Aiden picked up Noah's phone, pretty much reaching over him to do it and flipped it open, to lazy and tired to get his own. The screen glowed slightly, showing no calls or texts and a time that was clearly almost ten.

"Sure." Aiden let the phone fall onto Noah, hearing a grunt from his brother. "Get up. I don't really want to stay here longer than we have to." With that, Aiden pushed himself to his feet and headed toward the door before hesitating. Fingers inches from the handle as he stared at it, uncertain.

It's fine. He was being paranoid. He shook it off and opened the door, noting, with slight terror, that it wasn't locked.

"You didn't even ask me if it was safe." The Thing's voice reached Aiden's ears as he froze, staring past the doorway. "Thankfully, for now, you are."

He barely heard those last words as the scratches in the wood, eerily glowing in the morning light, caught his attention. "What—how?" He spoke, voice shaken. What the hell was with these… these things?

He heard the Ghost sigh as she fluttered in front of him, white dress settling softly around her as a golden eye stared back at him quietly. "You aren't naive." She spoke. "You can probably guess."

"Guess, what?" Noah yawned as he joined Aiden, peering over Aiden's shoulder before stilling. "Oh, I thought ghosts couldn't get inside?"

Aiden didn't miss the way Noah's voice shook, even as he tried to throw a faint curious expression on his face.

"Typically? No." The Thing floated backward as she turned, peering down the hall. "However, strong ghosts can break in, especially if they have a human connection like this one." Mia whirled, facing them. "I never clearly saw his face last night, but I was able to confirm it was a male." The Thing glanced toward Noah. "Thankfully, it didn't know I was here and, due to that cross," she gestured inside, "that room was protected… for now. I suggest, however, that you collect your belongings and we look for someplace else. I'm not in the mood to lose my chance of escape because of a possessed soul." With that, she vanished once more, leaving Aiden more than a little frustrated.

"That makes no sense," Aiden hissed.

Noah lightly patted his shoulder, brushing past. "Come on. I think we can trust her."

"You are too trusting." Aiden shook his head and let out a breath. "But I guess I agree. I don't feel comfortable staying here after last night but we don't really have anywhere else to go."

Noah had nothing to say to that. He pulled out his phone and his expression grew more tense. "I'm also getting worried for Dad. We haven't heard anything from him and I even tried texting him."

Aiden's gaze flicked to Noah as they walked to their room, Noah pulling up his own phone. Aiden heard the faint click and beep of Noah's phone as he dialed and put it on speaker.

"Hello, this is Rodger Raven. I am not available right now to take your call—" Before the voicemail could get any farther, Noah hung up, glancing toward Aiden worriedly. Aiden wondered if they should have left a message, but if Dad had his phone off and wasn't answering texts over a period of a few days except to say 'can't talk', then he wasn't sure what to think. Unfortunately, his thoughts couldn't help but to flit to Mother. It was too similar. He shuddered at the thought. What if they did lose Father? They still had quite a few more years until they were adults and they had no relatives that they knew of. Would they end up in foster care? An orphanage? He couldn't handle the idea and it was one he tried not to think about, especially after Mother's disappearance.

"It's probably fine." Noah's smile was shaky at best as he pocketed his phone. "I mean, it's Dad. He knows how to take care of himself. He's been in dangerous situations and cases before."

Even so, the silence still unsettled both of them.

Aiden let out a breath, changing his clothes and throwing the rest into a bin to one side. He thought about throwing some things into Dad's room, but, to be honest, he felt he was being paranoid. The man didn't find them, why would he come back?

It wasn't long before they headed out, storing away some money Dad gave them in case of emergencies.

As they moved down the dirt road back into town, Aiden's mind drifted toward the Thing. He shuddered at the idea of calling her, the Thing, by name. It wasn't her name, she wasn't human. Yet, he couldn't call her Thing anymore. She did watch out for them last night. She called that other monster Thing and he could agree with her that it fit much better. Ghost… he would call her Ghost.

The Ghost glanced at him, floating backward as they walked through the streets, her long hair curling around her as she tilted her head slightly. He couldn't read her expression and he didn't try to.

The sun barely peeked through the once more fairly overcast sky as they finally made it to Phen's house. They headed up the steps before Noah hesitantly knocked on the door, Aiden a few feet back.

There was the sound of faint footsteps before it opened to reveal the woman from the day before. She blinked before letting out a breath of relief. "Oh, it's good to see you two made it." She peered around the door, brow furrowed as she stared past them the way they had come. She murmured to herself for a moment, too soft for the boys to hear before turning back to them. "How are you feeling? Clearly, you made it home safely. Did you get any sleep?" She paused and smiled sheepishly. "I'm sorry, I shouldn't badger you two with so many questions. Come in, come in." She gestured.

Aiden didn't miss the way the tension in Noah settled slightly as they stepped inside the warm interior. The door closed as the woman bustled them forward, past a room on the left that was definitely a living room and a stairwell on the right to a kitchen dining room combo in the back. The faint scent of lavender filled the space, a candle flame wavering gently to one side.

"Mom? Who is it?" Phen's voice called from upstairs as the woman gestured for them to take a seat in the chairs. The hospitality was a bit surreal, but both accepted it, taking a seat as the mother bustled away toward the front.

"It's your friends! I'll take care of them, you just come down and say—" Before she could finish, there was the sound of running footsteps.

"Mom! Why didn't you tell me sooner?" Phen's voice was pitched slightly, as if embarrassed.

Aiden wondered why that was while Noah blinked, clearly confused, concerned and somewhat amused.

The mother returned, shaking her head, a faint smile on her lips pushing away the heavy air of grief. "That's my son. Though, I suppose, I'm content that he is happy to see you two." Her gaze shifted between them, expression soft. "Well, have you had anything to eat this morning?"

Noah shook his head as Aiden spoke a soft, "No."

Her smile faltered slightly before strengthening. "Alright, then, let me get you a hearty meal. It's more of a lunch at this point, but I think that will be fine for everyone." She turned toward the kitchen as faint footfalls caught Aiden's ears.

A moment later, a familiar figure slid into the room, literally. He caught himself, stumbling slightly as he almost tripped on the rug under the table.

Noah actually chuckled as Aiden shook his head.

Phen straightened, sheepish expression on his face. "Morning." He paused. "Um… it's good to see you guys again. Sorry about not being down to greet you and all." He glanced toward Aiden and quickly turned back to Noah. "I was helping my dad with something."

"Your dad?" Noah blinked. "Your mom mentioned that last night what—"

Phen's expression became drawn as Noah snapped his mouth shut.

"He took Lynn's death hard." Phen stared out the window for a moment and Aiden found himself looking away. Grief was one thing he still had trouble dealing with.

It was painful to lose a loved one, at least Phen knew the truth.

"So are you two ready to go out today?" Phen took a seat at the table, fingers lightly tapping on the wood. "There's a lot of a cool places I can show you, though it's mostly just sight-seeing. Not much else to do, really."

"Sure." Noah relaxed. "We could use that after the past couple of days." He paused, gaze flitting to Aiden.

To be honest, sightseeing might be a good idea. Maybe they would see Dad in the process. Aiden had a few choice words to give him for not contacting them back. Sure, he was sometimes bad at it, but this was getting a bit much.

There was a bit of silence after that before Phen's mother stepped in with some food, including an extra tray she took with her as she headed upstairs. Phen watched her go, shook his head, and chowed down on the breakfast sandwich with some cut-up fruit. It was surprisingly good and made Aiden feel both warm at the food in his stomach and cold at the fact that it was someone else's mother who gave it to them. Soon enough, they were heading out, Phen taking the lead with a slightly more chipper air then before. Though Aiden couldn't tell if it was fake or not.

However… "Why are you being so nice to us?" Aiden muttered quietly, not expecting the boy to hear as he walked a little ahead with Noah, chatting back and forth. Phen glanced back toward him, causing Aiden to almost stumble, surprised the boy heard him.

He didn't miss Noah's expression as Phen responded, "Because?" He seemed confused. "I kind of already explained and, well, it's not every day you meet someone who can talk to and interact with ghosts."

True… Aiden paused, half-expecting the Ghost to interrupt there, but noticed how he hadn't really felt her around lately, at least, not since this morning. For a brief moment, he wondered where she was before shuddering and throwing the thought off. He was somewhat relieved she was not with them.

"Sorry, we're not used to it." Noah spoke up hesitantly. "We appreciate it, really, it's just…"

Phen's expression shifted as he glanced between them. "Do you move around a lot?"

Aiden turned away, shoving his hands into his pockets as Noah shifted from foot to foot. "Quite a bit."

"Oh. Well then, if you are only here for a while, might as well make it count, right?"

Aiden turned to him, somewhat startled, and noticed Noah's expression showed the same. "Huh?"

Phen shrugged, fondness, yet heavy sadness shifted over his face. "Something I'm coming to terms with… enjoying the moments while I have them."

Aiden sighed, understanding. He supposed Phen would feel it even more after his sister's death.

"So, where to first?" Noah brought up after a little while of silence.

"Oh! Right, we'll start with the arcade. I know we're not supposed to go, but I'm curious. Then the library and I have to show you that ice-cream parlor—"

Aiden quickly tuned him out as they started heading down the road, noting as both Phen and Noah started happily chatting back and forth, gesturing about. Unlike the night, the day was serene. Blue filled the sky, the gray overcast morning having been pushed away for once which was a relief. Warmth gently fell over his skin from the sun. A few people were out and about, already busy with the tasks of the day.

Soon, they came across the arcade which very clearly had a closed sign hanging from the window. He could just barely see some machines inside that were being disassembled.

"I used to come here all the time with Lynn after she finished her occult club meetings." Phen glanced toward Aiden. "You know, I've talked with the others from the occult club and they all say the same thing, that they weren't there at the time. No one knew she was going to be there. So, I wonder why she was."

Aiden couldn't help but wonder that himself. They heard footsteps and turned to see a man stomp up to them, hair frazzled. "What are ya doing at my here arcade?" The man growled, a slight limp to his step. "It's closed, don'tcha know how to read the sign?"

"I was just showing my friends around," Phen said, a nervous quaver to his voice. "We weren't trying to intrude or anything."

"Ya better not be. I catch any ya trespassing, ya ain't going to be leaving happy." At that, he harrumphed and walked inside.

"He's—" Noah hesitated.

"Rude," Aiden cut in, knowing his brother was a bit too nice to say anything. "Or, I guess, a jack-ass works."

"Aiden!"

"What? It's not wrong."

"That's…"

Phen chuckled tiredly and sighed. "Yeah, he's something." He paused and peered over. "If it wasn't for the fact that he doesn't really leave the arcade much, I would suspect him, but…"

Aiden's gaze flicked to the arcade as they continued past. The man was strange and Aiden felt a little unsettled, but he had also seen a lot of grumpy old men with his father's job so he wasn't sure how to feel. Still, the fact Phen had some suspects wasn't a bad thing.

"He just seems like an old man." Noah winced. "And, well, trespassing isn't exactly legal." Both Phen and Aiden turned to him. "What?"

"You are something." Phen snorted and headed down the street as Aiden shook his head. "Come on, I'll show you the next town wonder, the haunted library." He chuckled. "Though I don't think it's actually haunted like your place was."

Aiden glared and sighed as Noah scrambled after. Aiden paused, glancing toward the arcade, only to shiver as he noticed the old man watching, gaze piercing, before he turned and disappeared into the shadows of the store.

Aiden was getting real tired of this whole town giving him the creeps. He wondered at Noah's naivety sometimes. Still, there was no actual evidence that it was the old man and he doubted someone like that could sneak into a school to kill someone. He turned and walked after the others before he lost sight of them. After a few more turns and passing by what seemed to be the middle of town, if the small selection of shops was any indication, they made it to the library.

Or, well, they would have, if Aiden hadn't gotten distracted by the small bookstore to one side that was next to a little cafe. There were a few chairs outside and one or two people reading while sipping tea and other drinks. He found himself staring through the glass windows to beautifully designed arrangements of all sorts of fascinating books. There was even a cat to one side, sleeping with its tail curled off the edge of the table.

He wanted so badly to go inside. He felt a tap on his shoulder and peered over to find that Noah joined him, clearly spotting something inside from the way he also stared longingly. "Let's keep going." He kept his voice soft as Aiden pursed his lips, realizing why.

They didn't have the money to spend on books even when Dad was around, it was even less likely to have a chance to get one when it was just them with some extra money just in case. With slightly slumped shoulders, Aiden let Noah pull him away, noting the confusion on Phen's face as they walked past him. He turned, hurrying up to them.

"You two okay?"

"Yeah, library, right?" Noah grinned, letting Aiden go. "We should hurry before it gets any later."

Phen nodded, clearly still confused before gesturing and leading them once more.

The library was small, but Aiden couldn't help the faint smile as he peered inside. Books were hard to travel with. He could only really bring a few with him, so usually, it was books for studying or school. He appreciated libraries, but it was cumbersome to get a library card every time. At least it was possible, unlike the bookstores where money was an issue. Though, it seemed like the library was closed due to a special event going on for the townspeople. Phen just led them away, shaking his head. Aiden followed, staring back dejectedly. Maybe he could get a chance to go in another time.

"So, I legit forgot there was a meeting going on in the library today so, let's head to the ice cream parlor, my treat." He grinned, tugging them along.

By the time they arrived, the adrenaline and fear of the night before had long since faded into a more content happiness.

Aiden, grudgingly, admitted that it was actually pretty fun. Though, he was starting to agree with Noah. The town wasn't large by any stretch of the imagination, so why was Dad not responding to their calls or calling them? It unnerved him more than he would like to admit. However, he wouldn't admit it out loud, he didn't want Noah to worry more than he already was. He hoped it was just because Dad was out of range, but who knew. What his father did was sometimes dangerous.

He scrunched up his nose when he noticed Phen grab the waffle cone layered in mint chocolate chip and chose a simple chocolate for himself. Noah seemed to debate for a while, to the point that the seller was starting to get annoyed, before eventually picking a chocolate chip cookie dough.

Aiden shook his head, amused as he took another lick of his ice cream, wiping some off his cheek as he felt it smudge against it.

Phen was watching both of them with amusement. They soon left, a cool breeze helping against some of the sun beating down. Didn't do much to stop the ice cream from melting, but it felt good.

"Oh, ice cream?" The Ghost's voice met his ears and he glanced up, tense, as the other two jumped.

"Yes." Aiden kept his word short, staring at her quietly, fingers curling around the cone, careful not to crush it. Why was she bothering him again? "Can someone like yourself even eat?"

"I should feel offended." She paused, deep in thought before sighing heavily. "Urgh… You aren't wrong." She ducked forward, almost getting in his face. "And I hate that I have to admit it to you." She swiped a finger at the chocolate, some of it coming off while some of it slipped past. Aiden took a few steps back, feeling his nose wrinkle up in a mix of horror and distaste.

She rolled her visible eye, stuffing the finger coated in chocolate into her mouth, annoyed.

She froze, standing in place, her feet firmly planted on the ground.

"Mia?" Noah asked hesitantly, taking a step toward her. She slowly tilted her head down as she pulled her finger away. Her attention firmly on it.

Aiden blinked, startled as something traced down her cheek.

"Oh, it's faint, but… I can taste it."

Aiden just stared. Was that normal?

"Uh, I think I might be missing something," Phen hesitantly called. "Mind explaining?"

The Ghost drifted back. "We are spirits. Food is not something that sustains us." She turned her attention back to the cone as Aiden realized, with annoyance, that she took a swipe out of the side he was working on, ugh… he was saving that part. "To taste it at all…" That same thing dripped down her face, following the path of the other.

Noah was the one who realized, shocked. "You're crying."

The Ghost paused, hand flitting to her cheek. She covered it, only a faint bit of a weak smile falling across her lips. "Oh, this is what it's like. No wonder he was being persistent last night." At that, she pulled away. "I need time to think." She darted away, surprising the three of them.

Aiden felt something drip on his hand and huffed. In the confusion, his ice cream melted all over the cone and onto his hand.

Because of course it did.

He wished things could make sense for once. He was getting real sick of this, plus, he lost his appetite. At the next garbage, he tossed the cone, wiping his hand down with a little water from the bottle he bought as well.

He turned his attention back to Phen, who watched the girl disappear before turning back to them with a strange expression. Aiden wished he understood these things a bit more. Sure, she was weird, but that was even weirder then usual from her and, strangely, it made him a bit worried about the situation, both her and what it was he and his brother were able to do.

He shook it off, trying to take a deep mental breath. Okay, the Ghost was acting weird, Dad was missing, Noah and Phen were interested in finding a killer…

Aiden sighed. All he could really do was keep an eye on them. He knew trying to persuade Noah to not do something was the equivalent of winning a cross-country marathon award.

Impossible for the two of them.

As the thoughts flitted through his mind, he found himself trailing the two once more.

Hopefully, the feeling eating at him was just the nausea of eating too much ice cream at once after not having it in a long time.

No matter how hard he tried to convince himself, he knew it was a lie.

Honestly, he just wanted to see Dad and go someplace else, anyplace else.

CHAPTER 16

Noah glanced back toward his brother, noting he was clearly lost in thought. He sighed and turned back to Phen, unsure what to really say.

"Your ghost… friend?" When Noah nodded, Phen continued, "is really strange."

"I've noticed." Noah glanced down the road. "But then, I don't even know if that's just the case with all ghosts."

"What do you mean?"

Noah tilted his head slightly and turned toward Phen. "To be honest, we didn't even know they were ghosts, that is, until we met Lynn."

Phen's eyes widened in shock. "Really? How could you not know?"

"They look like regular humans to us," Noah admitted. "Don't they look that way to you?"

Phen hesitated. "Sometimes, but most of the time, it's like they are faded, slightly translucent, which just makes it creepier." He shivered. "When Mia first 'introduced 'herself," he quoted, "she had this grin that split her face in a way that couldn't have been natural."

Noah frowned, curious. He saw those smiles, the ones where she was trying to scare them. They just looked like malicious grins, but the way Phen was describing it? "Do you mean, like, a wide grin?"

Phen shook his head. "No, more like the mouth became really wide, and almost sinewy and behind the strings of sinew was just black." He shivered and Noah blinked, startled. That was… really weird. Noah wasn't sure he wanted to admit to Phen that he never saw that before. "Just thinking about it gives me the chills. She looked normal after that, especially when Aiden hit her which actually helped a lot in making me feel a lot less scared." Phen paused. "It just makes me wonder, though, if Lynn would have started doing that if we never found her." He scuffed his shoe over the road, shoulders slumped. "How long would she have been trapped there before she was found? I guess I really should stop thinking of that and just be grateful we found her."

Noah turned away, rubbing his arms. Yeah, I guess it is better to know, he thought. After all, he was still wondering about Mom and he had a feeling he would always be wondering. It was something he hated. The fear and unknown of the situation just ate at him. He wouldn't wish it on anyone. "I can understand that." Phen glanced toward him and he quickly dropped his hands back to his side. "I am worried about Dad since I haven't seen him in a while."

Phen nodded, glancing ahead. "That's why I want to find this killer, to know who it could be so no one else disappears like my sister."

Noah couldn't argue with that. He peered back toward Aiden, noting he was falling behind a bit, lost in thought. Noah fell back too and grabbed his elbow, startling him. "Come on, at least keep pace." He tugged, walking forward and causing Aiden to stumble. He turned toward Phen with a grin. "Where to next?"

Phen blinked and chuckled. "It's not much, but we do have a central shopping area. We'll go there and then head back to my place. I know we passed it quickly earlier and you guys didn't go into the shops, but we can still look around. I don't know if you guys need to buy anything or not, but that is the place to do it."

"The only place we've been is the convenience store at the edge of town," Noah admitted, finally letting go of Aiden, who rubbed at his side before, this time, keeping pace. "Unfortunately, we're… lacking in money." He winced as Phen nodded. "At least, for things like that."

"Oh, the convenience store, yeah, that place is kind of creepy." Phen shrugged. "But mostly at night, because it's just the one clerk who many think is doped up at that point in the night." He paused. "I would help, but I don't have much of an allowance either, sorry."

Noah shook his head, gaze flicking in the general direction of the store. Noah felt a little bad for a moment, but shook it off. It wasn't his business.

•   •   •   •   •

It wasn't long before they were on the street Phen mentioned. It seemed to be the middle of town, something Noah and Aiden passed occasionally when heading to school and when they first arrived. They explored earlier, but it was interesting going through again, a bit later in the day. Like the rest of town, it was slightly dreary, but there were people out and about, going to the little stores that lined the street. Noah spotted an arts and crafts store, a little grocery store, and the book store from before, the one that caught both of their attention. Next to it was a tattoo parlor, or was that a nail salon?

The three moved between stores, talking about random things. At one point, they stopped at the bookstore again, and watched the little cat inside before it noticed them and, with a swish of its tail, disappeared back into the shop.

Eventually, with the day growing close to night, they headed back. Noah turned to Phen as they walked, raising an eyebrow. "There isn't much to do around here, is there?"

Phen shook his head. "Nope, kind of what I wanted to show. Once the arcade went out of business, it's been kind of boring. Sure, some of the kids are finding stuff to do, but I'm not interested."

Noah didn't need to guess what it was. He saw what happened to those his age who were bored and had nothing better to do. He and Aiden managed to avoid falling into those crowds, but only because they usually had each other and found ways around it.

Plus… he shivered. He'd heard enough stories from Dad to know to stay away from those things.

"So, where do we start?" Aiden finally spoke up, catching both of their attention. "Considering how small of a town it is, and since you are so darn determined to find this killer, where would you recommend we start?" He paused. "I would usually say the school would be a good bet, but I doubt we could just slip in."

Oh, so he had been thinking about it. Noah couldn't help but grin, getting an annoyed look from Aiden.

Phen seemed to debate on his words before turning around, walking backward for a bit. "That's a good point. Starting at the school wouldn't be a bad idea, I think."

"It isn't." Noah spoke up. "The thing is, you mentioned you were waiting for your sister, right?" When Phen nodded, Noah continued, "Most people avoid going into that courtyard and the only ways in are either climbing the fence from outside or the two doors on either side. We know she didn't leave because you were watching the front. This means that whoever killed her either climbed the fence and avoided the spikes at the top, came through the back door…"

"Or was already in the school," Aiden finished, causing Phen to stiffen. "To be honest, if it's the last one, it's a bit worrying, so I would rather focus on the first two options."

Noah had to agree.

"I don't think it's just the school." Phen sighed. "From what I've heard, there is no rhyme or reason to the disappearances. Sometimes it's a child, sometimes it's a grown man and sometimes…" he trailed off as Noah and Aiden exchanged looks. "The only consistency at first was location, but that's not even a thing anymore."

"Well, that probably negates that idea," Aiden muttered and Noah sighed. That brought them no closer to figuring out where to look or where to even start to figure things out.

He felt his phone vibrate and jerked, almost flinging his phone out of his pocket in his haste. He heard his brother yelp and glanced over as he wrenched his phone out of his pocket, utterly confused.

Noah blinked before glancing at his phone, then sighing. It was just another notification letting him know the battery was dying. He would have to charge it when he got home. He paused, noticing he had gotten another text at some point. It looked like it arrived during the day. How had he not noticed?

His heart skipped a beat. It was from Dad.

"Noah?"

Aiden's voice caught his attention. He turned in time to see Aiden staring down at his phone, clearly nervous. It seemed something caught his attention as well. Aiden's gaze flicked to Noah, who stiffened and quickly joined him, peering over his shoulder. Aiden's showed a similar text from Dad. It was sent early in the morning, when they were suitably distracted. Aiden flicked his fingers, bringing up the text for both of them to read.

That is worrying. I know you are not one to believe in the supernatural, but, listen to your brother and be careful. I don't like how things are going.

Aiden's gaze flicked to Noah as he tilted his head down to his own phone.

Noah's text that he received was clearly later then Aiden's, who hadn't received anymore. He pressed his, pulling the text up as he felt Aiden lean on his shoulder to read. They read it over carefully. The phone must have acted up, because all of the texts were said to have been received at the same time… did that mean the connection failed? Did something happen after Dad sent the message to Aiden? Why did Dad send the rest to him and not both of them?

This case is a bit more than I bargained for. I'm sorry I didn't text back sooner. I wanted to, but my phone has been acting up. I'm worried about what you said and I know it's scary. I'll come back as soon as I can. Stay safe, don't go out at night and stay in my room.

There was a pause as Noah flipped down to the next text with the same time.

I might have gotten myself in trouble. If I am not back by tonight, call the police and inform them. Find a way to stay with someone you trust. I know we've just arrived, but it's too dangerous for you two to be alone. Be careful at school and if you find someplace, put salt around the room like I taught you.

Another flip and pause.

Lbusgiojsjarhfaiufv… stay here children.
Let. Me. Find. YOU. Let. Me. Have. You. Give. Me. Power. Make. Me. Whole.

Then, there was nothing.

CHAPTER 17

Noah slowly pulled back the phone, shaken. Aiden just stared at it, gaze flicking to his own phone.

"Oh, that is not good." Phen's voice caused both of them to jump and Noah to let out a shriek, whipping around.

Phen pulled back, hands up defensively as an apologetic expression crossed his face. "I'm sorry. I didn't mean it, but your expressions said it was bad and I couldn't help but take a look." He slowly dropped his hands. "I only really saw the last text anyway and bits of the previous. I'm guessing that wasn't your dad?"

"No." Aiden spoke, voice hoarse. "Either he dropped his phone, which he never does, or…"

"Something happened to him." Noah found his voice cracking. He whipped around to face Phen. "Where is the police station?"

Phen blinked, startled, before gesturing. "This way." They hurried along, heading toward the police station. Silence pervaded the group as Noah thought.

All he could do was hope that Dad lost his phone and was still alright. He gripped his cross tightly. He wanted to run home and hide in Dad's room. But even Dad admitted it wasn't a good idea.

But could they trust the message before the last? They had to. Noah remembered Dad talking about the salt trick and Mia mentioning something. He could only hope that it worked. But where could they stay?

No one said anything as they hurried to the police department. It was a small building, probably only housing a handful of police officers. When they stepped in, the secretary at the front desk looked up. She seemed exhausted, her police uniform, once probably pristine, was slightly disheveled. No surprise with everything going on.

"Oh." She paused, glancing toward Phen before turning to Noah and Aiden. "I know Phen, who are you two and how can I help you?"

"Noah and Aiden Raven. Our father is missing." Noah spoke quickly, catching the woman's attention. "We received some texts that—"

She let out a sigh and straightened. "Let me see them." The woman gestured, cutting him off. Noah blinked, startled and glanced toward Aiden before handing the phone over with the texts open. The woman read through them, furrowing her brow. She reached under her desk, pulling out some papers before jotting some notes down. "What was your father's name again?" Her gaze flitted to them. "And can I have yours as well once more?"

"Roger." Aiden spoke up this time, voice even. "Roger Raven is our father."

The woman froze at that, her hand stilling with a slight screech on the notepad. "Oh… it's you two. Oh dear…"

Noah tilted his head, curious, as Aiden narrowed his eyes.

She sighed so heavily, it was almost concerning, her head drooping. "Not again…" She stood. "Give me a minute." With that, she turned and hurried toward the back. Aiden and Noah exchanged glances as Phen took a step forward.

"Do you really think the police can help?" He kept his voice low, getting their attention. "These disappearances have been happening for weeks, if not months. They are overworked as it is."

Aiden pursed his lips as Noah turned away. He knew that, but he hoped, maybe this time…

They waited in silence as the quiet sound of chatter echoed from nearby before the woman returned, handing the phone back over to Noah. "I'm sorry." She actually did seem apologetic. "We are stretched thin as it is. Your father is probably just investigating and lost his phone. However, if we do hear anything, can we have a number to call you two?"

Noah expected that answer, but he couldn't hide the disappointment as he responded with his number, which she quickly jotted down. Once done, she glanced between them. "Do you two have a safe place to stay?"

"They are with me." Phen spoke up, startling them.

Aiden's neck almost snapped with how quickly he turned to him. Phen ignored them, taking a step forward, hand to his chest. "Mom already said it's alright."

"Are you sure, Phen? You just…" The woman pursed her lips, almost upset.

"Yeah, that's why. Maybe their father is fine, but I would like to stay near them, from experience."

"Phen…" Noah wasn't sure how to respond to that. He hadn't expected the boy to suddenly step forward to help them. He shook his head and smiled to the woman. "He's right. We just wanted to see if there was anything you could do."

She actually flinched, the exhaustion more obvious than before. "We'll see what we can do."

Noah knew that was all he was going to get and, so, lightly grabbing his brother's wrist, who was still somewhat surprised at Phen's words, Noah tugged, catching his attention.

Aiden stumbled, before shaking his head and following after. "We should have expected that." Aiden peered over his shoulder as they kept moving. "Dad said the previous detective disappeared too and they haven't found him."

"I know, but I wanted to try." Noah sighed, slumping. "Plus, Dad told us to try anyway so it was worth a shot."

"Hey." Phen leaned forward, getting their attention. "Let's head to my place. I wasn't lying when I said you two can stay over. I doubt Mom would mind, especially considering how she reacted yesterday, and…" He trailed off before shaking his head. "It's getting late, with all the window-shopping and everything." He peered ahead. "It's probably getting close to dinner time."

Noah and Aiden exchanged looks before they nodded, following Phen. Soon enough, they arrived back to his place, Phen pretty much throwing the door open. "Mom! I'm home!" When there was no response, he blinked and shook his head. "Right, she probably went out to grab groceries and get the car fixed. We were pretty low on food." He glanced toward Noah and Aiden. "Well, come in."

"You sure?" Aiden finally spoke up. "This is a bit…"

"Odd?" Phen's smile slipped. "I know how it feels to be worried about someone who's missing, you two know that…" He trailed off. "I guess… part of me is hoping that you two don't have to deal with the same thing, especially since our situations are so similar." He paused at that before shaking his head. "Sorry, part isn't the right word. I don't want ANYONE to have to deal with that."

Noah relaxed, a faint smile on his lips. "Thanks, Phen." He peered inside, thoughts flying. "We'll be back, but we should get our things."

Phen raised an eyebrow, worry flashing on his face. "Isn't your house…"

"It's not safe, but all of our things are there." Aiden spoke up, catching Noah's attention. "We will… we will return once we've collected what we need."

Phen peered at him quietly before nodding. "I'll stay up just in case you need anything. Stay safe."

"Of course." Noah perked up. "We'll be back soon."

Phen peered between them before nodding. "Alright." He dug into his pocket, pulling out his phone. "At least, can I have your numbers? Just in case you need to call if something happens?"

"I'll give you mine." Noah spoke up quickly as Aiden stiffened. Noah reached in and quickly exchanged numbers before waving. Phen nodded, heading inside as they turned toward home.

"Thanks," Aiden said after a minute.

"It's fine." Noah glanced toward Aiden. "You really should accept a few numbers, though. Not everyone is going to—"

"I know." Aiden's gaze flicked to him. "I just…" He shook his head and the two fell into silence, neither really knowing what to say to the other.

Eventually, Noah spoke up as they rounded the bend that led into the woods around their latest home. "Aiden." Noah turned, nervous. "What are we going to do now? Sure, Phen's okay with us staying with him but where from there?"

Aiden's fingers curled into his pockets. "I wish I knew, but we're not Dad. We don't have enough information and now that Dad's in trouble?" Aiden tilted his head down. "There's no easy answer. What does that person want with us? Is it just us? Or were we simply unlucky last night?"

Noah turned away, unsure how to reply. Aiden's questions were solid and, while Noah wished he could argue, he found his tongue stuck to the roof of his mouth. The trees were dark and silent as the sun began to set, giving the air an almost unnerving feel.

"I think it would be best if we just pack our things as fast as possible and go back to Phen's," Aiden said as they approached the doorway. He tugged the keys from his pocket, the door opening with a clink. "I don't think either of us feel comfortable staying here."

Noah couldn't argue as he briefly noted the scratch marks on the door. Unfortunately, there was no blood or anything that could be used as evidence. Hell, he would take nail clippings at this point but that was only if they were dealing with a human.

Noah had a feeling that they weren't, maybe not fully.

How the heck was one supposed to find a ghost?

They headed inside, a chill filling the hallways and rooms with an unpleasant air. Aiden glanced over to one side as Mia floated quietly through a wall, turning toward them. She was perturbed, quiet.

"You're back." Even her voice sounded distant.

"Hey, Mia, you okay? Well, besides the obvious?" Noah asked as they headed to their room. Aiden already pulled a bag out, ignoring them. "And, really, we're only here for a little while to get everything together and see if Dad left anything behind."

Mia's lips quirked up slightly at that, though the expression was somber. "I've been better." She swooped around, settling next to Noah with a soft sigh as Noah took a seat on his bed, digging for his own bag. "Stay still for a moment, will you?" Her words were almost hesitant, edging toward pleading.

Aiden furrowed his brow, peering over. Noah quickly sent him a look, causing him to shake his head and sigh. Noah sat in silence, Mia's cold presence right next to him as she stared at nothing in particular.

Noah hesitated, but reached a hand up, lightly touching Mia's shoulder. "Hey, uh, want to, I don't know, talk about it?"

Mia paused at that before letting out a weak chuckle. "Do you know how strange it is to hear that directed toward me?"

"Probably very," Aiden mumbled, getting a hum from Mia.

"Not wrong." She paused. "I guess, I was just a little shaken and taken by surprise," she admitted, fingers lightly flitting over her dress. "I knew that creature was powerful, corrupting the second soul, but I hadn't realized how powerful a possession would be. I can… deal with most ghosts, but a dual soul like that? That thing is something else entirely. There is a reason I stayed with you last night. I could feel it, the waves of cold, of hatred." She shook her head. "I wondered why it was after you if it already had such strength, what purpose did it have to attack people who had just arrived? I pushed the question aside, brushed it off, if you will, until later when I realized I was able to actually taste. It was faint, but very familiar in a way I recognized. Like a distant memory that has long been lost. It left me wondering, that's all."

Aiden stilled at that, expression hard to read as Noah smiled weakly. "I guess it would make sense." He paused. "If he really is a ghost like you said, would you be able to help us find him?"

Mia tilted her head. "Possibly. It all depends. While I am able to go into this home and the school, due to your presence and the more open atmosphere of a school building, most other locations are still blocked to me. If the ghost is in one of those it would be hard to trace."

"Can you look for the living?" Aiden spoke up after a moment, catching Mia's attention.

"That's an interesting question." Aiden just stared, causing Mia to roll her eyes. "Just like how one would normally look. I check places, see if they are there, and move on to the next. It's the same. It's not like I, personally, can sense the living. Sure, some ghosts can, and they use that to drain the life from people, but I'm not like that."

Aiden shuddered at that and Noah felt a chill run down his spine. "Wait, ghosts can do that?" he squeaked.

"Of course. Thank limbo there are only a few who can. They are usually what we call Revenants, whose main goal is vengeance. If it's against a human who wrought them harm? Well, they have to have some way to affect and seek revenge against the still living human, correct?"

That was a terrifying thought and Aiden clearly agreed, because his shoulders were almost to his ears as he scrambled for the last few things.

Mia noticed and twisted her head some more so she was looking at Noah basically upside down. "You can always tell when a Revenant is near. The air itself will cry out, sulfur fills your nose and the chill is much worse than a normal ghost."

"Can you not do that?" Aiden choked out, one hand covering his eyes. "That is wrong in so many ways."

Mia righted herself with a faint giggle. "Ah, I knew that would make me feel better." She paused and turned toward Noah. "It's fascinating how you can just shrug it off."

Noah's expression turned sheepish. "I don't, not really, but I've seen some pretty gruesome things in manga and, at this point, I guess I half expect it from you. It's still really uncomfortable to witness though."

Mia hummed at that before nodding. "That makes sense." Her expression faded, becoming serious. "And what are your intentions as of now? This killer is very much not a Revenant, which is good, but you don't know where or what he is."

"You can't tell us?" Aiden huffed.

Mia outright pouted. "If I could, I would." Her expression returned back to neutral. "I have been like this for a long time, but there are still things I do not understand."

"If only we could just get a clue. Something."

"Yeah, all we have is what Dad texted." Noah gestured as he pulled out a few more items, stuffing them in his bag.

"Texted?" Mia blinked, hair swishing slightly. "What is this you speak of?"

Noah and Aiden exchanged looks as Aiden slung the bag over his back, his side of the room pretty much put away. He took a seat on the bed, waiting. Noah pulled his phone out and showed it to her. He knew they should be hurrying, but a part of him wanted to just stay there, to ignore what was going on. Mia squinted for a moment before leaning closer. "Text on a screen. I have seen it, but it is fascinating to see it so close and not just in quick moments of spying."

Aiden seemed amused at that.

"Is this from your father?"

Noah nodded, flipping to the last text. "This is the last thing we got. I have to ask, a ghost can't type on a phone, right?"

Mia pulled back. "No. Sure, they can affect technology, causing it to go haywire, but a text like that?" She turned to Noah, staring him dead in the eye. "Only the living can do that."

Noah stiffened. Aiden pushed himself to his feet once more, seeming ready to bolt.

"Someone… living? But didn't you say it was a ghost?" Noah tilted his head, fingers curling over the edge of the bed, tense.

Mia hummed, swaying side to side. "I did. I also said he consisted of two souls. Or so it felt."

Noah felt something clench in his throat as silence persisted.

"I'm not dealing with this." Aiden shook his head, hurrying toward the kitchen. "I'll start making something to eat and then we can go. Even if we are staying with Phen and his family, I would rather not put too much work on them." His gaze flicked to Noah. "Hurry up and pack up. It shouldn't take me long to whip up something quick and then we can go."

Noah nodded, watching him disappear out the door. He noticed that Mia was doing much the same, a strange expression of worry flashing over her face before disappearing. He cleared his throat and spoke up. "Could it be possible that he's possessed? Like Father talked about? A human that's been bonded with a ghost?"

Mia turned to him. "It is very much possible. I hadn't thought of such a thing since it is a rare occurrence. I simply believed it was a human that embodied the properties of the ghost, though I suppose possession and bonding does make more sense."

Noah just stared at Mia. "So, that's what we're dealing with, a human possessed by the supernatural." Noah felt a hint of curiosity run through him. That was actually really interesting, if it wasn't so terrifying. "That's why they were able to get into the house last night."

Noah rubbed his arms, suddenly feeling much more vulnerable. Wind blew against the plywood that was up against the shattered window. Right, that wasn't fixed, was it? At least the bookshelf was still in the way to keep it steady. Right, focus, Aiden told him to get everything together and he knew he should. He peered around their little room. He was really getting sick of having to quick pack all the time. Couldn't they just settle down for ONCE in their life?

"So, great. How does possession even work?"

"You will have to figure that out yourself," Mia admitted. "The process is different for ghosts and humans. I mean, I can tell you, but I doubt it would make sense, considering the situation." She shook her head. "My suggestion? See if there's some place you can do research. That brother of yours appears more like the studious type."

She wasn't wrong.

He paused as a faint sound of knocking caught his attention. Who would be knocking at their door at this hour?

CHAPTER 18

Aiden glanced up as he turned up the burner to finish the quick chicken dish he made to bring with them. A faint knocking met his ears and he frowned. He could hear the drip of water and glanced out the window. Rain clouds covered the sky, turning it a dark gray as some of it clung to the windows already. He dug into his pocket, checking to see if anyone texted, but didn't see anything. He stared quietly, tense. They only planned to stay there long enough to grab some food and their stuff and go. Noah wasn't even done packing. Who could be at the door?

He hesitantly turned, taking a single cautious step forward before freezing.

Something… he wasn't sure why, but his body screamed not to open the door, not to get any closer. A chill raced through him. He found himself taking a step back, feeling queasy, like his stomach was going to flip.

"Aiden, who is it?" Noah's voice reached his ears.

At that, the knocking turned into a sharp rattling SLAM.

Aiden stumbled back, a sense of terror running through him as his heart leapt into his throat. He spun, snagged up the bag he packed and darted toward the room Noah was in. He heard a quiet humming that was steadily growing louder… a familiar humming.

He raced into the room, startling Noah as the Ghost stared down the hallway. "We need to go," he said.

The Ghost froze for only a split second before leaping into the air. "Run," she hissed as Aiden grabbed Noah's wrist and tugged him to his feet.

Noah stumbled, confusion clear on his face, followed by worry as the sound of a slam echoed once more from the front door. The pounding of rain suddenly escalated, rattling over the roof as wind howled outside.

"Father's room." Noah gulped, pulling ahead, bag left behind as Aiden nodded, following him. "We should be able to get out through the window. Phen said he was waiting for us."

"Lovely." Aiden peered over his shoulder. "So we lead whoever is outside straight to him? We'll have to get him off our tail."

"I'm glad you at least realized you can't stay here," the Ghost cut in as what sounded like a chipping sound reached Aiden's ears. "He has a weapon. A door isn't going to stop him, not this time."

CRACK!

Aiden peered over his shoulder as they darted into Father's room. The faint gleam of silver from an axe head caught his attention as it slowly pulled out of the now cracked front door.

Noah, clearly having seen the same thing he did, slammed the door to Dad's room, locked it and raced toward the window. Aiden joined him as Noah attempted to unlock the window, pulling it up. He tugged, trying to wrench, but it didn't seem to budge, the wood swollen into the frame from all the recent rainfall. Aiden joined, trying to help as the two of them pushed, trying to slide the window up. It wrenched, shifting only a bit before catching again.

This was taking too long. Aiden could hear another shattering crash behind him and jerked, glancing back. Noah pulled back, wincing as a splinter dug into his palm from having caught a part of the window trying to open it.

Aiden pulled off his bag from his shoulder and, with a heave, swung it at the window just as lightning crashed and thunder rumbled outside.

He could see the glass splinter, but not shatter, and clicked his tongue. This was loud, but it would be faster than trying to open the stuck window.

"What are you doing?" Noah hissed.

"Trying to get us out. We can't get the plywood off the window in our room and the window itself isn't moving with how swollen the wood is, so this is our only option."

"But… damnit, I wish we could have just pulled it open."

"Believe me, I know," Aiden snapped as he pulled the bag over his shoulder and swung once more. "Our options are out there or staying in here, take your pick." This time, glass shattered with a loud echoing CRASH just as he heard splintering from the front door and the sound of a heavy footstep echo through the house.

They both jerked as the humming grew louder and wood splintered. Terror and cold shredded up Aiden's spine.

"Mia, can you possibly distract him?" Noah squeaked.

Mia glanced toward them and nodded. "I can escape him, no problem." Her brow furrowed. "Just run as fast as you can. One thing I do know about possession is that ghosts can give extra strength to a possessed human, their brains no longer limiting their abilities."

"Great, now we know." Aiden swung the backpack over his shoulder as he quickly brushed some of the shattered pieces away, some of the shards digging into his fingers and palm. He pulled himself onto the window sill, wincing as the remaining glass pierced his hand, a little blood dripping down the side, almost immediately washed away by the rain. He pulled himself through, dropping to the other side and turning, gesturing toward Noah, who was peering back and forth before tugging himself forward.

The rain pulled heavily at his clothes as Noah grimaced, struggling to pull himself through. He paused and peered back. "Mia, be careful."

"Just go, I'll be fine."

Aiden barely took notice as she darted out of the room. He helped pull Noah through, who was watching worriedly. Noah stumbled, almost slipping over the slick mud and soil as thunder clapped loudly in the sky, lightning flaring above, silhouetting the both of them.

And of course, this old house didn't have a stupid back door which would have been incredibly helpful. Aiden shook his head as his stomach twisted, the air cold and the humming heard loudly even through the pelting rain.

Noah steadied himself and the two bolted toward the surrounding forest, the window on the opposite side of where the road came in from town. They would have to circle around and neither felt inclined to do that near the house.

Aiden felt sick, the water clinging to his clothes and hair, almost blinding his vision as he brought one hand up. Everything was soaked through. Noah shivered, barely stopping himself from slipping against him as they jumped past the low fence and ducked into the trees, arcing around toward town.

The woods were, unfortunately, sparse, but the darkness of the growing night and the powerful storm hopefully lent them enough cover. Neither dared pull out a flashlight in case they were spotted, but that led to them tripping over logs and roots as they went.

The foliage caused them to slip more than once, unaccustomed to traversing through woods like this in the pouring rain. Thankfully, keeping somewhat close to the field, they managed to find the road, only slightly scrapped and bruised.

Aiden peered toward the house, noticing, barely, the splintered open door, swinging listlessly from its post as a loud angered cry echoed from within. He thought he caught someone standing to one side, but the figure vanished into the trees opposite barely a moment later, making him second-guess himself. Aiden shook his head, pulling Noah along as they hugged the trees instead of the path itself, keeping watch for anyone on the road. The few lights from nearby houses made it a little easier to traverse, but not by much.

Aiden could see frustration on Noah's face and wondered what he was thinking. Did he think they could capture the killer?

"Why didn't we try to do something?" Noah whispered, fists clenched as they turned their fast pace into a walk, catching their breaths. "He was RIGHT there."

"You know why." Aiden spoke evenly, knowing his brother would realize.

He pursed his lips before slumping. "I know." He sounded almost resigned. "We had no way to defend ourselves, no idea what was going on or how it worked." How it worked? What was he talking about? "And, of course, I have no idea how to stop a ghost-possessed human from doing anything."

Ghost-possessed? "Are you saying that person back there was possessed?" Aiden hissed. "That's asinine."

"What other way is there to describe that? I know the house is old, but he cut that door down in pretty much a few swings." Noah glanced toward him, expression tense. "Even Mia admitted he was probably possessed."

Aiden clicked his tongue, looking away. Of course she did. Aiden felt a hand reach for his and paused as Noah grasped his, holding tightly, shuddering. Aiden let out a breath and carefully pulled his backpack around, digging in. Most of what he packed was soaked, unprepared as he was for such a sudden storm, but he did manage to find the umbrella he put in there. He tugged it out, knowing it was pretty much pointless at this time, but wanting to at least avoid getting any worse.

They slowly moved through the streets, jumping at any sound that caught their attention. Noah gripped the flashlight in his pocket tightly. Thankfully, they didn't need it, Aiden soon enough finding the path to get to Phen's. They could only hope that they lost the man, but they weren't sure.

Aiden felt Noah tense, almost letting out a screech as something vibrated. Aiden winced, noticing his own phone vibrate as well, a strange, uncomfortable feeling settling in his stomach. Noah scrambled to pull out his phone with one hand as Aiden did the same. He flicked it on as he noticed Noah tense beside him. A single text lay over the phone.

Come out to play, little Raven children. I only need one of you, after all. Power. Give me your power. Make me whole. Whole. Whole...

Aiden pursed his lips as Noah shivered once more, not from cold, as the word, whole, repeated over and over again.

He just stared silently, shoving his phone back into his pocket, before tugging Noah forward. A silent promise of, we'll figure it out later, hung in the air between them.

CHAPTER 19

Aiden led Noah through the streets, noting how pale and exhausted he appeared now that he had time to pay attention, ignoring the faint twinge of pain in his fingers from digging into shattered glass. The street lights and pounding rain didn't do much to help. He brushed some wet hair from his eyes, attention peeled. Alright... a left up here. There it is.

It was stupid, reckless, but it was the only choice they had. They couldn't go to the police, the police would only try to get them to 'safety'. On top of that, what would they do?

He didn't have much hope, to be honest, with the way they looked now, he doubted they would be let in. Phen might somewhat trust them, but his mother had no reason to, even if Phen had talked to her about it. They literally met today and that was it and now they were barging on her doorstep, soaked and frightened. What could he even say? That they were being chased by the killer?

That would make her slam the door on their faces faster than he could even finish the sentence.

"Aiden?" Noah's voice was hesitant as they slowed, approaching the house. "Are you nervous?"

Of course he would notice. Aiden didn't say anything right away, thoughts churning, before he sighed. "We've come because we think there's something wrong with the house and hoped to spend the next few nights here while we wait for it to get fixed."

"Are you sure?"

"It's the only thing I can think of. Noah, if they find out the truth, we'll just be thrown out."

"You know, Phen said we could stay. I think we can trust him, at least a little bit. We don't always have to lie, you know."

Aiden glanced away, unsure how to respond. "Just… let me talk for now."

Noah sighed, shaking his head.

To their surprise, as they approached the door, it opened with a bang. "What are you two doing out here?" Phen's mother stood in the doorway. "I saw you through the window. You're soaked."

Noah shifted as Aiden nodded. "Sorry, we couldn't stay at home, we—"

"Phen told me, your father is busy with trying to find that killer, right? Get in here and warm up." She scurried forward, gesturing.

Aiden blinked, surprised, as Noah grinned at him, his expression pretty much screaming, 'I told you so.' Aiden wasn't sure what to think about that.

"Oh, my apologies, I never introduced myself. My name is Ellen." She lightly pushed them along, closing the door behind them. "I never really got to thank you for what you did for my family. For what you two and your father did in finding Lynn."

Aiden glanced back as Ellen pulled away, sadness in her gaze. "You know, Lynn's name was a play off of my name, that's how it is with first children sometimes."

Aiden was honestly surprised, not sure what to say as Noah's expression grew taut. Ellen shook her head. "Sorry, just… thoughts." She turned toward the stairwell as Aiden finished closing the umbrella, feeling a little uncomfortable with how much they dripped water over the floor. "Phen! Grab some of your clothes! Your friends are here."

"Who?" Phen called before Aiden spotted him peeking around the corner, up the stairs. His eyes widened in surprise. "Wait, Aiden? Noah? You literally just left."

"Some things cropped up and we had to leave home," Noah called up.

Phen blinked and nodded before heading back into his room. "I might have some old clothes you could borrow, hold on."

"You two, it's okay to come in." Ellen spoke up, catching their attention. Aiden hesitated while Noah nodded, stepping in toward the kitchen where they could smell something cooking. She peeked out the window and shook her head. "This weather lately has been terrible. I'm sorry you boys had to get caught up in it. Take a seat."

After taking seats, shifting uncomfortably in their wet clothes, Ellen handed them some cups of something hot. "Tea." She smiled. "I don't know if you drink it, but at least it'll warm up your hands." She got back to what she was doing, the rich smell from the kitchen indicated it was probably cooking. Aiden briefly wondered what happened at home, he turned the pan on to heat—He winced, he hoped he hadn't just accidentally set the house on fire.

"Ma'am, how did you spot us if you were cooking in here?" Aiden asked after a moment of centering himself, words soft as he took a sip of tea before staring down at it, startled.

"I was calling to make sure Phen was finishing up homework and happened to notice." She glanced over her shoulder. "So, Phen never mentioned anything about your mother. Where is she? And where is your father with the investigation?"

"Not sure." Noah spoke up before Aiden could open his mouth. Aiden pursed his lips, uncertain as Noah continued, "As for Mom… Mom disappeared a long time ago."

Aiden could hear the slight tremor in Noah's voice and wondered if it was actually a good idea to say anything.

"Oh, I'm so sorry." Ellen's voice was soft and somber. "As you know, I know what that is like, and to happen to children as young as yourselves…"

Silence pervaded the room. Aiden just felt uncomfortable. They shouldn't be here.

Footsteps echoed on the hardwood floor. "I got a change of clothes, I hope they fit." Phen's voice pulled Aiden from his thoughts and he glanced over. "Whoa… did I step in at the wrong time?" He glanced around. Ellen shook her head, soft smile on her face.

"No, thank you, Phen. Help me finish up dinner while they get changed." She turned to Noah. "The bathroom is the third door on the left. Just let your wet clothes hang over the shower curtain for now, I'll have Phen put them in the dryer later." Noah nodded and stood. Aiden wanted to change as well, but he figured he would just wait.

"You could use my room if you want. There's only one bathroom, but I don't mind." Phen spoke up, catching Aiden's attention.

He hesitated. "I—"

"It's no bother, if that was what you were going to say. The sooner you get changed, the sooner we can have dinner."

"Phen." Ellen gave her son a look.

"What? It's true."

Aiden glanced between them and slowly nodded. "If you don't mind." Phen smiled and gestured, leading him upstairs. There were only three rooms on the second floor and it was easy to see which one probably belonged to Phen.

Clothes lay on the ground, scattered everywhere. A pile of books were pushed up against the bed.

Phen suddenly looked sheepish, quickly picking up the clothes and muttering under his breath. "Sorry, should have thought about cleaning up. Didn't think I would be inviting you this quickly." He paused, stuffing some of the clothes into an almost overflowing dirty clothes basket, face red. "I'll, uh, be just outside." He scurried out of the room.

Weird.

Aiden quickly got changed, staying to the middle of the room so as not to disturb anything. The clothes were a little tight in some areas and loose in others, but he couldn't really complain. He bundled up his soaked clothes and stepped outside.

Phen, who must have been leaning against the doorframe while waiting, jumped. "Oh, done already?"

Aiden just watched him and Phen fidgeted gaze flicking toward him before turning away. "Right, sorry, stupid question. Let's go downstairs." He gestured and headed down. Aiden glanced toward the other two rooms. They were probably Lynn's and the parents 'room. He shook his head and moved downstairs. Phen took his clothes before going toward the bathroom to grab Noah's.

Aiden wasn't fond of the idea of just handing his clothes over, but he couldn't really argue.

"Phen, once dinner is done, can you bring your father's up to him?"

Phen nodded as he returned, taking a seat. Aiden sat next to Noah, unsure what to do with himself or where to go.

He briefly wondered if the Ghost would actually meet them and then wondered if she could get in. He heard a faint tap on the window and glanced over. Noah stiffened beside him and Phen glanced up, but it seemed Ellen didn't notice.

Good, because outside was the wet dripping form of their resident female Ghost.

"Why doesn't she come in?" Phen whispered as Ellen finished up dinner.

"She can't." Noah kept his voice low as Aiden watched her, floating quietly outside. "You have to let her in."

"Why don't you do it?" he hissed.

"Because we don't live here. I don't think it works if we do it, and, personally, I don't—" Aiden snapped his mouth shut as Ellen came back, taking a seat as she placed the food in the middle. It was a casserole of some sort that Aiden couldn't identify. He wasn't sure why he said something. After all, the Ghost freaked him out, but he did want to know what she saw and Noah was better at talking to her, so he couldn't argue with what he said.

"I hope you boys aren't allergic to anything, I didn't even think to ask."

"It's fine." Noah smiled, reaching forward to nab some bread. Aiden waited until the others grabbed what they wanted before getting some for himself. A home-cooked meal that he didn't have to make? He could definitely appreciate it.

"So, uh, how—" Phen cut himself off as Ellen glanced toward him. "Are we going to do sleeping arrangements tonight?" He chuckled nervously, causing Ellen to raise an eyebrow while Aiden just barely resisted slamming his hand to his face. Why did he think it was a good idea to talk about the literal spirit outside with his mom around?

"I'll leave it up to you three. If you need blankets or anything, let me know."

"Thanks, Mom." Phen relaxed, chowing down.

Aiden kept glancing toward the window, noting that now the Ghost was floating sideways, as if sleeping, arms crossed as her chin rested on top, staring inside. Her clothes and hair were once again damp, creating a very eerie appearance, but not one he outright feared. "You can come in," he quietly whispered under his breath. The Ghost cocked her head and reached out, poking the window. Her finger did not slide through. Well, that confirmed that.

She huffed and pulled back.

Phen must have noticed and he started muttering something. Mia perked up before whipping away.

Seconds later, a chill filled the house, along with faint dripping. Ellen glanced up. "I could have sworn we just had the pipes fixed."

"I'll check." Phen stood and hurried into the front room. Noah glanced toward him, curious. Aiden sighed; hopefully, the ghost wouldn't try to prank their current host.

He heard movement and glanced over just as Phen stepped back in, a mix of unnerved and trying desperately to hide it. "I think all the rain just made it sound like it was inside. I didn't see anything."

Ellen furrowed her brow. "Hopefully, you're right." Phen took a seat and Aiden was left wondering what it was the Ghost did. She did something, that was obvious, but it was always hard to tell with her. At least she wasn't chasing them like she did last time.

Soon enough, they finished dinner and, while Ellen was cleaning up, Phen headed upstairs with a plate of food. Aiden watched him go as Noah stood. "Let me help you." He grabbed up some plates and brought them over to a startled Ellen.

"Oh, no, you're our guests, you don't—"

"We intruded on your house, ma'am, let me help."

She seemed to debate for a moment before nodding.

Aiden watched for a moment before standing and leaving. He felt a chill and glanced left in time to notice the Ghost disappear into what could only be the living room. He hesitated for the longest time, almost wishing he switched places with Noah. Even now, even though he saw the Ghost guide them and help them, he still felt unnerved around her. Sure, she hadn't hurt them any time she was near them, which was a lot more than he would like, but he also didn't trust her a bit.

Still, he could tell she wanted to talk with someone from her quick glance toward him before floating in. He shifted from foot to foot before letting out the heaviest breath he felt in a while. Well, this was going to go great.

He slowly stepped inside, noting how cozy the room felt. There was an unlit fireplace to one side that was clean and rarely if ever used, but the light cascading from the different lamps gave the room a warm glow. Floating a little to one side was the Ghost.

"Took you long enough."

Aiden crossed his arms over his chest to stop himself from jumping as he turned toward the floating figure. "How would I know how the whole thing works? Plus, we weren't exactly going to sit outside, waiting for you, either."

"I didn't ask you to, but you could have at least warned Phen so I could get in," she hissed, getting right in his face.

The sudden movement made him backpedal. He grabbed whatever was on the side table, pointing it at her. "What the—Why do you do that?" he snapped unnerved. She slowly pulled back, her expression shifting slightly. "How do you expect me to react if you are suddenly going to get in my face?"

The Ghosts reaction, to Aiden's surprise, morphed into a sheepish pout. The expression quickly disappeared to be replaced with annoyance. "You really should get used to it. Your instincts are good, but I'm not going to hurt you. I've already promised that."

Aiden didn't believe her, but he did find himself slowly placing a coaster back onto the table. It wouldn't have really done much of anything anyway. "Alright, fine. Still, I get why you're frustrated, but so are we. Give us a break. We're trying to figure this out as we go."

"I'm aware."

Aiden pursed his lips, shifting his stance so it was still guarded, but a little straighter. "Well? You clearly wanted to talk. Did you see who it was?"

The Ghost actually hesitated at that before slowly, as if preparing, shaking her head.

A wave of disappointment and absolute annoyance flared through him and he took a step forward. "Seriously?" he asked. "You went to distract him! You would have clearly been able to see him after we escaped through that window, how—"

"Oh, don't you get started." She growled, dress flaring in her anger as the long black hair lifted slightly before settling back down. "Have you ever seen a ghost-possessed human? They are almost impossible to identify unless you know the person and, while I can certainly see in the dark, it means NOTHING if the person is decked in black with a mask and everything. There was nothing to identify."

"Nothing? Not even a build? or—?"

"No." The Ghost tilted her head almost ninety degrees causing him to quickly turn away or be on the verge of throwing up. Her voice continued in his ear. "The ghost who has consumed him shrouded his form with the ghost's own, merging the two. It's something only seen after a long term possession like this one and means the soul of the possessed is almost completely consumed."

Aiden wasn't sure how he felt about that, other than to shudder, one arm reaching up to rub the other at the idea of it. So, the killer or whatever was possessed… it would make sense, as much as any of this did.

He heard faint movement and glanced over as her neck snapped back into place, her gaze piercing his own, though her expression was much softer, to his surprise. "I will admit, I am glad you two managed to escape." That expression vanished to a mischievous one. "Though, you should be thanking me for helping to get him off your tail. I led him on a merry little chase before disappearing into the woods." She smiled, unpleasant. "And around here? The woods are my playground."

Aiden shuddered, but he couldn't deny the moment of relief that washed over him. "So he doesn't know where we are?"

"For now." The smile faded as footsteps sounded behind. Aiden turned as Phen stepped into the room.

Phen took notice of the Ghost and shook his head. "That still gets me."

"What, the Ghost or the one talking to the Ghost?"

"Yes."

Aiden groaned, shaking his head as the Ghost swooped around, chuckling. He turned to face the both of them, noting the odd expression on Phen's face.

"I'm guessing something happened considering your hand is cut up, even if you did try to hide it from Mom."

Aiden tensed and Phen smiled. "I may have heard the last bits of the conversation, but don't worry. I'm not saying anything." He narrowed his eyes as his gaze flicked to Mia. "You said that thing didn't follow anyone, right?" At the shake of the Ghost's head, Phen turned back to Aiden, who shifted at the heavy look, it wasn't a glare or anything, it was almost… thoughtful. "Then, fine, as long as my family isn't in danger."

"That's good." The Ghost took a seat in the air, leaning her elbow against her knee. "I need these two to stay alive, so any help is appreciated. Do not worry, I think we would be able to tell if he gets close."

Aiden pursed his lips, unsure whether to glare at the Ghost or not. Phen stepped inside, giving Aiden a brief once over before taking a seat. "You do know you can sit, right?"

Aiden peered toward him before sighing and taking a seat on the couch. The Ghost floated between them.

"So who is this HE that our ghost ally here helped get off your tail?" Phen watched casually, but Aiden didn't miss the curiosity as well as the hint of… anger? Worry?

He was probably reading that wrong.

They heard footsteps and glanced over as Noah came in, wiping his hands on his shirt. "Your mom told me to tell you that she was going to be upstairs for a while to make sure your father eats." He paused. "Is everything okay?"

Phen nodded. "Dad was weak to begin with. Losing Lynn, well…" he trailed off before shaking his head. "But never mind that, Aiden, here, was just telling me that you have a guy basically stalking you?"

"I didn't actually say that." Aiden spoke up, annoyed.

"Close enough." Phen waved.

Noah walked over, plopping down next to Aiden. "Basically." His gaze flicked up to the Ghost. "Oh, and thanks, Mia."

Mia smiled gently and waved. "Oh, it's no bother, but your thanks is welcome."

Aiden just shook his head, not sure how to feel about that, before returning his attention to Phen. "Do you feel comfortable talking in here?"

Phen rolled his eyes. "Mom and Dad are upstairs. I don't have anyone else who might overhear."

Noah winced at that as Aiden nodded. "Alright." He hesitated before shifting his attention to Noah. "It's pretty straight-forward. We learned, from the Ghost—"

"It's Mia, why won't you call me that?"

"—that ghosts can't actually interact with objects, such as cellphones." He turned back to Phen as Noah pulled out his phone and unlocked it, showing the text in question. "Which meant that the person we're dealing with is human."

Phen glanced toward the phone and did a double-take. "Okay... that takes creep to a whole new level." Aiden just stared as Phen raised his hands. "Pun not intended." He paused. "Mostly." Aiden let his expression fall into a deadpan. Phen smiled sheepishly before continuing, "Seriously, though, saying he only needs one of you to make him whole? That's some of the creepiest shit I've heard, ever." He furrowed his brow. "But, didn't we already suspect he was human?"

"No." Noah pulled his phone back. "Mia mentioned he was a ghost and the first time he attacked, he couldn't get into the room Aiden and I stayed in, though he probably could have rammed the door."

"That whole, ghosts can't come in unless they are allowed, thing?"

"That's the one." Aiden nodded, thinking through what Phen said. He couldn't deny it. He was creeped out upon seeing the text himself, but it just made him more uneasy, the more he thought about it.

"So how did he get in this time?"

"He's more powerful." The Ghost spoke up as she took a seat in the chair, leaning back against it. "On top of that, he was able to wield a weapon to break down the door." Her gaze flitted to Aiden as she continued, "That's why I was trying to unlock the window. While I broke through the glass, I wasn't actually inside the house, not until I had unlocked it, which you stopped when you swatted at my hand and then, subsequently, put up the plywood so it no longer acted as a window. In a similar way, that man managed to reach around and unlock the door. That home is no longer safe."

"So much to think about." Noah groaned. "This is almost too much at once."

"I'm trying to keep you alive," the Ghost snapped.

"O...kay." Phen observed them quietly before continuing, "Good to know. So we can't let him know you are staying with me, then."

"Basically." Aiden turned to him. "Only problem is, we don't know WHO it is. The Ghost—"

"It's Mia!"

"—didn't get a good look. All we really know, from the information we've gathered, is that he's a human possessed by a ghost who is looking for power to become whole and bears a heavy hatred towards probably everything."

"That totally narrows it down." Phen groaned, head in his hands.

Aiden crossed his arms over his chest. "It's more than we knew before. We also know he's after us now and that Dad must have figured out, or gotten close to figuring it out. If we can find Dad, we can find who this killer is."

"And you are sure it's the same one who killed Lynn?"

"Duh." The Ghost waved her hand. "Unless there are two killers in this town and I highly doubt that. Plus, I know a ghost attack when I see one."

"I'm not going to ask." Noah spoke up, getting a grin from the Ghost.

"No worries, I'll explain that one later. It's not really essential right now."

Aiden, for once, actually wanted to thank her. He wasn't sure he could deal with learning anything else right now. It was hard to keep track of what he did know, even though he didn't want to. He hated this stuff.

"By the way, Phen, thanks for having us, especially since you know what's going on and stuff."

Phen waved it off. "It's fine." His gaze flitted to Aiden, a quirk to his lips as he continued, "I don't mind. Ghost, human, a mix of the two? Doesn't matter because I'm going to find a way to take him down. Helping you is an added bonus."

Noah snorted as the Ghost chuckled. Aiden lightly slapped his face with a groan.

"Seriously, though, I'm not dumb. I know by doing this, I'll probably put my mom and dad in harm's way." Phen pulled back. "But what else can I do? We have no clues, no way of finding him, nothing."

"Just that he likes to send creepy texts," Noah pointed out.

Aiden paused and frowned before turning to the ghost. "Speaking of, I would think someone would notice a possessed human by now. Right?"

The Ghost hummed, tilting side to side before shrugging. "Yes and no. Like I said, I don't know much about the whole possession thing, just what I've told you."

"You've never possessed anyone?" Noah blinked innocently. Aiden could see her flare for a second before faltering.

"Ugh…" She shook her head. "No. I see no reason to. It's a complicated, annoying process unless under very specific circumstances." She pulled out of the seat. "Anyway, you guys should get some rest. With how quickly that ghost is growing in strength from the fear it's collecting around here, it won't take long for it to figure out how to track you, then you're screwed."

Track?

Yeah, nope, Aiden was done. Ghosts can go screw themselves, for all he cared.

"You mean, he can track Aiden and Noah? He really is a stalker."

"Yep, pretty much." Mia flipped upside down. "A strong ghost can track, at short range, any target they choose, as long as they see that target once. Don't ask me how it works, it just does. Other components, such as an aspect of the person, makes it even easier."

"Great." Aiden slumped in the chair, feeling like the world just dumped a heap of trash on him and said good luck regarding getting out.

He felt something land on his shoulder and peered sidelong as Noah slumped on his side, head resting over his shoulder blade. He seemed exhausted.

Aiden didn't push him off.

CHAPTER 20

Phen watched them for a moment before standing. "I'll grab some pillows and blankets." He paused. "I'll bring them down here."

"Thanks," Noah muttered.

The Ghost, Aiden noted, disappeared.

Phen nodded before hurrying away. There was a moment of silence that felt almost heavy to Aiden.

"Aiden?" Noah's voice was strained. "If that guy has Dad's phone and is after us, does that mean—"

"Dad's fine," Aiden cut in, even if he didn't fully believe it himself. He wasn't going to let Noah worry about it if he could help it. "It's Dad."

Noah remained silent for a moment, curling into his side. "I know, but I can't help but worry. Dad must know what's going on. So why isn't he contacting us? A note, a letter, using a pay-phone, whatever."

"We don't really have pay-phones anymore," Aiden pointed out, feeling a light smack against his side.

"You know what I mean." Noah huffed. "Still, you get my point." Aiden glanced sidelong, feeling as Noah shifted, hair brushing against his neck. "I wish those texts came through earlier, sooner. Maybe I could have contacted him back and told him to come home. To just get out of there."

Aiden wasn't sure what to say, there wasn't much he could say. "You know Dad." He kept his voice low. "He wouldn't leave anyway."

Noah snorted at that, but didn't argue. An agreeable silence fell between them as they waited.

"By the way, you're heavy. I think you need to cut your hair too," Aiden teased. Noah glared up before grinning and purposefully pushing harder into Aiden's side, almost causing him to fall over the side of the couch.

Aiden pushed him off, or tried to as Noah clung to his arm, holding fast. "You're just a light-weight."

Aiden smacked Noah in the head, causing him to stick out his tongue before pulling back. "Funny." Aiden didn't even try to hold back the sarcasm, causing Noah to smile.

"Did I interrupt something?" Phen's voice caught their attention. He was carrying a large bundle of pillows and blankets, almost hidden under the pile.

"Nope." Noah jumped up, hurrying over. "How did you carry all of this anyway?"

"Practice." Phen grinned. "We have a large family that occasionally comes over for holidays. Let's just say, this isn't the first time we've had to use the living room like this."

Aiden stood, taking some as well, noting as Phen glanced his way before quickly turning back to Noah.

Geez, he got it. He swiped up what he needed and found a place on the couch, plopping down. It would be nice if people didn't brush him off all the time to focus on Noah. He huffed, burying into the sheets, feeling a gaze settle on him. It was probably Noah.

A second later, he heard a thump and shifted slightly, peeking out. Phen took the floor between the couches, a heavy spread of pillows and blankets taking the spot to make it more comfortable.

"Are you sure you want to sleep on the ground?" Noah asked, having been arranging the other couch as if it was a bed. "I mean, aren't you sleeping upstairs?"

"Nah, it's more fun down here." Phen shrugged, hands behind his head, laying on his back. "Plus, well, crashing at my place isn't just for girls, you know."

"So you have girls over?" Noah teased.

Phen actually looked a little red. "Well, yes, but that wasn't what I was implying."

Noah chuckled. "I know, it was funny, though."

"I'm guessing you haven't stayed over at someone's place before, have you?" Phen peered toward Aiden, but it was Noah who responded.

"No. We travel with Dad too often. It's… well, we don't often have time or someone who is willing to have us over. It was not something either of us really thought of."

"Seriously?" Phen glanced between them. "Man, you two missed out on a lot."

"You don't have to rub it in," Aiden muttered.

Phen winced, pushing himself up into a sitting position. "Well, I'm not exactly the most popular in school, but I've had my share of staying over at people's houses. I guess it's just odd to me that you two haven't really experienced that yourself often."

Aiden sighed." It's not my thing, I just want to sleep."

Noah didn't respond, face buried mostly into a pillow, what could be seen of his expression was solemn.

"That's fair." Phen's voice came back, softer. "It has been a long day and, considering you mentioned that guy attacked you last night as well, I guess you would be pretty tired."

Aiden couldn't argue.

He heard Noah shift and, after a moment, said, "Yeah. Just a bit. Sorry for this."

There was a moment of silence before Phen responded, "You don't need to apologize you know. I invited you two so this works out."

Noah seemed to relax as Aiden felt a faint smile cross his lips. "Alright, whatever you say."

He heard a huff as a response. "I'm slightly offended you don't believe me." The words came out in a faint whine, though Aiden didn't miss the hint of relief and amusement.

Aiden slowly peeked out from under the covers. The lights were still on, which meant one of them needed to get up to shut it off. He noticed Phen staring at him, a strange, almost gentle expression on his face. He must have noticed Aiden watching because he quickly grew red and flipped over to face Noah, whose only visible feature was a tuft of reddish brown hair. Aiden actually chuckled at that as footsteps sounded nearby. He turned as Ellen peeked in on the three of them. She locked eyes with him and smiled before mouthing, "Good night."

With that, she flicked the switch as the lights turned off, leaving just a gentle glow from outside and the faint sound of rain. He heard the footsteps fade and curled into the sheets, a sense of sadness falling over him. How long had it been since Mom did that for them? He knew she was gone, but, for that moment, he couldn't help but miss both her and Dad. He rolled over, face burying into the pillows of the couch as he pulled the quilt tighter over him. He could only hope Dad wasn't going to end up like Mom… whatever that might have meant. He wasn't sure he or Noah could handle losing another parent.

As his thoughts raced, he heard the calming sound of the drizzling rain and soft breaths indicating the other two fell asleep.

"You can go to sleep too." A voice spoke softly above him, catching his attention. The Ghost gently lay over the top of the couch, her expression warm as she peered over the three of them, not particularly at him. Her brown gold eye glowed faintly, exceedingly gentle, to his surprise. "You are safe here. Get some rest."

Strangely, for the first time since he met her, Aiden felt like he could actually trust those words. It was a strange feeling as his body relaxed and his mind slowly stopped spinning.

"As I promised. I WILL protect you, you and Noah, with everything I have." Her words were even softer as he felt sleep pull at him, finally. "I won't let you two experience my fate."

Part of Aiden wanted to ask what she meant, but another part settled down as she started to hum a soft lullaby that sounded familiar, like an old nursery rhyme. It was soft and pleasant. Whatever lingering tension faded as the melody and the constant pitter patter of rain finally lulled him to sleep.

CHAPTER 21

Noah awoke as light fell over his face, warm against his skin. He rubbed his cheek, briefly reminding himself of where he was and slowly sat up. The blanket trailed down around him as he slowly took in his surroundings. Aiden was curled up on the other couch, still fast asleep and Phen was on the ground, basically spread-eagle, snoring faintly.

Noah picked his way up and around Phen before heading toward the door. He heard quiet footsteps and peeked out the door as Ellen headed toward the kitchen. She noticed him and almost jumped. "You're up already?" She kept her voice down. Noah nodded. She chuckled. "An early riser, huh? Wish my son could take after you." She continued on, Noah following behind. He felt a faint chill and guessed that Mia was nearby. "Need anything?"

"No, thank you, ma'am. Did you turn the lights off last night?"

"So you noticed." She turned to him and smiled. "I was coming down to say you guys should get some sleep, but you were already doing it." She lightly patted a chair before heading toward the fridge. "So I just turned them off for you. Sleep well?"

"Yes, thank you."

"That's good. I will say, I'm glad." Her smile softened. "I knew it would be hard. Phen was close to Lynn, so I was worried, but he met you two and you helped support him. Thank you for that."

"We didn't really do anything?" Noah blinked, confused, and Ellen chuckled.

"You were there for him when he needed someone to be there." She turned to Noah. "I know you're new here, so it's no surprise, but ever since these disappearances, people have been really particular about who they spend time with. Most people stay in their homes and only leave if it's to get something they need. As a result, well, people aren't as trusting of others." Ellen's smile faded. "I don't necessarily blame them."

"Oh." Noah paused before bowing his head. "Thank you for trusting us then."

There was a moment of silence followed by a quiet breath. "You're a child." Ellen's voice was quiet. "Even if you hadn't helped Phen and were there to find Lynn, I would still want to help. But the thanks is appreciated."

Noah tilted his head back up in time to spot a warm smile on the woman's face. He relaxed slightly, nodding.

There was the faint sound of movement behind him. Noah turned slightly, arm laying over the back of the chair as Aiden walked in, rubbing the sleep from his face, shirt half off his shoulder. "Morning," he muttered.

Ellen chuckled as Noah grinned, walking over. "Morning, Aiden." He lightly tapped his brother in the forehead. "Why don't you use the bathroom to wake yourself up?"

"Getting to that." He let out another yawn and paused, glancing toward Ellen before looking down. "Um, thanks."

"It's no problem, though, yes, why don't you head over? I'll be making breakfast soon and then I have to head out."

"To work? Where do you work?" Noah asked as Aiden headed toward the bathroom.

"At the library," Ellen responded.

"Oh, right, Phen did mention that," Noah said sheepishly as Aiden huffed.

"Whose the tired one again?" He let out another yawn. "Um, may we come over today? To the library? It was closed yesterday."

Ellen chuckled. "Of course you can. I'll see if we can get you a library card, if not, go ahead and use Phen's, just make sure to return anything you get." She tapped the side of her nose. "We don't want library fees piling up."

Noah winced, grinning sheepishly as Aiden chuckled and nodded, heading toward the bathroom. Admittedly, that happened once, where Noah forgot to return a book. Dad needed to ship it from their new house just to stop the bill from going up. Thank the heavens Aiden noticed.

Ellen's expression was beyond amused as she watched the two of them before she got started on cooking. Mia swooped above, settling down on the candelabra above the dining room table, chin resting in her palms as long hair dangled past, catching Noah's attention. "It's fascinating how calm you are now, even though you know you have a killer chasing you." She hummed.

Noah didn't reply, noting that Ellen didn't notice Mia. If she hadn't, he would rather not make a fool of himself by talking to the air.

Aiden returned soon after, casting a quick annoyed look up toward Mia before taking a seat as the smell of breakfast started to waft through the house.

The sound of stumbling feet caught their attention. The door opened as Phen almost fell in. "Morn'." He blinked, before suddenly straightening, adjusting himself slightly. "Uh, I didn't know you two were already up." His attention landed on Aiden before quickly turning to Ellen. "Hey, Mom, did you need any help?"

"Yes, actually, can you get their clothes from the dryer?" Ellen glanced back. "Breakfast will be ready in a moment."

"Right on it." At that, he hurried away. Aiden just shook his head as Mia chuckled above.

Once he returned, the twins changed and everyone settled in for a nice breakfast of french toast and bacon. Noah had to admit, Ellen was a good cook.

He wished he could remember what his mom's cooking tasted like…

Shaking the thought off, they got ready for the day. Ellen agreed that she would drive them to the library. Though, she had a couple errands to run first since the library wasn't supposed to open until after lunch. The twins, not sure what to do with themselves, just relaxed in the living room, Phen telling them a little about the place. Soon enough, though, they were on their way.

They piled into the little car, more upscale than Noah or Aiden were used to. It wasn't long before they arrived and Ellen walked up, unlocking the door before gesturing them in.

Aiden was the first one through, glancing around at the books in a quiet wonder. Noah followed a pace behind at Phen's side. Ellen hurried over to the counter and typed into it for a moment before smiling faintly. She pulled out a card and scanned it before handing one to Aiden. "Here you go. I must get going." With that, she pardoned herself, disappearing into the shelves.

Noah didn't mind, part of him wanted to head to the manga section, but he held off. Aiden turned and let out a breath. "Since your mom works here, you probably know the place, right?"

"Of course." Phen nodded. "I mean, sure, I'm not here often, but I come enough to wait for her with—" He snapped his mouth shut before shaking his head. "What do you need to know?"

"Where the section on paranormal is." Aiden spoke, expression straight.

Phen seemed to think for a moment before gesturing. "It's this way."

Noah followed, glancing over the library. It wasn't a large one, but it wasn't small either. He could just barely see a second story above. Shelves with all sorts of books lined finely dusted bookcases. Noah heard quiet chatter and the chime of the bell indicating someone just walked in. Guess other people did use this place in town. He could hear the faint footsteps of people moving around even though they had only just arrived.

They wound their way upstairs and Phen stopped, gesturing. "It's a small section. Well, not counting below where we have the fantasy paranormal, but we do have some archival."

Aiden nodded, already stepping up to the books, finger slowly moving over the spines as he flipped through. Phen watched him for a while before jerking and turning to Noah, slightly sheepish. "Sorry, what about you?"

Noah tilted his head, curious before shaking it off. "Do you have a computer I can use?"

Phen nodded and the two moved down the stairs once more. Noah briefly noticed that Mia hovered nearby, staying near Aiden, solemnly staring at the books. He spotted Ellen stopping in front of the desk, a customer pulling her aside before she could get behind it. She nodded and turned, leading them back into the shelves. He relaxed at that, no one was alone, that was good.

They stepped up to a few computers on the older side. He couldn't complain, a computer was a computer. "Thanks."

"No problem." Phen took a seat in the chair next to Noah, flipping on one of the computers as well. "I didn't know your brother was a fan of books."

Noah shrugged. "We both like them, but I guess he prefers them a bit more. He's not a book geek or anything, but sometimes it is nice to read when we're not sure what else to do, especially in a new place."

Phen's expression shifted at that and he sighed. "Right, moving all the time, I keep forgetting that." He swung, turning back to the computer before pulling up the internet. "So, what exactly do we want to research?"

"Anything we can find on possession and how to learn if someone is possessed."

"Aiden phrased it that way, didn't he?"

"Pretty much."

Phen snorted as Noah chuckled before the two fell into a companionable silence, typing away at the computers. It wasn't easy, to be honest, they had a lot of pages to flip through and it was clear everyone had a different way to show how possession worked. There were cases where people just attributed it to mental illness and other times when people said it wasn't even a thing.

"Hey, uh, Noah?"

"Hm?"

"Your brother, why is he always so quiet?"

Noah glanced over as Phen stared at him. He thought for a moment and shrugged. "It's just Aiden, he's always been that way, even when we were young. Why?"

"Oh, well, I was just—I was just wondering is all, and, I mean, I do want to get to know you two better since we are friends and… I'm not helping, am I?"

Noah just stared, unsure what to make of Phen's hesitant words.

Phen turned back to the computer, cheeks slightly reddened. "It was a stupid question, don't worry about it."

"Okay?" Noah shook his head, feeling a hint amused. This boy was so weird, but he couldn't hate him. "You know, you can always ask Aiden."

Phen's head dropped at that, body tensing for a moment before he let out a breath. "Right, that's fair." He paused. "Did you find anything?"

Noah took the change of subject graciously and frowned. "Unfortunately, no. I wonder how Aiden is doing."

Noah quickly observed the area in search of his brother. He didn't need to look far, noting as Aiden hurried down the stairs, book in hand, brushing past another person. Noah waited, watching as Aiden slowed his pace, walking over with a furrowed brow.

"I think I found something." Aiden flipped the book open, placing it between the two of them, almost squishing between them. Phen's face grew more red, but he quickly leaned toward the book, curious. Noah found himself both concerned and amused. He'd seen those looks before. He glanced toward the book, noticing there were newspaper clippings photocopied into the pages. "These are reports on incidents in the past of demonic possession. Not quite the same, but our resident Ghost says it's pretty close."

"Hm? What does it say?" Phen peered through the pages alongside Noah.

"Pretty straightforward, actually. Most cases of possession seem to indicate that, while the demon remains in the human's body, they can switch between the human's personality, and the demon's or ghost's. It's almost like multi-personality disorder, but it's not quite." Aiden pointed toward one article. "In this one, it talks of a girl who was possessed for almost a year. It was only discovered when the mother went to check on her daughter one night and found the daughter giggling while…" he paused. "Well, you can read it."

Noah didn't have to, and, from Phen's slightly green face, he was glad he didn't. "My guess is that, most of the time, the person will act normal, but, in spurts, the ghost will take control, more likely at night." His gaze flicked up to Mia who was hovering above, startling Phen. "Our resident ghost mentioned something interesting, how her strength grows when it is dark, either from cloud cover caused by rain or when it is night."

"Oh, so that's why he only came when it was night time." Noah frowned. "But wouldn't that exhaust the body of whoever the ghost is controlling?"

Aiden shook his head, pointing to another article. "No, it was determined that a possessed human doesn't have the same limitations as regular humans. Bodies need nutrients, water and sleep. The sleep is done for the brain while the human is, legit, asleep. The ghost simply controls the nervous system. Not sure if that is always the case, but it's something."

"Which is why he's able to hum, but he's never spoken." Noah blinked, startled. Fascinating and utterly terrifying.

"Okay, that's great and all, but does that mean we are literally dealing with an amnesiac Jekyll and Hyde?" Phen glanced over, causing Aiden to hesitate.

"It's plausible."

Noah groaned, head in his hands. Great.

"It's not all bad news though," Aiden pointed out, flipping a few pages. "While possessed humans seem difficult to decipher, they all have one thing in common." He grimaced and glanced toward Noah. "An aversion to crosses."

Noah's fingers shot up to curl around his necklace.

"That sounds like something mainly for demons, not ghosts." Phen frowned, turning in his chair to lean against the back, sitting at an angle.

"That's what I thought at first too, however…" Aiden pulled out his cross, dangling it between his fingers. "I wasn't wearing this for a while and our resident Ghost was able to touch me. Watch."

At that, he suddenly reached up toward Mia, who shot backward, curving around with a hiss before pausing. "I said you could do that once!"

"I needed to show them." Aiden frowned as Noah blinked, glancing back and forth.

"But, wait… I was able to touch Mia twice now and I wear one as well." Noah pulled up the necklace, showing it briefly before letting it rest against his chest. "Once when we shook hands and once when I put a hand on her shoulder yesterday."

"It has to do with his abilities." Mia glared down toward Aiden. "Like I said, Aiden's a magnet, but he's also more powerful so the aspects are probably enhanced both ways." She shrugged. "I can't say, however, why it was I can't touch you, but you can touch me, Noah. I'm going to assume that's something regarding your abilities."

Noah pursed his lips, not sure he liked that answer. It really wasn't one, but he decided not to worry about what she meant about his abilities for now. He swung around. "Well, for the cross, let's see if it's because of our abilities or if it's just universal." He started typing into the computer. Aiden leaned against the chair, arms crossed and chin resting on Noah's shoulder.

Noah heard Phen gulp and shift. "I'll, uh, help."

It took a while of flipping through a few pages, looking specifically for ghosts in regards to crosses before they were able to confirm what

Aiden said. Site after site seemed to agree that ghosts, whether they were demons, revenants or normal spirits, had an aversion to the symbol. No one knew why, but it was believed that it was because they feared what the symbol meant for them. The more deaths and problems a ghost caused, the more averse they were to the symbol.

However, when worn, it almost permanently, unless destroyed over time by repeated use, repelled all but the strongest ghosts from the person in question. The exception included ghosts that held no ill will or did no ill will, as long as it was made a certain way.

"Interesting, isn't it?" Noah poked Aiden's side.

"A bit overwhelming is more like it." Aiden shifted, catching Noah's gaze.

"I suppose." Noah peered back toward the screen. "You would think Dad would have mentioned some of this at least."

Aiden didn't say anything to that, just pulled back.

Phen let out a yawn. "Yeah, interesting. So, what? We just walk around, trying to touch everyone and see if they react like Mia did? Because, yeah, anyone is going to react that way."

Aiden frowned, before suddenly reaching out and poking Phen in the shoulder.

Phen stiffened, cheeks flaring red and Noah watched, amused, as Phen suddenly sputtered. "What was that for?"

"One, checking to see if you were a ghost, and two, to prove you wrong," Aiden pointed out, expression even.

Phen paused before quickly looking away, muttering under his breath. Noah chuckled before turning to Aiden. "He is right, though, we can't just go up to everyone and poke them. For one, it would take way too long, and for two, it would draw even more attention to ourselves."

Aiden seemed to debate for a moment before sighing. "I agree, but I'm running out of ideas. We have no clues, no leads, nothing."

Noah furrowed his brow, pulling up the texts again, hoping for something, anything.

"Dad said be careful at school." Noah paused and blinked. "I mean, that makes sense, but—"

Aiden smacked his face and groaned. "Noah, we're dumb."

Noah sputtered as Phen watched, shocked. "What?"

Aiden ruffled his hair, clearly annoyed. "Think about it. Where, exactly, have we been since we arrived here?"

"A lot of places?" Noah spoke quietly.

"Yes, but that was AFTER the first night when he tracked us down. Phen showed us around. Up until then?"

Noah frowned, unsure where his brother was getting at before he froze. "The diner, the market… and the school."

Aiden nodded.

"That means the person must have seen you at one of those locations. I doubt he would have just randomly picked you out in the street on the way to school." Phen spoke up, tone unnerved. "This goes back to our original idea of watching out for who killed Lynn… that could only really mean the school."

"The diner and market, while weird, are pretty much out of the question," Aiden muttered. "There were only three people who saw us at those locations and all of them saw Dad too."

"Well, we could try talking with those three," Noah pointed out. "To at least narrow it down so it IS only the school."

"I don't think you need to." Phen spoke, expression suddenly nervous. "You said your father mentioned to be careful at school. A school is supposed to be safe with teachers and staff watching all the time. So, why would he warn you about that place specifically?"

"Exactly." Aiden nodded before slumping. "It's circumstantial evidence at best, but it's all we've got."

"I'll take whatever I can get, if it means finding out who killed my sister." Phen glared, standing up. "However, if this killer is at the school, then why don't we just close it down, tell the police and—"

"That won't work," Aiden cut in.

"What, why?"

Noah spoke up this time, pushing his chair around to face Phen. "Because they have nothing to go off of. Just a text and some kids' words. The police have been at the school and never found anything. It's not so simple to go to the police and say, hey, the killer is at school, go get him." Noah sighed. "Believe me, I wish we could, but Dad's told us enough stories so we know what to expect if we try something like that."

"And, if it wasn't already there, we would put an even bigger target on our back." Aiden crossed his arms over his chest. "It's stupid."

"You don't have to be that blunt." Noah rolled his eyes, getting a huff from Aiden.

Frustration flashed across Phen's face, along with a quiet growl before he slumped. "No, that makes sense."

Aiden hesitated for a moment before finally speaking up. "Since we know it's probably someone at school, we can take precautions." He pushed away from the bookshelf he had been leaning against. "For instance, making sure we're never alone with someone we don't trust. On top of that, to avoid him figuring out where we are, we'll have to make sure he doesn't see us at school together. Noah and I are fine because he will expect that, but he might not yet suspect you, Phen."

"I'm not so sure." Noah gestured as Phen glanced down, debating. Noah watched him for a moment before facing Aiden, continuing, "That thing killed Phen's sister. If it is a possessed human, they probably are aware of Phen's involvement… he could be in danger just like us."

Phen stiffened at that as Aiden pursed his lips. "That's—"

"You know I'm right. Lynn said she got too close and Phen is following that same idea." Noah spun, no longer facing Phen, whose expression was twisted between contemplation and dawning realization. "Plus, it's dangerous for any of us to be alone. Phen is the only one we talk to at school anyway, us continuing to talk to him isn't going to change anything."

Aiden snapped his mouth shut.

"I know you are hesitant about it, but it's okay to rely on someone else." Noah kept his voice low, catching Aiden's attention.

"Noah," Aiden cut in, stance shifting, uncomfortable. "I'm not a talker, I would be better staying off to the side anyway—"

"That doesn't sound safe." Phen spoke up, annoyed, catching Aiden's attention. "Nor is that fair to you. I have people I can talk to, so does Noah. It doesn't matter. You shouldn't be by yourself and, like Noah said, let me…" He suddenly pulled back, choking before quickly catching his breath. "Let me help you to rely on me."

"Huh?"

"Um…" Phen stumbled as Noah watched him quietly, Aiden clearly confused. "I want you to be able to trust me." He straightened. "I'm not going to let you be alone, not right now."

Aiden watched him, clearly somewhat confused, before yelping as brown hair suddenly covered his face. He jerked as the hair just as quickly pulled away. He peered up to see Mia imitating landing on his head, arms crossed inches above his face. She grinned, expression clear with how close they were. "That one is right. While it's good to be observant, staying in a group is safer." She shifted, pulling back just enough so he could breath. "Plus, you need someone watching out for you anyway. You're not exactly the most observant one."

Aiden twitched. "Coming from you, I'm not sure HOW I feel about it."

"Haha, funny." She leaned forward once more, gold eye gleaming in the darkness cast by the long hair that once more covered his face. Through the curtain of hair, he couldn't see the other eye.

Aiden sputtered, brushing the hair aside as she chuckled and pulled back fully this time. "Until you call me Mia, I'll keep bothering you however I want, including calling you anything but your name." Mia hummed, tilting her head side to side, causing Aiden's hair to ruffle slightly from the presence.

Phen watched, before shaking his head and chuckling. "Okay, I can see the point." He frowned. "But what I said still stands. If you are still here after this is all said and done, I'm not going to just let you sit by yourself."

Aiden jerked, turning to him, surprised.

Noah wasn't. He felt a faint smile cross his lips.

For once, it seemed like they actually found someone who truly wanted to be THEIR friend, not just Noah's.

He just wondered how long it would last, until they pushed Phen away by accident like all the others.

CHAPTER 22

Aiden wasn't sure how to feel about Phen's response. The words still hung in his head as they left, deciding to go back to Phen's place. They waved good-bye to Ellen, Phen having a quick conversation with her in private. All of them felt uncomfortable with being out and about when they had no leads and, while Aiden knew both he and Noah were restless to find out what was going on with Dad, they couldn't just rush in.

There was nowhere to even rush in to. They could check the school, but Aiden figured it would be better to do it during the day to at least get a feel or a baseline. That way, when they checked at other times, they would be able to notice any major differences. Major differences like people actually wanting to sit near him.

Aiden smiled slightly. Someone wanted to sit with him that wasn't Noah. Was he just imagining it? Probably, but it made him feel happy in a way he wasn't used to. Almost giddy in the fact that someone WANTED to stay near him that wasn't Noah.

He was probably going crazy. He was trying hard not to get his hopes up, especially since there was no promises that they were even staying, once they found Dad, but—

Something jabbed into his side and he grunted, glancing over to see Noah's amused expression. "You were pretty lost in thought there. Everything okay?"

Aiden huffed and nodded, rubbing where Noah elbowed him. "I'm fine."

"You thinking about what Phen said?" Noah's attention flitted to the boy who was a few steps ahead, attempting to talk with their Ghost friend.

Aiden hesitated, and Noah's smile became gentler. "He's right, though, you don't have to keep silent. I know you're not comfortable talking with people, and that's okay. I just don't want you to be alone right now."

Aiden sighed, rubbing his arm. "I understand that. Believe me. But, I already promised myself that I would keep an eye on things."

Noah watched him for a moment before nodding. "Alright." He reached up, flicking Aiden in the forehead. Aiden instinctively covered his head and furrowed his brow as Noah continued with a grin, "People do like you, you know."

Aiden paused at that before tilting his head down, feeling his shoulders slump. He wasn't sure he agreed with Noah, but knew his brother would persist otherwise.

They made their way back to Phen's place, observing their surroundings as they went, the time now being late afternoon. Their Ghostly friend flitted around, keeping a more distant eye on things. Aiden had to admit, she was fast as a ghost, zipping from place to place, only the faint sound of running footsteps catching his ears.

When they made it back, Phen disappeared upstairs for a while, probably to help his father with a few things, leaving Noah and Aiden in the living room once more. There wasn't much they could do and both of them felt uncomfortable. To be honest, Aiden wanted to see if he could find a place to stay that wasn't Phen's. Wasn't there an inn or something they could stay in?

"Tomorrow, we should try to go home and collect what we can," Noah said, flopping down on the couch as Aiden took a seat on the other. "Maybe after school, we can head toward our place. We can grab our things and whatever Dad might have left and then come back. Sound good?" He waved at the end, turning slightly to peek over toward Aiden.

Aiden nodded. "I would love to, except if we do get followed… to an abandoned building in the middle of nowhere, where they already saw how we've escaped previously, how do you expect to deal with them?"

Noah raised a hand to argue and then promptly dropped it back to his side with a groan. "Ugh, good point."

"Don't ask me to do it. I can't carry things myself." The Ghost spoke up, hovering upside down between them.

"You're useless," Aiden muttered.

The Ghost just glared as Noah huffed. "Well, there went that idea."

"Wait, you were seriously considering it?" Aiden raised an eyebrow, getting a sheepish expression from Noah.

"What? We need all the help we can get. I mean, Mia could probably do more than just scout, you know. Which, by the way, we do appreciate your help." Noah glanced up.

The Ghost nodded. "I'm aware. You don't have to keep thanking me. I'm doing this for myself anyway."

Noah's expression shifted slightly to bemusement.

Footsteps echoed from the stairwell as Phen came in and plopped down next to Aiden, who jumped slightly in surprise.

There was a chair right over there. Did Phen have to sit right next to him?

"So, what are we doing? I mean, we can plan, but there isn't much to plan. We can spend the afternoon just doing whatever and head to school in the morning. It's up to you guys."

Aiden and Noah exchanged looks before Noah shrugged. "I'm pretty open. Just, I think I need to take my mind off of this for a bit, do you have any movies we can watch or something?"

"I know just the ones." Phen smiled, glancing sidelong toward Aiden. "Movie marathon, it is." His gaze stayed for a moment more before he stood back up. "I'll go get them and grab some popcorn… or, well, I should probably get us some dinner first. Aiden, uh, do you, um, want to help me?"

Aiden peered up, startled as Phen stepped to one side, awkward smile on his face. "I mean, well, you cooked the other day, so I was just wondering, that's all."

"You should," Noah prompted, catching Aiden's attention. He was grinning. "I look forward to see what you make."

Aiden debated for a moment before sighing and pushing himself to his feet. "Fine. Let's see what we have to work with."

They headed toward the kitchen, Phen keeping pace. Aiden could hear quiet chatter from the front room between the Ghost and Noah. He brushed it off, glancing toward Phen. "Your mother is fine with us using the kitchen, right?"

"Of course she would be. Why wouldn't she?" Phen's laugh was a little off, unable to make eye-contact with Aiden. "So, what are you thinking of making?"

Aiden shrugged, glancing in the fridge. He could probably whip up something simple. Oh, there was chicken stock, he could probably make some soup. That would be fine.

Soon enough, he got to cooking. It wasn't anything impressive, but he knew it would do the trick. He felt Phen's gaze on him, but when he glanced over, Phen was focusing on something else. At least he was helping, cutting up some of the vegetables. "Did you need something?" Aiden muttered after the third time.

"Uh, no. No I didn't—don't—" Phen hesitated before letting out a heavy sigh. "I just have a lot going on in my head right now that I'm trying to figure out and there are certain things that are making that difficult."

Aiden frowned, annoyed. "I can finish up here if you want to talk to Noah about it."

"No, it's not that. I mean, your brother is great and all, but no, it's not—well… just, don't worry about it, okay? I need to figure it out myself." He let out a breath. "I only really talked to Lynn about it before, so now that she's, well…" His words trailed off. He rubbed his hand down his face, his whole body deflating. "Without her to talk with and other things happening, it's hard to make sense of what I'm feeling, that's all. It's not negative to you or anything, don't think that."

Uh-huh.

"I'm not helping, am I?"

"You're making no sense, to be honest." Aiden flipped the chicken and then used the spatula to point. "I'm well aware I'm not the person to talk to about this. Whatever it is you're dealing with, I can't help you."

"I know." Phen glanced away as Aiden felt something stab into his chest. He brought it up, but Phen didn't have to so readily agree. "Like I said, I need to figure it out myself. It's just awkward, I guess."

Aiden didn't say anything to that, tilting his head down. He should apologize, say he's sorry, but the words clung to his lips, unable to be spoken. "Can you pass me the salt?" he muttered after a minute.

Phen jerked out of whatever thought process he was in. He handed it over and hesitated. "Did you need anything else?"

Aiden glanced toward him, taking the salt before lightly tapping some in. "Not really. I'm kind of used to cooking alone." He let himself chuckle, feeling it was a bit forced. "I don't trust Noah anywhere near the kitchen. Though, I do appreciate your help with the vegetables." He swiped them up, throwing them into the simmering cast iron pot he was using.

He briefly noted Phen's surprised expression. "Really? Noah's a bad cook?"

"Let's just say, he put the water on to boil, and got distracted so badly that when I came over and noticed, there was nothing left inside except for a burnt smell."

Phen snorted at that and then let out a laugh. "Oh man, I can see that." Aiden felt a small smile flutter onto his lips. Phen almost stumbled in his laughter, gaze suddenly on his. For a moment, he seemed almost… entranced? Aiden wasn't sure if that was the word, considering he just as quickly turned away, a flash of red shooting over his cheeks. "Anyway, I'll go cut up some bread and place the dishes and all that, sounds good? Sounds good." At that, he stepped away, leaving Aiden alone to finish. Aiden watched him go, feeling more than a little confused at Phen's reaction. Who was he to judge, though?

Silence enveloped the room as Aiden finished up. Noah joined them and they sat down to eat.

Soon enough, the evening passed without another word on the topic. Ellen came home not that long after, her expression showing her relief upon finding them home. She reheated the soup, taking some for herself and complementing Aiden on the food before bringing another bowl upstairs, where Aiden could faintly hear creaking and quiet sounds of chatter. Phen's expression grew tense for a bit before he sighed and quickly threw a movie in. Thankfully, they had decided to only watch one since the series was a long one that Aiden only ever heard of. At least Noah seemed to be enjoying it and, admittedly, the movie did have its moments.

But who thought a six hour movie as part of a trilogy that are all six plus hours was a good idea?

Ellen finally came down, convincing them to go to bed, which Aiden was kind of grateful for. Soon enough, they found themselves sleeping in the living room once more, Phen once again taking the floor between them.

·　　·　　·　　·　　·

The next morning woke bright and early. Noah was up and about, helping Ellen with breakfast. Phen quickly brought some up to his father before they all headed out. It was a school day and, while Aiden was usually fond of school, it really wasn't on the top of his list at the current moment. Phen was the first out of the car when they arrived, hurrying ahead of them as Ellen watched, amused. Noah and Aiden pulled themselves out of the car, as Phen waved at his mom. She waved back before driving off to work herself.

With the weekend having passed fairly quietly, the feeling of the school somewhat returned to normal, or at least, the normal Aiden felt when he first arrived, which was still dismal, but not necessarily as tense.

He headed inside, noting how the teachers were patrolling the halls. He glanced over to see the principal passing through, nodding to some students, talking to others and seemingly checking up on things. Aiden remembered spotting him the last few times, but he hadn't really been paying much attention. His secretary followed behind, expression even and clipboard in hand.

Aiden shook the thought off, heading to class. He had to admit, it was eerie, sitting in class while knowing there was a killer in the school, just out of your vision. It made him jump whenever he rounded a corner or entered a classroom, especially when he found himself lost. It was only the second week and while his sense of direction was solid, he hadn't exactly memorized the school. Thankfully, he shared quite a few classes with Phen, though somehow none with Noah.

He knew, however, that his brother would be okay. Case in point… he glanced over as they stepped into the lunch room, a few guys and girls chatting with Noah as he took a seat, laughing at some joke. Aiden shook his head, attention sweeping over the gathered students and few teachers.

Compared to the slightly more relaxed students, the teachers all seemed wary. They glanced over the students, walking through the room with an attempted air of casualness.

To be honest, if Aiden wasn't paying so much attention, he probably would have missed it. He took another bite of his lunch, some chicken tenders from the line, as a teacher passed by, gaze sweeping past his table.

He stayed somewhat close to Noah, but gave him space to talk with a few people. Every so often, someone would glance over to say something, only to pause and turn back to talk with Noah.

He finished up and stood, swiping up his and Noah's trays. Noah gave him a startled glance, followed by a grateful smile before he turned back to the others.

Aiden walked away, that familiar chill following him as he went.

"Hm… it's fascinating how different you and Noah are." The Ghost spoke quietly, flipping upside down as footsteps still echoed nearby, a disconcerting thing. "Though, I suppose it isn't too surprising. Just because two people look alike doesn't mean their personalities are the same."

Aiden honestly was just wondering why the Ghost was talking to him about this. He dumped the trays off, taking another glance around from his new position.

Nothing really changed.

"Ghost, are you sure you can't sense them?" He kept his voice low, tilting his head down as he returned back to his seat.

The Ghost huffed and glared. "I really shouldn't respond because I know you will have some annoying response, but… no, I can't." She flipped upright. "He's normal during the day. I've only sensed him before because the ghostly part took over." She tilted her head and kept tilting. "He hasn't sensed me either. At least, I do not think."

Aiden promptly looked away, just before the head went almost 180 degrees. Yeah, no, he hated how the Ghost could do that.

"Though, maybe someday, you and your brother would be able to sense them. I believe YOU already kind of do."

Those words caused him to freeze in place as the bell rang above. He jerked, glancing toward the Ghost who casually landed on the ground and walked past. "The strength of a human with connections to the dead is much stronger than one already deceased, after all." At that, she waved and vanished. He pursed his lips, unsure what to say to that.

He pulled himself from his thoughts, noting as the room was beginning to empty out. He quickly followed suit, heading toward his next class, a few paces behind a chattering Phen, who occasionally glanced back his way with concern before continuing on.

The Ghost's words thrummed through his head and he frowned. If it was possible for him and Noah to be able to sense them... how? What would he need to do to figure it out? It wasn't just that chill in the air, right? That wasn't really helpful.

Did he even want to figure it out? Why was he even bothering with ghosts? Ugh, ever since he spoke with Lynn and they found her body, his mind was a jumbled mess. Ghosts shouldn't exist, it shouldn't be the case, but now everything was showing that it was. Heck, even Dad's strange behavior and action made more sense now and it just annoyed him.

"Son, are you okay?" A voice caught his attention and he glanced over to see the principal. The secretary was a few paces behind. The secretary glanced up, watching quietly as the principal turned. "Are you lost? I know you just recently started."

Aiden glanced around and paled. He slowed to a stop at some point, not paying attention, and the Ghost hadn't tried to correct him. He winced. "Sorry, just thinking."

The principal nodded. "Do you need a guide to your room? I am busy, but I can take a moment."

"No, I'm fine. Thank you." Aiden nodded and hurried past, noting as the two men watched him go before continuing their path through the school.

He needed to get his head together. With the hallways empty like that, he could have been in trouble.

Stupid, it was stupid of him to not pay attention.

He hurried to the classroom, noting that the teacher was late, again. Why was that?

Phen, sitting in front of him, turned and glanced back. "Man, where did you go? You were right behind me."

"Got distracted," Aiden muttered, peering over the crowd. "Where's the teacher?"

"Ms. Fiona is always late." Phen waved. "There are all sorts of rumors but no one really knows."

Aiden couldn't argue, remembering seeing her come in quite a few times with messed-up clothes and a harried expression.

"Though…" Phen paused and frowned. "It is strange. Why is she always late? No one knows where she goes or anything, so could it be…"

Aiden glanced toward Phen, who tensed slightly. "Don't jump to conclusions," Aiden pointed out, causing Phen to frown. "We can keep an eye on her, but we can't necessarily say she is the one involved."

"Right, I know, it's just—I feel anxious. I NEED to know."

"We do too." Aiden wanted to snap, but kept his voice low and neutral. "Our father could be in danger and we're at school. I would rather be out there, but we need information."

Phen slumped in his seat, nodding. "Right, you're right. I'm sorry."

Aiden sighed, shoulders drooping. "As long as you understand."

The door snapped open and the teacher hurriedly walked in, quickly moving to the front and starting class without missing a beat.

It was almost impressive, Aiden had to admit.

CHAPTER 23

He heard movement and glanced over. Phen tossed something onto his desk. A piece of paper, crumbled up into a small ball.

He blinked, staring at it for a moment before feeling heat rise on his face. He quickly scooped it up and shoved it under his desk before the teacher noticed.

He didn't miss the way Phen quickly turned around, fidgeting in his chair either.

Idiot.

He unfolded the paper and quickly read it over.

Do you mind if we keep an eye on her? I want to know what she's doing. I just have a bad feeling. We'll track her after school. Does that work for you?

Aiden rolled his eyes and, half-tempted to throw the paper at the back of Phen's head, just waited until Phen glanced back before nodding and mouthing, "Talk later."

Phen grinned and returned his focus back toward the teacher as she turned from the board to the students once more.

Aiden just shook his head, unsure how to deal with Phen. He was so weird, but then, it felt like everyone in his life was weird, so who knows.

Thankfully, classes soon came to an end. Having shared his last class with Phen as well, he was basically dragged toward where Phen figured Ms. Fiona would be leaving. Noah soon found them, staying to one side. Aiden leaned against the wall, unamused, as Phen peeked around the corner, overtly spying on the door that led out of the classroom and getting a few odd looks from the students.

Aiden wanted to slam his head against a locker, but held off to save the few braincells that the group had left.

"Uh, Phen, what are you doing?" Noah asked after a moment.

Phen perked up and pulled away. "I want to know what is up with Ms. Fiona. I just think she's suspicious and, to be honest, I just need something to do."

Aiden mentally groaned. Of course. Noah just smiled, that awkward, unsure how to respond, smile. "Oh. You do know you're the one acting suspicious right now, right?"

At that, their resident Ghost companion, still out of sight, giggled. Phen jumped.

Yeah, that seemed accurate.

Phen glared upward before turning and peeking down the hallway. "She's leaving. Let's follow."

"How do you propose we do that?" Aiden pointed out, arms crossed. This was stupid, but at this point, an idea was an idea.

He wasn't going to remind them that that the Ghost mentioned it was a guy they were looking for.

Phen hesitated for only a second. "Mia, do you mind?"

"I'm not your personal scout, but fine." With that, the cold feeling faded. After a moment, Phen nodded and followed. Aiden hesitated before, noticing Noah going around the corner, he decided to join them. With the Ghost as their personal scout, it wasn't too hard to keep track of Ms. Fiona and stay out of sight.

Though it took a lot of effort for Aiden to stop both Noah and Phen from acting like thieves and hiding behind things like posts and trash cans. They were walking home from school, that was it.

Though he wouldn't admit it, but he did find it amusing when the woman paused and glanced back, only for Phen and Noah to whip around, appearing like they were walking the other direction, Noah practically pulling Aiden with him.

Their faces when he pointed out how even MORE suspicious they were was just the icing on the cake.

It definitely gave him a good chuckle.

Eventually, they agreed to walk even with him, pretending they were just going around town. Good thing too, because Aiden could tell Ms. Fiona was watching them.

He knew the Ghost would keep track of her, so he lightly veered them to one side, as if heading toward the arcade. He briefly noted the way Ms. Fiona relaxed slightly before moving on. He gave it a moment before turning and following at a slower pace, keeping the other two with him. At the distance they were and with it once again showing signs of rain, it was a bit easier to hide in plain sight. The streets were emptying out as they arrived at a small home on the opposite end of town from where Noah and Aiden lived.

Out front was a woman Aiden recognized, the girl who worked in the diner. Were they sisters?

"How old is Ms. Fiona?" Noah whispered toward Phen as they stepped to one side, moving behind a nearby home that seemed abandoned, many in this area were.

"Hm. I think she's in her thirties? I don't know, I don't ask that stuff." Phen waved.

"So, what is it you guys want to know? She's pretty normal from what I can tell." The Ghost floated over, startling them. "I didn't sense anything from her and, well, I can't get into their home, so I can't exactly do much else."

Aiden furrowed his brow. "Well? I'm just kind of following along."

Noah rolled his eyes before leaning back against the wall of the home, deep in thought. "Well, she didn't really do anything strange except head home. We already deduced that the diner didn't have anything to do with what's going on, so…"

Aiden shivered and frowned, glancing toward the building Noah was leaning against, noticing as Noah suddenly stepped away, a slight spasm going through him. He glanced over his shoulder, frowning slightly.

"Phen?"

"Hm?"

"This area of town, is there anything odd about this place?"

Phen blinked and furrowed his brow. "Not that I recall." He paused. "Though, actually, this is where some of the disappearances were taking place at night, like I said before. Many of the residents left soon after and no one really came in, so many of these buildings are empty. Sometimes the police find vagrants, but…" He paused. "I guess Ms. Fiona is one of the few who stayed, maybe that's why she's always harried."

"Could it be that she can't sleep at home due to what's going on and so sleeps at the school?" Aiden asked, glancing toward the building as the woman gestured toward the sky before hurrying into the house which, on closer inspection, was slightly more protected than Aiden thought. There were metal pieces across the windows like bars, and what little he could see of a side door was completely blocked off by random junk and thick metal.

"Oh, I didn't even think of that." Phen turned.

"If you can't leave, all you can do is try to protect yourself," Noah pointed out, pursing his lips as he stared at the home, moving away from the place they hid next to. "It would explain why she's late for almost every class, she's probably having to sleep between classes to get any sort of rest." He shivered. "This place gives me the creeps."

Aiden agreed, taking note of the darkening sky. "Let's get back to Phen's place. Tomorrow, we'll check around here, since we don't have any more leads at school."

"You do know the police have checked around here multiple times, right?" Phen pointed out, but followed suit as they headed back, street lamps flickering on in the growing gloom.

Aiden nodded as Noah furrowed his brow in thought. "Maybe, but I still want to check it out. I couldn't help but feel unsettled while we were in that part of town, like this persistent feeling of something being very wrong."

"That makes no sense."

"It's hard to explain, okay?" Noah huffed.

Aiden had to agree. There was no easy way to explain the feeling. "Hey, Ghost, you felt it, didn't you?"

"Hm?"

"That chill?"

"You'll have to be more specific." The Ghost landed between Aiden and Noah.

"Mia, I think my brother is being serious." Noah leaned forward. "You know what he's talking about."

The Ghost, as infuriating as she was, frowned. "Actually, no, I don't." This startled all three of them into stopping.

"Huh?" Phen turned.

The Ghost sighed, frustrated. "I don't feel things the way you do. A chill could mean the environment, it could mean location, it could mean a ghost is nearby or it could mean that negative emotions are clouding the air. There are literally too many options for me to know which one you are talking about."

Aiden wasn't aware of that. From his reaction, Noah wasn't either, because he blinked, startled.

"Oh." Noah pulled back. "Uh… It's hard to tell. What did you get from that area?"

The Ghost stopped walking, but continued to float forward, obviously lost in thought. "There's something there, but I don't think it's who were looking for."

"So there's not much point going back." Aiden leaned on one leg, watching quietly. "We don't need to put ourselves in danger just because—"

"But there's something there, right?" Phen gestured, cutting him off, a strange, almost desperate expression on his face. "That could be a clue. As I said, that's where a lot of the initial disappearances occurred, so maybe there might be evidence the police missed that we can find with ghostly assistance. We need to do something."

"Aiden, Phen is right." Noah gestured back the way they came. "You probably felt it like I did. There is something there and it's more than we've gotten up until this point."

Aiden debated for a moment, thoughts flitting back to what the Ghost mentioned about humans being better able to sense the deceased. He felt his whole body slump and the other two took it as the begrudging agreement it was if their exchanged glances of determination were any indication.

"So, tomorrow, after school, we'll meet here, and bring anything we might need to explore."

What is this, a field trip? Aiden thought, but pushed it off. He supposed they were right, a clue was a clue, it was something to grasp onto.

Plus, he had a feeling they were racing a clock anyway. The Ghost mentioned how that thing was becoming more powerful. Their father was still missing and the longer they took, the more worried and anxious they would become.

He knew rushing into things was a bad idea, but at the moment, it felt like it was the only option they had.

•　　•　　•　　•　　•

Noah awoke the next day to Aiden actually being up before him. He plopped into a chair next to Aiden, who was flipping through a notebook he probably borrowed from Phen. A pen tapped against his cheek as he debated before jotting something down. Ellen placed some slices of bacon and a good helping of scrambled eggs in front of Noah, who nodded gratefully before digging in as Ellen once more ran out the door for work.

"Hey, Noah," Aiden said, not even shifting his focus from the page.

"Hey." He leaned forward, chin in palm. "What are you doing?"

Aiden turned the page and gestured to the notes, written in clean script. Quickly flipping through, Noah took in the fact that it was all the information they had so far, not only on ghosts, but also on what clues they did have. "I'm trying to piece together what we have so far and compile it so it's easier to flip through. Can I see your phone so I can jot down the texts?" I think ours are the same, but I want to check anyway."

Noah nodded, pulling out his phone before handing it over.

Aiden flipped through it before quickly jotting them down. He paused, frowning as he glanced down.

Noah leaned forward, startled by the sudden lack of movement.

Aiden just shifted the phone slightly, making it easier for Noah to see the brand new text at the bottom of the page.

Where are you, little children? The little Ravens should come to me. After all, you are so close. Make me whole.

Another text below it.

Almost, almost… close, but not quite. The little raven, only a few minutes older, so… enticing. Give it to me. Give me your power. I can almost taste it. Give. It. To. Me.

Noah just stared, feeling the blood drain from his face.

"Oh, that is definitely not creepy in the slightest." Mia spoke up, peering between them. Aiden glanced over as Noah jumped, startled. "The obsession part is taking over. Might want to be more careful." She pulled back, frowning slightly. "The little raven, only a few minutes older, huh?" She glanced toward Aiden. "Last I checked, I believe you were the elder between you two? Seems pretty self-explanatory, eh?"

Aiden stared down at the text before handing the phone back to Noah. "It simply means he's a creep that we need to figure out before this gets any worse." He paused. "Though I suppose it's already bad as is."

Noah nodded, staring at the text with a frown. Did that mean—He froze before his gaze snapped up to Aiden. "Is it possible you were near him at some point?"

Aiden glanced toward him, frowning before paling.

"It's possible." Mia sung, humming faintly, the sound almost eerie, making Aiden shudder and pull backwards slightly. Noah just found himself shifting uncomfortably as Mia continued, "Why would he call the elder twin out? Either that, or he's just calling the elder twin out in general because he sensed that the elder twin might have some power already."

"You're deliberately calling me the elder twin, aren't you? You can't just, I don't know, use my name?"

"I could, but this is more fun." Mia chirped before settling down, expression even. "However, he is still calling you out for whatever reason. Whether it is because he knows who you are is a different story. Stay within sight of each other as much as possible."

Aiden stared at her for a moment before nodding. Noah glanced back down at his phone, lost in thought. Footsteps rang through the house, indicating that the rest of the family was up. Noah glanced over as Phen let out a yawn, stretching. He spotted them and paused. "Those expressions say a lot, you two okay?"

"Fine." Noah quickly stowed his phone away as Aiden just got back to his reading with a shrug. Phen glanced back and forth, worry clear on his face, followed by uncertainty. Thankfully, he didn't push. Soon enough they found their way to school.

CHAPTER 24

It was frustrating to Noah, because while he knew Mia was right, it didn't make it easy to accomplish.

Sure, he conversed with the other students, but it all felt hollow and his mind wouldn't stop thinking of the texts, or the utter gross chill he got when they followed Ms. Fiona yesterday.

Thankfully, the day passed relatively quietly. Soon enough, they were heading out of the school. Phen and Aiden led the way, a silence falling between them. Noah stayed a few steps behind, letting them lead as he hummed quietly to himself. Thankfully, because Phen's Mom worked late they could walk home themselves which made all of this a little easier to do. Mia stayed alongside, amused.

"Hey, Mia, it must be boring to sit at school all day." Noah glanced sidelong. "So, uh, why do you stay near during class?"

Mia tilted from side to side before shrugging. "I guess it feels almost nostalgic? Plus, your brother is quite fun to mess with." She paused as he narrowed his eyes and she quickly elaborated. "Don't worry, it's not to hurt him or scare him. At least, there is no intention of that. I know my limits." Noah's tense posture relaxed slightly as she shifted. "I just find myself amused by his reactions. He tries to hide them, but sometimes he fails miserably. And, best of all, he can't hit me with his pencil or something in the middle of class."

Noah snorted, trying to hide his chuckles. That was true. He relaxed even more; she definitely laid off a bit at some point. Too bad he never got to see when she did those pranks. He paused and glanced down the street. "But, seriously, you mentioned yesterday that it was hard to tell chills or feelings or whatever. What is it like for you?"

Mia paused for a moment before settling down to a walking pace beside him, footsteps clacking over the pavement of the sidewalk. "It's hard to explain. Ghosts like us are incorporeal. We have no real form or shape. We are held together by emotions and a soul." She placed a hand to her chest. "I don't know the specifics, but, because of this form, the soul is more fragile, but also more readily able to be aware of its surroundings. In a way, sensing is similar to feeling with touch. That skin-crawling feeling of webs against your body? The sensation of ragged edges of broken metal? That is how I sense."

"So, almost like you're touching whatever it is?" Noah shivered. "That sounds terrible."

"It can be." Mia paused. "But there are times when what we sense isn't bad." She tilted her head, single eye piercing Noah's. "You and your brother. What I sense is the feel of a warm blanket wrapped around after a long time of being out in the cold. A sense of touching grass brimming with life."

Noah stared quietly, unsure how to respond to that. It was hard to wrap his head around. "So when we talk about chill…"

"I don't necessarily feel a chill, just what is attached," Mia confirmed. "Yesterday, I felt a lot at once, for a brief moment. Which was why I was confused at your question."

"Yet, you can't touch things?"

Mia shook her head. "The feelings I attribute are from vague memories that remain. I could attribute your handshake with one but I couldn't feel YOUR hand. I think that's the case with all ghosts. We equate feelings and senses with the memories we still hold, the FEEL of those things. Your brother… makes an exception to that rule, from what I can tell."

Noah's thoughts flicked to how often Aiden hit Mia and, more particularly, Mia's reaction to the ice-cream. He glanced down. "Oh… that means someone with almost no good memories would also have nothing good to equate to if they end up a ghost."

Mia said nothing to that, but Noah didn't have to ask any farther. He couldn't help but feel upset for those who died and were stuck to this plane, only to constantly feel the terrible things they felt in life. For a brief moment he almost wished he could do what Aiden could, to help Mia make new memories like with the ice-cream. Sure, he could, for instance, hold her hand unlike Aiden but that didn't mean much if all she felt was a memory.

"Noah?" Aiden's voice caught his attention and he jerked, glancing up before faintly chuckling.

"Sorry, I guess we're here?"

Aiden nodded, watching him worriedly while Phen just gave a curious expression. Today was cloudy, but there was no smell of imminent rain or a pressure in the air, so hopefully, it was just overcast. He joined Aiden and glanced between them. "So, where do we start?"

Phen gestured to one house in particular, expression even. "This was the first house that had a disappearance. The family left soon after and the police did inspect it, but found nothing. It's now completely abandoned and, like most of the residences here, cordoned off." He grinned. "Doesn't stop people from going in though." At that, he turned and headed toward one side. Aiden and Noah exchanged glances before following after. "I talked to some of my more… adventurous classmates. They said they didn't find anything, but they left a window unlocked, just in case, for future dares." He stopped in front of a window that saw better days and pushed it up. Mia glanced around and pulled back.

"It's abandoned, but I don't think I want to go inside. I'll keep watch out here." She paused.

"You can't go inside, can you?" Aiden turned to her, furrowing a brow.

"You would notice." She cocked her head "You are correct. Most of these homes, I cannot enter." She didn't elaborate and it seemed Aiden didn't want to know any more, because he turned away.

Noah was still curious on why it was that she couldn't get into what was clearly an abandoned house. There wasn't even a for sale sign out front. It was as if the family just… left. So, why couldn't she get in? Was it because it wasn't for sale? Was it not fully abandoned? He wasn't sure how the process worked in regards to how ghosts are invited into or out of locations. He felt that maybe it was best not to ask for now. Mia had been very forthcoming with information as it was. He didn't want to push their luck.

Phen glanced between them, nodded and then pushed open the window as Mia trailed backward. He pulled himself inside. Aiden peeked in and frowned. "I feel like this is stupid. But here goes nothing."

Noah chuckled at that, lightly patting him on the back. "I'll be right behind you."

Aiden huffed, but didn't argue, pulling himself through. Noah did as he said, landing next to Aiden on a dust-covered floor.

"When did you say the first disappearance occurred?" Aiden glanced around the dimly lit room as Noah pulled out his phone, using the flashlight function to spread light over the dusty room.

"I never did." Phen walked around, confused. "But, well, a couple months ago now. Maybe about three? Still, it's surprisingly dusty, considering this is the room I was told others often came through."

"Dust does accumulate quickly." Aiden brushed a finger over one of the pieces of furniture. It was coated in a thick gray grime that almost clung to the skin. Noah twitched.

This place needed a good cleaning.

"This quickly?" Phen pulled out his phone, following in Noah's footsteps. Aiden brushed off the dust and stuffed his hands in his pockets.

"Either way, let's look around. Do you know which room belonged to the person who disappeared?"

"I think so, this way." Phen gestured and opened a door to the left with a faint creaking sound. The wood bent under the pressure as they walked out and into a long hallway. A stairwell was set to one side which spiraled up to a second floor. Phen took it.

The second floor was just as dusty and it made Noah's urge to clean heighten. He quickly suppressed it, reminding himself that there really wasn't any point to attempting to clean it.

Phen stopped in front of one room that had caution tape hanging uselessly to the sides. "Here it is. A few people have come inside, like I said, but they didn't find anything." Phen shrugged before pushing open the door. They stepped inside a room. It was probably a room for a girl, or a really girlish boy. It was hard to tell. The curtains were shut tight, casting the room in heavy shadow. None of them felt the need to turn the light on, not wanting to make their presence known considering they were trespassing. Aiden was staying between Noah and Phen, considering he didn't have a solid means to light his way.

Surprising, did he not think to bring a flashlight?

Aiden glanced over, probably noticing Noah's concern. He sighed and pulled his flashlight out, flicking it on. "I was trying to save the battery," he admitted. Noah could see why, it was a fairly powerful flashlight, stronger than their phones. When did Aiden grab it? When they were still home? Noah paused at that and groaned. Duh, it was when he was packing. He actually took time to pack while Noah sat and chatted with Mia.

Noah shook his head and the three of them split to examine the room. It was a fairly decent size with a bed, attached bathroom and a small closet.

It was also incredibly dusty.

Noah waved a hand, barely suppressing a sneeze as he pulled open the closet which was still filled with what were definitely girl's clothes.

"Want to give us some more details?" Aiden's voice caught Noah's attention as he noticed Aiden was kneeling, peeking under the bed, while Phen, as it was realized with him being the tallest of the three, was checking higher up.

"Don't have much more. Most of the disappearances were kept quiet to try to not scare the other people. I only know the basics of this one because it was the first." Phen glanced over. "Supposedly, it was some girl a little older than us. She went to bed and then, the next morning, she was gone. There was no sign of forced entry and the parents said she wasn't the type to just up and leave. It was brushed off until it happened to a man about a week later. After that? Well, don't really know much except where they took place."

Aiden nodded as Noah pulled away, frowning. There wasn't really anything that stood out. Other than the dust that clung to the air, he couldn't feel or see anything else.

"Nothing seems strange about this place." Aiden pushed himself to his feet, the flashlight passing briefly over the walls of the room. "If we have something to compare it to, it might help. Where is that second home?"

Phen perked up. "That would be about two houses down. You all set here?"

"For now." Aiden glanced around and Noah couldn't help but agree. There was no chill or odd feeling, there was nothing except the eerily quiet room and the faint sound of wind from outside. "I feel like we shouldn't stay in any place long."

Phen just glanced between them before nodding and heading out. Mia joined them briefly, but flitted away soon after once they arrived at the next location. The next place, Noah noticed, was similar to the first. To be honest, all of them were relatively similar so the fact that Phen knew which was which? Noah had to hand it to him. He did his research.

Slipping inside, they quickly found the room. In some ways, it was similar to the previous, almost undisturbed in a way that made it feel like no one lived there in a while, but made sure everything was tidy beforehand. Other than that, it was clear it was a guy's room from the clothes, to the books, games and posters.

Yet again, Noah and Aiden noticed that there was nothing inherently wrong. The dust sat heavy and thick and the silence dragged down at them, but nothing was out of place, odd or showed any indication of the person being taken by force. Aiden, after some time, suggested the idea of looking for scratch-marks, similar to the ones left behind at their home after that thing had attacked them the first time. While they didn't find anything in the rooms, they did occasionally find some outside the homes.

However, there was no set proof other than faint scratch marks near the windowsills of the respective rooms, hard to see with said rooms being on the second floor.

Noah glanced up at them, borrowing Aiden's light due to the gray overcast sky giving little illumination otherwise.

"Those look to be the same as what is in our place, like I thought," Aiden pointed out, getting an unnerved expression from Phen. Noah briefly noted that Mia was nowhere in sight and wondered where she disappeared too. He glanced around, but shoved the thought off. Of course she would be wandering, especially since she couldn't get into most houses. She was probably close by and would join up later.

"How did those scratch marks even get on the second floor?"

Aiden shook his head as Noah handed the flashlight back. "No idea. We know ghost-possessed humans are able to do things completely unnatural to normal humans, but this is utterly ridiculous."

Noah glanced back up before turning to Phen and Aiden. "But it also means that it's the same person that's after us. I guess you were right, Aiden." He shuddered. "Which means he's been around and possessed for a while now."

"So it probably is just one person." Aiden frowned before turning to Phen. "Next?"

Phen blinked and then pulled up his phone, tapping away for a moment before turning. "This way."

For the next while, they went house to house, sneaking in through open windows or just observing from outside. Mia would join them every so often before disappearing, easing Noah's worries a little. All the locations were the same, beds made, curtains closed and scratchmarks outside the windows.

Noah felt the hints of frustration, but Phen was definitely taking it the hardest, almost cursing. Aiden's expression turned neutral, if thoughtful.

"So, there is no actual rhyme or reason to the disappearances." Aiden leaned against the wall of the most recent house they checked in, the darkness of the sky dragging on to approaching night. "Male, female, old, young, it didn't matter much. The only similarity is that most of them were in this district."

Phen paced to one side, tapping at his phone. "Exactly! It makes no sense. We have a few more houses to check, but some are in other areas of town and the residents still live nearby, so they might question us if we do what we're doing now."

"What about that house we were near yesterday?" Noah glanced over. "When we were following Fiona?"

Phen paused and turned. "That's the thing, that's not one of the locations that a disappearance took place in. The person moved out, but that's it. It's not on the list or anything."

Aiden thrummed a finger against his lips, frowning. "It's getting late, we'll check it out tomorrow. Now that we know the general layout of where those others were taken, we might get an idea of what to—"

"But if we keep pushing it off, then we'll never find him!" Phen cut in, swinging around. "You said you felt something at that place, right? Yet you haven't felt anything at all at these other locations. Then why don't we check it out? We should have enough time to look through one more house."

"No." Aiden glared. "You and I both know it might take too much time. Plus, what would happen if it is his place? We would be walking right to him while he has strength."

"That's why I say, do it now. He's getting more powerful by the day. Who's to say he won't start being able to do this stuff during the day? If he hasn't already, like with Lynn?"

Aiden frowned, annoyance and frustration clear on his face, at least to Noah.

Noah honestly wasn't sure what to do. He agreed with both of them. He wanted to ask Mia, but the ghost was gone, out scouting again.

He desperately wanted to know what happened to Dad, but the chills he got from being near that house made him want to run the other way. He pulled out his phone, noting the battery was running low. It was late, almost seven o'clock. Though it was hard to tell in the dim light. Being early fall, the days were getting shorter just the slightest bit and, with how rainy this place tended to be, it was hard to figure out when sunset was.

He was grateful to notice there was no new text.

"Let's try it." Noah glanced up, noticing as Aiden stiffened. "Like Phen said, it's one house that isn't even that big. It's not a mansion or anything. We'll be in, out, and back at Phen's place quick enough."

"Noah!"

"Aiden, we NEED information. I can't stand not knowing what's going on with Dad and I'm not stupid enough to call Dad's number just to figure out who has the phone. If anything, you would think the police would have tracked him down, but they haven't! They haven't even contacted us since we gave them our number. We've learned nothing today except confirming what we already knew."

Aiden's expression was aggravated. "You and Phen are going to do it anyway, aren't you?"

Noah glanced away, not denying the idea.

"Aiden, I get your concern, but it won't take long," Phen pointed out.

There was a long silence followed by footsteps. "Whatever." Aiden headed toward the house, moving a bit ahead of them, startling both.

Noah watched for a moment before stepping even with him, only to flinch back at Aiden's stormy expression.

"Aiden, I promise it'll be quick and then we'll head back," Noah quietly spoke. Aiden's tense shoulders relaxed slightly.

"I get it. Believe me," Aiden muttered. "But…" He trailed off, not saying anything else.

CHAPTER 25

They headed toward the house in silence, a faint wind blowing through the streets. Noah glanced up as the soft sound of footsteps echoed nearby. He turned to see Mia glide over, amused. "I thought we were done." She paused, spotting something in Aiden's posture. She straightened, her entire mood shifting. "Ah," was all she said before slowly floating over toward Aiden, hovering around him.

"Ah?" Phen asked, confused.

Mia turned back to him, or, well, her neck did, her body continued to face forward. "Ah, as in, it obvious you've decided to do something probably stupid."

"You got that just from Aiden's expression?" Noah blinked, noticing Aiden glance sidelong toward Mia before quickly turning away.

"Uh, yes? It's easy to see when he's in a disgruntled, 'you guys are idiots', mood… and so far, in the little time I've known you three, he's usually right."

Phen clearly went to argue, only to pause. Noah didn't bother.

"They want to check out the house we felt a chill from the other day. Instead of going back to Phen's place and checking tomorrow when it's not almost night."

"Oh." Mia swirled around, neck snapping back into place. "Yeah, I see the issue there." She grinned, and Noah noticed the way Phen flinched. "Let's hope you two are right, and not this one." She lightly emulated tapping on Aiden's head.

Noah didn't miss the way Aiden twitched at that.

Phen shrugged as they stepped up toward the house in question. "We need information, and we haven't gotten a thing so far and, from your lack of reaction, you haven't felt him nearby, so we should be fine."

Mia hovered around Aiden for a moment before drifting away, turning to Aiden and Noah. "If there is trouble, just use your father's little gift. Though it won't do much good for Phen here." At that, she pulled back more. "I'll keep watch outside."

She vanished.

Noah kind of wished she would show him how she did that, but he shook it off, turning back to the building. They stayed on the far side, so as not to be in line of sight of Ms. Fiona's home. As a result, they were looking at the back side of the location. It was a two story like most of the others, nothing fancy, but not the smallest place either. All the windows were dark or curtained, and the back door, like with most of the houses, was barred shut.

"Have you heard anything else about this place?" Aiden cut in, tone icy.

Phen turned, hesitant. Noah wondered if he might be regretting pissing off Aiden. "Not much. Like I said, it's just another abandoned home on the street. But it wasn't part of the disappearances, so no one really bothered to check inside." He shook his head.

Aiden let out a breath. "Well, let's find a way in. The sooner we're in, the sooner we're out." At that, he stepped forward, over the curling and slightly longer grass. The paint was already worn from age, Noah noticed, and there was a set of metal doors at an angle that probably led to some sort of cellar. It was secured shut with an iron latch that was slightly rusted from all the rain, but very much still durable. He shuddered. Great, this house had a basement. He knew enough about the occult to know that was the place of nightmares. No, it was fine, this chill was probably just from the growing night.

They split up, searching for a way in. It was Phen who found it, a window that was slightly out of its frame enough that they could jimmy the lock.

Noah had to admit, he felt bad, trespassing like this, but that feeling was fading as he thought about his father and about the texts.

He was not going to let this creep get Aiden, or himself. If that meant breaking and entering? Well, then, he would deal with the consequences later.

Noah and Phen pried at the window as Aiden watched, occasionally glancing around. Eventually, the lock clicked and they pushed the window open. The chill Noah felt earlier, which he was somewhat ignoring, thinking it was because of the colder night air, shot up. Aiden took a step back, now much more hesitant. Phen was the only one who didn't react. He shoved the window up, making sure it stayed open.

"Ready?" Phen peered to them and paused. "Hey, guys, you okay?"

"No," Aiden muttered as Noah hesitated.

"I'm not sure." Noah took a deep breath and let it out. "But, let's go." He pulled himself through, feeling the need to run the other direction. Phen scrambled through right after with Aiden hesitantly crawling through a moment behind.

Noah barely paid much attention to it as he peered around. Mia hovered outside near the window, a strange expression on her face, head cocked.

A faint glow illuminated the otherwise dimly lit room as Aiden hopped in, shining his flashlight over the surroundings. The powerful beam cut over tables slightly out of place at strange angles that wouldn't have been noticed from outside. The chill in the air grew to the point that Noah shuddered almost without stop.

Phen glanced around and frowned. "Okay, yeah, this place is kind of creepy." He shook his head and walked forward, heading toward the nearest doorway. Aiden rubbed his arm, staying near the window as the beam of light cut across the gray and white of clothes and furniture. It was in a similar state of abandonment from the other surrounding locations, but something just felt… off in a way that Noah couldn't put a finger on.

Phen tried the door and, after a moment, swung it open. The hallway was dimly lit by the few pieces of light peeking through the heavily curtained windows and the stark beams from their flashlight and phones. Noah stiffened as Aiden's flashlight skittered over the walls.

"Oh… I think we found something, at least."

Phen glanced over his shoulder, having moved cautiously a little down the hall. He followed Noah's gaze, along with Aiden, before a resolute expression crossed his face. "Good, so I was right." He turned and started to march down the hall. "We're going to find something here, if those scratch marks INSIDE the building are any indication."

"Idiot." Aiden glared, but hurried after, with Noah keeping pace. The silence was eerie, only interrupted by their muffled footsteps and quiet breathing. A faint wind rattled the windows from outside, which did nothing to aid in the feeling of wrongness.

Doors lined the hall on the right, opposite the three or so windows that faced out toward a side street. Though Noah only knew that because Aiden, using his flashlight, pushed a curtain out of the way. Noah didn't miss Mia floating a few feet away, watching their progress quietly. She nodded and flitted forward as Aiden dropped the curtain back into place.

Meanwhile, Phen started opening the doors, taking his time glancing through rooms before moving on, closing the doors behind him.

With the other homes, they knew where to go generally, but here, they were stumbling around.

"Let's check upstairs, like with the other homes." Phen closed the final door and turned to them.

A faint creaking groan echoed through the house, making all three jump.

While Noah was always fascinated in the supernatural, horror was a different beast. He took a deep breath, trying to calm himself.

"It was just the house settling," Aiden muttered, though it wasn't hard to tell he was saying it to calm himself more than anything else.

Phen glanced around and nodded. "Come on." They headed around the corner into the interior of the home. To the left was the front door, sealed closed with a wooden beam that was nailed in. To the right was a stairwell that led up to the second floor and, past the stairs, was another hallway that appeared to lead into what was probably a living room. It was hard to see in the dim light.

Noah could have sworn he saw something flicker upstairs, but when he glanced up, there was nothing there, just a dim line of light from an upstairs curtained window.

"Let's not go up there," Aiden said, his voice slightly shaken.

"What? You want to go in the basement?" Phen frowned, turning to them. "That's the last place I want to check, you know that's where all the creepy shit is."

"I'm with Aiden." Noah started walking past the stairs toward the back living room. "Let's just finish this and go." He was already starting to regret coming in, feeling that anxiety churning in his stomach. Aiden joined him and, after a moment, Phen followed, letting out a groan. Aiden's light flashed over the walls of the living room and then the dining room, followed by the kitchen. All of them were immaculate, except for the layer of dust. Strangely, Noah didn't notice any cobwebs, as if even spiders avoided the place. Though that idea was ridiculous even to him.

That feeling of wrongness still clung to his skin as they stepped away from the last room, the back door sealed shut just like the front. To their right was a set of stairs into the basement, placed below the stairs leading up to the second floor. Phen looked hesitant, but nodded, heading quickly down the steps. Aiden and Noah exchanged glances before following.

"I still think we should just leave." Aiden kept his voice low and, though Noah was starting to agree, he didn't want to admit it. Aiden didn't have to be right all the time. Maybe he was just being paranoid.

The steps creaked and groaned as they descended. Phen reached around, finding a switch. To Noah's surprise, the lights turned on, dim, but visible, revealing the basement in all of its messy glory.

"Huh, the lights work?" Phen glanced over. "I figured power would have been cut since it's, well, abandoned."

"I guess not." Noah peered around as Aiden pursed his lips, even more tense.

"Or it's not as abandoned as we thought." He shook his head. "You better hope that thing isn't here."

"It's fine!" Phen called, quickly heading down the stairs. The room was cluttered with boxes from floor to ceiling. It was almost like a maze. Dust filled the air, making Noah want to sneeze.

Noah shuddered as a creak echoed from above. A moment later, a slight whining sound filled the air, followed by a clunk. Aiden whipped around, staring up the stairs as Noah slowly turned his head, following Aiden's gaze.

The basement door had shut behind them.

"You were saying?" Phen gulped.

There was no reply, Noah couldn't even find a voice to say anything.

"Okay, that's it, we're leaving." Aiden hurried up the stairs, pushing the door open. Noah let out a breath of relief, glad it wasn't locked.

"Wait! We need to check upstairs, there has to be something!" Phen rushed past Noah, leaving him partially on the stairwell, alone. Noah quickly remedied that, joining the others only a second later.

Phen caught Aiden's wrist, stopping him from bolting toward the exit leading outside. "Please, Aiden, it's just a house. You said yourself, it's old and probably settling. Plus, most terrible things happen in basements, we should be fine now, right?"

Aiden pursed his lips, wrenching his arm free. "I'm staying downstairs, you and Noah can go up if you want, I'm not stepping FOOT up there."

Phen sighed, before nodding. "Alright." Aiden blinked as Noah let out a relieved breath. Only to almost swallow it as the sound of multiple creaking doors caught his attention. The other two stiffened before Phen let out a weak laugh. "Probably just the wind."

Noah tried to steady his nerves, quickly hurrying past, heading toward the hallway that lead upstairs. "Yeah, let's go with that. Maybe we're just being paranoi—" His words caught in his throat as he stared down the shadowed hallway.

Phen came around the corner right behind him, phone light beaming over the doorways. "Uh, I didn't accidentally leave a door open, right?"

"No, no, you didn't." Noah breathed, that cold shooting downward, almost making his breath visible.

All the doors in the hall were open just a little, as if a faint wind pushed against them.

Yet, there was not even a breeze through the house.

"That's not good," Aiden muttered. "There's not really a ventilation system in here which would cause that."

Noah glanced sidelong to Aiden, noting he was growing pale, probably similar to his own countenance.

"Okay, yeah. I think I'm starting to feel a little off about all of this too." Phen gulped. "Let's… I know I said we should check upstairs, but now I think we should just get out of here."

"Get out of here?" a voice whispered quietly, almost into Noah's ear.

"Aiden, knock it off." Noah glanced toward Aiden. Aiden wasn't looking at him. He squeezed his eyes shut, both arms wrapped over his chest as powerful shudders ran through him. Noah couldn't help but feel like there was ice in his lungs, both at the sight and at the feeling suddenly gripping at his chest in dawning realization.

"Noah, no one—" Phen turned, light almost blinding Noah for a second. Phen froze, all color draining from his face.

"No one…" A voice whispered once more, this time feminine.

"Oh." Noah's voice climbed up a few notches as Aiden slowly started shifting toward the windows. Phen was completely stock still in front of him.

"No one. No one. No one." More whispers filled the room. Voices mingling, converging, overlapping.

Aiden grabbed Noah's hand and bolted, tugging him along. Noah jerked, turning in time to notice as Phen whipped around, startled at their sudden move. "Phen!"

Phen shook his head, stumbling after them when a figure shifted in front of him, finally visible in the phone's light. It was opaque with hard to define features, almost twisted.

"No one."

"Aiden!" Noah called, noting the utter fear and panic as Phen bolted the only way he could, up the stairs, away from the thing. "Phen! He's—"

"It's his own darn fault," Aiden snarled. "We need to go."

"You're just going to leave—"

"No, we're talking to Mia and finding a way back in once we know what the HELL is going on."

A figure drifted in front, hands reaching before recoiling back. Aiden darted around, down the hall with the now partially open doors where those creatures curled out, reaching through and towards them. Their words intermingled in a cacophony of voices.

"No one. No one. No one."

The echoes rang around the room as the twins raced toward the window that was thankfully still open, Mia hovering outside.

Aiden gestured, glancing over his shoulder for Noah to go through. The sound of screeching was what incentivized him. As soon as he was through, he turned as Aiden gestured. "Give me the cross Dad gave you."

"What?"

"No time, hurry."

Noah scrambled to take it off as Mia floated near him, tension ringing through her body.

Aiden grabbed it, turned and bolted back the way he came.

Noah recoiled as something slammed against where the window should be, as if there was an invisible barrier in place. Staring straight at Noah was a figure with wild eyes and blood seeping from multiple wounds, but there was no actual blood. Noah stumbled back as Mia fluttered in front of him.

"I thought so. That home… it's a prison."

Mia's words caused Noah to stiffen. Prison? And now Aiden and Phen were in there?

"Don't you dare think of going back in now. You would be at the mercy of those trapped within. You take one step, and they will be on you instantly." Mia drifted closer, curling around him almost protectively. "It's taking all of my will not to touch you right now, to take some of that life you hold, but that is something to worry about later." Her gaze shifted. "Let's just hope your brother gets to your friend in time, or we will have a mess on our hands."

Noah nodded, tongue stuck to the roof of his mouth as the figure continued to stare, a few more piling on top, hands pressed against a window that was no longer there.

CHAPTER 26

Aiden mentally cursed as he darted back down the hall. The ghosts, that's the only thing they could be, reached forward, their voices howling for attention.

They knew he was here, and he knew they were there, they weren't holding back.

But how could there be so many? He turned down the hall as another recoiled from him, the cross swinging in his tightened grip. This was god damn stupid, but it was the first thing that came to mind. If he could get this on Phen, there might be a way out. He knew Noah would be safe with their resident ghost friend, at least for a short period. That Ghost respected Noah, which was the only thing he could cling to in this mess.

"No one…" The voice coiled over him as he spun, darting up the stairs, almost tripping as one tried to get in his way. "No one, no one, no one!"

He shuddered violently, Phen OWED him if they got out of this. Gosh darn it. His gaze flitted around, his flashlight flickering wildly through the frosted air. Three doorways were partially open, leading to multiple rooms, he could hear the muttering and cries. He spotted something on the ground and jerked toward the door on the left. He quickly scooped up the dropped phone, recognizing it as Phen's and hurried inside, slamming the door behind him as another one of those things came up behind. He felt it was useless, but it might give him a moment to breathe.

He quickly looked around, taking in the room. It appeared ordinary in every respect. It was a bedroom with a bookcase on one side, books spattered over the floor.

Then he heard the whimpers and cries.

Sobs filled the air followed by screams.

"Let me go!"

"Stop, please."

"Don't hurt me—"

"Momma!"

"No! No. NO. NO!"

None of the voices were Phen's. Aiden saw a flash of a girl struggling as if trying to get away from something before she stilled, collapsing.

A boy who was curled up in the corner, gashes appearing more and more on his skin.

An older man, terrified behind a pole of the bed.

A young girl in the air, reaching desperately down as she held at something around her neck as if hanging from the chandelier.

A woman screaming as if struggling against bonds as tears trailed down her face.

All of them snapped toward him, four sets of glowing orbs and one that was just a black expanse of nothing pierced him in silence. The sounds stopping, frozen in the state they were when—He tried hard not to stop.

Though, he made sure to memorize each of their faces.

Not a single one was Dad. For a brief moment, utter relief shredded through him, followed by that increased anxiety.

These… these were—

He pushed the thought off, desperate to keep his mind steady as he walked through the room. Large as it was, it felt so confining, he couldn't breathe. The bookcase was shifted, the books having collapsed in heaps on the ground, clearly having been left there a long time. The eyes, both visible and not, followed him, but didn't move closer as he hurried into what appeared to be a room hidden behind the shelf. He quickened his pace, that ever present feeling of being watched clinging to him. He opened the door, noting that the room was still.

Though the room itself…

He took deep steadying breaths as the smell of decay and rot wafted toward him, mingled with the stale smell of urine and blood. Chains lay to one side, securely in the wall. There was fabric around the room, clearly making it sound-proof. He shuddered once more, stepping inside, gaze snapping from place to place. The sounds quieted, the house returning to its faint creaking, but he could still feel attention on him, watching, waiting. "Phen." He hissed. "Get out here, now."

The room here felt warmer, but not in a way that settled his nerves.

He heard movement and darted over, hearing a terrified cry from within the small pile of blankets and other things shoved to the side, stained in ways he didn't want to imagine.

"It's me." Aiden glanced over his shoulder. "Here, put this on. We need to go."

Phen cautiously poked his head out, blonde hair a tangled mess. "It was so close," he whispered, terrified. "They touched me, it felt like my skin was burning." Trembling hands reached out before he stiffened. His hands darted to his head and he trembled. "No… no, I don't want it. I do want it. Help!"

Aiden grabbed Phen by the shirt, pulling him up and shoved the cross over his neck, snapping it in place. "Here, it's yours."

Phen stiffened for a solid minute, mouth open in a strange twisted shock before he suddenly writhed. Aiden jumped, almost letting go as Phen grabbed at his wrists, holding tightly.

A second later, something shot away, screeching.

A boy of pale skin and eyes, screamed, "I almost had him! I almost bonded with him! Let me out!" He screeched, scrabbling forward, fingers clawing inches from Phen's face, but not moving any closer.

Phen stared up, frozen in absolute terror. "If I just had one more minute, I could leave this place!"

"Come on, let's go." Aiden grasped Phen's hand. "I don't know how long these neckla—" At that word, he heard a faint crack and glanced down, tugging out his own. Part of the cross splintered away, crumbling to the ground.

That was probably not a good sign.

The air shifted and his breath caught in his throat as the boy's attention snapped to him, before his head twisted almost ninety degrees. "You… You can let us out."

Hands clawed forward, reaching, grasping. Aiden glared before roughly pulling Phen to his feet. "We'll figure that out later." With that, taking one last snapshot of a room that was more fit for a solitary cell, he darted away. Phen stumbled after him, not saying a word, tears trailing down his face.

The ghosts drifted closer, gazes piercing him from all sides as he fled out the door into the bedroom.

"Save us." The boy from before shot in front of him, the others creating a horseshoe around them, blocking the path. "Let us leave. We just want to flee from this place."

Aiden took a tentative step back. With his cross starting to break, he wasn't sure how it would react now. "I have no means of doing that."

"You do." The woman who had been sobbing spoke up, head snapping toward him at an angle that wasn't right. "Just let us hold you, touch you, and we will be free of this place."

"And possess me again?" Phen yelped, holding Aiden's arm tightly. "Are you all insa—am I insane for talking to ghosts?"

At that, all of them hissed, the whole place darkening, the thick curtains slamming shut, extinguishing all light in the room as Aiden's flashlight dimmed and died. There was a faint glow throughout the room, not enough to see, but present. A breath washed over Aiden's face as a voice hissed. "If you do not help us, we will do so by force." He felt the air twist, everything in him screamed in sudden panic.

He felt a tug on his arm and found himself stumbling forward through the darkness. Aiden quickly pulled out Phen's phone, flicking it on. The meager light gave them enough sight to find the door, along with flashes of twisted figures, a woman whose hands were reaching and bloody, a girl whose neck was twisted in a way that made no sense, a young man whose eyes were red-rimmed and empty, weeping.

The boy, who flashed in front of them once more with his mouth wide, wider than anything possibly could be, as Phen raced past, pulling Aiden along.

Aiden almost tripped as they darted into the main hallway and down the stairs, sounds clanging in the air as desperate screams filled the house, reverberating off the wood and glass. A loud echoing SLAM reached his ears in the direction of where they were going. He heard another faint crack and his body thrummed, blood pounding in his ears, almost muffling the sounds. His legs burned and ached as they almost tripped down the stairs, barely illuminated as it was. The hallway was blocked by a man, the man from upstairs and the girl. Both stood side by side, twitching.

"Let us leave." They spoke almost in unison. "Let. Us. LEAVE!"

Phen's hand grasped the cross around his neck, already cracking and breaking. He thrust it forward, causing the two to hiss, retreating backward. Aiden felt something snap as they darted past.

"Child, give us power. Give us freedom!"

Aiden didn't look back, feeling the necklace crumble to the ground, his foot crushing down on it by accident as they flung the final door open and Phen practically threw Aiden forward into the room they started in only a little while before. Aiden stumbled as Phen turned. The ghosts were reaching through the doorway, attention glued on Aiden, but blocked briefly by Phen's form.

"Aiden!" Noah stumbled forward, hands pressing on the glass of a window that Aiden KNEW wasn't closed before. The frame was cracked, as if it had been slammed shut by force. A figure shot up through the floor, the boy from before. Aiden stumbled back, almost bumping into Phen as a wide smile crossed the boy's face that split it in a way that was NOT friendly.

"That pesky thing is destroyed, now help us." He stepped forward, the sound of the footstep ringing loudly in Aiden's ears as gurgling and groaning caught his attention. Aiden found himself taking another step back, almost pressing against Phen's back. "Give it to me. Your power. Give it!"

Aiden's attention shot toward Noah who was standing outside, something in his hands. He swung at the window, the glass shattering into the room. The spirit turned just as Noah reached through, unlocking the window that had very much been opened before. There was a dark and familiar hand resting on his shoulder as Noah shouted, "Mia! Help them!"

"On it." Another voice rang through the room and the boy stiffened as the air grew cold once more. "Oh, child, you are much too young for this." Their Ghostly comrade swooped forward into the room, curling around Aiden and Phen in the process, in a way that was not feasibly human. "You've become so twisted. This child's power will not help you, not alone and not at this stage. Let them leave."

The boy glared, though it was hesitant. "Why is one such as you protecting him? Why not just take his power?"

"That is NOT for me to answer, child." Their ally hissed, causing Aiden and the boy to stiffen. "This one is under MY protection. Now, do NOT anger me, let these two leave."

The boy glared and went to argue, only for the temperature of the room to drop in a way Aiden never felt before. The Ghost's form once more became soaked as she twitched, almost in a staticky way.

Aiden briefly noted the way Phen stared in horror, almost backing away from both of them into a corner.

The boy recoiled, trembling. There was a twisted terror on his face as a cracking sound echoed from the Ghost, followed by the spatter of drops of water on wood, strangely loud.

The boy nodded, trembling before gesturing to the others that must have followed. With a flash, he disappeared and the house settled.

Aiden felt himself collapse, trembling. Noah let out a breath, shoving the broken frame up before pulling himself inside. He stepped up to Aiden as a thump sounded from behind.

"Holy… That was—What the hell was that?" Phen's shaken voice sky-rocketed in panic. "What the hell did you do? What was that at the end?"

"Now is not the time. They are subdued for a moment, but it won't last long." The Ghost continued to curl around Aiden, almost like she was actually shielding him. "We must leave. Now."

Aiden stared at her, not sure how to feel, but nodded, letting Noah tug him to his feet, though his legs felt like jelly.

They managed to pull themselves through the window and, without really thinking about it, headed back to Phen's place. None of them said a word, the darkness of the growing night not helping their shattered nerves.

CHAPTER 27

They arrived back to Phen's. Ellen snapped the door open, ready to berate them, only to stop. She must have seen something about the way they held themselves. That annoyance turned to panic as she ushered them in, quickly checking to make sure Phen was okay. She threw so many questions around, no one really knew how to answer her. Eventually, she gave them some food, a warm bowl of stew, before having them take a bath. Once she was sure they were all okay, much to Noah's insistence being one of the few actually able to talk at the moment, she gave Phen a hug, startling him, before locking the door and heading upstairs. Phen watched her go, a distant look in his gaze as they settled into the living room, curling into the many blankets she pulled out for them.

The Ghost finally pulled away from Aiden, settling down to one side.

"What happened?" Noah finally asked. "We could hear sounds coming from inside and then Mia mentioned the house was almost groaning in pain, but…"

Aiden hesitated, but it was Phen who spoke. "Horrible," he said after a moment. "I thought I had gotten away. I felt searing pain for a second, but managed to pull away from something and found a room to hide in. It was when Aiden found me that, well…"

"He had been possessed." Aiden finally spoke up, he cleared his throat as he noticed his voice pitch up slightly. "I had to practically toss the cross on him."

"Oh, we are quite lucky then." The Ghost's voice was surprisingly soft. "Most likely, you were fighting it the whole time. I thought as much." She shook her head, eye gleaming in the dim light of the room. "If Aiden hadn't gotten that cross on you in time, we would be dealing with two ghost-possessed humans and that would not be good for anyone."

"What was going on with those ghosts?" Noah muttered. "Some of them were see-through."

"Those weren't the ghosts." The Ghost gestured. "Those were fragments, shattered memories of the real ghosts, which was why they could simply imitate. Their desperation to leave made them manifest and Aiden's abilities made them strong enough to leave their bound location and come down."

"The cross," Aiden muttered.

The Ghost's smile turned creepy. "Yes?" she asked, a slight lilt to her tone.

"It shattered." Phen glanced over, saying it for Aiden. He pulled out his, taking it off before handing it back to Noah. "This one is still somewhat intact, it's a little broken, but it's better than nothing."

Noah tentatively took it before turning up to the Ghost. "How?"

The Ghost hummed. "Those ghosts were desperate, the souls literally battering against the crosses themselves. With both of you having gotten so close to such shattered souls, the cross could only take so much." She tilted, a faint cracking echoing through the room. "Emotion is a powerful thing, after all, especially for spirits such as ourselves. A swarm of emotions, directed toward one place? Well, not much can handle that over long periods of time." She sighed. "And, to be honest, my presence probably hasn't helped. I'm able to restrain myself, but my being around you two has slowly deteriorated the crosses. I thought it was not something to worry about, but, well, you can clearly see that probably wasn't the case."

"That's why Aiden's shattered first." Noah blinked, pale. "You're usually around him."

The Ghost actually winced at that.

"So, you're the reason that ghost almost got to me." Aiden shuddered, still remembering the burning gaze. His attention snapped to Noah, where he glared, realization dawning on him. Aiden didn't have to say anything, Noah seemed to understand because he winced.

"I didn't think things would turn out like this when I first spoke to her," he admitted softly. "I'm sorry, Aiden."

"Do not be angry with Noah." The Ghost let out a breath, arms crossed under her chin, expression solemn. "If anything, he helped save your life."

Aiden nodded, realizing that, fingers curling up against his chest, tugging at the clothes.

"How did—what happened back there?" Phen asked quietly. "We were still stuck in the house and somehow the window we came through was closed, what—"

"They closed and locked it." The Ghost's attention drifted to Phen. "Many ghosts have the ability to affect their surroundings and, as I said, that place was a prison, for living and dead souls." She shook her head as Aiden swallowed, feeling a little sick. Noah seemed just as ill, face pale. "Noah here smashed the window and unlocked it, which was enough to allow me entry, though I was still somewhat weakened." She gestured. "As for what happened after? I do believe it might have been startling for you, but it was MUCH worse for that boy." A faint grin crossed her face, almost sinister. Phen shuddered. "While these two see my true image, you, Phen, see the projected." She tilted her head more. "The ghostly influence, the expression of the soul. My form is very much my own, but the way it can appear to others? Well, let's just say the mind has a way to perceive things when it can't understand it and ghosts utilize it to affect the mind."

"Oh…" Phen's voice was weak.

"So, what, you frightened him?" Noah blinked, confused. "How can a ghost be frightened?"

"Ghosts were once human." The Ghost's voice softened. "The image I projected was one that would spark the fears they hold, which is powerful and plentiful to those like them."

Aiden looked away. He was sick of hearing of all of this. He found himself curling up on the couch, pressing into the arm. He didn't want to hear anymore, but he also felt like his tongue was stuck to the roof of his mouth, unable to say anything.

"So, what would have happened if you hadn't… if the window wasn't shattered?" Phen asked, voice wavering.

"The ghosts in there? They would have used you until all of them were free from that place. For Phen, they would have simply possessed him to obtain a new body. For Aiden?" She turned, eye almost glowing in the evening light. "In your state, at your level of ability, even with all of that power, they would have drained you until you were a husk… It would have killed you."

Aiden felt his whole body stiffen as Noah shot to his feet. "What?" The strangled cry just barely managed to stay quiet.

The Ghost nodded. "He's powerful, as are you, but neither of you are able to control it. Sure, someday, you would be able to help their spirits pass on, but as you are now? They would just take from you and leave nothing."

Aiden found himself crossing his arms over his chest, fingers digging into skin. He couldn't be more curled in if he tried. Silence filled the room as the realization of what just happened settled over all of them.

"Shit. I screwed up." Phen's voice came out choked. "I thought everything would be fine. I'm… I'm sorry."

Aiden didn't have anything to say, he just slowly let out a breath before turning back to the Ghost. "How DID you save me? I get what you told Phen, but it was still a ghost, I doubt intimidation alone works." The Ghost tilted her head. "All you did was talk, but then you mentioned subdued…"

"Smart as always." She slowly grinned, flipping upside down. Her long hair fell past, half of her face still obscured by pieces of hair that clung on. "I've been a ghost a long time, a very long time. The longer we exist, the more powerful we are, at least, those who retain their obsession and form. Let's just say, those were young ones. My presence alone was enough to quiet them, at least briefly."

"So that's why he flinched from you." Aiden was trying to keep himself talking so as not to delve into the other topics running through his head. "And, well, it makes sense. There were six spirits in there." He turned to the other two. "And six disappearances, not counting Lynn, the prior detective and our father."

At that, both of them stiffened as horrified realization settled on their faces.

"But I didn't see a body!" Phen struggled.

"Spirits are trapped to where they die, not where their body is." The Ghost spoke up, voice wan. "Only a few have the privilege of being where they are buried."

Noah shivered as Aiden tilted his head down, thoughts racing. "So, they were captured and killed up there, and then dragged out and brought someplace else so no one would realize. Yet, that house is said to be abandoned." Aiden shook his head. "The room I found Phen in was probably a room to hide someone, it was small and held only the basics."

"Probable," the Ghost said. "With that many souls in one place, they probably spread throughout the second floor, though their room of origin was that room."

Phen convulsed at that, pulling his legs up. "Oh… oh god," was all he said.

"So, why did Lynn not end up there?" Aiden found himself muttering in thought.

"It was because I was waiting outside." Phen's voice was faint. "If the killer tried to come through the door, I would have noticed. Lynn said she was getting too close. Being part of the occult, she might have actually interacted with the others who were—" He snapped his mouth shut.

Once more, silence fell over the group.

"This is a lot to think about." Noah finally spoke up, voice wavering.

"What you three should do is get some sleep," the Ghost said, floating upward. "I'll keep watch tonight, but I do not believe there will be any major issues." Her gaze drifted over the three. "Discuss this tomorrow, once you all have your heads on straight." Her gaze lingered briefly on Phen, catching Aiden's attention. With that, she disappeared, only a faint brush of a breeze indicating she was still there.

Aiden shook his head and felt himself slump into the seat, suddenly exhausted. It was late as it was and he felt drained.

Footsteps echoed before something settled next to him. He glanced over as Noah plopped down beside him, pushing into his side. "I'm glad you're alright. Don't do that again, though, okay?"

Aiden didn't say anything, but he did find himself leaning against Noah. "Maybe listen to me next time?"

"Pft, you know I won't." Noah's voice was light and joking, something Aiden appreciated.

The couch shifted and Aiden turned as Phen stood up. His attention was anywhere but at the two of them, arms crossed tightly, his whole body shaking. Concern flared through Aiden as he noticed the boys tense posture, the tears at the corner of his eyes as he spoke. "Thank you for helping me back there." Phen's voice cracked slightly. "If you hadn't come, I don't know what would have happened. Yet…"

"Are you sure you're okay?" Noah asked, leaning around Aiden. "That was a lot."

A weak smile curled upward, though Aiden still couldn't see the rest of his expression. "I need some time to think, especially since I almost…" His gaze met Aiden's and he shuddered before hurrying away, footsteps ringing on the stairwell. Aiden watched him go and sighed.

"Aiden?"

Aiden shifted, noticing that Noah's weight felt a bit heavier against his side. "Hm?"

"Thank you for, well… I'm glad you are alright." Noah tilted his head down, pressing into his neck. "I think Phen feels the same and yet, I'm a bit worried."

"Because he didn't stay here? Like he has every night?"

"Kind of… yes." Noah let out a breath, curling inward. "I hope he's okay. He was almost possessed. I wonder if everything that happened is weighing on him. I know if I almost…" He shook his head. "I probably would have fled as well. I know I should be mad at him, but he's only been good to us since coming here, so I can't find myself hating him. So, well, I'm worried."

Aiden had nothing to say to that, though he found himself slowly uncurling on the couch.

"On top of that, seeing Phen walk away like that, seeing those specters or whatever and hearing what Mia had to say, I can't help but feel scared," he finally admitted, only startling Aiden slightly. "I'm scared of what might be happening to Dad as we speak, if he's safe… And it makes me think of Mom. Of where she might be right now. Is she dealing with this too?"

Aiden pursed his lips as Noah shook. "I could feel it, even from outside. That chill that made me want to run, screaming, and then you were there and Phen was there and all those THINGS were there—" he shuddered. "I'm sorry, Aiden. I should have listened—"

"I'll cut you off there." Aiden lightly pushed against Noah, startling him. "I'm not going to say it wasn't dumb, but information is information, and we can't change what happened." Or affect the past like with Mom. He shook his head, pulling himself to his feet, startling Noah. "I know one thing, though. Dad was NOT there." He smiled faintly as Noah blinked before a relieved, but weak grin blossomed. "For now, I'm tired and desperately need some sleep." Aiden paused, plopping down on the couch across from Noah. "We'll check on that idiot in the morning. For now, get some sleep." Aiden fell over, curling into the couch as he pulled a blanket over himself.

Noah blinked before letting out a faint laugh. "Alright. I think I can agree to that."

Aiden relaxed, relieved. There was a lot to think about and worry about, but for now he was just grateful everyone HERE was alright. He heard a sound like a thud and a quiet amused huff. "Good night, Aiden."

"Good night, Noah." Aiden curled tighter into the sheets. His mind was racing, but the exhaustion of everything that happened pulled him into a tired slumber.

CHAPTER 28

Noah didn't sleep well that night, images racing through his head. Aiden's terrified face was foremost in his mind as Noah was forced to stay outside, unable to do a thing.

He barely knew Mia, but he had to trust her to save his brother, but now… Now what were they going to do? What evidence did they have? Was any of that worth it?

No. He didn't think it was, even if there was a sense of relief that Dad wasn't there.

Movement caught his attention and he blearily sat up, noting Aiden was already awake, rubbing the sleep away. He at least rested, somewhat, which was good. Noah would take what he could get.

He heard a faint sobbing from upstairs and whispering. Noah jerked, glancing up before letting out a breath. Right… Phen's father. The sobs unsettled him more than he would like to admit. The sound of a door opening and closing caught his attention followed by a knock on another door.

He shook his head, noticing that Phen was nowhere in sight. At the moment, Noah was okay with that. He agreed with Phen's decision and even Aiden understood, but Phen bringing up going to that place almost got him possessed and Aiden killed. Noah couldn't help but feel a little… he didn't really have a word for it. Frustrated and angry would probably be the most accurate. He stood up and plopped down next to a startled Aiden, who eyed him warily.

"Are you okay?"

"No." Noah said, leaning against his shoulder.

Silence enveloped the room for a moment before Aiden let out a sigh. "You know we talked last night. Do you want to talk?"

"No," Noah muttered. "But I know I should."

"Hm." Aiden clicked his tongue, but didn't say anything else.

"What do we do now? That was a lead, at least, I think, but now we're back to zero and you're less protected."

Aiden let out a tired breath, slumping and finally relaxing against Noah. "I know." He seemed more tired than he let on, which made Noah feel somewhat bad he hadn't noticed. "I memorized their faces. I'll have to check if they match those who disappeared." Aiden suddenly felt heavy against Noah's side, but he didn't pull away. "Though, confirming it's them won't do much good, especially with no bodies there."

"Wh—" Noah immediately snapped his mouth shut. That was a stupid idea that came to mind.

"What?"

"Nothing."

"Noah…"

"Seriously, it's nothing." Noah pushed away, as Aiden sat up to turn to him with a narrowed gaze. "It's just a very stupid thought."

"Tell me."

Noah hesitated and then slumped, noting the curious, gentle expression. Geez… "Like I said, stupid. But, well, if they were that killer's victims, they would have information. Information we desperately need right now."

Aiden stiffened, realization dawning on him. "You're thinking of talking to them." His lips downturned into a scowl. "As much as I wish I could say that's dumb, it's not. However, I'm not letting you talk to them alone." His palm pushed against his face as he took in deep breaths. "Mom had a cross Dad always kept nearby, right?"

Noah blinked, before slapping his face. Of course, the cross in Father's room. They hadn't brought it with them when they fled before, but it was the only other one they had at the moment and he wanted Aiden to be protected. Even more so after THAT happened. "Let's do that." Noah spoke softly. "Phen still hasn't come downstairs and I think that sound was probably his father, so…" Noah trailed off. "I don't think they will miss us leaving right now and we need that. It's Mom's."

Aiden's lips quirked up. "I know." He let out a breath. "I'm not fond of the idea of going back, to either the house or where we were staying, but I'm also not in the mood to continue the farce of going to school when I know someone's there and we finally have some form of information. Hopefully the perpetrator is at school like they should be. If they are, that means we should be able to go back to our home without being followed like last time, as long as we're careful."

Oh, Noah hadn't even thought about that. Made sense though.

Aiden's gaze flicked to him before he shook his head and pushed himself to his feet. "Let's get something to eat on the way." At that, Noah stood, gathering the blankets that fell, placing them to one side. He hesitated before hurrying to the kitchen, returning with a few bars.

"I think this will be fine for now." He grinned, handing one over. Aiden just huffed, but took his as they slipped out of the house. They moved down the quiet street, the morning dew clinging to their skin. It was still early enough that others weren't quite up yet, but the light was starting to shine down. They munched on their bars solemnly. To be honest, Noah mostly wanted to get out of there. He wanted time to think without others nearby, not counting Aiden.

As usual, Aiden stayed silent, peering around with a wary gaze. Aiden ruffled his hair with a tired breath. "You know, Ellen is not going to be happy."

Noah blinked before mentally cursing. He hadn't really thought about that. Aiden chuckled as Noah slumped. "Ugh… I don't want to upset her, not after she took us in."

Aiden nodded, faint smile fading. "I know, she's only been kind to us as has Phen, but I can't stay there at the moment." Aiden rubbed his arm. "I'm not in the mood to try to answer questions I don't have answers TO. You know she's going to ask, she tried to ask last night, but we were too tired." He let out a breath. "I am SICK of these ghosts. The supernatural is just…" he grumbled, the last few words lost as a faint breeze blew past.

Noah didn't press, his attention shifting ahead toward the forest at the edge of town. He noted a certain lack of someone, curious. "I don't see Mia today, I wonder where she is."

"Don't know, don't care."

"You don't actually mean that." Noah peered sidelong toward Aiden. "I know it wasn't the best start, but she's not that bad." Noah shifted, fingers fiddling with his cross, feeling over the faint cracks in it. "She did protect you last night."

Aiden had nothing to say to that, just hunkered into himself more. He stuffed his hands into his pockets, shoulders almost up to his ears.

Noah turned away, pursing his lips, silence descending over both of them as the faint sound of dripping caught his attention. He peered up and groaned. The sky, looking like it might have cleared up, was once more becoming cloud-covered. Something landed on his cheek and he mentally cursed. He was so sick of this stupid weather and this stupid place.

"I'm surprised you didn't want to check on Phen or Ellen." Aiden spoke after a moment, catching Noah's attention. Noah winced, glancing down, remembering the worry and fear on Ellen's face last night when they got back to her place, looking like death warmed over.

"I did, but at the same time, I didn't," he finally admitted. "You know how I feel about Phen at the moment and Ellen made me think of Mom." He didn't have to say more, noticing as Aiden tensed at that.

"It's something else though," Aiden pointed out, catching Noah's attention.

He blinked and let out a weak laugh, of course Aiden would catch that. The laugh faded as he finally responded, "I guess I'm also just angry at myself. I wasn't able to do a thing back there and it was beyond frustrating. I guess I just needed time to think it over."

"Uh-huh. And?"

"It's only been a few hours." Noah glared back toward Aiden who nodded, not turning to face him.

"True. It has." He tilted his head. "But even I know you're not so callous as to NOT check on him after that. Something else is on your mind and I mean, besides Mom and what could have happened."

Noah felt his shoulders drop. Ugh, why was his brother perceptive now? "I think it's just… Everything is catching up with me. I know Phen lost his sister, but he still has his mother and father. Yet he's reckless. I mean, we both are, but… I guess it's just frustrating to KNOW that, to see that, and yet…"

Aiden watched him quietly before facing ahead once more. "Let's focus on collecting what we need. Who knows, Dad might have left us a clue or something during one of the times he was home. We didn't really dig into his room." At that, he picked up speed, causing Noah to stumble and jog after him. They continued on in silence, each to their thoughts.

It was stupid, Noah knew, but he couldn't help but think it.

Once again, he briefly wondered where Mia disappeared to, but brushed it off. It was fine, right?

Their footsteps clacked over the pavement as it shifted toward dirt road. The trees began to surround them on all sides as they followed the path. Soon enough, they turned the corner to their home.

Noah froze, staring in shock as Aiden tensed, horror flashing briefly on his face.

Wooden beams were crumbled and charred, one entire side broken and splintered. The door swung listlessly on a barely useable metal hinge and the roof was slightly tilted, dipping down where a fire had clearly broken out.

Aiden pushed forward, catching Noah's attention. He grabbed Aiden's arm to stop him. Aiden jerked back, startled.

"Could it be he…" Noah's words stuck in his throat. "Could that man have set our house on fire? Why?"

"I don't think he did." Aiden's words were faint as he stared toward the brunt of the damage. "That's where the kitchen was." He shook his head, pulling free and hurrying forward. Noah blinked, confused, and chased after him. Aiden stepped in first, pushing at the damaged door. It screeched, skidding over warped wood and ash. Everything inside was either charred or soaked. So someone had helped put out the fire, but didn't tell anyone. Noah heard a faint creak and winced as something cracked and splintered, crashing to the ground. Aiden quickly stepped back, the beam just missing him by a few inches.

The kitchen, or what once was a kitchen, was burnt black. Something sat, coated in rain and twisted beyond recognition on what was probably once a stove. The window shattered at some point, staining everything in either water or ash. The air still had a faint smell of smoke.

"I forgot." Aiden pursed his lips, staring at the stove. "I was about to start dinner when that Thing attacked. I never turned the stove off." He winced, glancing back toward Noah. "The house probably survived because of all the rain lately, but I'm not sure how the rest survived." He peered around. "It's as if someone put it out themselves, but who? This was probably a pretty big fire."

Noah shook his head, glancing around before stepping farther into the house, heading toward his and Aiden's room. He could feel the wood shift under his weight. Thank the heavens there wasn't a basement to this house. He wasn't in the mood to fall through the wood and down a floor. Whatever happened, the house was still standing, though barely.

Noah wondered why no one mentioned it. It made sense in some ways, especially since the house was a ways out. It was an older home and probably had defunct smoke detectors. So, who helped stop the fire? He briefly thought about Mia or that Thing, but shoved the idea off. Sure, Mia's appearance was always wet, but the water that dripped off was almost as spectral as her, and the Thing? He was a possessed human, why would he bother?

Noah shook his head, hurrying to the door that led to his room. He opened the door, or, went to, only to stop, noticing the handle was warped, pitted with the reddish tinge of rust. The door itself was almost yellow and bulged oddly, almost stuck. He tugged, wrenching for a moment before feeling it give. He stumbled back as the door opened. He had been ignoring it, but the lingering smell of smoke caught his attention and he covered his mouth and nose with his shirt as he peeked in. To his dismay, while the fire must not have reached the room, the lack of ventilation caused the smoke to settle. Everything had a dull yellowish color to it and what books he could see were curled up. He stepped in, picking up a manga, wincing as it cracked slightly, brittle and unsalvageable.

The bag he started to put together sat where he left it, next to the bed. He reached in, noticing a few things managed to avoid the same treatment. He grabbed up what little he could before standing up, peering toward Aiden, who was watching.

"Noah, let's go." Aiden spoke up. Noah nodded, keeping his breath shallow as they continued down the hallway to less damaged parts of the house.

Luckily, it seemed the constant rain helped, but it was still unnerving, seeing the stained walls, feeling the warped floor under their feet and noticing the pitted metal as they passed.

The fire must have been a few days ago and it did this much damage. He couldn't imagine what it would have been like if a full fire broke loose. Even though smoke still lingered, the air felt cold and acrid.

Unlike the rest of the house, Dad's room looked like someone took a battering ram against the door. The room itself was a mix between water-logged and torn asunder. Noah winced as Aiden peered around, eyes narrowed. He shook his head, slipping inside. "Noah, do you remember where you put it?"

Noah blinked for a moment, trying to remember what 'it 'was before he let out a huff. "Yeah, on the side dresser."

Aiden nodded, finding his way over as Noah peered around, taking in the room. Someone clearly went through everything. Papers lay, scattered over the floor, clothes strewn about with the bedding ripped and some things outright shattered.

Aiden parsed through the side dresser, gently picking up Mom's cross. It was the only thing untouched in the room, besides the side dresser it lay upon. Noah stared at it quietly, fiddling with his own as Aiden tilted it back and forth, uncertain.

"You know? I wonder why Mom used that for so long when she was never religious," Noah said. "I guess now it's kind of nice to know the reason."

"I still don't get how crosses can protect against the supernatural." Aiden laid it in his palm, staring at it with an odd expression. "How am I supposed to use this anyway? Do I just hold it? It doesn't have a hole for a necklace and I don't want to ruin Mom's—" he cut himself off as Noah joined him.

"Maybe we can find something to wrap around the top? It is extended outward so…"

Aiden conceded, placing it in his pocket before picking up one of the pieces of shredded fabric. He sifted through before picking up one that looked like it might have been from the bed. He pulled the cross back out, carefully wrapping it before slipping it over his head, tucking it under his shirt. It was a bit strange, almost like he was wearing a half scarf, but that was fine in Noah's opinion, it worked.

There was a sense of relief in knowing that Aiden was now protected, unlike before.

Aiden lightly touched his chest where the cross hung as a faint smile trailed over his lips before it was wiped away. "Come on, let's see if we can salvage anything." At that, they began to search.

Taking their time sweeping through the parts of the house that weren't damaged led to them finding nothing. No notes Dad left behind, no clues of who it was that might have attacked that night and, especially in Dad's room, almost nothing survived, either ripped to shreds or just gone.

Noah did manage to find some salt shakers that remained untouched that he took and a few crosses that were shattered in the same ways as Aiden's and partially Noah's.

He pursed his lips, as he thought over the rooms before hurrying back to Dad's, carefully pulling the still intact drawers out, mainly from the side dresser where the cross sat, untouched. This person… had he come more than once? Or were these shattered the first time this person arrived?

"Find anything?"

Noah shook his head and stood, only to pause as he finally got one of the top drawers open. It was filled with pens, paperclips and miscellaneous supplies. However, on top of all that there was a small file folder that looked like it must have been put here at some time and, with the cross on the desk, the person hadn't been able to get near. He flipped it open, and stilled.

It was Father's notes.

CHAPTER 29

"What's that?" Aiden joined him, taking some of the papers as Noah handed them over. He flipped through his, noting Father's familiar clean, yet somewhat scratchy hand-writing. "These are…" Aiden paled as he turned one of the notes around to show a boy around their age with pale features, just like the ghost within the home from the night before. "They are notes of the disappearances. Dad must have left this here the last time he came home, after we found Lynn." He stared back down at the papers, crumbling them slightly. "I guess Mom's cross, I don't know, protected the desk and, thus, these papers and everything within?" He shook his head. "That seems…"

Noah flipped through, realizing Aiden was right. Small, fuzzy pictures barely scraped together of each person littered the pages. There were little scribbles about strength, presence and relation. Even Dad had gotten frustrated at the lack of connection between the disappearances and the Thing that did them.

"Collect what you can and then we'll go. We can't stay here. Even with the person probably being at school, I would rather not remain in this place longer than I have to. Especially when it is unsound." Another crack echoed out near the front of the house, causing Noah to wince. Aiden peered over before continuing, "Not counting the smoke still lingering in the air. It's too dangerous."

Noah nodded, slipping the folder into his bag. Dad knew about the disappearances. Noah hadn't missed how anxious he was when he had to leave them, how Aiden had to convince Dad to get back to finding out what was happening.

Noah wondered if Aiden even remembered that and, if he did, how he was feeling now that Dad was missing. Noah shook his head, shoving it away. If Aiden hadn't realized, he wasn't going to bring it up.

Soon enough, they gathered what they could and slipped back out of the house. The damage was not something they could fix, not with just the two of them with almost no money between them.

The sun was high in the sky by the time they left. The dreariness of the morning faded, yet neither of them wanted to go to school or head toward Phen's house.

Noah was curious on where Mia went to and was kind of getting worried. She usually stayed at their sides, so for her not to be there, especially after last night? It concerned him.

To be honest, they were kind of avoiding talking about last night. Noah knew they should, but he wasn't sure where to even start. Aiden dug into his bag and handed over, to Noah's surprise, a wad of cash. "I grabbed some on the way out before and I figured you would probably be the one to use it before me."

Noah hesitantly took the money, shaking his head. That was Aiden for you. "Fine, I'll keep hold of it." He grinned. "We'll split it later."

Aiden rolled his eyes, but didn't argue as they settled into a more leisurely pace.

That made sense and of course Aiden would remember to grab it. Noah shook his head, letting out a breath as he threw it into his own bag.

"Plus, we can't just keep staying with Ellen and Phen. It's not fair to them or us," Aiden pointed out as he stopped to one side of the street, watching some cars pass. "Especially when they are dealing with Lynn's death, Phen's father and what almost happened yesterday." Noah winced at that. "If we can find an inn or motel, then not only will we no longer be questioned, but we would be able to work at our own pace."

"Are you sure?" Noah asked, voice somewhat faint. "I mean, I was thinking that too, but it's still pretty dangerous. I hate to say it but… will they even let us get a room?"

Aiden seemed to debate for a moment before slumping in what was clearly realization. "Ah… no. They probably wouldn't. I still remember the time Dad was getting out the boxes and told us to wait inside. I think you tried to get the keys and they were going to call the cops before Dad walked in to prove he was actually with us."

"Ugh, that time. I might have blocked that memory because of how annoyed I was. We're not THAT young." Aiden just raised his eyebrow at Noah's words, causing Noah to pout. "Okay, fine. Still, if we can't get a motel what are we going to do? We can't stay in one of those abandoned houses, not when they are THAT close to the prison house as Mia would call it."

Aiden shifted slightly before tilting his head down. "I… think we'll have to stay at Phen's house. I can't think of anything else. I hate the idea. I don't want to bother them or risk the killer finding us there but…"

"We'll put salt around the living room, how about that?" Noah leaned forward, faint smile crossing his lips. "We'll have to hide it from Ellen but it could work."

Aiden snorted but didn't argue, peering ahead. "I guess. I mean, I'm not an idiot. I'm well aware you and Phen are going to continue to try to do reckless stuff until we find the killer, or Dad, but I want to try to stop that as much as possible. I'm relieved Dad wasn't in that mess of ghosts back there, but I'm still worried. He's alive, but for how long? What if Phen or Ellen get caught in all of this. Would salt really work against a possessed soul?" Aiden's shoulders sagged with a heavy tiredness.

Noah couldn't argue. "So, like usual, you think Phen shouldn't have gotten involved with us in the first place?"

The melancholy expression Noah got back hurt. "Isn't it better that way? We only really need just us anyway. Having another person is only detrimental." He shook his head and continued forward once more. "Though, I suppose he already is in danger either way."

Noah turned away. He understood what Aiden was saying, but it didn't hurt any less that his brother thought such a thing. Having someone's help… it really was so foreign. He knew Phen probably felt bad for what happened, but he couldn't help but find himself agreeing with his brother. Less people would get hurt that way but, unfortunately, they didn't really have another option. Noah shook his head. No, he couldn't delve into those thoughts. If anything, last night showed that another hand wasn't always helpful.

Though, Noah wasn't sure he could fully say that. In the end, was it Aiden who was helping Phen, or Phen who was helping Aiden?

"I guess we could do that, stay at Ellen's as little as possible." Noah shifted. "But then what? We continue doing this? Look around during the day?"

Aiden nodded. "Yes. We're running out of time. People are starting to question us. Dad has been gone for too long and I am getting nervous on the fact that we have not gotten a word from the killer. Going to school did us no favors. So, we're going to try the opposite approach."

Noah nodded, though he was hesitant. The only thing was, they were out of options and out of time. It would honestly be nice if something they did worked for once. He sighed. "So, we're heading back?" Aiden stayed silent, clearly hesitant, drawing to a stop. Noah walked a few more paces before turning toward him. "Aiden?"

"I don't like the idea." He pursed his lips, face scrunching up in uncomfortable distaste. "I don't want to get Phen involved more than we have to. He knows what's going on and what's at stake. I don't think he'll argue if we tell him to stay home, especially after last night."

Noah wasn't too sure about that. He hadn't missed the way Phen was acting recently. He observed it enough times with other people that it was kind of obvious.

The boy had a crush on Aiden, that was clear. Noah wasn't sure of where it stood. As long as the boy didn't try anything, then Noah didn't mind, but if he hurt Aiden, well, he was still angry at Phen almost getting himself and Aiden killed.

However, that meant that he doubted Phen would just allow them to leave without knowing where they were. He would just have to wait and see. It could also just be his imagination and Phen really did just want to be friends, but it was hard to tell.

Even harder because it was Aiden.

"Noah?" Aiden's voice jerked Noah from his thoughts. "What's on your mind?"

"Just… thoughts."

"That's not good," Aiden teased, causing Noah to snort.

"Funny." He shook his head. "I was just thinking we should get food. And, once we know school is over, we head back to talk with Phen's mother and Phen. Then we find a way to take a look at that place and talk with the ghosts."

Aiden pursed his lips at that. "You still want to try talking to them?"

"Aiden, it is LITERALLY the only thing we have left. If we make a deal with them, they could give us information we need to find Dad."

"And do you know if they will even know anything?" Aiden pointed out, frown deepening. "Both Lynn and that ghost friend of yours admitted that their memory was gone. Lynn didn't remember how she died and that Ghost doesn't remember her own name."

"Why don't you call her Mia? She did save you." Noah's voice was quiet. "I know things have been rocky, but she hasn't done anything bad. She gave us information, has been there to keep watch for us and saved you from dying. I know you don't trust her, but she's not a bad person or, well, ghost."

Aiden pulled back, hesitant, before turning away. "I can't acknowledge it. I'm barely dealing with the fact that I can talk to, interact and be killed by ghosts of all things. Her? If I don't call her by name, I don't have to completely acknowledge the situation."

Noah blinked, startled by Aiden outright admitting what he was thinking. He was usually blunt, but he supposed the stress really was getting to both of them.

"Why can't you acknowledge it?" Noah kept his voice low, concerned as Aiden fidgeted, staring past him. "You know I've always believed in the supernatural and so did Dad, so—"

"That's exactly it," Aiden snapped, attention whipping to him, causing Noah to stiffen. "You and Dad always had this strange belief that I thought was just you two being insufferably crazy, not that I was the odd one out." He placed a hand to his chest. "It must be easy for you, but it isn't for me! It's the equivalent of me telling you that Mom is dead and we'll never see her again. I already realize, but—"

"Lies!" Noah stiffened, feeling a surge of anger as he slashed an arm outward. "She's still out there, I know it!"

"This is my exact point." Aiden growled and Noah backed off, realization dawning on him. "Now, what would happen if it turned out I was right? Now put yourself in my shoes about this entire stupid situation." He quickly walked past Noah, tension radiating off him. He didn't say another word.

"Oh…" Noah stared where Aiden used to be, unsure what to do or say. So that's what Aiden meant. It made sense, he supposed. He was still angry at the idea that Aiden thought Mom was dead, but that anger turned straight to concern as he realized that was exactly what Aiden was feeling now. He turned, quickly catching up. "Alright. I get it."

Aiden turned his head away, hiding his expression.

Noah watched for a moment before leaning forward. "So, uh, do you want to get some food? I'm starving."

Aiden paused before letting out a snort. "Alright."

Noah felt his lips twitch in relief. They shifted directions, away from Phen's house and headed to grab food.

CHAPTER 30

They debated on going to the diner, but agreed it would be too suspicious, due to the fact that they were supposed to be at school. It was part of the reason they hadn't gone to the police either. So Noah instead slipped into the convenience store to buy some things. Thankfully, the worker didn't much care. They briefly stopped by the bookstore Phen showed them before, wanting to avoid the library and Ellen. They peeked inside to see the rows of books. Noah kind of wanted to see if he could pick up copies of the books that were ruined.

They decided not to, on the fact that they only had so much money and, of course, the whole not being in school thing. When they found Dad and dealt with all of this, then they would pick up some new books.

By that point, people were starting to head home from school. Noah recognized some of the students that passed. A few gave them double-takes and confused glances. Noah coughed into his hand, faking being sick, causing them to hurry along.

Soon enough, they headed back towards Phen's place. Noah knocked on the door, waiting. They faintly heard the pounding of footsteps before the door opened almost violently. Ellen stood in the doorway, a mix of worried and, strangely, pissed. "You two!" she demanded, startling Noah and Aiden. "What were you THINKING sneaking out in the morning without letting any of us know you've left?

With what's going on with Phen, I have been worried sick!" She put her hands on her hips as Noah winced, curling inward slightly. "You two are still young, and it is dangerous out there. I don't know what your parents are thinking, more so your father, but this is inexcusable. Get inside, now." She just pointed.

Aiden stood stock still, shocked. Noah meekly hurried forward, tugging Aiden along. They slipped inside as Ellen let out a breath, crumbling slightly. "I'm glad to know that at least you two are alright. Please, can you tell me what happened yesterday?" She gestured, leading them to the living room. "Phen hasn't come out of his room all day and he locked the door on me. He usually isn't like this, so I'm worried." She glanced between them. "I know you're father is investigating what's going on, but why haven't I seen him?"

"He's busy." Noah finally spoke up, voice faint. "Dad's phone died and he's probably in the middle of tracking down the person."

Ellen furrowed her brow. "That is irresponsible of your father even if he is—"

"He's doing his best." Aiden spoke up, frowning.

Ellen didn't comment for a moment. She wiped down on her skirt, letting out a long and tired breath. "Alright, I won't press, but, please tell me everything is alright." She peered back up. "What did you three do last night?"

Aiden and Noah exchanged looks, uncertain what to even say. After a moment, Noah spoke up. "Phen was showing us around town and we got startled when we checked out the nearby forest, that's all."

Ellen frowned once more, but after some time, nodded, pushing herself to her feet. "Alright, well, I'm going to make you two something to eat." She peered up. "Hopefully, Phen will want to eat now." She hesitated before letting out a breath. "It's been so exhausting, taking care of my husband, I hope Phen recovers soon." She gestures to the twins. "Come on, you two, you can help me."

Noah hesitated as Aiden sighed. "Well, she's not kicking us out." He spoke softly.

Noah nodded, letting out a breath of relief, kind of glad she wasn't. She really was a good sort. They joined her in the kitchen. It wasn't anything grand, just some crackers, fruit and cheese, but it hit the spot after walking around for a while. Ellen picked up a bowl, heading upstairs. Aiden and Noah hesitantly followed when she gestured. "I want you to see if you can get Phen to talk to you." She spoke as they climbed the stairs. "He's gotten really close to you two…" She trailed off, shaking her head.

They reached the top floor where Noah realized that the door to the father's room was open and the sounds of a shower could be heard from inside. Ellen peered over, a moment of relief passing over her face before she turned toward Phen's door and knocked. "Honey, your friends are back. Can they come in?"

Silence met their ears and Ellen frowned, shifting her stance and knocking again. "Phen? Honey?"

There was a groan, followed by a soft, 'yes'. Ellen's expression drew taut, her hand shaking a little.

"Alright, honey." She turned to the two, handing the bowl to Aiden. "I'll be checking on my husband… please keep an eye on him for me, alright?" Once both nodded, she stepped into the other room, disappearing around the corner.

"Well, that doesn't sound good." Noah kept his voice soft as Aiden pursed his lips. He shifted, using one hand to hold the bowl while the other opened the door. He paused, didn't she say it was locked? It wasn't anymore.

Noah slipped past Aiden, stepping inside. Aiden quickly followed.

The room was cold, in a familiar way. Noah jerked, glancing to one side, noticing Mia hovering over something, she almost looked wan and tired, hair limply falling around her, the cold almost… lesser than usual, or maybe he was just imagining things. However, from Aiden's expression, maybe he wasn't. The sound of the door closing caught Noah's attention and he turned to see Aiden closed it, probably having felt the chill as well.

This was proven as Noah stepped toward the bed. Mia was sitting over the bed, hands lightly touching Phen's chest.

Phen, on the other hand, looked terrible, and it made Noah wonder how it was he even had the energy to say anything in the first place.

"What's going on?" Aiden growled.

Mia turned, both annoyed and strangely tired. "Took you two long enough." She let out a breath, her hair flicking as if alive. "I've been here all day giving him some of my energy to stabilize him and keep his idiot butt alive."

Huh?

Spotting their expressions, she continued, "You managed to get the cross on him in time to stop him being possessed, but his soul was still being torn apart by the ghost since he was fighting so hard." She shifted, her hands still resting right above his chest. "The soul is fragile and he's dealt with a lot lately. Let's just say yesterday was the final straw and his soul is inches away from fracturing completely."

Noah pursed his lips as he stepped over, noting Phen was out like a light, a thin sheen of sweat on his brow. *I guess it took the last of his strength to respond.*

"So what exactly are you doing then?" Aiden muttered, keeping his voice low.

"Reminding him what a single soul is supposed to feel like. There is a reason banishment is so finicky. You don't do it right, you shatter the soul and create space for a ghost to bond to the shattered pieces."

"Wait, are you possessing him?" Noah felt horrified.

Mia's head snapped toward him, almost off her shoulder. "No." She hissed. "This is different. I wouldn't expect you two to know." She didn't say anything else, just returned her focus to Phen. "Now, will you two do me a favor and grab his hands?"

"How is that going to help?" Aiden muttered, but took his hand anyway. Noah followed suit, curious.

Mia slowly grinned. "Because, with you touching him, I can utilize the energy you give off to complete what I've been trying to do and seal it. I had just enough energy to keep him stable, you will give me the energy I need to heal him. We'll talk more in a minute." At that, her eye, no, the whole place where her eyeball was turned black. Her hair fluttered in a nonexistent breeze, lifting around her as she spoke words that Noah didn't recognize. An old tongue, if Noah had to guess.

The air whipped like a tornado, tugging at hair and skin, though nothing else moved. The chill and cold increased before everything stilled.

A moment later, Phen shot up, squeezing their hands tightly to the point that Noah thought he heard a crack. He winced as Phen's head snapped from side to side.

"Wh-how-wher-" He froze and turned toward Noah and Aiden, realizing what he was doing. He suddenly pulled away, cradling his hands. "Holy shit, what just happened?"

Aiden shook out his fingers and grimaced. "I would like to know that too." He turned toward Mia who floated back, moving away from Aiden.

Noah didn't miss the way she flickered, as if struggling to maintain her form even more than before. Her voice, when she spoke, was more exhausted than the usual mischievous tone. "As I said, I remembered it recently when I saw Phen's state. While that one there helped save your life, he was unable to save every part of you." Phen pressed a hand to his chest as Mia swooped around, resting near Noah. "I noticed this morning. As I said, ghosts are made strongly of emotions, souls are influenced by emotions. A strong enough string of emotions against an already shattered soul?" She shook her head. "It's not like I can inherently see a soul, that's nigh impossible, but one can almost feel a shattered one when they are around a person enough."

Phen glanced down as Aiden frowned. "So, Phen couldn't handle what happened and… what? What is a shattered soul?"

Mia swayed side to side. "A shattered soul is a soul that has been torn apart by a mixture of things. It can heal, over time, but it's difficult. When a soul is on the verge of being shattered, ghosts are better able to manipulate the human, whether through talk or through possession. When it IS shattered… well… It's not the easiest thing to explain, but just know that, in his state and with that killer on the loose, not repairing it while we could was a death sentence for him."

Phen shivered, shock clear on his face.

Aiden watched for a moment before turning to Mia. "I get that. Why did we have to touch him?"

"Uh, because I can't touch you?" Mia, whose expression returned to normal, let out a huff. "That cross of yours is literally shoving me away. I barely managed to stay on Phen when you stepped closer. It's only the fact that Noah doesn't push me either that I could to be perfectly frank."

Aiden gripped the cross tightly.

"It was our mom's..." Noah spoke softly.

"Mom!" Phen scrambled, almost falling out of bed. "I remember her trying to talk to me." He got to his feet and raced toward the doorway. He opened it. "Mom? Where—"

Through the doorway, the two boys noticed as Ellen jerked up from where she was sitting on the other bed. She stared wide-eyed before shooting to her feet. "Phen?" Ellen's voice pitched up as she darted over, pulling him into a hug. Phen yelped, trying to wriggle away. "Wait, you're awake? Oh, I'm so glad. Are you okay? You don't have a fever or anything, right?"

Noah watched as Ellen checked over Phen, who let out a breath of relief, letting her know he was fine. Aiden's expression was taut and Noah... well...

Aiden's words from before spun in his head. He felt his fingers dig into his thigh. No, Mom had to be out there somewhere. He would find her and return things to normal... to this. Just like they would find Dad. Dad was safe, and so was Mom. He would prove it.

A gentle breeze wafted past and Noah tilted his head. A wistful expression passed over Mia's face.

"Thank you." He kept his voice low. "Whatever you did took a lot out of you, didn't it?"

Mia turned to him and nodded. "I've never had to do it before, though I heard of it." She shook her head. "A shattered soul is not something you want to feel." She put a hand to her chest. "It is… quite difficult, especially for one like…" she trailed off, fingers curling into her dress before she shook her head.

"So you can feel it?"

"Like I said, if you've been around a person enough, you can sense it." Mia paused. "Somewhat, but now is not the time to talk of that." Noah nodded as Ellen stepped in, Phen at her side.

"I don't know what happened, but thank you." Ellen sighed. "I know something weird is going on. I'm not blind. I don't know what you two are dealing with, but…" she hesitated for the longest time, as if debating. She hugged Phen to one side, who was watching her curiously. Finally, a faint smile crossed her lips. "You are always welcome here." She lightly patted Phen's back and headed downstairs. "I'm going to whip up something for everyone, a nice little desert. My husband sounds like he's hungry enough to eat one as well, actually." Her voice sounded much more chipper then usual and Noah wondered if it was because everyone was starting to recover now.

Phen watched her go before walking back over to the bed, closing the door behind him. His gaze briefly flitted toward Aiden before he turned away, taking deep breaths. "A shattered soul, huh?" He chuckled morosely. "Shit, I screwed up."

"I wouldn't think of it that way." Mia spoke up, startling all three of them. "While I am surprised you heard, I wouldn't say any of that is completely your fault. I mean, you did screw up, but not in the way you think." She elaborated, grinning.

Aiden rolled his eyes as Phen blinked, confused.

Noah wasn't sure whether to feel amused or bemused.

"The splintering of your soul? That was not fully your fault. You've encountered a lot at once. The death and interaction with your sister. A debate with yourself about things." She paused at that as Phen stiffened. Noah could guess what that was, but didn't say anything. "Then the possession, followed by learning you almost caused the death of someone impor—" She cut herself off when Phen gave her a sudden pleading look. "Who came to save you," she conceded.

Yep, that confirmed that. Aiden watched, confused, before letting out a quiet huff, shaking his head.

"All of that, combined with caring for your father who is clearly still struggling with the death of your sister and helping your mother deal with the grief? I'm honestly surprised it didn't splinter sooner than this." Mia shrugged.

Phen glanced down. No words were exchanged, though Noah didn't miss the way his shoulders shook.

Noah hesitated before gently standing. "We'll be outside." He grabbed Aiden's arm and tugged him up. Aiden just gave him a look, pulled his arm away and walked out.

Yeah, figured Aiden already realized. They stepped outside, Mia fluttering after them. The door closed moments before they heard quiet sobbing from inside.

"Poor kid." Mia's voice was soft, gentle. "I wasn't wrong, he really is going through so much in such a short amount of time." She turned to Noah and Aiden. "I'm not denying you two aren't, but at least you have each other to fall back on." She didn't explain further and Noah didn't need her to.

Sure, Phen liked Aiden, but that didn't mean he could rely on either of them and he certainly wouldn't be able to talk to his mom and dad about half of the things that happened to him.

Noah found himself taking a seat, staring at the stairwell. Aiden stayed standing, leaning his head against the wall as he observed the street from the second floor window.

The heart-wrenching sound from within pulled at Noah, causing him to curl inward.

Part of him wanted to join Phen and just cry. But he held off. He was fine, they were fine.

He was glad Phen was getting a chance to cry. He didn't look down on him for it, though he knew others would have.

"Hey, Noah?" Aiden's voice was soft, a little husky. "It would be nice to just get this over and done with. To find Dad and just get out of here. It's hard to listen." The last few words were said so quietly, Noah almost thought he misheard them.

Noah chuckled weakly. "Maybe, but I think I'll probably be in a similar state if…" he trailed off and sighed. "Never mind, but you are right. We have to find Dad. For now, I think it's best if we stay here. Mia's right, a lot has happened lately and it's getting to be a bit much."

"I get it." Aiden waved, the weakest of smiles on his face. "We'll check on him in a bit."

Noah nodded and glanced up. Mia curled above, turned toward the doorway, a strange mix of emotions on her face. Noah couldn't really pick out any of them. She spotted him watching and curled around him, her body bending in a way that wasn't normal. "Things will work themselves out, you know." She kept her voice soft.

"I know," Noah responded in kind, noting as Aiden observed them quietly, not saying a word.

Soon enough, the crying started to slow and then stop. Noah stood, pins and needles piercing through his legs as he tentatively opened the door. "Can we come in?"

"Ye… yeah."

Noah nodded and slipped inside, Aiden a few paces behind.

"You heard all that, didn't you?" Phen asked, head still buried on his legs, which were slightly soaked with tears.

Aiden nodded, before saying, "We're not idiots." He took a seat where he had before, tugging the chair over a little more. "We figured we would give you time, didn't mean we weren't still keeping an ear out for if you needed anything."

Noah noted how Phen's ears were now red, probably matching his face.

"Oh, uh, that's… thanks." Phen took a deep breath, wiped at his face and slowly sat up. "Sorry."

Noah waved it off. "I don't know who thought it was a good idea to tell people not to cry, I think it's kind of necessary."

Aiden gave him an exasperated expression that Noah promptly ignored. That didn't apply to him, alright?

"Uh… right." Phen glanced back down. Noah blinked as Aiden reached forward and lightly thwacked Phen on top of the head. "Ow!"

"Feel better?"

Phen glanced up, massaging the back of his head before nodding, a faint smile on his lips. "Yeah, actually, I do. You didn't have to hit me though." Aiden shrugged and pulled back.

"Good, your soul is finally mending itself." Mia took a seat in the air, cross-legged. "However, you are still in a precarious position. You're much more susceptible now and a cross isn't going to do much, even that one." She gestured toward Aiden.

Phen glanced toward the cross before doing a double-take. "That looks weird on you." Aiden stiffened and Phen quickly waved. "I mean, no, that came out wrong. It's fine. I was just startled since it's so big and I'm not helping, am I?"

Aiden shook his head, arms crossed over his chest to hide the cross.

Noah sighed. "Well, it's good to know you're doing better." He turned to Mia. "So, it would be best if he stayed home for now, right?"

Mia nodded. "Until this mess is taken care of, or he fully heals, whichever is faster." Mia shifted from side to side, almost at ninety degree angles. "Even with the speed of recovery, it'll still take a while, so probably not until after we get this case dealt with."

"What?" Phen shifted, almost jumping out of bed. "Are you kidding me? I'm not abandoning this now!"

"Yes, you are." Aiden spoke up, voice neutral. All attention snapped to him and his shoulders slumped. "Right now, the only information we have is to speak with the ghosts. You are literally in a state that isn't helpful right now." He sat up, staring Phen down. "Stay home, check on your parents. Noah, our ghost follower here and I will figure this out."

"I can help!" Phen snapped, placing one foot to the ground. "I'm not just going to—"

"If you want to help, then don't go getting possessed again because of recklessness." Aiden's glare was withering, making even Noah flinch back.

Phen stilled, anger brimming.

"I'm not saying you are useless," Aiden cut in, causing Phen to pause. "Just that right now, we don't need your help. It would be better if you kept an eye on things elsewhere while we worked."

Phen pursed his lips, but settled back down. "You said you were going to speak with those ghosts that almost possessed me, right? The same ones that tried to kill you?"

"Not necessarily." Aiden settled down himself, much to Noah's relief. "We're making a deal for information. We might need your help later, but for now, it would be best if only Noah and I did it."

Phen watched them quietly before sighing and slumping. "I guess it makes sense. I don't think I want to go back to that place anyway." He rubbed his arms. "Just, try to be careful, would you?" His gaze locked with Aiden who waved it off.

"No promises."

"What he means is yes."

"Noah!"

Noah smiled before turning back to Phen. "Get some rest."

"Sure, but what about you two? Are you staying downstairs?" He paused and shifted, glancing around. "I mean, I don't mind if you stay here. I did clean up the room and stuff so…"

"We'll be fine," Aiden said before Noah could get a word in edgewise.

Noah didn't miss the sudden despondent 'oh 'Phen gave.

Noah quickly cut in with a grin. "What he means is, we'll be staying downstairs. It's easier to slip out that way." He felt Aiden's glare as Phen just stared at him in surprise. "Plus, well, we already angered her a bit by leaving this morning. It's probably wiser to stay here for now."

"Oh, that was the yelling I faintly heard." He chuckled weakly.

"Pretty much." Noah chuckled as Aiden pushed himself to his feet.

"To be honest, we just came to talk with Ellen and, well, I guess check on you."

Phen watched them, startled. "Really?"

Noah rolled his eyes and stood, noting they completely changed topics, all well. "Why wouldn't we come check on you?" He shook his head. "Anyway, we plan to look around during the day instead of dealing with school. Hopefully, we can avoid the police if people start asking where we are. Though, I'm surprised there wasn't already news that we didn't go to school today."

Phen stared for a moment, pursing his lips before he responded, "I think that's because I was out as well. Mom probably called in and they just assumed…" He turned. "Hey, Aiden? I have Noah's but, what's your phone number? I want to keep in touch with you two, both of you." His gaze settled on Aiden before promptly going back to Noah, a hint of red on his cheeks.

"You hitting on us?" Noah teased, hands on his hips. Horror flashed over Phen's face as Noah chuckled. "Relax. I know that's not it, I just couldn't help it." He let out a breath as Aiden fiddled uncomfortably with his pants.

"Noah, that was cruel."

"Oh, hush." Noah gave Aiden a look before turning to a still bright red Phen. ""That's up to Aiden but…" Noah glanced sidelong. "He's terrible at actually picking up the phone so you would still have better luck just contacting me."

"Alright." Phen swallowed thickly before letting out a tired breath, cradling the phone. "I'll… call you." His attention stayed on Aiden for a moment before he shook his head.

Noah turned to Aiden. "Seriously, bro, you need to get used to using a phone soon yourself. This is awkward as it is."

Aiden winced though quickly turned into a shrug. "Who would I call?" He tapped his leg. "That creep? The only good it's done is letting me know he could text both of us. Great, right?"

Noah rolled his eyes, but decided not to argue. He gave up arguing ages ago.

"I mean, I know you were avoiding it, but couldn't you call the police?" Phen brought up, that blush returning once more. "Your father. A delivery service for food. I mean, you guys travel a lot, so…"

Aiden just stared. "Then I'll ask Noah to use his phone."

Phen blinked. "Uh, that's not exactly full-proof."

Aiden waved it off. "Whatever. We should talk to your mother and let her know we're heading out to take care of some things."

Phen glared, but sighed. "You're not going to agree, are you?" Aiden just turned and walked out the door.

"Believe me, I've been trying for a couple years now," Noah muttered.

"Why did you say that?" Phen asked, voice low and taut. "I didn't expect you of all people to tease like that."

Noah shifted, noting the glare on Phen's face.

"Because. For one, I wanted to see your reaction and for two…" Noah turned and leaned down, face twisting into an expression that seemed to startle Phen. "Aiden has had a rough time making friends. I know you are probably genuine, but I'm not going to risk him being hurt." Phen stared back, expression shifting from startled to even. Noah pulled back, trailing a hand down his face. "Just… I get it." He glanced past spread fingers, noting the way Phen fidgeted, both uncomfortable and very much unnerved. "I simply don't want my brother to feel betrayed because he trusted the wrong person. I know that pain all too well." At that, he turned and headed toward the doorway, leaving Phen to his thoughts.

Noah arrived in time to spot Aiden talking to Ellen. Her expression was difficult to read. "No. I don't think it's a good idea for you boys to go out again. It's getting late and I think it would be best if you stay here."

Aiden sighed, as if he already tried explaining something once. "Like I said, Dad will be there soon. He told us to get the place ahead of time and he would meet us there. When he's less busy, he'll come to you."

"I don't care. You can go in the morning and I'm not to enthused about your father anyway. I would rather make sure you two boys are safe. Your barely in your teens. It's too dangerous."

Aiden went to argue when Noah stepped over with a smile. "Ah, sorry. Aiden doesn't really like staying over other people's houses that much. He doesn't want to bother you but, yeah, we can stay." He gave Aiden a look which caused his brother to snap his mouth shut in annoyance.

"I get that, dear, but my point still stands." She glanced toward Noah before shaking her head. "Well, at least join me for dessert and than we can make sure the living room is set up for you again. Alright?"

Noah nodded, heading after her as she went through the door to the kitchen. Aiden followed quietly behind.

CHAPTER 31

Sitting down to eat, Noah appreciated the warmth of the moment. The joy on Ellen's face when Phen joined them, apparently feeling much better, was something that tugged at Noah's heart. It was both something special to witness, and heartbreaking to bear. Soon enough, they finished up their cakes as Phen brought some upstairs for his father.

Ellen was watching them like a hawk so eventually they found themselves settling into the living room once more, Noah managing to snag a salt shaker on the way. The rug was white so it allowed him to spill it over without too much showing once Ellen had stepped away for a bit. It wasn't perfect, but it was something.

Noah settled beside Aiden who was curled up in a blanket, staring at the far wall, lost in thought.

"What's on your mind?" Noah asked as he plopped down onto his couch, watching quietly.

Aiden paused, glancing up before sighing, rubbing his arms. "How much I hate this, all of this. Is it so hard to just wish for something to work for once and it does? We've been trying for days to get anything and our best solution is to talk to ghosts?" Aiden shook his head, his tense shoulders showing he was more than a little overwhelmed. "As I said earlier, I'm worried about Dad as well. I know he can take care of himself, but it's been too long since he last contacted us. What if—"

"I think he's still alright," Noah cut in, unable to hide the pain in his voice. "But, I agree. I hate this as much as you do." He glanced down and fell onto his side, half of his body intentionally landing on Aiden's lap. "We're learning all of this stuff, but still not getting any answers. I'm not really sure what to do anymore." He paused as Aiden grunted glaring down at him, only for the annoyance to shift to concern, probably spotting something in Noah's expression. "I'm worried about talking to those ghosts. It doesn't matter which one we talk to. I…" He shifted, fingers curling into the fabric. They sat in silence before Noah shook his head and pushed himself up. "But, you're right." He winced. "Oh man, I hate to say that."

Aiden huffed as Noah chuckled before sobering once more. "We really do need to talk to them, though. They are our best lead…" He hesitated, fidgeting. What he was about to say he knew his brother would say was reckless or even incredibly stupid but… "We should go now, as it's getting late."

"What?"

"I mean, Mia mentioned that they are stronger at night, right? It took them a long time to manifest when we were right there, in the house. If we want them to talk, we might have to wait until evening when they are a bit stronger so we can actually talk to them instead of those fragments or whatever." He winced, noticing Aiden's darkening expression. "I'm not saying go inside, but if we stand near the window I broke yesterday and converse with them? I think it might work better than trying during the day. Speaking of, I wonder how Mia was able to get in, but they couldn't get out. I thought Mia said shattering would work?"

"Maybe it's a different method for a ghost trapped inside." Aiden shook his head. "This shit is weird and I would rather not try to think about it or figure it out."

"Fair." Noah lips twitched up before dropping once more. "That's why I'm thinking we do it now."

Aiden groaned, clearly upset about what he was about to say, "It's stupid, and reckless and probably our best shot."

"When you say it like that…"

"You know what I mean." Aiden huffed. "Come on, before I decide I would rather sleep instead."

Noah paused for a moment before chuckling, adjusting his shirt. "Alright, let's leave our bags here for now and only bring what we need to. I would rather not be pulled down by a heavy backpack." He peered toward the door. "Once Ellen stops watching us like a hawk." He paused. "Speaking of, how are we slipping out unnoticed?"

Aiden frowned for a moment as both of them heard footsteps outside before Ellen peeked her head in. She smiled faintly upon seeing them still there before speaking. "Get some rest for tonight. I'll see you in the morning. I'll make us some pancakes, alright?" With that she waved and soon enough, after a few clicks of the lock, went upstairs.

"Well, great…" Noah muttered, annoyed. "We can probably unlock the doors without any issue but…" He sighed. "It's not breaking and entering if we're leaving, right?"

Aiden just snorted at that.

Noah groaned, that would be his luck. Well, all they could do was try. He didn't want to stay here tonight, not now that he had a plan of action. Hopefully they wouldn't wake Ellen. It would have to be enough.

Aiden peered out the window, as Noah swept to his feet, hurrying into the other room. Aiden got up after, peering up the stairs. Noah noted what he was doing as he peered over the locks. He could hear chatter from upstairs and felt a tap on his shoulder. Glancing back, Aiden put a finger to his lips, shaking his head. Noah frowned, but conceded. The two waited, listening for a few minutes before the sound of chatter faded. Noah grinned and slipped to the front door, quickly unlocking everything and, as quietly as possible, opened the door. Aiden slipped past.

With a gesture the two hurried down the road as the flicker of the lights above cast long shadows over the road. Noah saw Aiden shiver and peered over to see Mia settle beside them. "Took you guys long enough, at least you two remembered the salt this time. I had a heck of a time getting in. So, anyway, I was only half listening, why were you two gone today and why did you two think it would be a good idea to go to the prison again so soon after almost dying?"

"Do we need to tell you?" Aiden leaned back, giving her an annoyed expression.

She rolled her visible eye. "It would be nice to know so I know what I'm doing to keep you two somewhat safe."

Noah lightly elbowed Aiden before responding, "Oh, hi Mia. Actually, we went back to the house to collect some things. We were going to try to find a room for the night but…" he shrugged, smiling sheepishly.

"And then you plan to speak to those ghosts later?" Mia swayed slightly side to side. "It's obvious you realize the implications of doing that, so I am not going to point them out. Instead, I have to ask, are you prepared?"

"Prepared as we can be," Aiden muttered, placing a hand to his chest. "It's make-shift, but it'll do."

Mia hummed. "And you think those children will be able to give you answers? They are angry, hurt and vengeful."

"They are also desperate." Aiden finally turned to face her. "To be honest, you said yourself that you wished to go home and, after being here for so long, I'm surprised you aren't as desperate as them."

Mia's expression shifted, her visible eye flashing black for a moment. "How astute. However, you are quite wrong." Aiden paused as Noah slowed to a stop, confused. Mia settled onto the ground, her feet touching the earth lightly. Her hair trailed around her and Noah noted, he never saw the other side of her face, even when she flipped upside down. Mia turned to both of them and cocked her head. "I have been here a very long time. Obsession is a powerful thing in ghosts, but over the years, I've learned to curtail it. Patience is often key, and yet so few remember that." She walked forward, Aiden glanced toward Noah who shrugged and walked beside her. Noah could hear Aiden huff, and follow behind. "My desire to go home has not faltered, nor has it subsided." She tilted her head, almost snapping her neck to turn toward

Noah while she continued to walk forward. "You do not understand, nor will you ever, the sheer force of will it takes to suppress that desire. It was wise of you two to obtain that cross, and for me to stay with Phen throughout the day instead of following after you when you left this morning."

She cocked her head to the side, hair almost completely obscuring her features except for the one piercing golden eye. "Know this, do not, for a moment, think that my desire, my desperation, to return home has faded. It has only grown. Be aware of that when you talk to them. They are but children, unable to contain the emotions like an older ghost might. They will take you for all you're worth." At that, her head snapped forward once more and she hummed, swinging her arms and continuing forward as if she hadn't just said all of that.

Noah found himself at a halt, Aiden stepping up beside him. Noah glanced sidelong at Aiden, unsure what to do. If Mia was so desperate, then what was she doing helping them?

Sure, he had made a deal with her and she followed through with that deal, but why? He and Aiden had no idea how to use whatever this was. He trusted Mia, a lot more than he expected, considering she was technically still a stranger to them. He just... he couldn't help but wonder.

Why didn't she take their power or whatever when they didn't have the crosses to protect them?

He shook the thought off. The more he learned about ghosts, the more the supernatural unnerved him. He was starting to understand Aiden's hesitation, though he didn't feel the same. After all, Aiden probably didn't trust her at all at this point, but, then again, Noah knew that he probably never had.

•   •   •   •   •

Aiden shivered, the cold wind blowing past as they continued down the street. At least the salt thing worked. Good to know. Still, even with that Ghost showing that there was nothing to fear with Mother's cross protecting him, there was still too much he didn't know about these creatures that put him on edge.

Of the things he did know, it didn't make him feel any better.

It was getting late now, the amount of people on the streets dwindling to almost nothing. They walked and talked, Aiden pulling out the papers they found earlier in the day. They peered over the papers and debated on which person might be their best bet. "I think it's him." Aiden gestured to one picture showing Peter, a once smiling and happy looking boy of blonde hair and piercing blue eyes. "He was definitely a sort of leader of the group. He might be the best to initiate the conversation with."

"But isn't he the one who attacked you?"

"They all did." Aiden chewed on his bottom lip in thought before shaking his head. "The other reason is because he was one of the latest ones to be captured, so he might have seen something different."

Noah winced, but didn't reply. Aiden felt a chill and noticed the Ghost watching them quietly, her expression was hard to decipher but there was almost a hint of concern on her face which he slotted away for later.

Soon enough, they found themselves approaching the home once more. The streets were completely abandoned, the moonlight just starting to peek past the dark clouds lingering above. A cold wind blew through, causing Aiden to shiver and pull his sweatshirt tighter around him. The Ghost floated above, silent as the night, wary.

Aiden steadied himself, mentally preparing the questions they decided to ask Peter as he moved up toward the shattered window. Thanks to where it was, no one had yet to notice it. The surrounding homes were all abandoned and it was placed on the side.

He pulled out Peter's sheet. He stepped up to the window and spoke. "Peter Williams, are you here?"

Silence met his words, but he waited, the seconds ticking by in his head. Their Ghost ally and Noah both mentioned that it might take some time and Aiden wouldn't be surprised. It took a while last time as well. He lightly placed his hand against the wall, wondering what the hell he was doing.

He felt movement and turned as Noah bumped up against him, grinning before leaning in through the window. "Peter! We want to talk to you," he almost shouted into the room. "We know who you are, now can you talk to us?"

Once more, a quiet stillness settled over the home.

Aiden listened carefully along with Noah, a chill curling over his neck, getting worse as the time moved, only noticing Noah's sudden stiffness a second before he heard it.

Creak. Both gazes snapped toward the doorway as it slowly shifted, opening just a crack.

Noah pulled back so it was just the two of them pressing against the windowsill and not actually inside.

There was nothing there.

There was a shift, a groaning sound echoing through the house as if it was resettling. The moonlight disappeared, shadows arcing over them. Aiden took a step back, flicking on his flashlight. Noah followed suit with his phone, both of them wary.

They figured they would be fine outside, but Aiden was starting to second guess that.

Their Ghostly ally flitted around them in a slow circle, just watching. It was eerie, and though he didn't want to admit it, it was also strangely comforting to have her there.

He just wished he knew what her true intentions were.

He didn't trust her, not at all, but he was well aware that she did want to help them. Gain for gain, he supposed was the case and, if that was all it was, he could handle that.

THUD.

Aiden jerked, flashlight beaming over the remains of the glass and straight into a pale face, hands having slammed on the area where the window was. So that was the thud he heard…

He barely held in a startled sound, Noah let out a quiet screech and stumbled back.

The boy, the same one from yesterday who tried to possess Phen, tilted his head, features so different from the happy go lucky picture.

"You." He hissed, hands pressed against the window that was no longer there. "Why are you here? How do you know my name?"

Aiden shook it off, it was fine, the ghost couldn't get to either of them. He pulled up the sheet and turned it around. "This is you, right?"

The specter straightened, slowly pulling back from the window. "Yes, that is." His eyes narrowed, flicking briefly to Mia, where he stiffened. Aiden could almost feel the way she waved, the movement over exaggerated. He promptly ignored her, turning back to Aiden. "And what good will that do?"

Aiden took a deep breath, stuffing the paper back into his pocket. "We're trying to look for the one who did this to you and the others."

The boy, Peter, jerked, twitching before leaning forward once more. His face was twisted in an expression between utter glee and withering hatred. "What good will that do us? We are still trapped here. Unable to say good-bye, unable to rest with our own bodies."

"We want to try to find a way to stop any more people getting trapped in there." Noah cut in, words a little shaky, but strong. "To be honest, we're looking for our father—"

The creature hissed, causing Noah to snap his mouth shut. "The lives of another don't matter to me. Let me out of here."

Aiden grimaced; this was going as well as he expected.

"Peter, calm yourself." Another voice spoke up, a woman's. Noah and Aiden shifted, glancing beyond Peter as he straightened. Behind him was the woman Aiden remembered seeing chained down. He also remembered seeing her picture, an older woman holding a child as she stood next to a man, face hidden by the cut of the picture. Yet, here, her arms were still bloody and scarred. She stopped to one side of Peter, head cocked. "You are the boy from last night. The one who could see us fully."

Aiden hesitated, unsure whether to nod.

"Veridian, that's your name, right?" Noah asked, glancing between the papers and her.

The woman cocked her head the other way. "Why, yes." There was a faint hiss in the air. "I believe you came back for more than just a chat and to bother us like this. Why don't you come inside?"

Aiden shook his head. "We'll continue to talk, but we will not enter. Not right now."

The woman swayed side to side for a moment before nodding. "If you don't mind, I will help the others come down so they can speak as well." At that, she turned and moved away, disappearing through the door.

Peter pulled back, silent. A strangely neutral expression on his face.

Soon enough, to Aiden's disdain and fear, the room was filled with the other ghosts. The little girl clung to the ceiling. The other boy was against the wall. The man floated behind the woman and the girl sat crosslegged near the window.

All attention was on Noah and Aiden.

"We're here." The crosslegged girl spoke, voice even with a quiet sound of static. "Why do you torment us like this?"

Noah shook his head and took a hesitant step toward the window. Neither of them were touching it, but they weren't far from it either. "We want to find a way to deal with the person who did this to all of you." Noah spoke, voice a little more hesitant this time. "You see, our dad was trying to find him and disappeared. If we can find our dad, he might know a way to not only stop the man who did this to you, but also help to free you."

At those last two words, all of the specters perked up, heads snapping, literally, toward Noah.

"And why should we believe you?" Peter hissed. "Believing him was what got us into this mess."

"Believing him? What happened?" Aiden finally broke in. Information, that's what they needed.

Peter's lips smashed shut.

Silence filled the area for a moment before Veridian stepped forward. "There was this strange humming sound that we heard, outside our window."

"What are you doing! They haven't made any deals to help us."

"No, but I would rather not have another child end up here," Veridian said, shooting in front of Peter, causing the other to back off. Aiden heard a faint whistle from the Ghost next to him, clearly impressed. Veridian instantly pulled back and turned to Aiden. "The stories are relatively the same for all of us, so I'll tell mine." She hummed, a tune that caused both Noah and Aiden to stiffen.

"They recognize it." The boy curled up in the corner spoke, the only one who wasn't watching them. Aiden didn't need to guess why, noting the empty sockets. What happened to that boy's eyes? "They have heard it as well, and yet they still live."

Veridian slowed in her hum, an eerie tune that made Aiden want to run. "This song, we all heard it." Her gaze flitted toward the boy who noticed Aiden and Noah knew the tune, before turning back to the twins. "You have heard it as well, but neither of you were dragged here. How was it that you could resist its pull?"

"Pull?" Noah asked, confused. "What are you talking about?" He shook his head. "I want to run in the opposite direction."

The creatures all glanced toward each other, a silent whisper of a conversation echoing between them. Finally, Veridian turned back and floated forward. "We wonder, does that have to do with the power that emanates from you? Even at night, we usually would not have the strength to speak or be seen like this. That power, it is what is making us strong right now, correct?"

Aiden was honestly not sure and their Ghost ally wasn't saying anything.

"Maybe? Honestly, we really don't know much about this power thing." Noah hesitated. "But you said you felt called? Do you mind explaining?"

Veridian hummed, a different less eerie tune this time. "We all walked over to the window and opened it. Then, the next thing we knew, we were being dragged outside, cloth over our mouths." She shook her head. "When we woke up, we were in that room you saw above." Aiden noticed the way quite a few of the ghosts were stiff. He doubted it was a memory that was easy to talk about.

Though, he was curious how it was that the ghosts remembered as much as they did.

Veridian pulled back. "We never saw who did it. We were always bound, gagged and blindfolded." Veridian shivered. "I don't remember what happened, none of us have clear memories of the time, but…" Veridian turned to the empty-eyed boy. "One of us did see the man who did this to us, for a moment."

The boy tilted his head up. "Me." He turned to Aiden and Noah. "That's why he took my eyes. That blindfold. I managed to pull it off." Aiden tried hard not to shiver as he noticed the blood trailing from the empty sockets. "He laughed as I screamed, this echoing double-layered voice. My mind still plays tricks on me, but I know I've seen him before." He twitched. "At the school. I don't know his job, or what he does, but he works there."

"Do you remember anything else?" Noah's voice was quiet, prodding.

"He smelled of cologne, a strange, horrible mix of oranges and cinnamon. He was tall, appeared taller with the fact he was looming above me—" The boy stopped, rocking side to side. The girl floated over and settled next to him, neither saying a word.

The tension in the room skyrocketed, but also settled. A strange combination that was hard for Aiden to understand.

"Well, that is what we know." Veridian turned back to Aiden and Noah. "As for this man you speak of, your father." She floated forward, fingers lightly touching against the glass that no longer sat there, the pieces shattered. The jagged edges the only indication of what was once a solid pane. "Your father was brought here, for but a moment, but our killer could not touch him except through rope or bags."

"Wait, you saw the killer after your death? Don't you have a description?" Aiden took a step forward, frustrated.

The woman shook her head, gaze piercing. "We see that man, the one who did this to us, as he wants us to see him, not as who he is. We flee when he arrives and return when he departs. A few have tried to attack him, but the end results…" Her gaze turned to Peter who pulled back fully now. "Are less than ideal." She returned her attention to Aiden. "Your father, however, felt different. He saw us and it seems like our killer is using him for something. Last I knew, before he was hauled off in a bag, was that your father was still alive… something none of us have seen happen before. He's always dragged our bodies out AFTER we're dead."

"That creep didn't kill us right away either," Peter argued. "That bastard took his time."

Veridian didn't argue and Aiden shivered, not wanting to imagine what it was these creatures went through.

For a moment, he felt something brush just in front of his cheek, and he pushed back, terrified.

Veridian just smiled, her hand through the window. "That power you possess, that LIFE… he wants it so badly and now I see why." Her grin grew and Aiden found himself taking another step back, Noah doing the same, fear slashing across his face.

"Okay, time to go." Their Ghostly ally circled back down, curling around them. "I hope you got what you wanted."

"Just stay a little longer," Veridian pleaded, though her voice sounded strange. "We've almost finished receiving it, that beautiful power, that beautiful LIFE."

"Why are you guys so obsessed with our damn power or whatever!" Aiden snapped, feeling both frustrated and fearful. He noted the other ghosts were pushing forward, no longer shying away. Another hand poked through, then a leg.

"Okay, let's go, move." Their Ghostly ally growled, air growing viciously cold. Aiden felt Noah grab his arm and wrench, racing away.

Screeches filled the night air, along with angered wails and cries.

"Keep going," their Ghostly ally said. "All the way back to the house. Stay there tonight, in the living room. We will talk tomorrow." Aiden didn't argue, racing down the street with Noah pulling him along. The cries echoed in Aiden's ears, even from so far away.

The run felt long as they darted down the road, that ever present feeling of cold shredding down Aiden's neck as they finally spotted the house. It took all of Aiden's efforts not to slam the door open as he raced up. Noah hurried inside, gesturing as Aiden quickly closed and locked the door, twisting and turning all of the locks before they bolted into the living room, pulling Noah with him who had stopped in the main hall, trembling.

"Oh… holy. What was that?" Noah's voice pitched upward, barely stopping from being loud enough to wake anyone. "We were talking just fine and she suddenly just became deranged." He turned to Aiden. "Why was Mia so insistent we leave? How were they doing that? What is this power we have?"

"I would like to know that myself." Aiden let out a breath, feeling his own pounding heart start to subside. "Let's just rest for tonight and figure it out tomorrow." He paused, thoughts racing. "We did learn some things though."

"I would say a lot." Noah perked up. "They saw Dad! He's still alive."

"But he's also in the hands of a killer." Aiden pursed his lips, finally taking a seat on the couch. "A killer who tortures his victims before killing them. On top of that, the killer needs Dad for something, but what?" Aiden gritted his teeth, frustration foremost. "Damnit. The worst part is, the only new lead we have is the cologne he wears and confirming he works in the school. That does absolutely nothing!"

Aiden heard footsteps and froze before he realized they were Noah's. He could hear faint snoring from upstairs and felt relieved they didn't wake anyone with their sudden barge back into the house, even if Aiden was as careful as he could be with the door. he felt the couch dip next to him. "It's more than we knew." Noah spoke up, voice faint. "At least we know Dad is still alive."

"But for how long?" Aiden muttered, receiving silence in return. "I knew it was urgent, but I guess I hadn't quite realized. I hoped he simply dropped his phone and got away, but to know that wasn't the case?" Aiden let his head fall forward into his hands with a tired groan.

A palm gently patted against his back before something leaned into him.

"I'm just glad to know he's still alive. Mia's right, we should try to get some rest tonight. Being exhausted won't help anyone."

Aiden knew that, but with his thoughts racing as they were, he wasn't sure he would be able to.

He wasn't sure why, whether from exhaustion or from a need to annoy, he found himself falling sideways, earning a yelp from his brother, causing the two of them to tumble off the couch, Noah barely catching himself from landing flat on the ground, dragging blankets down with him. Aiden chuckled though it was more out of a strange tiredness than amusement. "Are you okay?"

"Ugh… just hand me the damn pillow and get off."

Aiden rolled onto his side, head on Noah's stomach as he reached up onto the couch, grabbing a pillow. He knew he should get up, but even rolling over felt tiring. Thankfully there was still some blankets on the ground from the night before that cushioned the sound of their fall. He managed to drag the pillow down, feeling it smack into his face. Huh… maybe he was tired. "We need to sleep, right?"

"Did you have to knock me over to do it?" Noah groaned, lightly tugging at the pillow while pushing at Aiden. Aiden didn't think he was that heavy. Aiden noticed that neither of them moved and sighed. He probably should get up.

He frowned slightly, his eyelids fluttering closed as a sudden wave of drowsiness swept over him. He was laying on Noah's stomach, this wasn't even funny anymore. Ugh, this was awkward, he only meant to be annoying.

He felt hands lightly push at his side "Aiden," Noah whined, tone achingly tired. "Get up, will you?"

"Trying," Aiden muttered, managing to push himself up enough to flop off of Noah but without the strength to get back on the couch he ended up falling right next to him. He wasn't sure why, but he felt utterly drained and exhausted, as if he was hit over the head with a sudden dose of sleeping pills. He felt Noah shift, but his mind slipped into a tired darkness as he curled into himself.

He needed to get up. They were thirteen, they had no reason to share a bed, or, well, the floor, but his body wasn't listening to him and neither was his mind.

For a brief moment, before sleep took over, he wondered if their ability to help ghosts had anything to do with it. If it did, then it would explain why they were so exhausted.

The thought terrified him.

CHAPTER 32

Noah awoke with a crick in his back and neck. He could tell he was curled around something… a pillow? His mind was slow to catch up as he curled into whatever it was, hearing a quiet grunt and whine.

He blinked blearily, his brain finally catching up with the night before.

It took him all of two seconds after that to realize he curled up around Aiden, Aiden pressed against his side, waking up in a similar state of confusion.

It took another second for Noah to roll over, almost slamming into the living room table with a painful yelp.

"What the—" Aiden pushed himself upward, holding his head. "Ugh… we didn't try one of Dad's drinks again, right?" he muttered before stilling. "That was a stupid question." He peered around, utterly confused. The faint sound of cooking echoed from the kitchen along with humming that promptly stopped at Noah's yelp. Footsteps sounded before Ellen peeked her head in worriedly.

"Are you boys alright? I know there are a lot of blankets on the floor, but I thought you would use the couches…" She frowned slightly. "You two didn't go out, did you? I heard some banging early this morning."

Noah barely stopped himself from widening his eyes, shaking his head instead. She relaxed before that frown vanished. "By the way, you two looked so comfortable, I guess you boys needed a good rest, especially since I couldn't wake you even when I called to you. Same happened to Phen so I figured I would let you boys stay until you woke before you headed to school. Feeling better?"

Noah felt heat rise to his face as he scrambled to his feet. "What are you talking about?" He yelped quietly.

Ellen chuckled into her hand, faint smile on her lips. "It's fine. I was going to wake you two but I figured I would let you two sleep, obviously you needed it like I said. Phen should be just waking up soon so why don't you join me for breakfast?" She glanced toward her watch. "Unfortunately, I won't be able to drive you three to school since I'm already late as it is for work, but I can at least get you all some breakfast."

"That's fine. Thanks, just give us a minute." Noah was still bright red and noticed Aiden was being suspiciously silent. Ellen gave a little nod and wave before walking away. After she was gone, the sound of humming returning once more, Noah turned slowly to Aiden with a quiet embarrassed horror. "Did you knock us both out just by falling over?" Noah asked as Aiden, who had buried himself under a blanket Ellen must have put over them last night, poked his head out, clearly a little embarrassed himself.

"Not my intention," Aiden muttered. "Ugh, I'm going to leave the pranks to you from now on."

Noah blinked and felt a wide grin cross his face, only to quickly wipe it away when Aiden glared at him. "Seriously though, Aiden, what was that? I suddenly felt exhausted."

Aiden nodded, palm pushing into his temple with a grimace as he climbed to his feet. "I was realizing this as we were falling asleep. I think I know why our Ghost friend was so adamant about us leaving." He shook his head. "We need to talk to her. See if she can come in."

Noah shrugged, pushing himself to his feet and stumbling over before coming to an abrupt halt. "Shouldn't we, I don't know, get cleaned up first?"

Aiden paused at that and groaned. "Right, yeah, let's do that."

Noah quickly brushed his teeth and got ready for the day, changing into another set of clothes.

They were so exhausted, they hadn't even changed. Thankfully Ellen didn't ask as she handed them some breakfast before glaring up the stairs, annoyed. "Ugh, that boy. How is he still not up?" She waved to them before hurrying up the stairs.

In that moment, Noah glanced around before calling out, "Mia?"

Mia swooped down, probably having been on the roof, and settled down in front of him, watching curiously. "Yes?"

"We need to talk."

"Was I correct in assuming you collapsed soon after getting back?"

"You knew it was going to happen."

Mia rolled her eyes and leaned forward. "Yes, yes, I did." She pulled back. "I've told you before, with you two not understanding how your powers work, it is easy to be affected by a ghost. Your father probably protected you from it and, with your abilities, one or two ghosts won't make much of an effect. However, that was six in there, slowly feeding off of your energy as you were just chatting."

Noah gulped. "Wait, is that why they suddenly went crazy at the end?"

Mia smiled, it wasn't a nice one. "Oh, they were crazy from the get go. That Veridian woman did a fantastic job of managing to hide it, which helped the others, but underneath? They were all deranged." Mia sighed. "Not surprising, considering how and where they died. I talked about shattered souls before, this creep shatters the soul, messes it up just enough and then kills the person before they can mend." She grimaced. "It leaves the ghost tattered. I hadn't noticed before, but while you were talking and while I was listening, it was easy to pick out the tell-tale signs. I'm not sure if you noticed, but all of them were slowly moving towards you two the entire time, not just the two or three you were speaking with."

Aiden shuddered as Noah rubbed his arms. He thought he saw it, but also thought it was just his imagination. After all, every so often, one would shy away, so… To know they actually were doing exactly that? He wasn't sure what to feel about it.

"So, even if we wanted to, we couldn't free them." Aiden frowned.

"No." Mia shook her head and sighed. "A shattered soul like that? The only freedom you can give them is banishment."

"But why? Is there no way for them to recover? They just want to go home like you—"

"We are not the same," Mia hissed, surging forward before promptly pulling back. "But, no, there isn't a way that I know of to recover a damaged soul like that. You and Phen could heal because you still have a mortal coil that protects the soul and gives it life and nourishment. Ghosts like us?" She put a hand to her chest. "If our soul is shattered, well, there is no recovering from that. We are only parts of our original selves. You noticed all the wounds and markings on them, correct?"

Noah nodded as Aiden said," I was wondering about that… Phen mentioned he often saw things that we couldn't. Yet, those ghosts? I saw the wounds, the…" He shuddered and Noah knew exactly which ghost he was talking about. "Yet with Lynn and yourself, we haven't."

Noah felt a little better, knowing he wasn't the only one who noticed that.

Mia nodded. "That is because Lynn was a pure soul, the killer hadn't gotten a chance to shatter hers, because she was simply in the way, or so I would assume. If he managed to capture her like the others, then it would be possible, but I believe with what Phen and Lynn said about her getting too close, he got desperate and, as a result, sloppy." Mia shook her head. "I believe I told you before that our forms and our souls are expressly linked."

Aiden stiffened. "That's how you could tell." Mia grinned. "You mentioned we see your true form. That was their true form. Broken."

"You, admittedly, didn't see the worst of it, but, yes." Mia crossed one leg over the other and leaned against the side. "In that state, they can only crave, but never be satisfied." She turned to them, eyes narrowed. "If you hadn't fled when you did, if they had gotten a chance to escape, they would continue to haunt this town, constantly searching for something that can no longer help them."

Noah glanced away, hugging himself tightly. "Even with this power, there's nothing we can do?"

Silence enveloped the room for a moment, before Mia let out a sigh. "Maybe someday." The words sounded fairly distant, off. "But as you are now? No." The floorboards creaked. "Simply to escape their confines, those ghosts drained you of almost all of your energy. It was only adrenaline that kept you going. Once you relaxed? Well, you saw the results."

"That explains a lot."

Noah glanced away, feeling his cheeks redden. It was embarrassing to think about. "So, uh, we know that if we're near ghosts for long periods of time, don't try to prank each other, or knock each other off the couch."

Aiden turned to him and rolled his eyes. "We can't use that as a reference, besides, you've done that to me enough times, it's fair."

"You didn't wake up with a crick in your back!"

"No, but I did wake up to you almost trying to suffocate me." He glared, causing Noah to feel heat rise even more. Gah.

"Oh? Did I miss something interesting?" Mia giggled, rocking back and forth where she stood in front of them.

"Not really." Aiden shrugged as Noah viciously shook his head.

Mia raised an amused eyebrow, but didn't push. "If you say so." She lounged back as if in a chair and sighed. "So, what are you planning to do now?" Aiden shrugged as Noah frowned, unsure. What were they going to do now? Going back to that building was apparently suicide.

He winced, all those ghosts… all those people who were ruined by one possessed person. How was that possible?

They heard footsteps and peered back to see Ellen descending the stairs, peering at her watch with a frown. She hurried over to the stove, finishing breakfast before placing down three plates stacked with pancakes. "PHEN!" She shouted, annoyed. "Get down here!"

Footsteps sounded above followed by a yelp and stumbling. It wasn't long before Phen hurried down the stairs, almost tripping on the bottom one. He peered over, blinking in surprise. Ellen who had put some glasses filled with orange juice down, walked over and patted his head. "Make sure you get to school, mister. I've already called, telling them you three would be late but don't skip entirely. I need to go, make sure you get there as soon as you finish breakfast, understood?" She lightly kissed him on the forehead, startling him. She waved before hurrying away as Phen quickly brushed his hand against his head, grimacing.

Noah couldn't help but watch with a hint of envy at the interaction. A moment later, they heard the rumble of the car before it pulled away.

Noah wondered if Ellen wanted to stay home but couldn't. If she was the only one working, she probably couldn't risk losing too many hours at work. In a way, she was similar to dad. They wanted to be there, but work made it difficult.

Noah shook his head as Phen hesitantly walked over. "Hey guys, how are you two? Did you… did you go out last night? I could have sworn I heard the door early this morning."

"Yeah… that was probably us." Noah winced. "Long story but, how are you feeling?"

"Better after a good night's rest," Phen admitted, glancing between them. "So, I was thinking, you mentioned how you were going to see those ghosts again, right?"

"Already done."

Phen blinked and shook his head, expression somewhat impressed. "Of course. That's why you said long story." He paused before glancing back up. "So, you obviously would have learned something, right? As you know, I know this place pretty well. I might be able to figure out any clues you might have."

Aiden furrowed his brow. Noah hesitated for a moment before turning to him, telling him everything that happened the night before, though changing up how they fell asleep. No one needed to know about that.

Once done, Phen, whose brow furrowed deeper with each bit of news, let out a huff as he put his fork down, having been eating while they were talking. "Okay, so that's a thing. Good to know." He glanced toward Mia and turned away. "Thanks for that, Mia, I don't want to imagine becoming something like them."

Mia just nodded. Noah shuddered, agreeing. To be unable to move on, but also be unable to resolve whatever it was that plagued you. It sounded horrible.

"However, the fact that your father is stuck with that guy?" Phen shook his head. "How are you two not panicking right now?"

"Oh, we're panicking," Aiden said.

Phen blinked, staring as Noah smiled sheepishly. For once, Aiden was actually right. His mind was in a frenzy and he was trying his best to keep calm. It wasn't working very well.

"You two…" Phen shook his head, amused. "Still, that gives me some ideas. We have clues on what he's like. There aren't that many male teachers or workers in the school and, to be honest, if that person was our age, I think someone would have realized by now. He would probably be recognized if it was a teacher, especially with such distinctive cologne." Phen curled his nose up in distaste. "I mean, I like oranges and cinnamon separate, but together? Who thought that would be a good idea?"

Aiden shrugged as Noah actually thought it over. True, that did actually sound quite disturbing. Maybe it could be a good smell, but he wasn't sure about that.

"It's probably a faint scent." Aiden spoke up. "Something you catch if you were close like…" He winced as Noah shifted uncomfortably. "Well, putting that aside, we now can confirm it's someone who works there, that isn't a teacher or a student, but is there often enough to be somewhat recognizable." Aiden pursed his lips, debating. "That does narrow it down a bit. Custodial, secretarial, things like that."

Phen hummed in thought, lightly tapping his cheek before nodding. "We might be able to figure it out." His gaze flitted to Aiden. "We know what cologne he uses, that it's a male which… whoops?" He chuckled. "I should have thought of that when I was following Ms. Fiona the other day."

Noah blinked and then slapped a hand against his face with a groan. He hadn't even thought about it. Aiden's lips quirked upward in amusement. Smartass, of course he thought about it and didn't say anything.

"But other than that, we can narrow it down to anyone who is support staff." Phen narrowed his eyes. "This person is specifically after you two. If he has your father, there has to be a reason. It's strange he hasn't used your father to drag you out, to be honest."

Noah stiffened and tugged his phone out, only to sigh. There were no new texts which was both upsetting and relieving at the same time.

"That is odd." Aiden furrowed his brow. "I highly doubt this ghost-possessed human is dumb. It would make sense to just send a picture to drag us out, like you said."

"Maybe he knows we would go to the police? Or find a way to do something against him?"

"Either that or he's specifically not contacting us for a reason." Aiden glanced up. "It's possible he almost exposed himself with one of the texts. He hasn't texted or even attempted to call since the last one calling me out." He shook his head. "Speaking of the police, it's lucky no one has really been curious and Ellen has been covering for us unintentionally. Most of the time, but the rest of the time, the police should have been suspicious." Aiden glanced between them, as Noah stiffened in realization.

"Which means that the police were never notified."

"Exactly." Aiden grimaced. "Of course, that just solidifies the idea that it's not a teacher. Even if one didn't say anything, another would, so…"

"It's someone higher, or with an easy way to slip in and out." Noah pursed his lips as Aiden nodded.

Phen watched, curious and concerned. "So, if they didn't call the police and are not contacting you, then what are they up to? Are they trying to find you themselves?"

"I don't know about that." Mia spoke up. "Think of what happened to the others. They were all lured out and then ambushed."

Aiden pursed his lips while Noah placed his face in his hands with a groan. Geez… Could something PLEASE make sense for once?

"Okay, so a stalking, ambushing, ghost human with a heavy desire for capturing these two. That's totally not creepy or gross in the slightest." Phen's voice indicated his disgust pretty well, in Noah's opinion. "However, I think we do have what we need to maybe figure this out."

"Huh?" Noah perked up. "What do you mean?"

Phen grinned, arms crossed over his chest. "Simple, actually. We have criteria now. Everything we discussed should narrow down who the culprit could be. I'm going to call some of my friends at school and ask around. Once we have an idea, we each take turns either being near the person, or talk to him while the others remain nearby. We are literally the only ones who know this much."

"It's valid." Aiden spoke, finishing up the breakfast with a quiet clatter. "While I would love to go to the police, they would ask how we found out this information and we can't exactly say we talked to the dead ghosts of his previous victims."

"Dead ghosts." Phen snickered, causing Aiden to glare. Noah chuckled as well, getting an annoyed sigh.

"You idiots know what I meant."

"Yep, it is funny though," Noah pointed out before settling. "Alright, so for now, we wait while Phen does his research or whatever and then what? We head to school?"

"Basically." Phen gestured as he pulled out his phone, tapping at it briefly. "Also, Mom will know if I don't go to school. She just… she just knows. I think it's a mother thing. Now, give me a sec."

The phone rang before clicking in. "Yo, Phen, Whatcha doing. Ya sick again?"

"Yeah, just going to stay home for the morning." He let out a cough which sounded somewhat fake before continuing, "Hey, man, can you do me a favor?"

"What this time?"

"I got a friend here who's curious on some of the male school workers."

"The teachers?"

"No way. Student-teacher relationships are illegal anyway. Nah, this is something else."

Noah blinked as Aiden let out a quiet groan, slumping. Mia giggled.

"Oh... Hm... does this have anything to do with Lynn?"

Phen stiffened, smile freezing before he responded, "It may."

The person on the other side paused before continuing, "Alright, I'm in. Just give me some information. I'll get ya some names. I'll ask Janice, ya know she keeps tabs on all the guys. Even has tabs on those twins ya always around."

"Gerald!"

"What? Ya near them right now? Dude, relax."

There is someone keeping tabs on us? Noah mouthed, causing Aiden to groan.

"It's the typical shizz. You know collecting data is her thing, she's been more adamant about that since what happened to your sister," Gerald said. Phen snapped his mouth shut as the guy on the phone quickly continued, "Dude, sorry. That was insensitive." The other boy paused. "So, anyway, give me the deets."

Phen shook his head, quickly describing everything they realized to 'Gerald'.

"Got it. I'll talk to her, see what she can dig up. Get back to you in a jiffy." At that, he hung up and Phen huffed.

"Who was that?" Noah asked, curious.

"Eh, an old buddy of mine. Cool enough guy, but..." Phen shrugged. "We're friends and all. Janice was Lynn's friend, and part of the occult club so they are in the highschool part. A few years older than us. She keeps track of everything going on at school." Phen winced. "I'm honestly kind of worried for her."

"Do you think she's in danger?" Noah stiffened. "Because she knows too much?"

Phen pursed his lips, but didn't argue.

Aiden leaned back, lost in thought. "Okay, so now what? We wait for them to find something? I highly doubt they'll get back to us right away."

"You underestimate Janice's persistence and Gerald's impatience, especially since it has to do with Lynn and we actually had information. They'll get back to me."

"So, why haven't we met them?" Noah blinked, glancing between the group. "You seem pretty close."

Phen winced. "Well, you have probably seen them at school with me a few times, but they are actually in the upper grades, so they are mostly in the high school wing. Like I said, Janice was Lynn's friend." He paused, a somberness pulling at his shoulders. "I miss my sister, but I'm glad I'm able to find ways to help her."

Aiden turned away as Noah let a weak, but genuine smile cross his face.

Phen responded in turn, the weight lifting just slightly. A silence fell over the home, the faint sounds of rain echoing outside, indicating it was once more letting loose.

So much rain, as if even the town itself felt bad for its residents. Noah was honestly curious if ghosts had any effect on the weather, because it certainly felt like it. Either that, or it was just really bad luck.

Noah wasn't sure how long it was, but soon enough, the phone rang once more, startling the group.

"Hey, Phen, took some time, had to work with class and all." The voice on the other end sounded more than a little amused. "Ain't staying home like ya."

"Ha-ha, so, what did you find?"

"I talked to Janice. She said she would text you what she had, though she wasn't sure about the whole cologne thing. That would be a bit weird to be sniffing everyone. Though she mentioned something interesting."

"Interesting?" Phen tensed as Noah fiddled with his cross, feeling over the cracks, worried.

"Yeah, she keeps feeling like she's being watched." A quiet gasp. "Of course, there's also the fact that she mentioned how weird the guys are acting lately. Don't know who she was talkin 'about, but hopefully, that list will help." He paused. "Whateve 'you're doing, be careful, Phen. Something weird is going on and I don't like it."

"I don't either," Phen whispered. "Keep an eye on Janice for me, will you?"

"Try my best, but ya know how she is." Gerald spoke as a beep sounded from the phone.

Phen flipped to it and nodded. "Looks like Janice sent it." He paused. "Did she really have to send photos like that?" Phen's face was red.

"Oh, she probably grabbed the best ones she had. You know how picky she is with her photos."

"How does she even get photos like these?"

"Don't ask me, I just appreciate."

"The fact that she doesn't care who, male or female, only makes it slightly better, I guess…" Phen groaned. "And, uh… if she…" Phen glanced up, catching Noah's eyes before suddenly jerking. "Never mind. Talk to you later."

There was a pause and then a faint laugh. "Yeah, talk to you later, dude. Feel better, man." A click sounded through the phone as Phen sighed and glanced up.

"That was an interesting conversation." Aiden raised an eyebrow.

"Hehe… uh, don't worry about it." Phen coughed into his hand. "Anyway, they were able to slip out of class and send me the information. Janice pulled through." His expression evened out. "Though I would rather get this done sooner rather than later. It sounds like Janice is being watched as well."

Noah pursed his lips, not sure what to say to that as Aiden tilted his head, lost in thought.

"So, what are our options?" Aiden glanced back. "Who does she have?"

"Three." Phen flipped his fingers up and slowly pulled them down as he talked. "The first one is the secretary, a man who never really talks. You probably met him if you went to the principal's office. Speaking of, two is the principal himself. Though, I would rather that not be the case." Phen shook his head and continued, "The third is the school janitor, Mr. Williams. Hadn't seen him much lately, so honestly forgot he was there."

"What do they look like? Can we see the photos?"

"I guess." Phen hesitated before flipping the phone around.

Instantly, Noah understood why he was so hesitant. The photos were clearly candid shots that one might see in a glamour magazine or something.

"She is quite the photographer, how do you even get those angles? Makes me wonder who you were going to ask for." Mia giggled, slight smirk on her face.

"No one!" Phen cut in, averting his gaze from both Noah and Aiden.

Noah's eyes widened and he quickly pulled out his phone. "You said she had pictures of us like that? Can you tell her to get rid of them?"

Phen jumped, fumbling, glanced down and winced. "Eh…" He spoke aloud. "Gotta talk to Janice about that, I have no say in what she does."

Noah pursed his lips, getting a raised eyebrow from Aiden. "Don't worry about it."

"That only makes me worry more, you know."

Noah shrugged. "It's just something I realized. It has nothing to do with you." He turned to Aiden. "Though I do have to say, the candid shots show she's really good."

"Good enough to stay out of sight," Aiden muttered, deep in thought. "She would also be good at observing things to wait for the perfect moment to take a picture. Can you text her back and tell her to watch those three and give us any information on what might seem odd?"

"Uh… sure?" Phen typed into his phone for a moment, then waited. It wasn't long before he nodded. "She said she would try." He typed a bit more before putting his phone away. He continued, "I told her to be careful. However, we should use this chance as well. I would love to borrow the library computers, but Mom will get pissed that I am not at school."

"So, who should we start with?" Noah leaned forward, curious. "I feel like the principal and secretary would be the hardest, since they would usually be together. So, the janitor?"

"It's worth a shot."

"Alright. Noah and I will try to watch out for them. You—" Aiden pointed at Phen, startling him, "are supposed to stay out of this and AWAY from the possible killer because of the state you are in."

"That's—"

Aiden's glare shut Phen right up.

Noah felt a little bad for Phen, though he had to agree with Aiden on that.

Phen pursed his lips, expression pissed before taking a deep breath and letting out a sigh, slumping in his seat. "Okay, yeah, I get it." He debated for a moment. "I'm still going to school with you, though. It'll look suspicious if I keep missing classes. I'll point the men out to you and stay near Janice, will that work?"

Aiden seemed to debate for a moment before nodding. Noah smiled, relieved, only to pause and groan. "Ugh, that means we have to go back to school."

Aiden actually chuckled at that. "Oh, come on, it's not that bad. You're not going to be paying attention anyways."

Noah rolled his eyes, but didn't argue.

Aiden pushed himself to his feet, glancing over toward Phen. "Well?"

Phen blinked, confused, attention snapping between them. "Well, what?"

"I think Aiden means to ask if we are going or not." Noah joined Aiden in standing, getting a glare in return. Mia chuckled, curling above them in amusement.

Phen took all of a second to recollect himself before nodding. They left, heading out the door and toward the school. It was late morning, that much Noah could tell, but the meager light that managed to slip through the ever present clouds did nothing for their moods.

Arriving at school was even worse. Noah wasn't sure why Aiden had a liking of school in general. Noah tolerated it, but this whole situation made him want to just run the other way. With a quiet sigh and a weak smile from Aiden, which Noah could appreciate, they separated and made their way to class.

It was clear the teachers weren't happy with their late arrival even with the call and Noah could hear the whispers and conversations happening. When one of the girls asked where he had been, he just waved it off with a bright smile and mentioned how things were hectic. They simply lost track of time and were sick the last few days.

Noah could only imagine how Aiden felt about all of this.

He pushed the thought to the side. There were three people he had to keep an eye out for. Now, he just needed to figure out how to do that.

CHAPTER 33

Aiden felt uncomfortable walking through the halls of school, especially when none of them had a class together, except one or two with Phen, and they had to go separate ways. It was unsettling even with the movement of people through the halls and the quiet chatter that often filled them.

The feeling was not helped by the fact that Aiden could feel the Ghost nearby, that female ghost kept flitting near him before disappearing. Maybe she was checking on Noah? He winced, it felt like he was intruding by just taking Mother's cross, but at the same time, the thought of her helping to protect them and find dad was both a chilling and warming thought.

Aiden wished he traded the cross with Noah. Noah should have Mother's last gift, not him.

He pushed the thought away as he moved through the halls, keeping quiet and observing. It was easy to tell the entire school was still unnerved. The students had a quicker gait and glanced around with a paranoia which was very much warranted, even as they smiled and laughed about nonsense. He did not miss the glances sent his way, uncertain and wary. Not surprising.

His gaze flitted to one side as Aiden spotted an older man wandering through the crowd, someone he hadn't paid much attention to before.

The janitor.

If someone could be qualified as plain, this person was the epitome of it. Mostly unremarkable in every way that made it easy for Aiden to realize why he never noticed the man before. The janitor held a mop in one hand and a bucket in the other and was dodging around the students with an ease that showed how long he had been doing this.

Aiden found himself intrigued and glanced toward where he knew the Ghost was. "I know you said you didn't really see the killer, but do you know how to sense him?"

"I think we've discussed this before." The Ghost settled on the ground beside Aiden, turning between him and the man in question. "I didn't get a good look and sensing when the demonic-like presence isn't there is difficult."

Aiden clicked his tongue, debating on what to do. How were they supposed to find information on who it was if they couldn't even equate them with anything? The main thing they needed was evidence and not just of the damn supernatural.

Aiden frowned before letting out a long sigh. He supposed he could just watch them. For now, he would keep an eye on the janitor. He knew Noah could better get information through conversation than himself, so he would trust his twin would follow through on that end.

Aiden cautiously followed after the janitor, who moved through the halls with a practiced ease. Aiden knew class was starting soon, but, to be honest, he had no interest in attending. He acknowledged it was rare to feel that way, but Aiden just wanted to know where his father was and classes were behind anyway. Aiden kept his pace even, watching from the corner of his eyes. Unfortunately, he could never get close enough to get a scent. The janitor never looked his way and didn't react as the students brushed past him, hurrying to class. The Ghost watched him briefly before flitting away once more. Eventually, the janitor moved into the west wing, the wing where they found Lynn and that was supposed to be forbidden for students.

Aiden narrowed his eyes and went to follow when footsteps caught his attention. He turned, startled as the principal's secretary came to a stop a few feet away from him. The man watched him quietly before speaking. "You should be in class."

"Oh, sorry. I got lost." Aiden turned toward the secretary, somewhat peeved to be losing the janitor's trail, but acknowledging that this was another person he was supposed to watch out for.

"Is that so." It wasn't phrased as a question. The secretary just stared before turning, walking back the way Aiden came. "I believe I recall your schedule. This way." Aiden hesitated before following. The halls were eerily silent as they winded through. Aiden frowned, unsettled. The school wasn't that big, right? Did the bell ring without him noticing?

Aiden almost leapt out of his skin when the sounds of heavy footsteps rounded the corner ahead. The principal stood, startled. "Oh, I did not realize you were away from your desk, Mr. Clark."

The secretary, Mr. Clark, nodded, fingers twitching just slightly. "Mr. Henderson. I spotted this student on the way to the west wing. I figured it was best to bring him to class."

"Why, of course." The principal, Mr. Henderson, gestured. "Move along now."

Aiden watched warily. Considering both of them were here, he felt a little safer, but that didn't mean much.

At least Aiden now had a general visual of everyone as the principal walked away, stopping at the next intersection, hands on his hips as if observing something. Aiden pulled out his phone, quickly sending a text to Noah. He hit the send just as he noticed that Mr. Clark stopped.

Aiden barely avoided running into him, side-stepping to avoid hitting him.

"This should be it."

Aiden paused, glancing up and frowning. This was—

That's when Aiden felt it, a sudden, familiar and terrifying surge of cold.

His entire body stiffened, panic racing through him before he whipped around, bringing his arms up just as something slammed into his side. Aiden let out a pained cry as he found himself thrown back, tumbling through a nearby doorway as it shattered around him. Pain flared up his back and sides and he felt a trickle of blood slip over his right eye.

"Of course the little Raven would notice." A voice spoke that Aiden had trouble recognizing in his dazed state.

Aiden struggled to his feet, trying to grab at something, anything. In his addled mind, he realized he was tossed into a janitor's closet, a mop and other items along the walls, held up simply by hooks. He grabbed at the mop, ripping it from the wall and placing it in front of him. The darkness made it hard to know what was in front of him, alongside the dizziness.

"Who—"

The man, whoever it was that attacked him, chuckled and started to hum. That cold flickered back and forth. It had to be the secretary, he was the last one Aiden saw before this started, but the figure was a bit too big to be him. Was it because of ghostly properties?

"No one for you to worry about, little Raven." The man hissed. Aiden sharply pulled in a beleaguered breath, trying to push away the dizziness. The mop was clasped tightly in his hand as the figure reached forward. "To be honest, I expected you to be knocked out, but you sensed me at the last moment, how fascinating."

Aiden felt the cold wrap around him and suppressed a heavy shudder as the figure took another step forward into the room, making it feel almost suffocating. Aiden struggled to pull in a deep breath, feeling himself sway slightly, pain flaring up his spine with the movement. He needed to get out of here.

"Now, give me your power." A hand reached forward, fingers curled in a strange, twisted way that wasn't human. "Give me your life."

Aiden swung, hearing a wet slap and the crack of wood as the base shattered against the arm of the figure, the mop head curling over the shoulder and part of the face, causing the man to spit and sputter.

Aiden didn't expect it to do much, considering, but he knew it would give him a moment of surprise, which he took, pushing off the back wall and darting around the stumbling figure. Good thing too, because he felt a rush of wind indicating someone tried to grab for him. The person howled as Aiden wiped at the blood, trying to get rid of it and the dizziness. He stumbled, only for a hand to catch his arm. Aiden wasn't sure if it was there to catch him, or stop him. He jerked, trying to get away.

For a moment, the grip held. Aiden turned, vision shifting slightly in pain. Who… The figure let him go, to his surprise. Aiden didn't give it another thought, said thoughts tumbling and shifting as it was. He darted away, that cold feeling present behind him, confusion and pain running through his mind. He wasn't going to be able to keep this up. That hit almost knocked him unconscious as it was. He ducked into a room that was hopefully empty and crouched to one side, holding his head with trembling hands. Pain throbbed through his body and skull and it was taking everything in him not to let darkness take over. He might have a concussion. Aiden pulled out his phone, shaken. It was hard to read the bright screen, but he found Noah's number and quickly typed into it once more.

Footsteps sounded nearby as his adrenaline spiked. He had to get out of here. There had to be a way out. Aiden held his breath as the footsteps paused by the door. A voice echoed through, sounding strange. "He's nearby, I can feel it," the person whispered. "So close… So close to being whole again."

Aiden heard movement and then a sound before the footsteps raced away, down the hall. For a brief moment, he felt a familiar, almost comforting chill. Was that the Ghost? Aiden stayed put for a moment longer, thoughts drifting. He had to stay awake. Just a little… longer…

CHAPTER 34

Noah stuffed the phone back into his pocket, thoughts panicked as he raced out of class, throwing some random excuse toward the teacher before bolting. Mia saw his expression and darted away as well.

Aiden. That thing was after Aiden. How did it happen already? Was he alright? Did he… Noah shook it off, glancing around. Aiden said he was near a janitor's closet, but that didn't help much since there were a few different ones. Considering how messed up the text was, and how hard it was to decipher, Aiden was probably pretty out of it. Okay, think. The first text mentioned he was following the secretary, having lost the janitor in the west wing. Supposedly, Aiden was heading to class. Considering the time between texts, Aiden was probably not in the west wing anymore; if anything, he might be in the east. Noah raced that way, moving through the halls, keeping his eyes peeled.

Aiden could take care of himself, but… Noah was not about to risk it.

He spun around a corner, noticing some splintered wood and traces of blood. Noah raced up, peeking inside the room where a door swung weakly, splintered and cracked barely staying on the damaged hinges. There was no one there, just some blood on the ground and shattered and broken wood. Noah looked around wildly, trying to calm himself and think. If Aiden was injured, which he clearly was from the damage

Noah was seeing, Aiden wouldn't be able to go far. The text was sent only a few minutes ago, which meant, even if the killer got him, they couldn't have gotten out of the school yet. Noah took deep steadying breaths, continuing down the hallway, peering around. He heard movement and stiffened, turning to a doorway. He swung it open. "Aiden?"

There was a moment of silence.

Noah didn't need more than a moment as he spotted a figure to one side, squatting over another. Noah lunged forward, tackling the first person. "Get off him!"

The first person, a slight man in janitors clothing, let out a startled yelp and hiss. "Get off me. I was trying to bandage him."

Noah scrambled to his feet, pulling back enough to spot the person on the ground. The open doorway only gave meager light and the curtains were closed, so it was hard to tell, but Noah didn't miss the blood coating one side of Aiden's face, the bandages already being wrapped around a deep head-wound, some of the bandage now lying limp. Noah scrambled, shifting so he was near Aiden's head, panic flaring through him as he inspected the damage. There was a quiet sigh as the person he tackled stood, hurrying to the door and closing it once more, almost no light coming in.

Yet, it was enough to confirm that the person Noah tackled was, in fact, the janitor. The janitor stepped back over and squatted next to Noah and Aiden, clicking a flashlight on.

"You must be his twin," the man said as he got back to wrapping the wound while Noah held Aiden carefully. "I noticed this one following me earlier. That's when Mr. Clark caught his attention. There's been strange things happening, especially around the school, and I couldn't help but find curiosity in the fact that Mr. Clark was out and about, so I followed. I'm not a very conspicuous person, after all." The janitor spoke as he worked.

"Did you see what happened?"

The janitor shook his head. "I got distracted and, when I arrived, all I saw was a small note on the floor near the door with two quickly scrawled words on it. Help Him." The janitor pulled the note out, handing it to Noah, who took it. The penmanship was shaky and clearly rushed. "I have to wonder who wrote it. Though, I have to say, it does eerily resemble Mr. Clark's handwriting, if I had to guess. But why would he write it?"

Noah stared down at it quietly. So, someone knew Aiden was in here. Maybe the secretary or maybe someone else, but why didn't he help Aiden himself?

"Unfortunately, considering this one is unconscious, he may have a concussion." The janitor spoke, glancing toward Noah. "He'll have to go to the hospital."

Noah stiffened, terror running through him. Neither of them much liked hospitals, and now, thinking back on it, Noah had a good feeling he knew why.

But if Aiden really did have a concussion, then… Noah nodded, pulling out his phone. The janitor didn't stop him as he dialed 911, a number he was getting way too used to calling lately. To his relief, it didn't take long for an ambulance to arrive. He directed them inside over the phone and glanced up as a few paramedics hurried in, along with a familiar female police officer. It was the same woman they talked to a few days ago about their father's disappearance. Noah also felt a strange presence which he could only assume was Mia.

The officer and paramedics asked some quick questions as they inspected Aiden, putting a brace around his neck before carefully placing him onto a stretcher. Noah wanted so badly to follow, but he knew he had to stay.

He had to find the person who attacked Aiden.

The officer watched him quietly before gesturing. "You should go with them. We'll take it from here."

Noah quickly shook his head, stepping back away from her and the paramedics who were too busy getting a ventilator on Aiden. That looked so strange on him.

"I have to stay here." He gestured. "I have information."

"Look, Noah, right? You are a kid, leave this—"

"Here!" He shoved the note into her hands, startling her. "We're not sure who wrote this, but we believe it to be Mr. Clark."

By that point, the paramedics had pulled Aiden out on a gurney, racing toward the ambulance. The officer let out a sigh, shaking her head before taking the note, peering over it. "We will take Mr. Clark into custody for now." She radioed over the information before turning back to Noah. "As for you." She pointed at the janitor who was now on his feet, brushing himself down. "I need you to come in for questioning, since you were the first one at the scene."

"I figured." The janitor spoke, being carefully escorted away by some of the other police officers. Noah barely noticed, thoughts churning.

"Noah, right? Why didn't you go with your brother? We could have—"

Noah jumped, turning back to the female officer. "I might know who did it." He gestured. "I—"

"I know you want to help, and to keep an eye on your brother, but you shouldn't be getting involved in this. You should have called as soon as you received the text and note. You are a child."

Noah winced, but couldn't help but understand where she was coming from. The female officer sighed and squatted down slightly to look him in the eye. "It's dangerous right now. We're lucky nothing worse happened, but for now, it is best if you head home, or someplace safe. Understood?"

Noah stiffened. If he left now, he might lose track of who it was that attacked Aiden. He couldn't do that. "I'll leave in a moment, I left all my stuff in—"

"Which we can get later, please, follow me." She gestured. "Clearly, whoever attacked your brother could also be after you. We can't risk—"

"But—" Noah snapped his mouth shut, noticing the heavy look on the officer's face. He was lucky she was distracted while the EMT's were here or he would have been forced to go with Aiden… unable to check on the last person. "Can I at least go the bathroom first?"

The woman sighed, slumping. "That's the oldest trick in the book." She straightened. "We're not trapping you or throwing you in jail. It's just for safety."

"I know." Noah felt a faint chill and noticed as the officer shivered. Noah turned, spotting Mia and stilled.

Mia took a deep breath, seeming to concentrate, before the temperature dropped. The officer shuddered, glancing around wildly just as Mia reached forward, lightly tapping her shoulder as she started to grin, water once more dripping from her figure.

The officer glanced over her shoulder and froze.

In that moment, Noah darted away as a scream cut the air.

He mentally thanked Mia, briefly wondering how she did that, as he quickly moved around the corner, mingling with the crowd of students who heard the scream and were being ushered away by teachers. He shifted through the crowd, meeting Phen's gaze briefly before he broke away into a quieter hallway.

He took a breath, leaning against the wall as a faint whisper of wind and footsteps met his ears. Phen and Mia slipped around the corner as Noah watched.

"Noah, you okay?" Phen hurried over as Noah nodded, peering up at Mia. She settled on the ground, her clothes drying once more and her expression solemn.

"Your brother was smart." She spoke softly. "I arrived just in time to distract HIM."

Phen stilled, glancing at Mia with faint horror.

Noah ignored it, staring dead at Mia, who actually flinched. "Did you see him this time?"

Mia sighed, hair actually floating slightly in clear frustration. "No. I didn't have the time. I could sense Aiden and so could he, good thing regular ghosts catch his attention as well." She gestured to Noah. "With Mr. Williams, the janitor, being with the officers and Mr. Clark, the secretary, being pulled in for questioning, that leaves only Mr. Henderson out and about."

"But Aiden thinks it was the secretary. He mentioned it in the text."

"It might be." She stared, almost as if peering through him. "It might not. It's best to make sure we know where all three are. Especially considering this happened in broad daylight in the middle of the hall."

Noah winced, nodding.

"What happened to Aiden?" Phen cut in, panicked and clearly worried.

"He's alright." Noah pursed his lips, a fierce anger thrashing through him at the thought. He hadn't felt it before, but now, seeing his sibling unconscious and bleeding made him want to curse out whoever thought it would be funny to do something like this. Mia actually pulled away, arms wrapped around herself as she shuddered. Made sense, she said she would keep Aiden safe and didn't, but… "He will be alright."

"Oh." Phen's voice was faint before he shifted his shoulders, standing a bit taller. "So, he must have encountered the killer and survived."

Noah nodded, a weak feeling of relief at the thought pushing away some of the hatred. "Considering the janitor was bandaging Aiden up when I found him, I'm going to guess the janitor is not involved."

Phen nodded. "That makes sense." He sighed. "Mr. Williams never seemed like someone who could kill, or be possessed. I just didn't want to assume anyone at this point."

Noah nodded as they continued through the halls, surveying the area, but not heading back to class. Mia floated nearby, staying quiet and thoughtful. "We need to find Mr. Henderson." Noah finally spoke up. "I would like to keep an eye on him for now."

"What about the secretary?" Phen glanced toward Noah who shook his head.

"The police brought him in for questioning." Noah showed Phen the note.

"So, doesn't that mean they have the killer? I mean, if I was a killer, I would totally write a note like that to give myself an alibi since I would have probably realized I was caught." Phen shook his head. "A simple 'help him 'would make it look like I was trying to get someone's attention and mislead when, in fact, I was the one who did it."

"Probably, but I'm not taking any chances." Noah narrowed his eyes. "Whoever the killer is HURT my brother and probably has my father." Noah sighed. "It's more likely Mr. Henderson, but what you said makes sense as well. Unfortunately, considering how long this is happening, this was rather messy."

"He's getting desperate." Mia spoke up, settling next to them, expression still as solemn as before. "He's at the end of his rope and is doing anything he can to get what he wants, even if it leads to him more likely getting caught." She sighed. "I can understand the feeling, even if I don't agree with it."

Noah pursed his lips. "So, maybe it is the secretary."

"I think you are correct to keep your options open." Mia spoke up. "But…"

"Let's just take a look." Phen gestured. "There isn't harm in it. If the secretary is the killer, then the police have him. If it's someone else, well, at least we will know."

Noah nodded and turned to Mia. "You're a bit faster than us, do you think you can try to find the principal?"

Mia nodded, clearly angry herself. Was it at herself or the person who did that to Aiden?

Mia darted away out of sight as Phen and Noah stayed together, searching around the school. They decided not to split up, recognizing it would be a bad idea. Who knew Aiden would get caught during the short time between classes?

"I've found him." Mia spoke up, catching their attention only a few minutes later. Noah would usually jump, but his attention was a bit too focused to do just that at the moment. "The principal's toward the back of the school. I'll lead you."

Noah nodded as Phen followed. They moved quickly, slowing down once they got closer and Mia put a finger to her lips. This was probably stupid, but Noah just couldn't let it go.

He peered around the corner, noticing the principal staring out the window, arms crossed over his chest. Noah ducked down a bit more to try to stay out of sight.

"What is he doing?" Phen asked quietly.

"Staring out a window." Mia's voice held a heavy sarcasm. "If we knew, then we wouldn't be doing this, now would we?"

Noah briefly noted how Phen glared up at her, but ignored it. The principal was murmuring to himself, faint incomprehensible words.

"Should we get his attention?" Phen asked.

Noah hesitated, unsure. Usually Aiden would be there to dissuade them from doing something stupid, but he wasn't here this time.

Phen must have noticed something in his expression, because he stood and walked over. Noah stiffened, pushing back to watch. Mia narrowed her gaze, but settled near Noah.

"Mr. Henderson?" Phen spoke up. The principal glanced over, but didn't turn.

"Ah, Phen, wasn't it?" His voice sounded a little off. "I'm sorry, I'm still a little shaken by what transpired. The police just told me the situation. It's awful something like this happened at my school and for my secretary to be the cause of it." He shook his head and sighed.

Noah frowned. Had the police mentioned telling the principal?

There was no certainty that the secretary did it so why did he say that?

"I thought he was just brought in for questioning?" Phen asked, probing in a way that worried Noah, but made him grateful. He had the same question.

The man stiffened slightly, startling Noah. "I suppose that is true. You certainly know a lot, young man."

"It happened to my friend," Phen cut in, hands on his hips.

The principal paused for a moment and nodded before turning to face back outside. "Either way, you should head home. School is cancelled for the rest of the day."

Phen didn't say a word, arms crossed over his chest. After a moment, he huffed and moved away, heading back toward them. Noah pushed himself against the wall, letting Phen pass. Phen briefly glanced toward him and nodded before continuing, just in case Mr. Henderson was paying attention.

Noah let out a breath and glanced around the corner once more, that murmuring returning once again.

"No, no. I can't do this anymore. But… I get that, I know it's necessary." The man sighed, head slumping against the window.

Mia shifted, settling right next to Noah. The principal stood and headed toward the backdoor, no longer talking. Noah glanced toward Mia before quietly following. Phen would catch up when he got the chance. Keeping his steps as quiet as possible, Noah headed toward the door as it swung closed.

Noah peeked out through the door window as the principal walked away, passing over a low stone wall. The door was probably a one way, similar to an emergency exit. He waited for a moment before pushing it open, slipping out. A mix of curiosity and a need to know kept him moving. It was probably just something stupid, but he wasn't going to risk it. He waited near the stone wall as Mia peeked over before gesturing. Noah followed her as they headed toward the distant trees, slipping into the surrounding forest. The brush of flowers from the meadow almost seemed maddeningly different from his mood, even the sky was bright and sunny for once.

What was with that?

He stayed as hidden as possible, wondering why the principal was walking so far into the forest. Noah stopped as Mia put a hand up, the other hand pressed against her lips in a shush motion. Noah crouched low, peering around through the brush. He froze, realizing he couldn't see anything or anyone. Where did the principal go? He was right there!

His gaze snapped over the area, taking in everything he could. While there was no sign of the principal, he did spot something strange in the dirt near one edge of the clearing. It appeared to have been recently upturned and he could swear something gleamed from that direction as sunlight beamed through the trees.

Noah slowly shifted, moving over to it. It would have been hard to spot normally, but, as Aiden liked to point out, he tended to be more observant. He listened for any crackle of leaves or snap of branches as he used the trees as cover to move around the clearing, getting as close as he could without entering.

He took a deep breath. He hadn't heard anything, so, maybe the principal moved farther into the trees? Well, crap, that wasn't good either. If he had, Noah wouldn't be able to track him. He shivered, frowning as a faint waft of cold caught his attention. It reminded him a bit of when he stood near the house with all the trapped ghosts.

His gaze snapped to the little piece, which he could now see, from this angle, was a trap door.

He heard shuffling and jerked.

"Shi—" Mia's word was cut off as a hand lashed out. She was sent tumbling through the air. Noah's breath caught in his throat as he stumbled forward, just managing to avoid the other hand grabbing his jacket. He spun, shifting in the direction of the trap door. The principal, appearing almost… twisted, stepped out, a wide grin on his face. The lips were curled up in a way that wasn't natural, head jerking side to side as a faint eerie hum reached Noah's ears. Splinters decorated his arm, which Noah hadn't noticed before.

The principal took another step forward, and Noah couldn't help but wonder how he had gotten behind him. Noah gulped, noticing the small piece of pipe that could be easily hidden against one's side.

"I thought I sensed you." The man grinned, the words dual-layered and heavy. From where Noah stood, way too close for comfort, a faint smell wafted to his nose.

A mix of orange and cinnamon.

CHAPTER 35

The man shifted his head, a CRACK echoing through the forest. "You stupid spirit, how dare you interfere."

Mia shook her head, catching herself as Noah took another step back.

The principal's attention snapped back to him and that's when Noah noticed the bright red eyes glowing in the shadows cast by the large trees. The principal swung out his pipe, pointing it at Noah. "Now, I'm not sure if I should be happy or annoyed." The dual voice made it difficult to tell who was speaking. "That brother of yours escaped and my secretary was captured due to incompetence, but here you are, ripe for the taking."

What?

Noah yelped, trying to pull back, only for the pipe to slam down, just missing his feet by inches as he tripped, crashing down hard on his butt.

"Oh? I thought you figured it out, since you were watching me with that other one." The man pulled back, tilting his head with another loud CRACK. "A little blackmail can go a long way."

Noah stiffened as horror filled his thoughts. No wonder Aiden didn't realize. The secretary was working with the principal. He was so dumb for not even realizing or thinking about it. He scrambled to his feet, partially wondering where Phen disappeared too.

"I would leave him alone." Mia spoke up, shifting forward, and halting between Noah and the principal.

"I acknowledge you are powerful, but you can't fight me, not as you are and not as I am." The principal lifted his head, peering down in distaste.

Noah slowly pulled himself toward the trap door as Mia straightened up, hair and clothes billowing. "Really? I have many more centuries than you."

"But I have a human body." The principal grinned. At that, he swung. Noah didn't stay to watch. He ducked away, lunging for the trap door. He didn't want to run away from here, knowing if he did, the principal would probably just disappear, or go after Aiden who was very susceptible in the hospital. Plus, that cold feeling was even stronger and that meant only one thing. He grabbed the handle and tugged up, releasing a cloud of dirt.

He felt a presence behind him as something slammed into his back. He let out a startled scream as the ground slipped from under him and he tumbled, falling into the sudden pit below him, completely missing the ladder. He crashed to the ground with a groan, head spinning, and glanced up just as the door slammed shut above him. Crap…

Darnit, how had he not noticed the man kicking out toward him? He recognized a boot to the back well enough. He shook his head as the darkness pressed against his sight. He quickly pulled out his phone, hoping it hadn't gotten destroyed in the short fall. At least nothing was sprained or broken.

He flipped the flashlight on and froze.

The little place he fell into was not as little as he thought, and that cold was now even worse. The room was fairly large with cells placed around it. In the middle was an inscription on the floor and a circle burnt into wood and stone. He heard a groan and turned toward one of the cells, scrambling up to it, desperately ignoring the others as he noticed strange shifting and that ever present cold.

The light shone inside, revealing a pile of shifting rags... familiar rags.

"Dad?" He grabbed the bars as his father slowly lifted his head, emaciated and exhausted.

Terror flashed on his father's face as Dad caught Noah's gaze, blinking away the light. "Noah? Oh... oh god, what are you doing here?" He struggled to his feet, collapsing as he moved. "You have to leave, you have to get out of here."

Noah knew his father was right, but the suddenness of the situation and the relief and terror of finding his father down here was not helping. Noah glanced around wildly, spotting a set of keys to one side. He darted over, flipping through them as fast as possible. He could still feel the general presence of Mia above and could only hope she was keeping that creep occupied as best as she could. He found the right key, stuffing it into the lock and twisting. The doorway clanged open and he darted inside, catching his father as he went to stand up again.

Thin, badly-scraped arms wrapped around his neck as Noah practically dragged him out. His father was out of it, clearly, and Noah was seriously panicking. The trapdoor was off to one side and up a ladder. There was NO way either of them could climb. There had to be another exit, right?

"To the right." Dad spoke weakly. "You're acting just like your brother. I get you're trying to think on your feet like he does, but it's not working."

Noah didn't say anything, unable to argue with that assessment. Aiden wouldn't have ended up tossed down through a trap door.

He froze for a second as the sound of scrapping reached his ears. When he peered to one side, a gaunt face caught his attention, a hand reaching through the bars desperately. "Let me out!" The man called and Noah felt his throat seal as he felt something scrap past his t-shirt. He jerked, peering over to see someone in broken shades clawing toward him, face pressed harshly against the bars.

"Ghosts, just go." Dad hissed, startling him.

Wait... those were...

He jerked toward the last cell where he saw another figure sitting, a badge glowing in the weak light of his phone. The man twisted his face up and, with that, Noah turned and scurried forward, dragging Dad with him. It took everything in him not to gag in horror of the missing jaw, clearly ripped off before the other detectives death, tongue gone as well, leaving just… throat.

He heard scrambling from above and the clang of the trapdoor. "You stupid ghost, let me get my prey or you will be next."

"He is not yours." Mia's voice echoed, sounding dangerous. "You have no claim to either of them. Now, give up and accept your fate."

"No! I will not go down to the hells! If I do, I will take this soul and all the others with me!"

"Too bad, the hells would welcome a soul like yours." Mia hissed and a deathly chill filled the chamber.

Father clicked his tongue, wincing as Noah managed to find a doorway pressed into the earth. He fiddled with the keys, made more difficult with the fact he could only use one hand, which was shaking badly with the images now seared into his head. If Dad hadn't told him they were ghosts before, he definitely would have figured it out with that last... soul? Spirit? Whatever it was.

A clanking sound echoed from the chamber with the missing detective. The chill increased and a haunting chatter filled the air as Mia spoke. "I can hear them now."

"Noah… we need to leave. Now." Father's voice was strained as he stared behind him at the cells. Bars rattled and shook as a strange sound like wailing and a faint gargled cackling filled the air. Noah stiffened, recognizing it.

Just like when they were in that home, words were starting to echo around, repeating over and over like a litany. He hurried his movements for the key, quickly shoving it into the lock and throwing the door open as a loud sound echoed behind them like feet crashing down on stone and dirt. Noah didn't need to look back, he could FEEL the change in pressure. He scrambled forward and almost flipped as the door suddenly slammed shut behind him, howls filling the air, along with curses. Dragging a practically limp body bigger than him was draining, but adrenaline and pure fear was pushing him to move as fast as possible. Something dove through the ground and he barely stopped himself from letting out a shriek before Noah realized who it was in the dim light. Mia gestured and shot down the tunnel. Noah followed, footsteps echoing loudly down the passage. A chill slithered up his spine and it took everything in him not to shiver as the stench of turned earth and rot filled the air. He could feel the ground slope. A door caught his attention up at a sharp incline, only a thin amount of room on either side. He pressed against it, trying to figure out how to make it budge. There was a moment of panic before it slid open sideways. Mia settled down in front of him, expression even as she watched them both. Her hand was up as if she just pressed something. She let it drop and drifted away.

Wait. Noah thought she couldn't do that. She said herself she couldn't—he paused, maybe something changed because of what happened with Aiden. He shoved the thought away, finding it unimportant in the moment. After all, she tapped that police officer on her shoulder, how was this any different? He stepped inside the room and frowned. They were in the principal's room. There was a clanking sound and, when he peered back, the shelf moved back into place, runes flaring briefly on the ground.

Wait, runes?

"A ritual," Mia said, her tone of voice strangely off. Noah just nodded, heading out the door. He would ask her later.

CHAPTER 36

Dad must have gone unconscious at some point, due to exhaustion. Noah, however, felt uneasy and exhausted. His dad was heavy and bigger than him which made it difficult to carry him. After so long without answers, that felt rather quick and way too simple.

The principal knew they were following, so why did he lead them to where Dad was? Did he honestly expect to catch Noah down there? Had he hoped to just drag Noah in there?

There were too many questions and no good answers. Still, he couldn't stay here.

Where the heck was Phen?

"This is not good." Mia stared out the floor to ceiling windows. The sky, so bright on the way through the forest, darkened. Clouds coated the once blue expanse as lightning flared above though no rain fell.

A quiet groan from Dad met Noah's ears and he quickly headed out the door.

The halls were quiet, empty. The students must have been escorted out completely by now. He didn't think he was gone that long, but it wasn't too surprising.

Dad was coming to as they moved through the halls, pained sounds escaping his lips. After a moment, his fingers curled around Noah's. Noah stopped, pulling them to one side into a room, both to hide and rest, breaths short at this point. Making sure the door was closed, they took a seat on the ground.

Dad pulled away, pressing his back against the wall and taking deep shuddering breaths.

"Dad?" Noah's voice quivered, worried.

Dad stirred. "I wasn't having a nightmare."

"Sorry." Noah shifted uncomfortably. "We were trying to find the killer, but we're not like you, we couldn't find information—"

"You found me."

"Only because the killer led me there." Noah shook his head. "I don't know why."

Dad closed his eyes, leaning back. "You two..." He slowly let out a long breath. "I'm proud of you." Noah pursed his lips, unable to respond. "I sense another one. Is she safe?"

"Yeah." Noah found his voice shaking slightly. So he can sense Mia?

"I will trust you are right for now." Dad turned to Noah once more. "Where is your brother?"

Noah winced, voice faint and tired. "At the hospital. The principal attacked him."

Dad stiffened and tried to push himself to his feet. "Did he get any blood?"

What? "I don't know. I wasn't there." Noah scrambled to his feet. "Aiden was bleeding badly, but he escaped."

Dad let out a breath and shook his head. "This is not good. We have to get to your brother."

Huh? "I mean, I know he's in danger, but he's—"

Dad turned to Noah. "That man will know where Aiden is. He knows you have escaped and the ritual is almost complete. We don't have time."

"What ritual?" Noah pleaded. "I don't know what's going on!"

"Ghost." Dad turned to Mia, who shifted back, startled. "I noticed you were fighting the principal off while Noah got me out. What is your association with my children?"

Mia seemed surprised before her expression shifted. She settled onto the ground, clothes and hair blowing in a nonexistent wind. "They agreed to help me return home and, in turn, I agreed to protect them to the best of my abilities."

"A full pact?"

"Correct." Mia grinned, fingers to her lips as she cocked her head to the side. "They had no idea and still don't."

Dad clicked his tongue as Noah stared, confused.

"Well, then, a slight addendum. In exchange for the rescue of Aiden and the banishment of this fiend, I wish to have you occupy my body until said time when the banishment is accomplished to MY whims or you NEED to leave in order to rescue one of my boys from the possessed human once I have sight of Aiden. My soul is not to be touched under any circumstances. Is this deal agreeable to you?"

"Hm, you have made deals before." Mia stared, contemplative, her gaze flicked to Noah before turning back to Dad, nodding. "I have no argument. I will accept your terms until you see fit."

"What?" Noah glanced back and forth as Mia stepped forward and kept walking right into Dad, as if settling into his skin, disappearing from sight.

A moment later, Dad straightened, pulling from Noah's grasp. "No wonder he wished for me to take control." Mia's voice echoed from Dad's mouth as she peered over Dad's arms, gingerly fingering at one bruised section. It was surreal, seeing Dad's body, but hearing Mia's voice. "A reckless bargain that could go terribly wrong if I so wished. He must be desperate. No surprise though. He is incredibly weak. It's a miracle he was even able to walk out of there or, well… he was dragged out of here after we got to the principal's office." Mia —or was it Dad? Noah wasn't sure, so decided just to stick with Mia, since Dad was probably unconscious again —turned to Noah. "However, his part of the deal does match with the one made. And since I failed a part of the deal, I will make sure, with his addendum, that I do not fail this time." She peered toward the door, determination flaring on her face, along with… anger? It was an expression Noah never witnessed before on

Father's face. He hoped to never see it again as Mia said, "Well then, we need to get to your brother."

Noah couldn't help but stare, freaking out. "Wait. Are you possessing my dad like with what almost happened to Phen?"

"Different." Mia spoke as she headed toward the door. Noah scrambled after her. "This is a temporary occupation of mutual benefit. I can better interact with the real world, and in return, I give strength to the host body. It is rarely done except in times of need." She peered toward him. "Clearly, you can't see me, only your father, correct?"

Noah nodded hesitantly.

"That is because I am operating his body under my whim. His soul is safe, since I am specifically avoiding that part of him. I am simply, I guess you can say, operating the vehicle."

"That's even weirder." He swallowed thickly. "And what is this deal you both were talking about? I mean, sure, I discussed stuff with you when we first met, but—"

"Now is not the time to explain." Mia's gaze flitted to Noah. "Unless you want your twin to be used as a sacrifice, to finish a ritual that should be forbidden. We must hurry."

That shut Noah up. He nodded as they headed out of the school. To Noah's surprise and relief, Phen was standing outside, pacing heavily. He seemed surprised upon seeing Dad, but relieved on seeing Noah.

Phen ran up, catching Noah's hands. "I'm so glad you are alright." Pain flared across his face. "I'm sorry I couldn't help, a teacher caught me when I rounded the corner and I couldn't get away. She pulled me out of the school and, well… Anyway, I'm glad you found your father, I think?" He glanced over briefly, pulling them toward a car to one side, running idly.

"Ah." Noah pursed his lips, glad to know what happened. "Phen, he's still out there."

Phen stiffened, glancing toward Dad who walked right past. "Wait, you mean it was the principal?"

"Yeah. It's a long story." Noah shook his head. "What's the quickest way to the hospital?"

"Mom's nearby, she can drive us." He gestured as they approached the car.

Mia increased her step. "Then let's go, we have no time to waste."

Phen nodded, startled. He glanced toward Noah, who shook his head, mouthing, "I'll explain later."

He agreed and they hurried to the car.

"Phen, what were you thinking running out of the car like th—" Ellen's yell cut off, startled.

Phen winced before sheepishly asking, "Mom. Can we go to the hospital?"

"What happened?"

"Aiden, he's hurt." Phen hesitated. "This is his father, by the way."

Ellen's attention snapped toward Dad as anger flashed over her face. Not even a moment later, it vanished as she seemed to realize the state Dad was in. "I can see the resemblance." She paused, clearly noticing the desperation. She sighed. "We will talk about this later, Phen." At that, she gestured. "Well, then, go on, get in."

"Thank you, ma'am." Mia spoke, using Dad's voice. Or maybe it was Dad, Noah wasn't quite sure how it worked. Mia said she was just 'driving 'Dad's body. So did that mean Dad was aware? How did a possession like this even work?

They piled into the car and Phen asked Ellen to step on it. They quickly pulled away as rain suddenly let loose, crashing over the ground, thunder cracking loudly above. Ellen cursed, but didn't say anything else as they quickly drove through the strangely empty streets. Wind howled outside. Dad was twitchy and Noah just felt wrong.

All he could do was hope and pray that Aiden was alright.

CHAPTER 37

Aiden slowly opened his eyes, the headache from before having dulled. A gentle beeping was overpowered by the loud echoing sound of rain on the nearby windows. The air smelled of sanitizer and cleaning supplies. Lightning flashed, almost blinding him as thunder crashed soon after, making him wince.

A nurse with a scar around her right eye glanced over, watching him worriedly. She stepped up, checking his head. He shivered, feeling a bit chilled. "Are you alright?"

Strange question. A nurse should know that.

"I'm asking because I want to check your speech and hear if anything else hurts," she responded after a moment of Aiden not saying anything.

"Oh." He spoke after a moment. "Fine." The words felt strange, but he did feel a little better than before. Was his head wrapped? Something pressed against his forehead and hair, so he supposed it was wrapped. He glanced down to his arms; an IV was placed under the skin. On the side table, he could see his clothes and, on top, Mother's cross. Next to it was his phone, screen cracked and clearly broken. He guessed it caught some of the brunt of the hit. He was surprised it worked after that attack, but it seemed it might be in need of repair. He wasn't sure how useable it would be until he could turn it on, if he could.

The nurse walked over, gently pulling out the IV and wrapping his arm, a warm smile on her face. A sense of comfort washed over him and he relaxed.

"That's good. That's very good." She reached up, lightly touching his head. The touch felt strangely cold. Did he have a fever?

"Thank you." She backed away and bowed her head. "I've been able to hold the barrier, but my time is almost up."

What?

"Ah, he's awake!" Another nurse came rushing in. "You shouldn't be taking your IV out like that!" She hurried over, before pausing. "Though, all signs are steady and it's been properly wrapped." She stopped, confused, and reached a hand forward, just like the other nurse had. To Aiden's surprise and sudden fear, her touch was gently warm.

He slowly turned his head toward the nurse at the end of the bed, who was smiling, hands clasped in front of her.

"Who…" He kept his eyes on the first nurse with the scar, probably confusing the one who charged in.

"Um, my name?" the second nurse asked, uncertain. "Are you okay? You aren't looking my way."

Aiden stilled at that, realization and faint horror dawning on him. Yet, that sense of comfort still remained. His gaze returned to the first nurse, who placed a finger to her lips and smiled.

"Thank you, raven child."

A gust of warm, soft wind blew through the room, almost dulling the sounds of the storm outside. The nurse, that ran in, yelped. Aiden quickly covered his eyes and, when he brought his arm down, the first nurse was gone and so was the gentle cold feeling. She said barrier…what—that didn't matter, she was clearly a ghost, his horrified mind realized. He winced as cold energy spiked nearby, making him shudder. Was that woman protecting him somehow?

"What was that? Did one of the windows end up open?" The nurse that still remained looked around and frowned. "Weird."

Aiden turned to the nurse in question and debated before asking. "Is there a nurse that works here with brown hair, cut short, and a scar around her right eye?"

The woman stiffened, startled. "How…" She shook her head. "Yes, well, she used to. She died a month or two ago. Was she a relative of yours?"

"No." Aiden spoke softly. "Just someone I met." The living nurse just nodded and quickly went over the charts as that cold fluctuated.

"Well, considering you are speaking okay and there is no slurring. That's a good sign. Do you remember what happened?"

"Vaguely, I was very dizzy at the time," Aiden admitted, not wanting to lie. The less he lied here, the quicker he could leave this place. "I have a concussion, don't I?"

The nurse nodded. "You are correct, but thankfully, it's a mild one. Get some rest and you should be out within a day or so."

Aiden pursed his lips. A day or two in the hospital? No thanks. He only ended up in one once before and, from what he remembered, Dad had to convince the staff to set up salt and other things around the room. There were a lot of strange sounds that night. He couldn't help but wonder if the barrier the scarred nurse mentioned kept out other ghosts. If so, why did she decide to help him? Why did she thank him?

The nurse jotted down some things and glanced up. "Do you feel hungry? I can bring some food in, if you need it."

Maybe, but his stomach was twisted in knots. Were Noah and Phen alright? Did that guy catch them?

"I'm fine."

The woman nodded, noting down a few more things before bringing the paper to her chest, observing him carefully. "There is a button over here to press if you need anything. Don't hesitate to call if you start feeling dizzy, lightheaded or nauseous, understood?"

When Aiden gave a short nod, wincing slightly, she turned, heading for the door. "I will bring in…" She paused. "Oh, never mind. I guess someone brought some water in for you earlier." Aiden glanced toward the side-table, only slightly surprised. The woman stepped out, closing the door behind her.

Aiden reached over, picking up the cup. It was slightly cold to the touch. He glanced in. Pure water.

His throat, at that point, let him know just how dry it was and he took a sip, relieved.

So, that other nurse was a ghost. What was keeping her here? Was she gone? He had too many thoughts running through his head, which did not help his headache. There was a strange desperation clawing through his veins like something was wrong, but he figured it was just because of where he was.

He hated this. He wished ghosts just didn't exist. Why did he have to deal with this stuff? He closed his eyes, taking steadying breaths as he held the cup, both to take a sip, and to wake him if he accidentally fell asleep.

That's when he heard it. His whole body stiffened as he slowly turned his head toward the window. Lightning flashed as a face stared in at him, soaking wet, grinning and humming a familiarly eerie tune. Aiden's entire body felt like it locked up just as a click sounded from nearby.

Like a lock turning.

He practically threw himself out of bed as the man pulled a hand back and crashed forward. Glass shattered as wind howled into the room, tugging at Aiden's gown and hair as the man reached through, pulling himself in. Aiden raced toward the door, head throbbing and heart pounding. He tugged desperately, realizing with horror that it was locked.

When did it get locked? HOW did it get locked? How did it get locked on both sides? It did, right? He didn't see a lock on his side so maybe—

A quiet chuckling sounded from behind and Aiden turned. Noticing his clothes nearby, he snatched up the cross, holding it in front of him like a weapon. Would it even work that way? He had no idea.

"Now, now. Little raven child. The ritual is almost complete. Just come here and I can finish it."

"Frick that," Aiden hissed, back pressed against the door as lightning flashed once more, illuminating the figure. "You… then—"

"Just like your twin, I guess you hadn't figured it out either." The principal grinned, blood dripping from one side of his mouth. Lacerations crisscrossed over his hand from smashing the glass and catching a mop on the arm. "No matter. I've locked the door behind you for both you and them, a fun little ability I still have in this human form, and, while it took a while to find you, the barrier has fallen. That little guardian spirit can't protect you anymore and that other nuisance is nowhere nearby."

Little guardian spirit? Aiden's thoughts flickered to the nurse and realization flooded through him. She had been watching over him in multiple ways.

"I just didn't want anyone else to die to him." Words faintly echoed into his ears, as if spoken from far away. "Help is coming, I can feel it." The nurse's words caught Aiden's attention. He clung to the thought, desperately hoping she was right.

CHAPTER 38

Not wanting to waste whatever time the nurse gave him, Aiden used his other hand to continue to tug at the door. Sure, the man said he locked it from both sides but there had to be some way to get it open. To one side, he saw the button that nurse pointed out to him. It would alert them if the shattering glass hadn't. Did he call for help, or try to hold him off? Seeing the principal take a step forward, Aiden didn't have time to debate.

He lunged to one side, slamming down on the button as the figure reached out, grasping. Fingers curled into his clothes and tugged.

Aiden, desperate, slashed out with the cross. The figure wailed, letting him go and stumbling back as a sound echoed through the room. Not even a second later, he heard hurried footsteps and the turning of a handle.

"What the—" A voice echoed from the other side as the principal glared, red eyes glowing even as most of his face was obscured from darkness.

"Pesky child." He hissed. "Drop that thing. I will enjoy draining you of your life to fuel the ritual."

Aiden withheld the need to gag, gulping as a heavy slamming sound echoed from the door, shaking it. The figure's gaze flicked to the door as it rattled again.

"Tch. Humans." He turned back to Aiden. "If you are hoping for rescue, I'm going to have to say, you're not getting it."

Aiden had a feeling he was right, but held out a bit of hope. Sure, a complete stranger said help was coming, but he couldn't help but feel she knew what she was talking about.

Noah would find him.

There was only one other avenue he could think of, but he was sure that jumping from whatever story window he was at would not end well for him.

Considering the principal climbed up without a ladder or anything and easily grabbed people from second story windows? Well, he wasn't sure what his chances were.

The principal stalked forward, a wide grin on his face, twisting his features as blood slipped from his nose and down his ears, dribbling out of both sides. A small part of him half expected blood to be coming from the eyes as well, but they were simply glowing a piercing red. Aiden pulled back. He hated the feeling of being a cornered animal, he realized, because terror was causing him to scramble back toward the window, cross out in front of him. He briefly peered toward the window as wind and rain crashed through, water pooling on the ground near his feet, soaking through the thin socks.

"Out of the way!" a voice shouted from the other side of the door, causing both of them to pause. That voice!

The door suddenly snapped, crashing open and flinging pretty much across the room. It barely missed the principal as he moved out of the way, the fragments smashing against the other window and splintering with a CRASH. Standing in the doorway, leg still up, was, to Aiden's surprise, Dad.

The principal straightened, turning to Dad in annoyance. "Well now, you got a body of your own. One that would not let me take him over or break him myself."

Aiden glanced over as Noah darted forward. The principal pulled something from his side and tossed it, causing Noah to slide to a halt, just barely avoiding being hit by what was probably a pipe, from the looks of things. In that moment of startled silence, the principal turned and lunged. Aiden stumbled back, thrusting his cross forward. To his shock and terror, the principal slapped the hand away, causing the cross to go spinning to one side of the room as he continued forward, bodily smashing into Aiden.

Aiden twisted at the last minute, catching the corner of the window, as his knees cracked harshly against the sill. The timing of Aiden's turn made it so he wasn't flung out the window, but the principal's momentum was strong enough to send him flying forward past Aiden. Fingers grabbed onto Aiden's arm, realization dawning in split second horror as the principal was flung over the sill. He had all of a second to realize what that meant before he felt a sharp tug. A pained cry and an echoing CRACK met his ears as he was jerked forward, almost falling out of the window as gravity asserted itself, his arm feeling wrong under his skin. The principal dug into his forearm, fingers gripping so tight as to pierce the skin. He heard a faint scream from behind him as rain slammed onto the back of his head and neck, drenching his bandages, hair and clothes. The sill cracked as he tried to hold himself inside, but the creature's weight felt unusually heavy, and he could have sworn it was growing heavier as the water soaked both of them. He wasn't sure what would give out first, the sill or his arm.

His knees locked under the sill as he heard a shout from behind. "No, you don't!" Dad's… no, the Ghost's voice echoed as Aiden tried to fight back. His fingers and legs shook from exertion as the storm grew stronger, rain and wind battering at his exposed skin. Half of his body was pressed out of the window, glass digging into his side. It was now he could clearly see the dizzying sight of the four story drop, so close and yet so far. He was going to fall like this.

It was clear the cross did something. Burns littered the man's body from where he got close, the hand that smacked it away almost black. Pure anger flared in the prin—no, creature's gaze.

"You will PAY for that." His voice echoed up to Aiden, the words slithering over his ears, his body feeling slimy and gross at the sound. Blood pounded in his ears as he felt the glass shatter under his grip, his body leaning just that little bit farther forward, feet almost slipping off the already wet floor.

He heard another crack as the man's hand snapped up, catching his throat. He choked, trying to push away, arm shaking as he barely kept himself from being dragged out. Pain was all Aiden knew for a moment, but adrenaline kept him conscious, along with a very livid fear of death. Below him, the creature laughed, the sound echoing over the storm.

"I'm going to drag you to hell!" he cackled, snapping a hand up once more, the one that was gripping his forearm, catching his shoulder in an iron grip and tugging him farther forward. Aiden tried to shove with his now free hand, but his vision was going fuzzy and the grip felt like it paralyzed that arm. Either that, or the dislocated shoulder made it impossible to move. "Human, I'll be human again!"

Aiden could feel his legs trembling, dizziness catching his attention as much as the horrified realization of the four story drop did earlier made worse by his clearly imminent death. He couldn't fight this thing, he was barely holding on. A fall from this height—

"AIDEN!" Noah's voice caught his attention as his fingers slipped on the soaked sill and he found himself almost flung out. Noah caught his waist, grunting as gravity tugged at both of them. "Let him go!"

The creature hissed. "I will take you both!"

Noah yelped as Aiden felt another tug, vision now failing. A nurse rushed over with another, trying to pull the arm away from his throat, but the creature wouldn't budge, red gleaming in the darkness as wind and rain plunged down.

"Let. Them. GO!" A female voice cracked as a familiar feminine form surged out and down, slamming into the creature.

Lightning flared as a chill that froze Aiden's very BONES clawed through the air. The Ghost shifted, howling.

To Aiden's shock, fear, for the first time, shone over the creature's face. "Wait, it's not possible. You are—"

"You should have not dared touch them." An echoing voice shook the air, a mix between a guttural growl and an out of tune radio. Aiden noticed as the nurses flinched away, suddenly stumbling back as if terrified. "You should have listened. You caused me to BREAK my agreement. To FAIL in my deal to protect this child. Let the hell's rejoice in your coming. For none will care for your parting. So, now... Suffer." The Ghost hissed, and, for a split second, Aiden could have sworn he saw both eyes, the second one a searing bloody red with a scar tracing over the skin, pulsing as if fresh. "You will never touch him again, because this one is MINE."

Aiden felt his vision dip, darkness taking over as he tried desperately to get any air in. A moment later, the hand on his throat loosened and he sucked in a harsh breath, coughing.

That quickly turned into a choked gasp as an earth-shattering scream echoed through the place, causing Aiden's ears to ring. The grip loosened.

The weight was gone.

The sudden change of force caused Noah to stumble back, pulling Aiden with him, the two crumbling to the ground. Aiden's heart was pounding in his ears, head ringing with pain.

A second later, he heard a loud thud from below and shuddered, feeling sick. The nurses bustled around, quickly checking on him and Noah while a few went over to Dad, who slumped against the wall in a daze. One raced out the door, probably to get a doctor.

Aiden had a hard time keeping track after that. With the adrenaline of the moment leaving him, everything felt like it was spinning and he felt tears trail down his face from a mix of pain and terror. Why him? He hated this stupid ability or whatever. He never wanted this.

Arms wrapped tightly around him, pulling him against a familiar chest, a pounding heart echoing loudly in his ears as he felt a hand hold his head close. Noah's worried voice reached his ears as he found himself shuddering, instinctively pulling himself closer even as his vision faded.

CHAPTER 39

Noah sat in silence, thoughts drifting to the few hours prior to finding himself sitting in a chair next to two occupied beds in a brand new room.

Aiden collapsed against him as wind and rain lashed into the room, crying. Aiden never cried. Yet, Noah found himself pulling his brother close in a hug he knew Mom did before when they were terrified. His fingers shook as he held tight, feeling Aiden suddenly slump against him, unconscious. "Someone get the doctor!" one of the nurses shouted while others hurried away. Not in a panic like before, Noah noted, this time, it was more coordinated.

However, the thing that stuck in Noah's mind was Mia.

More specifically...

Noah grasped onto Aiden's waist, wind and rain buffeting his face as Aiden tried desperately to push the man away, the two of them just barely avoiding plummeting out. He couldn't see Aiden's face, but he could practically feel the terror and fear. Everything froze as Mia charged out. For a brief moment, Noah saw a flash of something, though he wasn't sure what, and then Mia's hand, fingers curled to resemble claws or, actually, were claws, pulled out of the middle of the man's back, blood pouring down as he let out an agonized scream.

Mia leaned close, as if talking into the creature's ear, before his entire body seemed to become paralyzed in fear. The air twisted around Mia for a moment, as if a cloak billowed around, before the principal, creature, whatever, suddenly let loose, falling to the ground. Peace settling over his face.

Noah was certain, even with that expression of relief and serenity, that he was dead before he hit the ground.

The image burned into his mind. Dad mentioned banishment before, what happened back there with Mia and the principal definitely was NOT banishment.

A gentle chill fell over the room before Mia floated in, her appearance back to normal, though Noah still flinched as she settled down beside him, watching Aiden quietly.

"You have no need to be scared of me." Her words were gentle and filled with a strange sadness and warmth. Her gaze turned to Noah, curious. "As I said, I've lived a long time. That one realized too late, I suppose."

"Dad was supposed to banish the ghost." Noah spoke, tongue firmly stuck to the roof of his mouth. "Not kill him."

Mia nodded, turning back toward Aiden, who was fast asleep. "That is correct. However, I could not risk him taking one of you with him and your father understood that, according to our agreement. I could not risk THIS one dying. My deal would be broken, completely, and I would lose all chance of escaping this place…" she trailed off. "I would have lost so much."

"But…"

Mia turned back to him, expression soft. "To be honest, that man's soul was so consumed at that point that, even with the banishment, he would not have lived more than a day. At least this way, both of their lives ended at once."

"But, is that ghost really gone?"

Mia nodded, turning toward the windows, alight with bright sunlight, the remaining bits and pieces of the previous rainstorm just clinging to the windows. "In killing him while he was still bound to the human, I was able to end his existence on this plane." She paused.

"Not necessarily an easy feat, but one I am able to do, I suppose."

"He recognized something about you."

Mia closed her visible eye, tilting her head down before turning to Noah, grinning. "As I said, he hadn't realized how old I am." She chuckled. "And, he went a step too far in trying to kill in the way he was. He clearly forgot, in his fury, that such a death would have been meaningless in giving him what he wanted."

Noah turned back to his brother, thoughts flying a mile a minute. Mom's cross sat in Noah's lap and, while it hadn't completely helped Aiden, it gave him a chance to defend himself.

Still, Noah had been so close to losing his brother. If he had been a moment slower. If Mia hadn't broken down that door that was so firmly shut. If Aiden hadn't caught himself when the principal charged at him, trying to fling them out and succeeding in at least one of those objectives…

He couldn't imagine it.

He peered toward his dad. His hands reached out to either side, grasping their hands as best as he could. It was terrifying, how close he came to losing both of them.

How close they were to disappearing just like Mom.

He felt tears forming and quickly pushed the need to cry away. He couldn't cry. Not now.

Silence descended over them for who knew how long. Noah's arms grew numb from staying in one position. The nurses came and went, bringing in things for him and checking on Dad and Aiden.

It was a while later when a knock on the door caused Noah to glance up. It opened, Phen peeking in hesitantly. Phen seemed relieved as he stepped in, walking over. "How are you?" he asked, gaze flicking to Aiden before returning to Noah, who finally pulled his hands away, settling them in his lap.

"I've been better," Noah admitted.

Phen smiled weakly. He grabbed a chair and pulled it over, sitting across from him as he stared at Aiden. "I'm just happy he—they are still alive," Phen said. "I don't know how I would deal with another person dying on me."

Noah stared down at Aiden, seeing the pain on Phen's face out of the corner of his eye as Phen continued, "I just feel so useless. I was so determined to help you and Aiden and, instead, I did nothing. I wasn't there when that creep attacked either time and I wasn't there for you when you found your father. What was the point?"

Noah glanced away, unsure how to respond as Phen bent his head down, trying and failing to take steadying breaths. "I'm sorry. I shouldn't be saying that."

"I don't see a problem." Mia spoke up, hovering between them quietly. "No one knew what was going to happen. A lot of it happened so fast." She flipped over, staring up toward the ceiling. "I have a feeling that a bit of that creature's human soul was what led us to Noah's father, as a way to atone."

"Huh?" Noah glanced up, startled.

Mia nodded. "I realized it during the slight conversation we overheard. The human soul was still fighting the ghost."

"That's why he had that expression when he fell," Noah whispered, shocked. "He was relieved for it to be over."

Phen shuddered, wrapping his arms around himself as Noah glanced toward the window, feeling off. Sure, the room was different, but he couldn't help but still picture the shattered glass, the trails of blood and the crash of the storm heard loudly through the room.

"Most likely." Mia sighed. "The living human soul is a powerful thing. As I said before, it can heal itself in time and helps develop the core of ghosts, even once the body is long dead. Most likely, he was subconsciously leading us to your father in hopes that you might find a way to end it. But, well, we'll never know that now."

"That's…" Phen spoke softly. "That's horrible."

Mia just nodded, staring up at the ceiling once more. "You need to remember, ghosts often don't hold a sense of humanity in them, just emotions, and obsessions. Sure, there are ghosts out there who only wish to help, but there are others, many others, who desire to harm. Thankfully, the one advantage living humans have is that they are not as susceptible against a ghost's influences, even less so if they cannot even interact with the dead. There is a reason there aren't as many possessions as one would assume."

"So the stronger the connection, the more a ghost can influence and interact," Noah whispered, pursing his lips, as his fingers traced over his arms.

"That's why I'm not quite sure about you two," Mia admitted, flipping onto her stomach. "To have such a connection to the dead, and yet to never know about them. Your father did a good job keeping them away from you as a result."

Noah glanced down, unsure how to respond.

A quiet whine sounded from one side. Everyone turned, practically snapping to face Aiden, who slowly opened his eyes, blinking blearily.

"Aiden." Noah quickly grabbed up his hand, relieved. "Oh, thank god you're awake."

Aiden turned toward Noah, lips turning upward in a rare, genuine smile. "I'm fine, Noah." He coughed slightly, one hand shakily reaching up to rub his throat, that was also lightly bandaged.

"That's good to hear." Phen smiled as well, a little sadder. "I'm glad you are alright. Sorry I wasn't there."

Aiden glanced over and shook his head, wincing slightly. "Hey, Phen." His words were hesitant, though Noah wasn't surprised. "It's fine. I was kind of taken by surprise." He shut his mouth, peering toward the window, lost in thought.

Noah lightly poked his shoulder, catching his attention. "At least we don't have to worry about him anymore."

Aiden nodded, relief falling over his face. "And I guess you found Dad."

Noah perked up, grinning. "Yep!"

He chuckled tiredly and turned to Phen. "Thanks for coming."

Phen glowed red and glanced down, fingers pressing against each other. "Of course I would come, no matter what. I mean, you're important to m—a good friend."

Noah leaned forward, just staring at Phen with a raised eyebrow, causing him to blush even deeper.

"So, we really are friends." Aiden's shoulders, tense a few moments before, slowly loosened. "Even with—"

"Even with the killers, and ghosts and all that stuff." Phen nodded, blush fading into a neutral expression. "Even if you change your mind, I will always want that."

Aiden blinked, startled before a warm smile fell over his face. It was a long time since Noah witnessed such a cheerful smile. "Thanks, Phen." He let out a yawn, settling back against his pillow. "And… thank you, Mia." At that, he fell back to sleep, soft sounds falling around the suddenly silent room once more.

Mia stared, shock on her face as Noah watched her quietly. Her expression shifted before she slowly moved forward, hesitant. She stopped, as if unsure.

Then, with tears curling down her cheek, she swept forward, hands on either side of Aiden's face as a smile fell over her lips. "Geez, took you long enough," she whispered. "You're welcome… I will keep my promise to you going forward. I will do what I can so that this doesn't happen again, you hear me, Aiden?"

She leaned forward, forehead pressing against his as her whole body shimmered, a sense of warmth and comfort settling over the room. Silence fell over the group for a moment before she pulled back and quickly left.

Noah watched her go, turning to Phen, who smiled sadly.

"You do realize—"

"Yeah." He glanced toward the windows. "I get it. With this, after you all heal up, you'll be leaving."

Noah followed his gaze for a moment before he held a hand out. "Give me your phone."

Phen, confused, pulled it out. Noah took it and, shifting to the contacts page, typed in a number. "He doesn't like giving it out, like I said before, but, here." He handed it back as Phen's eyes widened, staring at the numbers.

"He's not going to block me, right?"

Noah actually snorted at that. "I don't think he would know how, even if he wanted to." Noah shook his head. "No, this is so we can stay in contact as long as his phone still works." He paused fingers finagling with the cross settled around his neck. "You know? I think one thing that could be helpful, if you want, is to continue looking up information if we run into situations like that again."

"Don't you mean when?" Phen joked before nodding, voice just a bit softer. "Yeah, I could do that. I want to help, however I can."

Noah flashed him a grateful expresion before letting out his own yawn.

"Speaking of, I should get going. You definitely need some sleep." He gestured. "I think they might be kicking you out soon, why not stay the night with us?"

As if on cue, a nurse came in, gesturing toward the door. "Visitation hours are over. You can see them in the morning." She spoke kindly, and Noah had a feeling she understood. He pursed his lips, hesitating before he stood, joining Phen in heading out the door. He gave one last look back to his two sleeping family members.

As she said, he would be back tomorrow. He glanced up toward the ceiling and whispered quietly, "Mia? Keep them safe."

"I will," she responded, voice faint and filled with emotions. Noah relaxed, following both the nurse and Phen as they left. It was kind of nice, knowing that both of them would be safe. He trusted Mia, even if the others didn't. Sure, he was terrified of what he saw, but she did it to save his brother. No matter what, he couldn't hate her for that.

CHAPTER 40

Aiden slowly shifted awake, the early morning light beaming in. He could hear his father's soft breaths, still fast asleep. Goosebumps hit his skin along with the faintest chill. He glanced up to see Mia floating to one side, sitting as if in a chair, hands to either side and legs one over the other as she stared out the window. She tilted her head, glancing toward him.

"Morning." She smiled brightly. Aiden let out a breath, slowly sitting up, pushing against the headboard. He was mostly exhausted at this point, though his shoulder ached fiercely. At least it was reset.

"Noah's gone?"

"He's been gone for a while, visitation hours ended hours ago." She chuckled, turning around, still in the same pose, clothes curling down around her in a wave. "It is good to see you awake."

"That's surprising."

Mia rolled her visible eye and leaned forward. "I'm in too much of a good mood to take your bait." She chuckled, startling Aiden. "But that's something we'll talk about once your father is up."

Aiden glanced sidelong toward Dad, thoughts churning before he turned back to her. "So… what was that back there?"

"You'll have to specify." She actually looked apologetic. "A lot happened, so I'm not sure what you are talking about."

Aiden frowned, unsure how to explain himself. "I mean, the principal, I think, is something we all need to talk about but… something strange happened before you all arrived."

"Hm?"

Aiden's gaze flicked back to her. "There was a woman, a nurse. She was like you."

Mia furrowed her brow before realization seemed to dawn on her and she perked up. "Oh! A Guardian."

"Guardian?"

Mia nodded, twisting so she was laying on her stomach, kicking her legs up behind her as she put her chin in her hands. "Yep! I thought I sensed something briefly when we were arriving." Her expression softened. "Guardians are rare ghosts that form under specific conditions. Most likely, that young woman lost someone to a ghost and died herself not long after. While many like that turn, some find the strength to hold on to their… humanity, I guess you might call it, and decide to protect others from that same fate." Mia shrugged. "That's pretty much all I know about them." She glanced toward the doorway, expression hard to read. "Most likely, she was a nurse that died here. Hospitals are… terrible places for those with connection to the dead, and there are MANY with that connection in these places." She turned back to Aiden. "You probably feel it, the whirlwind of emotions that gathers here. Ghosts are made of emotion, so it is often overwhelming. If it was a guardian that you met, she was hiding you from the ghosts that dwell here, and is the reason that your father, Noah and I were able to get to you before that man found you."

"He found me anyway." Aiden frowned, shuddering at the memory.

"Yes, but he was also a human possessed. Those are stronger than most humans and even ghosts. That woman was clearly powerful in her own right since he DIDN'T find you right away, even though he knew he put you in the hospital to begin with."

"Oh…" Aiden rubbed his arms.

"Well, enough of that." She smiled. "I will just say, it is good things ended the way they did. It was pure fortune you met a guardian of all things during that mess." The smile disappeared. "If you hadn't, we would not be speaking right now."

Aiden pursed his lips, attention shifting away from her at those words. She let out a breath and he heard a faint cracking sound. "For now, I'm going to continue keeping watch so that no ghosts try to take advantage of the situation. The sooner you and your father are out of here, the better." With that, he felt the chill fade and realization dawned.

He really could feel when she was nearby. He wasn't sure if he appreciated it or not.

•   •   •   •   •

It was a few days later when Aiden felt the joy of being allowed out of the hospital. Dad finally woke up about a day after his talk with Mia, though it was another day or so before he was even close to leaving the hospital. Knowing he was now awake relieved him to no end, though he knew Noah was even more ecstatic. He stood, wearing his normal clothing once more, the jacket sitting comfortably over his shoulders in place of the hospital gown. His throat still felt sore from the grip, making it difficult to talk and his shoulder still ached, though it was already healing.

Dad was allowed out of the hospital as well, the main issue having been malnutrition and dehydration. He was already looking better.

Aiden joined Dad as he pulled himself out of bed, chuckling.

"I'm fine, Aiden. It's good to see you up as well."

Aiden snorted, but couldn't help the faint smile on his lips. "I think that's mutual."

Dad let out a laugh at that and pushed himself to his feet. "Come here, boy, let me give you a proper hug for once." He reached out, pulling Aiden into a tight hug.

"Dad," Aiden whined, coughing slightly, but didn't pull away.

"Hush now, I'm going to spoil both of you with affection, alright?"

Aiden couldn't help but pout at that, especially as he heard the door open, followed by footsteps.

A chuckling voice sounded from behind as Dad let him go. Noah stood nearby, grinning from ear to ear. "Well, that was surprising."

Aiden glared as Noah shrugged.

Noah didn't seem to notice as Dad walked over, pulling him into a hug as well. Aiden barely stopped himself from laughing.

"You think I wouldn't get you too?" Dad chuckled as Noah huffed, before giving him a hug back.

"It's good to see you too, Dad."

Dad let him go, turning to both of them. "Well, I think we've been in this place long enough. Let's grab our things, get paid and get out of this hell hole."

"The one you dragged us into. Just a reminder," Aiden pointed out, stepping up to his side. "Let's pick a bit better next time?"

"I don't know, I had fun," Noah teased.

Aiden rolled his eyes at that.

"That's enough, you two." Dad led them out the door, stopping by the reception desk to make sure everything was in working order before leaving. Aiden was glad they were leaving, not just because he was sick of hospitals, but also because whenever he or dad were awake, besides that short conversation with Mia, they were being questioned by the police to find out what happened. Dad told them the truth and, when they laughed it off, he just smiled and asked how a normal man could climb to a fourth story window in the rain without any rope or anything. Then hang on to a child while lunging through a window. It shut them right up, acknowledging how impossible that was.

When they asked why the principal attacked Aiden, Dad just shrugged and said, "That one, I don't know, maybe he wanted to take one more victim with him and, since Aiden got away, he decided to go after him, I couldn't tell you."

After some debating, they accepted that and let them be.

The only thing that was a little weird was the secretary, but Aiden did manage to learn that the poor man knew about what was going on and was blackmailed into helping the principal. He was probably the one who left a note, letting the janitor know where Aiden was and, from what Aiden gathered, he was also there to help against the fire that started while the principal was looking for them in their home, which was why it was only partially burnt down.

Still, Aiden was grateful that it was, pretty much, over and that they were leaving. The other problem was the constant chill he got while they were there. Thankfully, it never got worse and, much to his chagrin, Aiden had a feeling it was because of Mia's watchful presence. Then again, she outright told him that so he couldn't really say one way or another.

So, seeing the sunlight from outside the hospital was refreshing for Aiden in multiple ways. A car pulled up in front of them, two familiar figures in the front seat. Phen rolled his window down and waved. "Figured you could use a ride and convinced Mom to take you."

Noah perked up as Aiden couldn't help but smile.

"Thank you, young man." Dad spoke, nodding before opening the back door. Aiden ended up going in first. Noah followed with Dad getting in last.

Ellen peered over her shoulder. "Good to finally meet you in not as desperate circumstances."

"Of course, I hear you looked after my children while I was captured."

"I was not aware of your situation," she admitted, tone apologetic while also giving Phen a glare. "But they are sweet kids, I couldn't just leave them, and Phen trusted them. Though, I will say, they did lie to me about your situation."

"My apologies on that, I suppose I can't blame them though." Dad chuckled as Ellen sighed.

"No, I suppose I can't either and I guess I can't be mad at you either for leaving them." She shook her head. "Still, you do have some precious kids to go through all that to find you."

Aiden barely managed to push away the blood rushing to his face, but Noah didn't seem to manage it, smiling awkwardly.

Dad let out a laugh. "Well, I'm happy to hear it. They are the world to me so I am so glad they had someplace safe to stay." His laughter shifted to a warm smile. "If there is anything I can do to repay you, please, let me know."

Ellen chuckled. "Considering they were there for my boy during this whole mess, I'll take that as thanks and repayment enough. How about that?"

"If you wish." Dad leaned back against the car seat at that. Silence fell over the car for only a moment before Phen leaned over and started to just talk. The main topic of conversation was about how the old man at the arcade had been so rude to everyone because he was surprising them with a new and improved version of it. So, now, they had something to do. Noah jumped right into the conversation. Aiden listened quietly, amused.

He did note, however, that he hadn't felt a certain Ghost in a while. He wondered where she was.

It wasn't long before they were dropped off at the house. Phen stepped toward the back of the car, opening up the rear compartment and pulling out the bags they left at Phen's house. Aiden managed to hide his embarrassment, Noah didn't even try. Dad just laughed, taking Aiden's.

"How long are you staying?" Phen asked as Dad threw Aiden's bag over his shoulder. "I mean, your house is in pretty bad shape." He peered around them toward the still splintered and waterlogged front door.

"Probably only a day or two," Dad admitted. "I already got a call for a job about a hundred miles from here with a deadline on when I need to get there."

"Oh…"

Dad relaxed and reached forward, ruffling Phen's hair, startling the boy. "Thank you for being there for my sons. I know they appreciate it, even if they won't admit it out loud." He gave Aiden a look, causing him to quickly turn away. "Keep in contact, alright? I think they would like that."

"Of course!" Phen perked up, smiling brightly. "I'll come by when you guys head out, sound good? Or, if I can't, I will at least contact you."

"Sure," Noah piped up, glancing sidelong toward Aiden. "We would like that."

Phen nodded and scurried back to the car. Ellen drove off, heading back down the road.

The sunlight was warm on their skin as they headed toward the house. There wasn't much to get, but they still wanted to get some things and just talk.

They moved to the barely ever used living room that managed to avoid the fire, a place Aiden honestly forgot they had, and settled down in peaceful silence. With fresh air having blown through the multiple shattered windows and front door, most of the smoky smell was gone, but whoever got this place had a lot of work ahead of them.

It wasn't haunted anymore, at least.

Dad let out a heavy breath, slumping into the lumpy chair as Noah and Aiden took a seat on the couch.

"That was not what I had in mind," Dad admitted, tense shoulder relaxing. "I'm proud of you boys, if a little peeved."

Noah nodded as Aiden shifted, leaning against the arm. "You really hid a lot from us, you know." His words were pointed, causing both Dad and Noah to flinch.

"I wanted to protect you." Dad leaned forward, hands clasped between his legs. "After your mother's disappearance, I wasn't sure what to do. It was her skills and abilities that kept ghosts away." He glanced toward Aiden. "It was her cross, that she imbued with her abilities, that helped so much, so I'm very glad you boys kept it on you. I only knew the basics, a simple investigator turned ghost whisperer. I figured if I kept going, I would find out what happened to her. That's why I couldn't just stop investigating. Plus, I didn't trust to stay in one place for too long, worried what would happen to you two."

Aiden and Noah exchanged glances.

"I wanted nothing more than for you two to live normal lives, as normal as I could give, but I suppose I was wishing for too much." He smiled sardonically. "I should have known that one day, you would realize. That I wouldn't be able to protect you like I wanted to. I guess it came sooner than I hoped."

"Oh." Noah spoke quietly before glancing toward him. "I want to know. Do you think Mom is still alive?"

Aiden stiffened and Dad shifted uncomfortably. "I truthfully don't know. That's why I'm looking, searching. Every case I take, every chance I have to find out what happened, they all mean something to me."

"So you're still searching for her," Aiden said quietly. "You haven't given up."

Dad shook his head. "I want you to have your mother back and if it truly is the case that she is gone, to know the truth of what happened to her."

"So…" Aiden tilted his head. "What would have happened if we met a ghost who wanted us dead or worse and you weren't there? What did you expect to happen?"

Dad actually winced at that. "I hoped that, with the constant moving, and the fact that you had no idea ghosts were real, that it would help protect you from them, give you an extra layer."

"A solid plan, but a flawed one." The Ghost's voice echoed from above as she floated through, landing on the table delicately, facing the three of them. "A powerful enough ghost would be able to break past the barrier, but, I suppose, a powerful one would also be something you couldn't deal with."

"You." Dad glanced up, tired. "The ghost from before."

Mia smiled, though it seemed a little strange. "Yes, Mr. Raven. My name, given by your son, is Mia."

Dad's eyes widened. "Is that true? Did you actually give this one a name?" Dad turned to Noah, who nodded, confused.

"I had no memory of my actual name, so he deigned to give me one." Mia bowed her head. "That is where the beginning of the deal came into place."

"Oh." Dad sighed. "I suppose I shouldn't be surprised. Of all the ghosts they could have met and made a deal such as that with, I suppose I've definitely met worse."

"I'll take that as a compliment."

"Deal?" Aiden sat up straight, unnerved. "What are you talking about?"

Mia turned to him, a strange happiness on her face. "If you recall, I said I would protect you as long as you helped me escape this place and return home. You or, well, your brother agreed. I'm not sure the importance on the name, but it feels important." She shrugged. "However, basically, think of it this way. In agreeing, you basically made a deal—"

"With the devil." Dad chuckled. "Or, at least, that's how some people would call it. Ghosts are notorious for their terminology and words. One thing to watch out for, which I didn't even think about, were deals. However, I guess you two were careful and lucky. You made a deal with her without realizing. I'm not sure the extent of what that means, since you were probably aware you were making a deal, but not the… importance of it." He rubbed his temples for a moment. "Deals made with ghosts are binding and, if completely broken, can lead to catastrophic results." His gaze flicked to Noah. "Death is the best option in that case. Still, if you were aware you were making a deal of such magnitude, it would change things."

"Exactly." Mia turned back to Dad. "The deal was pretty much a real one, but not completed due to only Noah accepting said deal. Thus, it very much is a full deal, however, there are means of breaking it without completely facing the consequences… though as you surmise, there will still definitely be problems if it is broken." Her gaze flared for a moment, hair swirling around before settling. "Still, I wish no harm on them, as you can see. Imagine, however, if they had unwittingly made a deal with a being not as friendly as myself."

Dad pursed his lips, clearly agreeing. "I thank you for keeping with your deal appropriately. I did hear you, faintly, though I was slipping in and out of consciousness. You truly wish to protect them and that's something I'm forever grateful for, though pardon my hesitation at the fact that this happened at all. Too often have I encountered ghosts that wished to harm or twist words, avoiding keeping their end of the bargain, so this came as a surprise."

Mia frowned at that. "I have heard of many a ghost like that. A deal is a deal, I see no reason to try to act otherwise, even if they were unaware."

The tension in Dad's posture seemed to dissipate as he nodded.

"But we didn't know that was a thing, these deals," Aiden snapped, annoyed. "How can we make a deal we are unaware of? I mean, sure, Noah shook your hand and stuff, but—"

Mia turned. "Because of how powerful you are." She sighed. "I didn't realize either until I said it and Noah here agreed. Thankfully, one thing I DO know about deals is that you can't have more than one. Which means Noah can't accidentally make another with a dangerous ghost unless this one is broken completely or completed." She paused at that, thinking something over before continuing, "Though someone can add an addendum, like your father did, since it still fit within the parameters of the deal." She pulled back, hair flowing gently around her. "Even as old as I am, there is a lot about ghosts that I still do not fully understand, and the same goes for humans with powers like yours. But, Aiden." Aiden jerked, startled. "You spoke my name, the name Noah gave me. For that, I am grateful." She peered over. "It's strange, your acceptance. I hadn't realized you were blocking me out until you accepted me like that." She smiled faintly. "I think with that, I might be able to finally leave this place."

"Really?" Noah jerked, sitting upright in surprise as Dad narrowed his eyes. "That's great!"

Mia nodded, relief on her face. "Of course, I am still stuck with you, but yes, I can feel the tethers breaking even as we speak."

"So, my sons 'power is that strong." Dad spoke softly. "It is not easy to destroy the tethers ghosts have on the mortal realm, especially ancient ones."

"You are correct." Mia gestured to herself. "As I told your sons before, their energy is one of 'life'. Something so powerful is a boon to ghosts or a detriment, depending." She closed her eye, putting a hand to her chest. "So, to complete the deal and make sure no mishaps occur, I will continue to do what I can to protect your children and guide them with what knowledge I do have. In exchange, I need your family's help to find my way home."

"I suppose that is reasonable." He massaged the bridge of his nose. "Though, then again, even if I disapproved, I wouldn't have the skill to banish you. So, I guess it's good I don't mind, especially since my children clearly do like you. To be honest? As soon as you got Aiden's respect, I couldn't hate you even if I tried. He's a good kid, but not very trusting."

Aiden only felt slightly affronted by the words.

Mia's smile was both brilliant and a hint mischievous. "I can understand that and, you are correct, you are strong in your own right, but not enough to banish me." She relaxed. "Still, it is good to know I have your trust as well."

"Yes, though I will not partake in the deal, if you don't mind."

"Of course, I have no qualms about that. It mainly only was for these two anyway and this leaves you open to make your own deals if necessary."

Dad nodded as Aiden pursed his lips, watching the exchange.

Dad turned back to Noah and Aiden. "I guess I have to start teaching you boys what I know, especially if we're going to continue like this."

"So, we are going to help Mia?" Noah smiled widely. "Awesome!"

Aiden just let out a groan and turned to Dad. "Just make sure to collect the money from the mayor this time?"

Dad almost pouted at that, almost. "That happened once, Aiden."

"And I'm not going to let you live it down," Aiden pressed, amused. Noah let out a laugh.

This, Aiden could handle.

CHAPTER 41

The next day, Dad collected the money, slightly reduced due to it being a death instead of capture. Dad didn't mind and Aiden just didn't care by that point. He wanted out of that town. Dad made a few calls, mentioning that he was still a bit too weak to banish the multitude of ghosts created by the killer. Aiden found himself a little frazzled at the idea that there was an entire association of people who focused on ghost cleansing or banishment, whatever it was called. Still, as long as his father wasn't in the center of the mess, he just shoved the thought off. That was something he would figure out later if it was necessary.

Once everything was put into place, the family got ready to be on their way, making last minute arrangements. Noah sat in the back seat this time, only to make sure Aiden didn't re-injure himself due to all the boxes moving around, or so he said.

Aiden settled into the front, peering out the window before glancing toward Dad. "So, where are we going next?"

"There is a report that a man is cheating on his wife, but there are no leads. The wife is paying a handsome sum to figure out the truth. She wants us there in the next few days."

"Is that the closest thing?"

"No, but it's a thing that doesn't sound as dangerous as this one," Dad admitted as he turned the car on, the old thing chugging to life. "I think I could use an old-fashioned cheating case after this mess."

Noah chuckled as Aiden snorted at that, shaking his head before staring outside once more.

"So, we ready to go then?" The Ghost settled down on the middle console between Dad and himself, floating over it as if sitting, though there would normally not be enough room for that. Dad twitched and Aiden saw him reach for his pocket before relaxing.

"You are going to keep doing that, aren't you?"

"Uh, duh?" Mia flipped upside down, hands behind her head. Noah shifted uncomfortably in the back, pointedly not looking their direction. "Where's the fun otherwise?"

"You are quite the mischievous one, aren't you?

"You're just realizing?" She grinned before flipping around, settling down as if sitting properly between the two once more. Her expression was more solemn as she stared ahead. "To think… I'm leaving this place."

"How do you feel about that?" Noah asked, curious.

Mia stayed silent. "Some might say bittersweet, but of the few memories I have before my death? I'm glad. Glad to be leaving this hell-hole, as your father so aptly put it."

"Well, we'll see." Dad sighed. "I've never seen a ghost that can break its tethers completely."

Mia just nodded, gripping onto the car tightly, as if she could actually hold it. Aiden felt a vibration against his leg and almost leapt out of his seat. He scrambled, pulling his damaged but still useable phone out and glaring back to Noah, only to pause when he noticed Noah wasn't holding his phone, his hands were held up innocently.

Aiden narrowed his eyes before turning back to the text, only to backpedal in shock, or attempt to. It only led to him pressing himself even farther into the seat.

"I heard you are heading out today, Aiden. I figured, well, that I would say good-bye like this. That way, you also know, as cheesy as it is, that it's not really a good-bye. Okay, this is sounding stupid, but I'm glad to have you as a friend. Don't forget to text me when you get out of this dump. You hear me? And, well, if you are interested… I wouldn't mind you calling me when you get to the next town. Oh, and if you were wondering, your brother gave me this number. Just don't blame him for that. Okay, you know what? This text is already long as it is, so… How about this. Take care, Aiden, and say see ya to Noah for me. From your penpal, I guess, sure? Let's go with that, Phen."

Aiden stared down at the long rambling text and felt a smile slowly cross his face. He was not going to admit that he felt a few tears prickle at his eyes. He quickly blinked them away and glared back at Noah, who just grinned, hands behind his head.

"Oh, come on, you know you're not that upset."

Aiden sighed, because, well, Noah was right.

Heh, to think, he finally had someone to talk with besides Dad and Noah.

"Ah, so he picked up two partners, he's moving up in the world," Mia teased, though the smile on her face spoke volumes. She imitated poking Aiden in the shoulder. "Hey, guess you can call me big sis, since friend is probably already taken in your book."

Aiden swatted at her hand, causing her to chuckle, shaking it out, only wincing slightly.

"Big sis, huh?" Noah teased. "Does that mean we get to poke fun at you?"

Mia glanced over her shoulder. "Don't you already?" Noah seemed startled as Aiden huffed.

"I'll stick with Mia for now."

Aiden didn't miss the way Mia absolutely brightened at that, hands clasped in front of her chest with a happy little smile. "Ah, thank you, little brother."

"Okay, yeah, no. I WILL go back to calling you Ghost if you do that." Aiden twitched as both Noah and Mia laughed. Dad just shook his head, though amusement shone on his face as well.

A moment later, Mia stilled, staring ahead. Her eyes widened, as she lightly touched her chest. If ghosts could breathe, she seemed breathless.

Aiden peered ahead, noting as they broke through a set of trees, passing into a main road. Meadows and fields took up either side of the long straight road. A few strains of wheat waved gently in the breeze.

Aiden glanced over, startled to see tears tracing down Mia's face, as she continued to stare out over the area.

"I'm guessing you've not been this far before." Dad spoke softly.

Mia slowly shook her head, hands to her mouth as tears continued to roll down her cheeks. "I never thought I would." Her voice sounded choked slightly. "Thank you… thank you so much."

Aiden glanced away, peering out over the landscape, the sun shining brightly above. He held the phone in his hand gently as the quiet sound of sobbing filled the car.

They had a lot on their plate going forward. Dad's search for Mom, Mia's search for her home. Noah's search to find a place where all of them could settle down and call home.

All he needed was to figure out what he wanted in all this.

Though, he supposed, he didn't have to figure that out yet. He was just happy to have his father back and to be leaving. A companion in the form of a ghost and a new friend? Well, he wasn't going to forgo a gift when he received it.

Maybe there was hope that things could improve.

He felt something lightly brush past him and glanced over to see Mia curling up between him and Dad, a happy little smile on her face as she relaxed for the first time since he met her.

He glanced back toward Noah, who gave him a look full of warmth.

He supposed, for now, he was just happy to be with his little family again. Who knew what awaited, but, at least, they were a bit better prepared this time.

That was his only hope.

ABOUT THE AUTHOR

Tea, cake, and a good book are often the cornerstones of a comfortable evening for Julie. A writer and artist, she likes to spend hours at a time working on projects, often being distracted by her cat, Nelson. She listens to a variety of different types of music and will often be seen playing D&D with friends.

NOTE FROM JULIE BOGLISCH

Word-of-mouth is crucial for any author to succeed. If you enjoyed *The Raven's Crux*, please leave a review online—anywhere you are able. Even if it's just a sentence or two. It would make all the difference and would be very much appreciated.

Thanks!
Julie Boglisch

We hope you enjoyed reading this title from:

www.blackrosewriting.com

Subscribe to our mailing list – *The Rosevine* – and receive **FREE** books, daily
deals, and stay current with news about upcoming
releases and our hottest authors.
Scan the QR code below to sign up.

Already a subscriber? Please accept a sincere thank you for being a fan of
Black Rose Writing authors.

View other Black Rose Writing titles at
www.blackrosewriting.com/books and use promo code
PRINT to receive a **20% discount** when purchasing.

www.ingramcontent.com/pod-product-compliance
Lightning Source LLC
Chambersburg PA
CBHW031435200726

48289CB00001BA/261